FOR MOTHER'S DAY . . .

You can send her flowers. You can give her chocolates. You can say "I love you" with a bottle of her favorite perfume, dinner in her favorite restaurant, maybe even a surprise party. Or you can say "I love you, Mom" with that most special gift of all—a book.

So here's a very special book for mothers— and daughters, grandmothers and grand-daughters, too—a special collection of stories to celebrate Mother's Day, to read and to treasure, written by six favorite TO MOTHER, WITH LOVE authors . . .

TO MOTHER WITH LOVE

JANE BIERCE   MARIAN OAKS
STACEY DENNIS   GARDA PARKER
MARTHA GROSS   CLARA WIMBERLY

ZEBRA BOOKS
KENSINGTON PUBLISHING CORP.

ZEBRA BOOKS

are published by

Kensington Publishing Corp.
475 Park Avenue South
New York, NY 10016

First Printing: April, 1993

Printed in the United States of America

CONTENTS

A Different Kind of Love

by Jane Bierce

Professor Laura Parsons smiled confidently at the three young women students clustered in the tiled hall outside her classroom, unlocked the door, and left it open for them. That they were too involved in their hushed conversation to follow her immediately was of no concern to her.

Laura dropped her purse and briefcase on the desk in front of the green chalkboard. When she turned on the overhead fluorescent lights, she paused to check the number of student chairs ranged in precise ranks and files before her. Too many. That would never do.

She decided to push a few back beside the long table at the far end of the room, removing them from the straight and formal configuration to present a less intimidating environment.

With a little effort, she dragged the molded

plastic seats with their fake-wood writing arms across the dull utility carpet into two rows of six chairs, in a sort of arc centered about the podium. The enrollment for this course was rarely more than twelve, which suited her style of teaching very well.

Experience had taught her this was the most comfortable setting for her students and herself. No one had to raise his voice above a normal speaking level; no one missed the jokes, everyone got involved.

Laura reached for a piece of chalk to write her name and the title of the course, then dusted the residue from her fingertips.

"Oh, good," one of the girls whispered to the others as they entered, her voice carrying in the silence of the room. "Dr. Parsons. My sister took this course from her and loved it."

"Comp 1001?" another girl asked, then groaned. "Not very likely. I'm just taking it now because I need to get back into the mindset of studying."

As she turned away to remove her teaching materials from her briefcase, Laura tried to keep from nodding and smiling at the remark.

It was the summer quarter of Palm Community College, and it was admittedly hard to raise full classes for the session that started in early May and staggered into the third week of June in the Florida heat, not yet tempered by the summer rains. It was too early for the fresh crop of high school graduates to enroll, but it was convenient for those who had failed Comp under other teachers and had to fit it in before the fall semester. Or they were re-entry students who'd been out of school for some time, housewives whose small children were old enough for day care or whose husbands had left them in need of a livelihood, or truck drivers and mechanics who decided they should have gone to college in the first place.

Actually, Laura loved the challenge. These were people who had a hard time putting one word after another on paper. If there was anyone she didn't want in this class, it was the brilliant child who'd gone to a prep school and been drilled on obscure points of grammar.

The school had a policy of testing students and exempting them from this class if they had minimal skills in composition, so Laura rarely had to salve skittish egos that had been crushed by exposure to true talent.

She scanned the computer-printed roll list to see if there were any names she recognized, then realized she was also holding another piece of paper she'd found in her campus mailbox that morning.

. . .inform you that you have thirteen students in your eight o'clock class and only

eleven in your afternoon class. If you can convince one student to switch from morning to afternoon, it will not be necessary to cancel the one o'clock session.

Laura frowned and slipped the message under the roll list on the slanted surface of her podium. Then she looked up to take a quick head count of the students who straggled into the small classroom.

There was little chance of convincing anyone to take this class for two whole hours in the afternoon heat. No, these were the people who wanted to get out early to go to a job, the mother who hoped the sitter wouldn't have too hard a time coping with getting the kids up for breakfast before she could get back home.

Laura was just about to clear her throat and begin her usual opening speech when a pretty young blond woman walked tentatively into the room, searched for a seat in the back, then reluctantly took the chair squarely in front of the podium.

"Good morning," Laura said, trying to smile at everyone with equal encouragement. "This is officially Comp 1001, but I call it White Knuckle Comp. I congratulate you all for having the good sense to take this course in the summer quarter. To avoid cutting into your jobs or beach time, we do almost all the work during the two hours you're here in the classroom, except for a short term paper which is due just before the end of the quarter."

There was a general groan from the twelve people in front of her. She counted heads again—twelve people. A no-show. The one o'clock class was in real jeopardy. Well, there was no sense fretting over it right now.

"Don't buy the textbook for this class unless you think the campus bookstore needs the money more than you do," Laura went on, eliciting a nervous titter from the class in response. "But you might want to invest in a paperback dictionary, particularly one that has a summary of the rules of grammar in the back. You'll need plenty of paper and a redundancy of writing instruments. Park your fear of writing outside the door and we'll try our best to get you through this course with a C at the very least."

The blond girl sitting in front of her suddenly grinned. Her face lighted with an incandescence that reached from her bright blue eyes to straight teeth between innocent lips and engaging dimples.

Laura paused to look at her, thinking, as she always did, that this young woman could have been her own child, if she and Tony could have had a child.

She clapped her hands once, having the effect of getting everyone's attention and clearing her own mind at the same time.

11

"Now, let's get to work."

She forgot about the ominous message from the front office until the last few minutes before she would dismiss the class. As she suspected, no one was interested in changing classes, and the thirteenth student hadn't turned up anyway. Perhaps her afternoons would be free this session. If she didn't need the money so badly, she would be relieved.

The girl in the seat in front of the podium, whom Laura could now identify as Becky Houseman, scribbled something on the page she had been using as a worksheet, then frowned. She dawdled when Laura dismissed the class.

"You mean the other class will be canceled?" she asked, falling into step with Laura as they left the classroom.

"I'm afraid so."

"And you won't get paid—"

"Well, no."

"I mean—you must not get much, considering what I paid for the class, multiplied—and—you probably don't get all the money. See, I have a mathematical mind. This writing business is hard for me."

"If I can reduce it to a mathematical formula, would you feel more at ease?" Laura asked, trying to steer Becky away from her own doubts about the other class.

"Oh, you've already helped me get a grasp on

some of it," Becky said, beaming.

They were approaching the plate glass doors of the building. Laura had decided to go home for lunch and come back to campus later for the afternoon class rather than spend the time in her office.

"Oh, there's my father," Becky Houseman said with a sigh. "I swear, he's going to make a lot of enemies parking the car there and making people go around him. He's just not used to — doing things like everyone else. I'll see you tomorrow, Dr. Parsons."

Laura watched Becky dash toward the white Mercedes convertible which was in the no-parking zone at the end of the walkway and seemed to be straining at a leash to be moving again.

The man sitting behind the wheel was straight and distinguished looking, a man of great presence. She noticed how the sun glinted off his light hair, close-cropped in what had popularly been called a Prussian when she was in college — now the mark of a military man.

Laura watched for only a moment, then turned toward the shade of the oak trees that sheltered the walkway to the library.

Colonel Charles Houseman, U. S. Army (Ret.), looked up from the paperback mystery he'd been reading while he waited. Marking his place with a scrap of paper on which he had sketched some directions, he dropped the book to the leather seat.

He looked at the elaborate watch that nestled against the wiry pale hairs on his tanned wrist.

It was ten-hundred. If Becky came right out of class, it would take ten minutes to drive to the auto registration office, about twenty minutes to process the paperwork on Becky's car, and they'd be back home by eleven-hundred.

But why? There wasn't anything more to do today, or any day.

Charles Houseman glared at the entrance to the building where he had left Becky precisely two hours earlier. A few jean-clad students straggled toward the entrance, a few others hurried out. They all looked so terribly young.

He glanced at his watch again and checked his rearview mirror. A noisy coupe with a customized paint job came up behind him, and when Charles didn't move, the driver honked the horn.

Charles waved him around. The kid made a face at him as he passed.

Then Charles gritted his teeth and turned his attention back to the entrance.

Becky appeared at the glass door, pushed it open, and waited for a woman to precede her out into the bright sun. The woman was of average height, but she had a certain elegance about her, even in a dress that had a split skirt. Her brown hair was graying at the temples. When she moved, it was with the grace of someone so comfortable in a setting that her mind could be on other things.

At last Becky reached the car and let herself in.

"Sorry I'm the last one, but I wanted to talk to the professor," she apologized, buckling her seatbelt.

"Was that your instructor?" Charles asked, slipping the convertible into gear.

"Dr. Parsons," Becky answered with a nod and a quick smile. "The students say she's a whiz at helping students get over the fear of writing. And I thought she had some very interesting exercises."

"I hardly think you're qualified to pass judgment on instructional techniques," Charles said, easing to a stop at the end of the drive and then turning onto the main street.

"Well, if I can apply any pressure at all, I think I can ace that course," Becky said cheerfully. "The only work outside of class that she requires is a term paper, and the girls I talked to during the break said that the types of topics she's looking for are a blast to write."

"Humph!" he said. "You can't learn much from writing lightweight fluff. When I was in West Point—"

"You had to practically dig up the general you wrote about," Becky supplied from memory. "Yes, sir, I know."

Her voice had a little edge to it. He'd rarely heard it until he'd retired from the service and they had moved to Florida a few weeks before. She had cultivated a new attitude, and sometimes he could barely tolerate it.

The problem was that Becky was all he had left of the life he had known for thirty years.

Doris, his wife since the year he'd graduated from West Point, had abandoned him on three June the previous year, just when he was starting to count the days until he would be out of the service.

Doris didn't want him anymore and left while he was still at full pay so a divorce judge would see she was adequately provided for. It was a calculated move, and he smarted from it. Yet, it showed a certain backbone on Doris's part, something she needed to be able to get on with her life.

". . . so I thought, since that publisher is after you to write that book, you should enroll in Dr. Parsons' one o'clock class," Becky was saying, cutting into his reverie.

"What!" he barked, unable to remember what she had been saying previously.

"Dr. Parsons needs another student in her one

o'clock class or it will be canceled," Becky explained with elaborate patience.

"Don't be silly!"

"You've been having trouble sitting down to write your book," she pointed out.

"I don't have a deadline. I haven't even actually signed the contract," Charles said, feeling sweat pop out on his upper lip.

It did that even in the dead of night when he thought about writing that stupid book. He was sorry he'd even considered the idea of exposing even one operation of his long career in military intelligence to his own scrutiny, let alone literary analysis.

"From what I saw of Dr. Parsons' techniques, she could have you writing your book just like that!" Becky snapped her manicured fingers and grinned back at him.

"I'm a graduate of West Point," Charles replied, as though that were the end of the discussion.

"When I was reading the material about enrolling, I noticed that Comp 1001 is a class that anyone can take, even without a high school diploma," Becky countered. "You can take it as an audit. You pay your money and sit in a chair. You can leave after the instructor draws her pay! But she could help you get started on that book, sir. I know she could."

"When I've thought it all through," he argued,

"I'll probably be able to just sit down and write the whole thing, start to finish. It's probably just a matter of organizing everything logically."

"Then why haven't you started it?"

Houseman made a noise in his throat which was supposed to be an answer.

"You've got to do something!" Becky said with barely controlled exasperation.

He was writing out the check for the registration on Becky's car when it struck him that Becky now had her freedom. He no longer had to chauffeur her to the supermarket or the tennis court at the country club where they were enjoying guest privileges until his name could be submitted for membership. She could be gone all day, not around to talk to him at all.

It was a scary thought.

He felt a panic in his gut that was totally foreign to him. He had to do something. In the past few weeks, he'd tried golf and fishing, tennis and walking around his new neighborhood. His knees hurt and he was bored. He resorted to reading books he'd read before, mostly spy thrillers and murder mysteries.

He had to do something.

He looked at his watch.

"What time does that class start?" he asked Becky as he tucked his checkbook into the pocket of his slacks.

"One o'clock." The look on her face was Cheshire-like.

Thirteen hundred. He could just make it.

It was already hot when Laura reached her classroom after her lunch break. There were several students clustered around one young man whose long sun-bleached hair straggled from a ponytail at the back of his tanned neck.

". . . So I spiked the ball so hard the sand flew up just as the dude lunged at it and he got a mouth full!" He regaled his listeners, his words emphasized by expansive gestures. His sleekly muscled arms and shoulders were exposed by his tank top shirt, showing a tan that had probably been in place since childhood.

When the students realized she was there, several found seats and settled into them. Three other young people entered the room, taking their own sweet time.

There was still an empty seat at the center of the back row, between the beach bum and a young woman whose black hair frizzed around the sunglasses pushed up on her head.

One student short, Laura thought to herself, mentally preparing to make a speech she'd given many times before. But this time she would have to add the preface that if the class did not pick up another person in the next few days, it would be canceled and they would all have their afternoons free again.

She checked her watch against the clock on the wall and started toward the door.

But as she was about to close it, a tall, distinguished-looking man stared back at her from the hallway, startled. He looked very familiar, but Laura couldn't immediately place where she had seen him before.

"Composition 1001?" he asked, glancing down at the computer-generated slip in his hand.

"Yes," Laura said, surprised that she was able to muster a voice when she was so stunned by the clear blue of his eyes, the forceful set of his jaw.

"Good," he responded, adjusting his grip on the well-worn briefcase in his other hand.

The twelfth student! Would wonders never cease!

Laura moved aside and motioned toward the one vacant seat in the room. The newcomer assumed his place with a definite economy of motion, his erect posture providing everyone in the room with an example of discipline.

Several heads turned to watch him open his briefcase and take out a legal pad, but when he raised his eyes, they all looked away.

It was then that Laura placed the bearing, the telltale signs of the military man. This was

Becky Houseman's father.

The lines of his face gave him a certain distinguished, capable expression. His knit shirt and cotton slacks looked anything but casual as they encased his well-built physique.

Relieved that she would not have to say anything about the class being canceled, Laura gave her usual little introductory spiel.

She couldn't help but notice that Houseman was taking notes furiously, as though every word she uttered was of extreme importance. She certainly wasn't used to being accorded this kind of attention, and it made her uneasy.

Houseman's presence seemed to make everyone nervous. It certainly put a damper on the spontaneous responses Laura counted on to move the students through the basic exercises she used to break the ice and get them to drop their inhibitions about writing. When she called on him, he spoke in clipped, authoritative responses which were short, full sentences.

Halfway through the class, she had become annoyed, wondering why he was there. Clearly he needed to take a freshman composition course about as much as she did.

Because the man in the center of the back row was so intent on completing every task as quickly as possible, the kids fell into his pace. When the exercises she had planned were completed ten minutes before she could justify giving the class its break, Laura reached deeper into her bag of mental tricks.

"This time I want you to write a general noun on a piece of paper and hand it to someone else," she suggested.

Trying to keep a straight face, she watched the exchange in the back of the room. The beach bum handed his sheet of paper to Houseman, nonchalantly, as though it were a matter of no consequence. Houseman reciprocated with disdain.

"Add a word, but leave enough room for four other people to make increasingly specific contributions to this page—" Laura instructed. "Do it as quickly as you can, with a minimum of thought."

One of the girls in the front giggled over the third round of words, but quickly stifled her laughter, glancing back over her shoulder toward the other students.

By the time the exercise was reviewed and she let the students take their break, Laura was wondering if there was any hope of salvaging her reputation for teaching a painless method of learning composition. She didn't want to hear any grumbling in the hallway, and certainly hoped that if the students did grouse, the front office wouldn't pay any attention.

She followed the students out of her classroom and hurried down the hall to the soda machine. Dropping two quarters into the slot, she punched a button and gave the machine a thump with her fist when it sputtered. The machine delivered a can and she retrieved it, relishing its coolness in her hands before opening it.

When she turned back toward the classroom, Houseman was standing a few feet away, studying her.

"You have very interesting instructional techniques," he said with an impersonal tone.

Laura wanted to tell him that he had blown her lesson plan out of the water, but she was willing to give him a little more leeway. She had long ago learned that patience went a long way toward understanding.

"This class is generally for students who are afraid to write," she told him. "Some aren't even comfortable speaking in class. My job is to make it easier."

The man bought a can of soda from the machine without having to give it a thump.

"That's what's wrong with this country," he pontificated. "We're watering down our education so everyone thinks he can read and write just because he has a degree from a little community college. We try to make everything entertaining and fun—"

It was when he took a drink from his can that Laura noticed the ring on his right hand. It bore the insignia of West Point. She'd seen one like it before, years ago, when she'd ordered her college ring.

It was obvious that he'd been a man of some rank, but Laura hesitated to guess just how high.

"For many students, this is the best education they can afford," she said defensively with some pride. "I think the teachers here try as hard as anywhere else to prepare our students for life beyond these walls."

He looked back at her with a glimmer of surprise. "Sorry if I offended you," he said, lowering his voice a bit. "I—I'm taking this class because my daughter thought it would help me with—an assignment I have."

"Oh?" Laura asked, suddenly intrigued.

"Becky is taking your morning class," he said. "I'm Charles Houseman."

"Yes, I know." Laura took a sip of her soda and waited until the fizzing in her throat had stopped. "Now I'm wondering why both of you are taking my class. She seems very competent with her language skills and you're a graduate of West Point. What's this all about?"

"Becky doesn't test well," he said, looking away, as though he couldn't maintain eye contact and talk about his daughter. "She freezes up. That's probably why they didn't exempt her from this course. She was very impressed with you, told me you'd probably be able to get me past this—this block I have. I've been asked to write a book."

"How nice," Laura said, burying her professional jealousy under a layer of well-bred manners.

Houseman frowned lopsidedly. "I don't want to do it, even though the agencies have cleared it."

"That's probably why you have a block, not because of any inability to put one word after another." She tried to be encouraging without getting personal.

He sighed. "No doubt."

He seemed reluctant to say anything more, so Laura started walking back to her classroom. She was relieved that he didn't follow her. There was something about him that drew her to him, but then there was his stiff discipline, which was off-putting. She was confused by her own reaction, and in such a situation, it was best to be cautious.

The students walked back into the room behind her.

"I know the signs say that you aren't to have food and drink in these rooms," Laura said, placing her drink carefully on her podium. But this is summer and you can't very well sit through a two-hour class and study if you're fighting dehydration. I'll overlook your transgressions if you overlook mine. I find it works best if you don't have more than half a can to spill. Please be very careful."

Everyone seemed relieved that she was so liberal, but Houseman scowled at her. She couldn't understand why he seemed so hidebound about her breaking a silly little rule. After all, he had a can of soda on the floor beside his chair, too. Maybe he thought he was the only one who could break rules with impunity.

Laura worked mightily to raise the level of spontaneity in the class and was quite pleased with the results by the end of the session. There were a few times when even Charles Houseman seemed to smile when the other students laughed at the outcome of an exercise.

The room emptied quickly less than an hour later, when she announced that class was over.

Laura had reached the solitude of her office at the far end of the hall and dumped her briefcase onto her desk when there was a light knock at the frame of the open door.

Charles Houseman stood there, glaring at her impatiently.

Sighing, she motioned for him to enter. "What can I do for you?" she asked automatically.

It was the way she always responded to students at her office door, and for a moment, she wondered why she had not long ago adopted the various discouraging phrases other instructors used.

26

"For one thing, I'd like to know why you do those stupid exercises," he said, taking a step into the tiny cubicle, filling it with a nervous energy.

Laura motioned toward a molded plastic chair between the filing cabinet and the crammed bookcase and sat down behind her desk. He sat erectly, his feet squarely on the floor, his briefcase nearby.

"I'm sorry if they seem lacking in intellectual challenge," she said, marveling at his self-discipline. "But I'm trying to make the students comfortable using the language, learning shadings, and then fitting expression into whatever framework they function in most readily. Your daughter seems to think she's better in a mathematical mode, so I'll encourage her to see a sentence as an equation." She shrugged. "Sometimes it works, sometimes it doesn't."

"So." It was a statement, denoting thoughtfulness.

"You have to understand that the students in this class are usually people who've been told they can't write," she explained. "I try to get them past that and keep the lessons as painless as possible."

"That's certainly—untraditional," Houseman grumbled.

"Um. Tradition isn't always effective."

Houseman stiffened.

Laura chuckled to herself. She admired self-control and accomplishment, concepts this man was no stranger to. He was clear-eyed and principled, to say nothing of distinguished and handsome. She could have compared him to a fine steel coil, tightly controlled and about to spring in all directions—and she would take a blue pen and edit the line from her text as too florid.

"I'm certain you didn't come here just to complain about my unorthodox teaching methods," she said.

"No. I told you earlier I've been asked to write a book, and it occurred to me that you could help me." He was definitely trying to smile. "The contract is generous. I could pay you well."

Laura leaned back in her chair and studied the piercing eyes that confronted her.

"I make it a practice not to respond to requests along this line," she said, finding comfort in long-established principle. "No matter how interesting the outcome might be."

Interesting. As attracted as she was to this man, she knew in her heart she should resist any involvement in his project. He exuded an air of discipline and control. She'd had enough of people who were self-indulgent and only as moral as they needed to be.

For a moment, he looked as though he would

say something more, but he slowly got to his feet. "I'm sorry I took your time."

"Mr. Houseman," Laura said, "it's nothing personal. I couldn't possibly do a good job of writing something for someone else. I hope you'll learn something in class that will help you over your problems."

She sighed. "Besides, it's not wise for faculty to become too involved with a student, or a member of a student's family," she said. And as she spoke, she realized she didn't take his status as a student as seriously as she regarded his daughter's.

He scowled and left the office. She heard his precise footfalls receding down the hall, then the distinctive groan — grate — wheeze — clank of the door as he exited. The silence echoed after him through the hard, empty areas of the building, and into a void within Laura.

Pausing before she sorted through the paperwork on her desk, Laura reconstructed Charles Houseman in the chair across from her. He was lean and stern, as though he would actually prefer ten laps around the football field to dessert.

What did she find in him, then, that was so — attractive?

Annoyed with herself, she put the idea aside. But she realized she could not concentrate. There wasn't anything to do here that she couldn't pack into her briefcase and take home with her.

Abruptly, she got to her feet and determined to brave the late afternoon sun to walk the short three blocks to her apartment and work where she could enjoy an enormous glass of iced tea.

She did some of her best thinking while she strolled under the oaks and palms that lined the walks of the flat campus. Unfortunately, when she tried to address the problems that faced her, all she could think about was Houseman.

It had been a long time since she had felt an attraction to a student, although it hadn't been so rare when she was younger. She'd never acted on any of these impulses, having recognized them as the trap she'd been warned against in her instructional courses in college.

As she got older, the age difference between her and her students grew wider. Besides, there had been Tony.

Charles Houseman sat in his car for a long time, trying to ignore the heat of the upholstery as it burned through his slacks and shirt.

He didn't often make a fool of himself, but he certainly had just now. He should have known there'd probably be some professional injunction against Dr. Parsons helping him with his book.

Damned if he knew what to do. He just

wasn't cut out to be a civilian. He should march back in there and apologize.

Then again — how?

He tapped his fingers on the steering wheel, then looked out across the campus, back toward the building he had just come from.

A flash of blue caught his eye as Laura Parsons left the doorway and strode along a walk. Strange, there was no parking lot in that direction. He knew because he'd toured the campus extensively before picking up his daughter at ten that morning.

Why would Dr. Parsons be going in that direction?

Houseman turned the key in the ignition and the car's motor purred to life. He carefully swung it around and followed at a discreet distance, allowing her to leave campus by the western gate without seeing him. A block further she turned down a narrow street lined with apartment buildings, so he passed the lane and looped back by going around the next block.

Yes, there she was, letting herself into the street-level door decorated with the wreath of dried flowers. Ferns spilled from urns on the porch. Aha!

He hesitated, backed into a driveway, and left the lane without actually passing her door.

He could easily get into trouble, but his training was taking over. There was an objective to be overcome.

The apartment was stuffy because Laura had not left the ceiling fan on. Air-conditioning was too expensive to run when she was not there. For that reason, she tried to spend as much time as she could on campus, absorbing the coolness of her office or the library.

But there were times when there was no other place to go. There was work to be done in what should have been her living room. The room was an office itself, with a computer, file cabinet, and extensive bookcases constructed of bare planks and cement blocks. It was functional rather than stylish, meaning that it was generally cluttered, occasionally chaotic.

Laura dropped her mail onto the keyboard of the computer, merely in passing, without looking through it. She was on her way to the small kitchen and the pitcher of tea in the refrigerator. Luckily, there was enough for two glasses, enough to tide her over until a new pitcher could be brewed. Enough ice, accompanied by the puff of cold air from the freezer compartment to cool the perspiration on her neck.

Life could be bearable for a few hours longer—until the sun set and the sea breeze would take over.

She couldn't stand the dress, hose, and shoes a moment longer, so carrying her glass of tea, she went upstairs to her bedroom and found a flowing Indian gauze dress and a pair of sandals which were much more comfortable.

Laura paused to open the broad window that looked out on the communal garden below. At this time of year, she was one of the few residents who stuck out the sweltering summer, who witnessed the rampant wild verbena that clung tenaciously to the gravel around the palm trees. She made a mental note to harvest some of the flowers and dry them for her potpourri before the lawn service mowed them under.

Somehow, she had always thought she would have a home with a larger garden where she could grow flowers and vegetables, the way her mother and father had. There was such a feeling of rightness about eating your own tomatoes and lettuce, a luxury in unlimited bouquets of common flowers throughout a house.

She took a long swallow of her tea, then reached overhead to turn on the ceiling fan over her bed. There were only a few concessions to comfort in her life. It was not easy to live as she did, yet she had few choices.

As Laura walked slowly back down the stairs to the living room-cum-office, she thought again of the conclusion she had recently reached that life was not going to get any better, that she ought to be more accepting of her fate.

If Tony had lived and recovered, maybe it

wouldn't have been so hard. But Tony, dear Tony, had turned bitter when his illness overtook him. He'd refused her wish to have a child—afraid he would pass on a tendency toward his illness to an innocent young life, even though Laura pleaded that she would be able to withstand the challenge.

Of course, he had been right. She would never have been able to raise a child alone on the salary she made as a high school teacher and then as a college professor. It cost too much to stay current in her field. It cost too much to write.

Carefully putting her glass beside her computer, she sank to a steno chair and picked up her mail. No bills—she lived a frugal life. Advertisements.

She was about to open an interesting-looking envelope from a magazine publisher when her doorbell rang. Wearily, she got to her feet and walked around her desk to reach the door. Looking out the peephole, she saw the last person she had expected to see.

Charles Houseman.

What the hell is he doing here? Drawing a quick breath, she threw the envelope back down onto her desk and opened the door.

"I wanted to make an official apology for my stupidity," Houseman said, as though he'd been practicing. "I hope this will—speak for me."

He handed her a bouquet of mixed flowers,

exactly like the ones she always stopped to admire, but was too frugal to buy when she went to the nearby supermarket.

"I—ah—don't know what to say," Laura stammered, taking the flowers and touching a large pink carnation which centered the bouquet. "Come in. I'll—explain."

Houseman took a few steps into the room and stared at her computer, it's cyan-colored screen glaring back at him. "What—"

"I eke out a living writing magazine articles and tracts on teaching communications," Laura began. "I really can't take on anything more. I have a few article contracts to fulfill. If I stop contributing to my usual outlets for any length of time, I'll lose my momentum and recognition."

"I see," Houseman said. "I thought you were just one of these teachers who are all method and no substance."

"I don't claim to be infallible as an instructor," Laura replied. "I've just had exceptional success doing what I do and write extensively about it to help other teachers. My focus is a little narrow, I confess, but—" She shrugged.

"Hm! Well, I bow to your wisdom," Houseman said stiffly. "I see you're working. I'll—get out of your way."

Laura suddenly didn't want him to leave. But

she had nothing more than one glass of iced tea to offer him.

"I — ah — don't mind, I wish I had something to offer you."

"I wouldn't dream —"

"If I can help you, later," Laura offered. "Once you get started."

"But how do I start?" Houseman pleaded.

The easy answer that came glibly to Laura's lips died there when she saw the pain in Houseman's eyes.

"Do you write longhand?" she asked.

"I'm used to dictating," Houseman said. "Letters and so on."

Laura was not surprised. "Well, then," she suggested, "buy a little tape recorder, take a walk, and talk into it."

"Just — like that?" he asked. "That doesn't seem like writing."

"Ah-ha! You're just as afraid of writing as those kids in the class," she observed. "You've got an image in your head of writing being some mysterious, ephemeral courting of a muse. Believe me, it's not that romantic. Find a word to start with and go from there."

"A word?"

"I suggest *the*. Works for me every time."

Houseman looked down at her doubtfully for a moment, then reached for the door. "I'll think about it. You'd better put those flowers in water."

"Yes," Laura agreed. "Thank you. I'll see you tomorrow."

She stared after him as she closed the door behind him.

Then she realized that she didn't know how he had found out where she lived. She'd have to ask him. Tomorrow.

Houseman left his car in the curved driveway of his bungalow in a fashionable suburb. The sun was still hot against his shoulders.

Dropping his keys into the pocket of his slacks, he strode through the house and out to the swimming pool. Becky was collecting her magazines and the remnants of her snacks from the deck where she liked to sunbathe.

"I was beginning to worry about you," she said, tugging at the hem of the oversized T-shirt covering her skimpy bikini. "Your class was over at three and it's almost five."

"I—I said something to your teacher and had to go back to apologize," he said. It never served any purpose to hide his faults from Becky. Her blue eyes bored into him, and he knew she could read his soul.

"Oh, Dad," she groaned, moving past him toward the kitchen.

"I took her a bouquet of flowers. I think that made up for what I did."

"What did you do?" Becky called over the din of soda cans being dumped into the recycling bin.

"I asked her to help me with my book," he said, following her back to the kitchen.

Becky turned back toward him. "That's not why I suggested you take her course!"

"I know!" he agreed. "It just came out. I know you don't think I'm susceptible to such things, but for some reason, I just lost — all sense and discretion."

Becky shook her head slowly.

"I learned a lot about Dr. Parsons," he went on. "She lives just off campus. She writes — magazine articles, I guess. She has a computer, quite nice, really."

"I've got to take a shower," Becky said, but her face told him she thought he was hopeless.

"Want to go someplace for dinner?" he asked. "I need to go to the mall. Need a few things for that class."

"Sure," Becky called back to him before she slammed her bedroom door.

He started to pour himself a drink, then remembered that lately Becky had flatly refused to fill the ice bucket at the bar. It was a silent reminder that she had been thoroughly disgusted with the bender he went on when he'd retired. In his stupors, he could forget that his wife had left him. But reality always came with morning.

Becky had been right. There were times he had come close to cursing her, but she was his daughter, flesh of his flesh. He'd often wished for a son, but a son would not have stuck by him through the last few months.

A son would have split, grown his hair long, and had his left ear pierced in defiance of everything military—and he might have been justified.

Life was a mess. Civilian life. Without structure, without order. He needed order.

He hadn't realized that he'd picked up a heavy crystal cocktail glass. His chin puckered pensively. He returned the glass to the mahogany surface of the bar with a resonant thud.

Then he went to the master bedroom and laid out a change of clothes. It was hot and even with air-conditioning, he had found himself taking three showers a day. Sometimes it was the most constructive thing he accomplished, he thought. He wasn't coping very well. Not well at all. It wouldn't be long before he'd be talking to himself, answering himself, debating and arguing—

Get a grip, he urged himself.

Becky sat across from Charles at a table in a restaurant they had decided to try. Nothing fancy, just a place that had a friendly-looking hostess and hanging plants in the solarium where they were seated.

She perked up when she saw the waiter nearing their table.

Houseman stiffened.

The kid's blond hair was pulled back from his face into a tight ponytail, and he was wearing a tucked white shirt and neat black trousers, but he was unmistakably the same kid who had sat beside him in Dr. Parsons' class.

"Good evening," he said, handing menus first to Becky and then to Houseman. "My name is Greg and I'll be your server tonight. The soup of the day is gazpacho and the special is grilled chicken with Noodles Alfredo. Can I get you something to drink while you look at the menu?"

"Iced tea, and I'll have the special," Houseman said, wanting to get the kid away from the table as soon as possible.

Becky dragged her eyes away from the waiter and opened the menu. "I'll have iced tea, too," she said slowly. "I've heard the burgers here are good. The—Garden Burger and onion rings."

She looked up at the kid with one of the flashiest smiles in her repertoire and it was returned in kind.

Houseman felt himself scowl as he handed his menu back, but the kid didn't seem to notice.

It was a Monday night and business was slow.

The service was good; Houseman had come to expect that when he went anywhere with Becky and there were male servers. She was the kind of girl who turned guys' heads, but to his knowledge she didn't abuse her power. Maybe later she would take advantage of it, and he dreaded the day she played games like that. He wouldn't know how to tell her that life wasn't a game, that it was serious stuff.

A dark-haired boy came by and filled their tea glasses before they were half-empty, and Houseman suspected he had just wanted to get a closer look at Becky.

The server brought extra bread with Houseman's dinner and found a fuller bottle of ketchup for Becky's onion rings. *Damn, I'd be falling all over myself, too,* he thought, *if someone like Becky showed me the least encouragement.*

He felt lonely, very lonely. As though his useful life was over, and there was nothing left to him but to struggle with his memoirs. With any luck, he could draw the project out for years.

"I'm so glad you're taking that class," Becky was saying between bites. "I get such a good feeling from Dr. Parsons. I don't think she's married, is she?"

Houseman shook his head. "No. It seems she lives alone."

"The word around campus is that everyone

loves her. I know that could sound kind of — suspect. But I haven't heard a bad word about her."

Houseman nodded.

Becky paused between halves of her Garden Burger and looked up at her father thoughtfully.

"Do you mind if I send Mom something for Mother's Day? It's Sunday, and I'll have to mail it tomorrow if it's to reach her."

Houseman shrugged. "Do you need any money?"

Becky's eyes narrowed slightly, then she touched her napkin to her mouth. "No. I can take care of it. I didn't have anything expensive in mind."

"It's fine with me," Houseman said. He didn't want to think about Doris anymore.

The dark-haired kid with the iced tea came by and would have refilled their glasses, but Houseman waved him away. The boy insisted on clearing the empty bread basket and salad plate from Houseman's place and retreated just as the tall, blond kid returned and asked if they would like dessert.

Becky shook her head. "Some other time," she said.

The kid left the bill and smiled.

"He's very cute," Becky observed.

"He sits beside me in Dr. Parsons' class."

Becky's blue eyes flashed. "Maybe we should trade classes."

"Not on your life!" he said and tossed an extra dollar down on the table. Maybe if he tipped more than usual, the kid would know he wanted to put some space between them.

They went to the Radio Shack in the mall, and he bought a tape recorder he could hold in his hand and take with him when he walked around the yard. He always thought better when he was pacing. He bought more tapes than he would ever need and extra batteries, then quizzed the manager of the department about the latest computers. He'd probably need one if he decided to write his book.

Becky was bored and excused herself to look through a shop across the concourse which specialized in cheap jewelry and hair ornaments. When she returned carrying a shopping bag, he was talking about printers.

Tilting her head, she let him know she was amused, but only for so long.

"I do have homework," she whispered.

"So do I," he answered, then took the salesman's card.

He had something to do, he realized with exultation, if only briefly.

Houseman left the top of the car down on the way home, even though there was distant lightning in the sky. There was something about the breeze brushing past his cheeks that made him feel good again. It was the successful completion of a brief skirmish, perhaps, and not the victory of a battle or a war, but it was something to build on.

Laura had let herself into her classroom a few minutes earlier than usual, suspecting correctly that the previous evening class would have left the seating arrangement in disarray. For some reason, she was not surprised that Becky Houseman showed up early, also, and pitched in with the chore.

"I have to apologize for my father," Becky said, picking up a piece of notebook paper from the seat of a chair and crumpling it in her fist. "He never should have asked you to work on his book with him. That's not why I suggested that he take this class. Now he's made it very awkward for all of us."

Laura took a deep breath. She hadn't slept well the night before, and it hadn't been the whirring of her overhead fan that had kept her awake.

"I'm sure your father can do whatever he puts his mind to," Laura said.

Becky giggled and took her seat in the middle of the front row. "This morning, he's pacing around the house, saying *the* into his new tape recorder. Over and over again." She shook her head.

44

"That's probably my fault," Laura admitted with a sheepish smile, straightening the podium.

"No, I'll take responsibility for that, too." Becky ran her hand through her short blond hair. "I'll try to smooth all this out as well as I can. I've been picking up after him ever since Mom left a year ago. So help me, he couldn't so much as make a cup of instant coffee for himself. Mom and I both knew he would be helpless, so when they divorced, I stayed with him. Besides, Mom was used to being on her own most of the time anyway. Dad was always off somewhere or other, and when he was home, he'd be preoccupied and wouldn't be able to talk to her about — what he'd been doing. Maybe that's part of what's bothering him. He's never been free to talk to anyone about anything before."

Laura was uncomfortable hearing so much about the man whose face had been so much on her mind during her sleepless night.

"You're very perceptive for someone so young," Laura said, trying to address the Houseman who was present and forget about the absent one.

"Army brats specialize in trying to figure out the best route to survival," she said, lowering her voice as another student entered the room.

"Are you an Army brat, too?" asked the girl who had just entered the room. She sat down tentatively beside Becky, even though that wasn't the seat she had taken the day before. "Have you ever lived in Germany?"

Becky shook her head, but her expression was friendly as though she had just recognized someone she vaguely remembered.

Becky would be all right, Laura knew.

It was time for class to begin, she told herself.

Houseman had seen unorthodox instructional techniques before, but Laura Parsons' seemed to border on the insane. He shook his head and tossed his pen down on the writing arm of his student chair with disgust,

Ironically, the kid beside him, hair once again unfettered and earring dangling, was straining forward in his seat, intent on Laura's every word.

He thought of her as Laura, not as Professor or Doctor Parsons, as the students addressed her. He viewed her critically, as he had been trained to, looking for habits that signaled weaknesses. But all he could see was her total involvement with the process of teaching, a give and take of ideas and energy.

Laura's delicate features took on a luminosity when she was reacting to the students' enthusiasm. This was clearly her passion, the thing which kept her going. Knowing as he did that her home was merely an apartment, probably just a place to work and sleep, he extrapolated that teaching was the touchstone of her life.

He envied her having a touchstone, having any anchor or rudder or foundation. He had none—no marriage, no career.

Only Becky.

He leaned back in his chair and fiddled with the mechanism in his pen.

God, it was too much to expect Becky to be the focus of his life. He was already too judgmental when it came to her. It was all he could do to keep from ordering her around. "Don't stay out in the sun too long," he wanted to say. "Be careful when you drive. Don't date that kid. For God's sake, don't—"

The kid beside him responded to something someone else said, then laughed and shook his fist in the air. "Yes!" he hissed jubilantly, then turned his triumphant grin toward Houseman.

Houseman blinked away his reverie and tried to concentrate on Laura, but he had missed too much of the train of thought.

Laura looked straight at him, as though she knew exactly what had happened—that he'd been woolgathering and was totally lost. Her delicate hands spread wide to calm the class, then grasped the podium.

"Let's summarize what we've just discussed," she said, then covered for him by saying, "for the sake of your notes."

Houseman scrambled to find a fresh sheet of paper in his notebook and scribbled to keep up with Laura's dictation.

"This is a good time to take our break," Laura said, closing her notes. "Good work, everyone. Very good work."

The students got to their feet and filed from the room with varying degrees of energy. The exertion of learning seemed to have taken some of the ginger out of the kid who sat beside Houseman. Greg, that was his name. He stood and stretched, then shambled out the door, tugging at the ponytail of the girl ahead of him. She turned and looked up at him coquettishly, then disappeared into the hall.

Houseman sat there, feeling his own inertia. Too late he saw Laura walking toward him.

"So—" Laura said, sitting down in the seat ahead of him and draping her arm over the back of the chair. "Are you having a hard time getting into the swing of things?"

He frowned.

"I sensed you losing your concentration," she went on.

He sighed. "I didn't know you had such a grasp of what's going on in the class," he said. "I've done some instructing, and I never—"

Laura smiled. "In a small class like this, I know when someone gets lost. I just have to

48

teach around him, then catch him back into the fold at the first opportunity."

Her fingers fluttered gracefully then tapped against the back of the chair.

"Do you need help with something?" she asked.

"Yes, but I don't know what it is."

"Becky said that you spent the evening trying to begin your book by dictating into the recorder you bought."

"Yes." He got to his feet wearily. "I felt like a fool saying *the* into the blasted thing a thousand times."

Laura stood and looked up at him with an expression she probably intended to be encouraging. "That's a start."

"I'm not getting anywhere!"

"Your heart's not in it," she said. "Figure out why not. Then you'll understand—"

"I don't intend to be emotionally involved with what I'm going to write. It's an assignment!"

"Ah! That's the problem!" Laura told him, as though he had touched on something she could understand. "I'll deal with that in our second hour. Go take a break. You need to clear your mind and come back fresh."

She was mollycoddling him, he knew. But, damn! It was just what he needed at the moment.

Outside the classroom, Becky Houseman waited for her father, an anxious expression on her face. Laura noticed that she seemed uneasy. She didn't particularly want to be drawn into the scene, but there was only so much space in the hallway, and the other students had already established their enclaves.

"Your agent called," Becky said, handing her father a slip of paper. "He wants you to call him immediately."

"Did you take care of that errand?" Houseman asked, as though there was something very important which took precedence over whatever it was she presented to him.

"Yes, sir," she replied in an automatic gesture, but her focus would not be diverted.

"You can use the phone in my office," Laura offered, reaching for the key in the pocket of her skirt.

"No," Houseman said, looking around. "I'll use the pay phone down the hall."

Becky watched him stride down the corridor then turned back to Laura.

"He's really very upset with all of this," Becky said. "I don't understand it. I thought it would take his mind off leaving the army and — the divorce. He's a great storyteller and a very articulate speaker."

Laura smiled. "Articulate. Excellent."

Becky giggled. "I've always known the big words, Dr. Parsons. It's just that I feel that you've given me permission to use them. What do you think—about my father's writer's block?"

"I don't know enough about it, dear. I just know what I would do, and what I do changes in each situation."

"I don't care if he ever writes a book. He doesn't have to, you know. It's just that I can't bear to see him in such pain."

Laura bit her lip and looked to the end of the hallway, where Houseman was still on the phone. Pain was something Laura knew about— the deep-down, immobilizing pain of an unseen wound for which there was no surgery, no dressing, no analgesic. It was usually more complex than anyone else could understand. There was never a simple solution.

"I'll see what I can do," Laura murmured, as the members of her class, as if on some unspoken cue, began to move back toward the classroom.

Greg Swensen, the tall young man who sat beside Houseman slowed his steps and looked down at Becky as he neared them. Laura had seen that expression before.

Becky glanced up at Greg and smiled.

Suddenly feeling excluded, Laura smiled and

left the knot of people around the door. She hurried down the hall to the vending machine and bought a can of soda, trying to ignore Houseman's heated phone conversation.

Returning to the classroom, Laura was amused that Greg was still outside the door, talking to Becky. Laura was sensitive enough to body language to know that Houseman didn't think much of Greg—and that Becky was absolutely taken by him.

She shook her head slightly, hoping it was not enough for anyone to notice. The more life changed, the more it stayed the same.

Laura stalled, allowing the students to settle down of their own accord, waiting for Houseman and Greg Swensen. Houseman came into the room, obviously controlling some anger. Greg was last to return, closing the door behind him, his attention still somewhere out in the hall.

"Before we go any further," Laura said, "we have to face the inevitable. Assignments. It's a word that strikes terror in most hearts, including mine. I'm going to share some of my techniques of sneaking up on the little buggers and finessing them into submission. You might want to take some notes, and I'd really like you to share any of your ideas with us."

She could see Houseman hunch forward in his chair, ready to take extensive notes. Greg

Swensen seemed lost in his own thoughts.

As the hour wore on, she was able to refocus their attention on the class discussion, but not without receiving some strange looks, not only from Houseman and Greg, but from the rest of the class.

Soon she had everyone participating in the exercises again. Charles Houseman was becoming more comfortable with the rest of the class. At one point, the rapid-fire exchange of ideas became so lively, Laura caught a glimpse of the man behind that stone facade.

And when he laughed with the rest of the class, she knew that the fascination she had begun to feel the day before had turned to something much more profound. And dangerous.

Laura wasn't surprised that Houseman followed her to her office at a discreet distance.

He stood in the doorway, tall and spare, his face too serious to be handsome, yet she had seen glimpses of his smile and knew it could be devastating.

She steeled herself with a breath and motioned for him to come in and sit down.

"I'm asking for your help one last time," he said, his voice low and controlled. "My agent has to have an answer by Friday. You are the only person I know I can turn to—"

"All right," Laura said, raising her hand to stop him. She quickly glanced at the work on her desk and tried to assess the tasks she had waiting for her at home for the rest of the day. "I can give you a few minutes . . ."

Charles Houseman glanced around the office and appeared to be listening. "Blame it on my intelligence training, but I don't feel I can talk to you here. I'd rather it be at my place. Don't worry. Becky will be there. We'll—have dinner. I'll come by for you at six."

"Oh. Well, yes, that'll be fine," Laura agreed, thankful for a reprieve, of sorts.

Sitting at the round glass patio table and trying to feel less than overwhelmed by the Housemans' elegant bungalow and swimming pool, Laura lowered the pages of the contract she was reading. For a moment, she tried to digest the terms, all couched in elaborate legal language.

"I know writers who would kill for a contract like this," she said, directing her remarks toward her host.

Charles Houseman stood a few feet away, grilling steaks on the gas barbecue. With a long-handled meat fork clutched in his hand, he turned toward her, his eyes narrowed in an unasked question.

"Not literally!" Laura laughed, guessing at his thoughts. "At least, I don't think so."

Charles looked visibly relieved.

"Still, the terms are very generous," she told

him, then shook her head. "I suppose—the publisher knows what he's doing—"

He laid down the fork and returned to the table, leaning on the back of a chair with his muscular arms tensed. "That's why I wanted you to read the contract. Is it too good to be true?"

Laura shrugged and laid the document on the tabletop, leaving her hand on it so it didn't blow away. "It's in black and white. Once you sign it, you get paid, so long as you write a book that meets the requirements, and they seem fairly lenient."

"Have you ever written a book?"

"I've never sold one," Laura told him, making a distinction. "I've sold lots of magazine articles, though."

"And this is more than generous?"

"Yes," Laura replied, pushing a lock of hair out of her eyes. The wind was freshening and heavy clouds were moving in from the water.

"That's what bothers me," he explained, pulling the chair from the table and sitting down abruptly. "To write this book, I've been told I'll have access to materials which had been highly classified. See, I suspect someone wants the story to come out for some political purposes. I'm afraid someone intends to stand over my shoulder—or the shoulder of whoever is going to edit it—and make sure the right things are left in and the wrong things are edited out."

"I see," Laura said, studying the seriousness in his eyes.

"I've tried to steer clear of politics in the service," he said. "It wasn't easy. I did my job and did it well. I tried to find the purpose of the greater good. But now that I'm no longer in the service, I don't want to be used to further someone else's political ambitions."

"Then I think you should follow your instincts," she advised.

"And not sign the stupid thing?"

"If that's how you feel deep inside."

Houseman's smile was tentative, but he seemed relieved. "I've never rejected an assignment before," he said. "In the service, it's not an option. It feels strange now. This is the first time in my life I've been free of the pressure of being under orders. Sometimes I just wish someone would tell me what to do."

"I'm not telling you to turn down this contract," Laura pointed out. "I'm only telling you that it's not going to be the end of the world if you do."

"I know that," Houseman said. "But it's good to have your advice."

Becky came to the patio door, a concerned look in her eyes. "The weather report on the television says there's a storm heading this way, sir," she said. "I think I'll set the table inside rather than out here."

"Fine," Charles agreed, pushing his chair back. "But the steaks need to grill a little longer."

"Can I help with anything?" Laura offered, getting to her feet.

"No! You're a guest!" Charles said, reaching for the meat fork again.

The wind was beginning to swirl across the patio, swaying the hanging pots and scattering fallen leaves across the deck.

She picked up the contract and took it inside to the safety of a small desk in the living room.

Laura had caught only glimpses of the house when she arrived. Charles had invited her out to the patio while he grilled the steaks, and she could not very well have lingered to appreciate the spare modern furniture and eclectic objets d'art. Even now, she stopped only a moment to glance at a painting before searching out Becky in the kitchen to offer her help.

"I don't know what to do!" Becky spouted, slamming cupboard doors. "It seems silly to put grilled steaks on the china, but the everyday dishes look out of place on the linen table-cloth."

"Go ahead and use the china," Laura advised, trying to be helpful. "Or would you rather just set this table here in the kitchen?"

"You wouldn't mind?" Becky asked, as though holding her breath.

"I'd love it, really," Laura assured her. "Here, let me help."

"I'll have to —" Becky said, immobilized by indecision.

"Shush!" Laura hissed, seeing what a nervous state Becky was in. "This is really the easiest thing to do."

"My mother would never entertain anyone in the kitchen," Becky told her. "She was as by-the-book as my father."

"Maybe it's time to throw the book away," Laura suggested gently, taking the pile of everyday dishes from the girl's hands and placing them on the woven mats on the round kitchen table. "It's hard to live your life by someone else's standards, especially when you don't know the rules."

Becky nodded in agreement, her face tense as she distributed the silverware.

"Oh! We're eating in here?" Charles asked, coming into the kitchen with the platter of steaks.

Laura looked up at him and smiled. "It's still a cookout," she told him, picking up the salad bowl from the counter. "Becky, I just love salads like this."

The look Becky gave her said she thought she was being patronized, that she wasn't exactly certain that everything was going to be all right. Just as they had begun to eat, the lights flickered and threatened to go out.

"Oh, no!" Becky exclaimed, jumping to her feet. "I'll get some candles. I hate storms."

"We get them almost every day in the summer," Laura said.

The girl returned with some votive candles in little glass holders that diffused their flickering light. "We probably won't need these," she said, lighting the last one, but just then the power dipped again. After a heartbeat, the lights returned to their normal intensity. Becky sighed as she resumed her seat. Laura smiled at her encouragingly.

"Those candles are lovely," Laura said admiringly.

"Better safe than sorry," Charles said. "Eat. Eat."

He suddenly seemed more at ease, as though he had settled something overwhelming in his mind and could now go on about the mundane motions with less strain. Laura knew that feeling, too.

"Dr. Parsons says I can turn down that book contract and forget about it," he told Becky.

"That's — that's probably the best thing to do," she agreed tentatively.

"But I think I'd still like to write," he added. "Nothing so lofty as the book for the contract. I'd like to learn to write, keep on taking the classes. Do it the right way, not just jump in with some impossible contract serious writers would resent."

"What would you write?" Laura asked. "War stories?"

"No!" Charles said. "I think the reason I can't feel right about writing my own experiences is that some of them are too painful. I'd rather write fiction, like mysteries or space fantasies."

"Really?" Becky interrupted. "That would be awesome."

"Do you think so?" he asked her. "I've had such a hard time finding anything I could get my teeth into, that would challenge my mind. That's what I miss. I imagine golf and tennis can be intellectual, but I just haven't mastered them. I think I want to learn to write before I have to fulfill a contract and get stuck on something I should have learned in the beginning."

Laura couldn't restrain her sudden nod of approval.

"You'll have to put up with me in your class for a little longer, then," Charles said apologetically. "I was going to drop out toward the end, I thought. But I never leave a job undone. It's contrary to everything I've ever learned. What will I take when I've finished your class?"

"I don't know," Laura replied thoughtfully. "The usual creative writing course won't be offered next fall because of the budget cuts.

Maybe you can find an informal course somewhere else."

Houseman's eyes were suddenly dubious. "Do you mean that someone else teaches writing?"

"Oh, sure," Laura said, surprised that the concept threw him.

"Well, I thought — I'm sure you could teach me everything I need to know."

Laura laughed gently. "That's a flattering thought, but no one knows everything about any one topic."

Charles Houseman stared back at her. Then he looked away.

"I've noticed that there are some books lying around that are lighter reads," Laura said, not quite comfortable letting them know of her penchant for close observation. "Maybe you could start by scribbling down a few ideas along those lines."

"Dad, you'd do great with a mystery," Becky said. "You know all the ins and outs."

The look Charles gave his daughter might not have been meant to cut her off, but it did. She looked back at her plate as though she had been censored.

"Maybe you're right," Charles said quietly. He took a deep breath and cut another bite from his steak. "Eat up! We have cheesecake for dessert."

The telephone at Charles Houseman's elbow rang, but he almost ignored it. It was Becky who reached for the phone to keep it from ringing a third time.

"Houseman," she said automatically. "Oh! Hello! I—ah—didn't expect you to call—. Wait a minute. Can I put you on hold and pick up the phone in another room? Good!"

She smiled apologetically toward her father and Laura, then picked up her dinner plate and left.

"I'd be angry if I weren't so pleased that she's obviously finally made a friend," Charles said, pausing to poke his fork at a slice of cucumber.

"There was a girl in class today who said she was a service brat, too," Laura remarked. "I think it might be she."

Houseman nodded, then smiled slightly. "That would be good. Someone to understand what she's been through. Although Doris and Becky didn't have to move around very much. I was stationed at the Pentagon most of the time I was in Intelligence, so we lived in Arlington. Still—"

His smile grew a little, although he averted his eyes slightly, "I don't mind her going off that way if I have a chance to talk to you alone a little more."

For a long moment Laura studied his face in the light of the little candles. This was a setting she would have envisioned had she married when she was young. Dinner in the kitchen on a stormy night, candles fending off the threat of darkness. A pretty daughter off furthering her social life after helping with a simple but lovely meal.

The last thing she wanted was for Charles Houseman to ask her detailed and extensive questions about writing his book.

"Is there something specific you wanted to talk about?" she asked, taking the initiative.

Charles shrugged. "You probably already know a lot about me—about us. And I know almost nothing about you."

"I'd have thought you'd done your usual intelligence protocol to find out everything there is to know about me," Laura said with a playful sidelong glance.

"No!" Charles protested. "I know I offended you when I followed you yesterday. It doesn't take more than one instance to send me a message."

"Mm!" Laura said with a grin. "You have potential. It takes minute observation to be a writer."

"I'd rather you just come right out and tell me what you want me to know about you, and I'll let it go at that."

Laura laid her fork down on her plate and studied the flame of one of the candles for a moment. "I've been teaching for twenty-five years, the last seventeen at the community college. As you've probably guessed, I live alone and eke out my stipend by freelance writing. On the surface, I guess my life looks very narrow and boring, but I find every day, every hour filled with the excitement of learning about my students and my writing. The years have gone by so quickly, I'm constantly amazed. I just can't think that I would want my life to be any different."

Charles studied her face for a long moment, almost disturbing her.

"Yes," he said finally, "I can see that. You've never married?"

"No," Laura answered, taking a deep breath. "I may as well tell you the story. In college I thought I was very much in love with a young man who was a year ahead of me. Tony. When he graduated, we'd begun making plans to marry. But toward the end of his finals his senior year, he was complaining of fatigue. We thought it would let up if he took a few weeks and rested, but it didn't go away. It was diagnosed as leukemia.

"I said I'd drop out of school and we'd get married so I could take care of him. Both our families objected, and Tony was easily persuaded that he should go home and allow his family to look after him. I fought to go through the legality of being married. I so wanted a child! I kept telling Tony that if I had his child, a part of him would live on. But he refused, afraid that he'd pass on some defective gene. He kept saying I wouldn't be able to cope with a drastically ill child if I was alone. It was years after his death that I concluded he was probably right.

"I wasn't so much in love with Tony as I was in love with the idea of being in love, of making a great sacrifice for my ideals and the person dearest to me. So I've spent the years doing what I love doing, teaching and writing."

Charles reached for her hand. "You've been very brave."

"No," Laura countered. "Sometimes I think I've been the coward, hiding away out of the mainstream of life."

Charles Houseman sighed, and in the mixture of dimmed electric light and flickering candle-light, he seemed to let down his guard a little. "It sounds—inviting," he said.

He glanced around the room, then got to his feet and refilled their iced tea glasses from a pitcher on the counter. As he returned it, the lights flickered and went out.

When the darkness lasted for a long moment and there seemed no relief except for the flashes of lightning beyond the windows, Charles reached for a decorative candle that graced a centerpiece on a sideboard in the dining room and lighted it from one of the little candles that flickered on the table.

"I'll take this to Becky," he said. "Will you be all right?"

"Of course," Laura replied confidently.

Charles was gone for only a few minutes, returning with a very angry daughter.

"He's really very nice," Becky was protesting. "He seemed very concerned about you this afternoon when I went to take you that message. Dr. Parsons, what do you think of Greg Swensen?"

"Oh! Greg Swensen. He's the fifth Swensen I've had, I think. They're all hard-working young people. The first one went on to be an accountant, I think. Charles, don't let the flippant attitude influence you. They all have very inventive humor and are nice kids."

"I don't know about this—" Charles muttered.

Becky scowled and took the candle from her father's hand, placing it firmly on the counter to illuminate the space where she intended to work. "The reason you don't like him is he's so much like you," she observed, putting her empty dinner plate beside the sink.

Laura rose and removed the dinner plates from the table. "If I may interfere—blatantly," she said and turned to face Charles. "It wouldn't do any harm for Becky to form some friendships with young people whose families are well-established in the community—which isn't a

66

knock on the young lady who told you she was a service brat. I'd advise you to find a variety of friends, Becky. You certainly can't stay isolated in this house for the next few years."

"There's that, too," Charles said, thoughtfully. "Oh, all right, but I really wouldn't want you to go out tonight."

"I know. I told him we have company—but I didn't say who," Becky said, then chuckled. "I wanted to, but I didn't."

"Good," Charles said, as though from a great distance.

For a long moment, they worked in silence to clear the table for dessert.

"At least the water is still running," Becky said as she rinsed the dishes to put them into the dishwasher. "The lights have been off a long time, haven't they?"

"Don't worry," Laura reassured her. "It's something you'll have to get used to."

"I suppose so," Becky said. "Gosh, I'm glad you were here."

"Thank you," Laura said, and couldn't resist patting Becky's shoulder. It was about the most intimate gesture she allowed herself with one of her students, although many times she restrained herself from being more expressive. She relied more on verbal praise and encouragement.

Charles took a bakery-shop cheesecake from the refrigerator and handed it to Laura.

"Can I trust you to be fair?" he asked, and as the light in the room increased, she saw a smile creep into his eyes.

"Oh, I think so," Laura said seriously, then laughed. "I can cut this whole thing into three pieces, right?"

"That might be a little too generous," Becky laughed, taking a knife from its holder on the wall.

"I'll use my best judgment, then," Laura promised.

They were just beginning to eat dessert when the lights came back on. Becky was about to blow out the candles when Charles stopped her.

"Leave them," he said. "You know, the more I think about it, the more I have to change my mind about that young man."

"Greg?" Becky asked.

"Hm," Charles responded. "If Laura thinks he has potential, he might be all right."

Becky looked at Laura then back at her father. "A limited approval! Fine!" she said with an edge to her voice. "Then again, that's the best I've ever gotten. I'm not planning to run off and live with him."

"Well, it's always in the back of the mind, isn't it?" Charles asked.

Becky didn't say anything for a moment, then murmured, "Possibly. Is it always in the back of *your* mind, Father? When you meet a woman?"

Charles laughed, nervously. "Possibly."

"Dr. Parsons, what do you think?" Becky asked.

"I think this is a lovely cheesecake," Laura offered, sidestepping the issue.

Becky laughed and got up from the table. "Since the lights are back on, I'd better go do my homework."

"Homework?" Laura asked.

"My history teacher doesn't have your sympathy for students who want to enjoy the beach," Becky said, disappearing.

"Sometimes she's impossible." Charles remarked.

"Ah, you don't know what impossible is," Laura argued with a sympathetic laugh. "She's sweet and loving. You're very lucky."

The lines of his face deepened for an instant and then relaxed. "Yes, I am. Becky seems to like you—more than—another woman I took to dinner a few months ago."

Laura glanced up at him suddenly and saw a distressed expression she hadn't anticipated. "That—that's why—that little conversation about—motives?"

Charles grinned a bit sheepishly. "I'm a mystery reader, Laura. When I pick up a book, I can't help sneaking a peek at the ending. I like to know there's going to be a logical ending, even if it's a twist. I need someone in my life, a relationship. But I'm so old-fashioned, I can think of only one meaning for relationship, and that's marriage. So, I'm giving you a peek at the ending I want. You're a self-sufficient woman, with your career, and you obviously get a lot of satisfaction out of teaching. I understand I'm jeopardizing that. I'll walk away for a few weeks until the course is finished, but I'm very attracted to you."

Laura took a deep breath—and then another.

Charles got to his feet and walked over to the sink, then returned. "I said that badly."

"There are things that can't be said gracefully," Laura told him gently. "But I'm pretty old-fashioned, too, I guess, because it's a comfort to know we think the same way."

The telephone rang, and Charles merely raised his head and glanced in the direction of Becky's room. When the next ring was merely a little bleep, he grinned.

"It's getting to be like old times around here," he said. "I only hope it's not that Swensen boy. I'm not quite up to being understanding. Come. Let's sit in the living room where we can talk."

They were halfway to the sofa when Becky poked her head around an archway and reached the cordless telephone out to her father, carefully holding her palm over the mouthpiece. "It's Mom," she said in a stage whisper. "She says she's getting married to Fred."

"The financial planner?" Charles asked.

Becky nodded, her eyes wide with glee. "Can you talk to her?"

Charles took the telephone and turned slightly away. "Doris? You're marrying Fred? . . . Well, you know I want you to be happy. . . . Of course she can come, if you're waiting until July. She's taking two summer classes. I'll send her on the plane about a week before so she can help you get ready, then she can come back before you leave on your honeymoon . . . Sorry—force of habit. I'm pleased for you. We'll talk later."

When he'd handed the telephone back to Becky and she had returned to her room, Charles sank his hands into his pockets and looked out at the rain washing over the patio for a long moment.

"Is everything all right?" Laura asked, making herself comfortable at the end of the sofa.

When he looked back at her, a smile slowly came over his face. "I suddenly feel so free," he said. "I'm almost ashamed of the way I feel. I've decided to send the book contract back to the agent, I've liberated my daughter to make her own decisions, and now my ex-wife is marrying someone else! What I thought would be negatives have all turned positive."

"It's all in your attitude," Laura said, noticing a change in his posture as well as his face. The release of the tension he'd projected since the

71

first moment she had seen him seemed to leave him almost giddy.

Laura couldn't help the smile that began from somewhere inside her and reached out to Charles.

Sitting down beside her, Charles tentatively took her hand in his. "What would happen if someone at your college knew — that we were friends — if we became close friends?"

Laura thought awhile, experiencing the warmth and strength and gentleness of his fingers clasping hers.

"You know, it makes less and less difference to me," she said softly. "I don't want to stand back anymore and just look at life while other people live it. There was a time tonight when I wanted to reach out and hug Becky — and I think she needed it — and I held back, for professional reasons. There was a moment when I thought, if I get involved in your project, if our relationship comes to that ending you gave me a peek at, I'll lose my job. But right now, I don't mind risking it. I've played it safe for so long, it's time I lived closer to the edge."

"Are you sure?" he demanded, his hand applying a comfortable pressure to hers. "This is a decision you might not be able to back away from later on."

Laura took stock quickly and nodded affirmatively. "Maybe it's time I took the leap of faith to make my writing my career. I got a letter from an editor yesterday asking me to consider writing a series of four articles, and I was wondering how I could handle it in the few weeks between sessions. Now I can say to myself, 'Go ahead; it's not a problem.' "

"We're in agreement, then," Charles said, abruptly dropping her hand and bounding to his feet. "Becky! Come here a minute!" Then he chuckled. "Please?"

Becky appeared around the archway, her expression questioning.

"Angel, we're going out. Will you be all right?"

"Thank you for a lovely evening, Becky," Laura said, trying to touch all the bases, knowing that Charles was used to being in charge and deciding to let him take the lead.

"It was great to have you here," Becky said dutifully. Then her expression changed to a mischievous smile. "Is something happening here?"

"Yes!" Charles said decisively, reaching out to tousle her short blond hair. "Can you be discreet about what happens in our home?"

"Mum's the word!" Becky cooed, reaching out to hug her father. Then she looked at Laura, and her confusion in the face of the situation was plain.

Laura spread her arms to encompass Becky. Words weren't necessary. They exchanged a look that communicated understanding and support and a promise of solidarity in the future.

Outside, the rain had stopped and the evening was fresh and cool, bright stars glimmering in a twilight sky.

"If you tell me it's not going to rain again, I'll put the top back down," Charles said.

"Oh, let's risk it!" Laura proposed.

"Have you ever thought of starting a mystery with a line like *It was a dark and stormy night?*" he asked, unsnapping the canvas roof of his convertible.

"That's terrible!" Laura laughed, pitching in to help him. "How about this one? *It was a night when anything could happen.*"

"That has real possibilities," Charles agreed.

Repeat Performance

by Stacey Dennis

Mary tugged the hem of her white dacron top down over her ample hips and sighed. Ten pounds. Ten stinking, lousy pounds that she just could not lose! It made her crazy. At least it did when she thought about it, which fortunately wasn't that often.

"No, only every time you try to get into something you haven't worn in a while, or when you're foolish enough to look too close in the mirror, Mary, old girl," she told herself. Then she laughed. Oh well, there was a lot more to life than being ten pounds overweight, a lot more than excess poundage to worry about.

Mary leaned close to the mirror and concentrated on her make-up. She'd always enjoyed wearing make-up, and that hadn't changed, even with all the trauma she'd gone through in the past few years. Raymond's suicide. It had been such a devastating shock. Oh, she'd known her husband wasn't himself, and hadn't been for a long time, but he'd been a private person, not one to open up to anyone, even his wife of twenty-eight years. So he carried his disappointment and feelings of failure around with him until one cold night in January he just couldn't cope anymore.

Mary shuddered, then shook herself from her reverie. That was all behind her now. Raymond had made his choice, and now she had to live with the result: widowhood.

Amazingly enough it wasn't as terrible as Mary had feared. Once she got over the terrible shock and the grief started to dull a little, she found she liked her new freedom. If she went out and it got late, she didn't have to worry about calling home. If she felt like a peanut butter sandwich for dinner instead of a cooked meal, there was no complaining. She had no one to please but herself.

And best of all, she had her job, she mused as she screwed the cap back on her new lipstick, a coral shade called "Salmon Satin."

Working at Easton's Animal Hospital had been her salvation. It kept her sane in the beginning when all she wanted to do was curl up in a closet and cry, and now it not only provided a modest living, it also gave her a reason to get up in the morning.

As she picked up her jacket and purse, Mary chuckled. And she enjoyed her co-workers, too. You had to be a little crazy to work in an animal hospital. And now, today, they would finally meet the new veterinarian, Dr. Thomas Warren, who was replacing the retiring Ed Rogers.

"He's probably young and cute with tight buns," Mary's co-worker said, giggling as she poured them each a cup of coffee a half-hour later. "Oh, I do admire tight buns," Jesse said, rolling her blue eyes heavenward.

Mary laughed. Jesse was about the same age as her youngest daughter, Sunny, and almost as fresh. "You need your mouth washed out, young lady," she threatened, "or should I clean out your mind?"

Jesse tossed her head and gave Mary a haughty look. "Don't try your mother act on me, Mary Jeffrey. Don't you have enough kids of your own to work on?"

"More than enough," Mary said, nodding, "only they're not here and you are."

"Well, get with it, Mary, old girl," Jesse said. "We women like to look at men just as much as they like to look at us. They check out our boobies, we admire their buns. No difference, see?"

"Good morning, ladies. This must be the right place. I was warned that this clinic was practically crawling with beautiful women."

"Oh! Dr. Warren? You *are* Dr. Warren, aren't you?" Jesse blurted, then lapsed into a stupefied silence as Mary stared.

This was the man who was taking over Dr. Rogers practice? Why, his hair was snow white! He was at least fifty-five or six, and they had all been expecting a much younger man, possibly someone just out of veterinary school. Mary felt her cheeks flush. How many of Jesse's outrageous remarks had he overheard?

"Ladies?" the stranger queried, looking puzzled. "Is there something on my jacket? Leftover food in my beard?"

Mary didn't see any food in the snowy beard, but she decided she wouldn't mind searching to make sure. Good Lord, her reaction was even worse than Jesse's! But older than she'd expected or not, this was one good-looking male!

"I'm sorry," she managed, after swallowing a couple of times. "You must think you've stumbled into a nest of idiots. It's just that . . . well, we were expecting someone a little younger. I mean since Dr. Rogers is retiring and all . . ."

Mary hadn't been this shaken since eighth grade when she'd had to read an essay aloud in English class. This man definitely wasn't young and yet he wasn't old either. Dr. Rogers was old. He shuffled when he got tired, which had become more and more frequent in the past few years, and sometimes he'd even sounded old, like his voice box was winding down or something. But this man . . . even with white hair he looked youthful and vigorous, as if he could run circles around all of them, young Jesse included. And he had the darkly tanned skin of an outdoorsman. And good Lord, the eyes! They were rich chocolate . . . to die for!

Dr. Warren was smiling. "Let me assure you right now that I won't be retiring for a long, long time, and my name is Tom, at least when we're not with patients. And you ladies are . . ."

"I'm Jesse Myers. I'm the receptionist. Of course, I can fill in and assist in simple procedures if Mary is busy, but she's the real assistant."

"Well, Jesse and Mary, I'm pleased to meet both of you. Ed told me he had a good crew here. There are two more employees, aren't there?"

"Yes. Linda Green and Pete Evans. They'll be in shortly. Linda helps Jesse out front, and Pete will work with you. He's on summer break right now, but he's going back to college in September to get his degree in veterinary medicine," Mary explained.

"Sounds good." Tom sniffed, then grinned almost boyishly. "May I have some of that coffee?"

"Oh, sure," Jesse said, jumping up before Mary could move.

Mary excused herself and went into the examining room to make sure everything was ready for the first patient. She smiled. It was Bingo, a lovable, Benji-type mutt that twelve-year-old Gary Brooks had rescued from the animal shelter.

"Well, you're very efficient, Mary," Tom said a few minutes later, his dark eyes flickering over the examining table. "Jesse tells me our first patient is a real ham. Bingo?"

Tom's eyes sparkled with good humor, and Mary felt herself relax a little. She'd always been an upbeat person, at least until Raymond's suicide. But now, almost two years after that tragic day, she was starting to feel like herself again.

"Bingo is one of a kind. You'll see."

Tom laughed. "I've always had a soft spot

for animals, ever since a baby bird fell out of its nest when I was about eight. I put him in a box lined with cotton and tried to feed him with an eye dropper, but he died a few hours after I found him. I guess that's when I decided to become a veterinarian."

Mary smiled as she busily checked instruments and supplies. She could almost picture a sandy-haired little boy peering into a cotton-lined box, and grieving when a baby bird died.

"Wait until you see what comes after Bingo," she said. "It's a potbellied pig, and she really does have a pot belly. Penelope is expecting."

Tom put his hand to his head and groaned. "What an initiation! A pregnant pig! What ever happened to all the nice, normal little kittens and puppies?"

"You'll have those, too," Mary assured him. "All in due time."

Pete came in and Mary introduced him to their new employer. Then Gary arrived with Bingo. Boy and dog walked into the examining room and when Gary stopped, Bingo immediately sat by his side. "Say hello, Bingo," Gary commanded.

Bingo promptly sat up and extended one paw.

Shaking his head and smiling, Tom shook

the paw. "Hello there, Bingo. How are you to-day?"

"Woof!" Bingo responded, his plume of a tail wagging enthusiastically.

Gary grinned and Mary followed suit, convinced that there were even more freckles on the boy's nose than there had been the last time.

"That means he feels fine and can't imagine why I brought him in here," Gary explained to Tom.

"Why did you? He looks great to me."

"Oh, he is, but he . . . well, my Mom said I have to be a responsible pet owner and have him neutered. I could take him back to the shelter and let them do it, but I'd rather have it done here. You won't hurt him, will you?"

"No way," Tom said, deftly lifting Bingo onto the table so he could do a quick exam. "He'll be asleep when we do the operation, and it's a simple, easy procedure. I'll put in a few stitches, and he may be a little uncomfortable for a couple of days, but that's it. And your Mom is right, Gary. Being a responsible pet owner means making sure that your pet doesn't contribute to the overpopulation. You're doing the right thing." Finishing his exam, Tom nodded. "We can take care of Bingo this afternoon if you want to leave him here now. He'll spend the night, and you can pick him up tomorrow morning."

Gary relinquished Bingo's leash, but he looked worried, and Mary couldn't resist putting her arm around his slim shoulders and giving him a quick hug. "Bingo will be fine," she promised the boy. "We'll take good care of him for you."

Gary left and Mary turned to find Tom watching her. Their eyes met and he winked. "You looked right at home with that boy," he remarked.

"I've had lots of practice."

Next came Penelope. Technically, she was considered an exotic pet, but since there were no exotic animal clinics in town, Dr. Rogers had agreed to look after her when Neil Andrews first brought her in.

In a state of advanced pregnancy, Penelope snorted and wheezed, and looked thoroughly fed up.

"Nice pig," Tom said, gently feeling Penelope's distended belly. "First litter?"

"Yes," Neil answered. "She's only a year old." Neil Andrews liked the unusual, hence Penelope, and soon, her progeny.

"I understand potbellied pigs make great pets," Tom said pleasantly.

"Penelope is not just a pet," Neil said, looking indignant. "She's a member of our family. Animals have deep feelings, you know."

Tom valiantly kept a straight face and shot Mary a quick, sideways look. "Certainly," he said. "I agree. What I should have said is that potbellied pigs make great family members."

Neil nodded, smiling with satisfaction. "Can you tell when the babies will arrive?" he asked. "I'm getting impatient, and so is my wife."

"Well, I can't be absolutely certain, but I'd guess it could be any day now. Do you have a litter box prepared?"

"Litter box? For Penelope?" Neil looked as if he might faint on the spot. Mary took a quick step in his direction, prepared to grab his arm if he started to tilt.

"What Dr. Warren means is that you should prepare a clean, quiet place where Penelope can give birth in comfort, Neil," she said diplomatically. "What about that nice family room you fixed in your garage?"

Neil beamed. "That would be perfect. Our bedroom is nearby, so Barbara and I will be close if Penelope needs us."

"Nice going, Mary," Tom said when Neil left, Penelope waddling along beside him. "I didn't do so well with that one, did I?"

Mary brushed lint off her white jacket. "You just need to get the lay of the land," she said.

"Neil is a very nice man. He's just a teensy bit overboard about his pet . . . whoops, I mean, family members!"

Tom grinned and rubbed his short, silvery beard. "I think I'm going to enjoy this even more than I anticipated."

"What did you do before you bought this clinic?" Mary asked curiously.

A shadow passed over Tom's face, and for a minute Mary thought he wouldn't answer. Then he spoke, but his voice was tight and clipped. "Nothing nearly so interesting as this," he said evasively. "Okay, where's the next patient?"

They worked through until noon, then Tom stripped off his disposable gloves, washed up, and shrugged out of his white coat. "I'll be back around one-thirty," he said. "I have a surgery scheduled for two p.m., don't I?"

"Yes, I think so," Mary answered, "but you'd better check the time with Jesse. Appointments are her department."

Tom nodded, and suddenly he looked older, harassed, anxious. "I'll be going home for lunch every day," he explained. "Jesse has my home number in case of an emergency; otherwise, I'd rather not be disturbed."

"Certainly," Mary said, feeling as though she'd been chastised. What in the world did the man think she was going to do, follow him home and sit on his front steps while he ate lunch?

"So, what do you think so far?" Jesse asked between bites of a chicken salad sandwich. "He's a good-looking devil for an older man, isn't he?" She peered at Mary from beneath thick, dark lashes.

Once again Mary was reminded of her perky, pesky daughter, Sunny. "He's okay," she said casually, lifting a forkful of potato salad. "I think he'll be pretty easy to work with, even if he did fly out of here on the dot of twelve as though a herd of rampaging elephants was chasing him. I wonder what he's got waiting for him at home that made him so anxious to get away? And he made a point of saying he didn't want to be disturbed unless it was an emergency."

"Mm, sounds like a young wife to me," Jesse murmured, her eye sparkling mischievously. She pulled a small bag of potato chips from her brown bag. "Or maybe just a live-in lover."

Maybe. It was definitely a possibility, Mary knew, surprised at the sharp disappointment she experienced as she thought of Tom with a young, beautiful woman. Silly, she chided herself silently. Silly and pointless. Tom was a nice-looking man, and so far he seemed to be a competent veterinarian. And he was a professional, certainly too smart to even dream of getting involved with an employee.

Good heavens, what was she thinking of? After only a few hours of working with the man she was already weaving fairy tales. He was probably happily married with six children and dozens of grandkids. And hurrying home to a nice quiet lunch with his faithful wife of thirty-odd years. But he wasn't wearing a wedding ring. Mary had noticed that when she handed him his disposable gloves.

At twenty-seven minutes after one, Tom walked in the back door of the clinic, whistling.

Mary frowned. He was certainly in a better mood than when he'd left. He looked calm, relaxed, and ready to go back to work.

Mary could feel her gray eyes narrow suspiciously. There were several things that could calm and relax a man in a short period of time, but at the moment she could think of only one, and she didn't like the pictures that danced in her imagination.

Once again she chided herself. Get a grip, Mary! This man is your new employer. He's not your beau. He doesn't belong to you. It's none of your business what he does on his lunch hour, or even if he takes more than an hour. Mind your own business, Mary!

"Well, are we ready to repair the broken femur on that collie?" Tom asked brightly, looking from Mary to Jesse. "Where's Pete? Does he have everything all set up?"

"Everything is ready," Mary said, nodding. "We were just waiting for you."

"Not late, am I?" Tom asked, checking his wristwatch.

Good grief, how could such a simple movement be sexy? Mary asked herself. Or did it just seem that way? Was she that deprived? It was more than two years since she had been with a man. Within a year after Raymond's death, even her children urged her to "get into the swing of things," but in today's society, dating was scary. Mary had been out of circulation for more years than she cared to count, but she didn't need a degree to know that most mature men wouldn't be satisfied for long with chaste good-night kisses. As much as she missed the intimacy of being with a man, she was scared to do more.

"Mary?"

Tom's voice brought her back to earth. She shrugged. Here she was practically drooling over her employer. She'd even, and now she felt her cheeks flame, checked out his buns!

"No," she said. "No, you're not late at all. It's just that Dr. Rogers always came back at one. It's what we're used to."

"Well, sometimes change is good," Tom said. "All right, let's get to work, shall we?"

The operation took almost two hours. Mary was fascinated by Tom's surgical skills. He worked carefully, but swiftly, and when he finished he didn't even seem tired.

"Now we better take care of Bingo," he said. "I'm sure Gary will be here bright and early tomorrow morning to pick him up."

"Will you want Pete to stay tonight until both dogs are out of anesthesia, or shall I?" Mary asked.

"Neither," Tom replied. "As soon as Bingo's stitched up you can both go home. I'll stick around for a while."

Mary glanced at her watch. Neutering Bingo wouldn't take long, and an early night sounded great. "Thanks," she said. "I do have some errands to run, not to mention my own lonely little pet waiting at home."

Tom smiled. "Not a potbellied pig, I hope."

"No," Mary replied. "Just a sweet, playful little pup someone left here on the doorstep a few months ago."

"I don't understand that kind of thinking, but then people dump children the same way, so I guess we shouldn't be surprised that they do it to animals." Tom looked grim now, and some of the anxiety Mary had noted before lunch seemed to creep back.

They took care of Bingo in silence, and as soon as she washed up, Mary gathered her purse and jacket. "Are you sure you won't need me?"

Tom shook his head. "I'll be fine. Good night, Mary. I enjoyed working with you. You're an excellent assistant. I think we'll get along great." He winked then, and Mary felt more like an awkward teenager than a forty-nine-year-old grandma.

She drove slowly, moving cautiously in the after-work traffic. She was a bundle of confusion. Why on earth was she so physically attracted to Tom? Sure, he was good-looking. There was no denying that, and he had a good physique for a man his age, but she'd met nice-looking men before. For that matter, she'd had a few of them offer to take her out in recent months. But she'd always declined, and it had never really bothered her, until now. Something about Tom was different. There was a magnetism she simply could not ignore. Mary laughed softly, glad there was no one to see her agitation. If Jesse knew what she was feeling, she'd say Mary was suffering severe deprivation. But the younger generation viewed things differently. They believed in taking pleasure where they found it. Mary knew she could never do that. When and if she ever slept with another man, it would have to be someone she had deep feelings for, someone she respected and loved. She couldn't just hop casually in and out of bed. It wasn't her style, and she was just too darned old!

Later that night her son Jason called to tell her he was being promoted to sergeant. He had enlisted in the army right after high school. At first Mary had been devastated, but now, hearing the new maturity and pride in her son's voice, she decided he'd made the right decision.

When she hung up Mary poured a glass of wine and dropped a capful of bubblebath into the bathtub. She turned the water on full force and watched as the tub filled with sweetly scented, iridescent suds. Then she stripped off her clothes and climbed in, setting her wine glass within easy reach.

As she sank down in the warm, soothing bubbles, Mary sighed. Maybe this was what she needed, to pamper herself more often. Like tonight. She'd been too tired and distraught to cook, so she'd settled for a half-dozen crackers spread with cheese and an apple. Hardly a balanced meal, and certainly not the best way to maintain a trim, slender figure. She chuckled, imagining herself fat and flabby, curled up in front of the television with a five-pound box of chocolates, Rascal curled at her feet.

Mary slid further down in the tub, thinking of the mixed-breed pup she and Jesse had found shivering on the clinic doorstep a few months earlier. He'd been a sorry sight, all right, and her first inclination had been to take him to the animal shelter on the other side of town, but then she made the fatal mistake of picking him up. His tiny pink tongue flicked out and licked her cheek. She looked into his dark, limpid eyes and she was a goner.

Now Rascal ruled her with an iron paw. He lazed around the house like he owned the joint, ate her out of house and home, and took up half the bed at night. He also lowered her blood pressure, gave her a way to vent her leftover motherly instincts, and generally made her feel needed.

Sipping her wine, Mary found herself wondering if Tom had a pet. Probably. She hadn't known many vets who didn't have a houseful of animals. It went with the territory. Her thoughts drifted back to the years when her kids were growing up. They'd certainly had pets then! Dogs, cats, gerbils, goldfish, hermit crabs, even a parakeet. You name it and it had probably lived in Mary's house at one time or another. And out in the backyard were countless small graves.

Maybe that's why she hadn't been able to bring herself to put the house on the market, Mary thought. It wouldn't be just a house she'd be leaving, it would be a whole lifetime. But she knew she had to make a decision soon. Her property taxes had gone up twice since Raymond's death, and she was sure they would continue to climb. Even with no mortgage payments, the house was still expensive to keep up. Taxes, repairs, and maintenance. It all added up. And what did she need all this space for anyway? The kids were all on their own, and she hoped it would stay that way. Jason seemed intent on making the army his career, and David was ensconced on Wall Street, working his way up in the world of finance. Her oldest daughter, Donna, was happily married and expecting her second child. Even Sunny had flown the nest, working her way through college on a scholarship. She wanted to be a teacher and work with handicapped children.

Mary was thinking of how proud she was of all her children when she realized the bathwater had cooled. She downed the last drops of wine and stood up. Critically, she looked down at her naked body. Not perfect, but not bad for forty-nine either. She shivered and wrapped a thick terry towel around herself. She really would have to find out if Tom was single.

Tom closed the book he'd been reading on animal husbandry and rubbed his eyes. Time to call it a night. But it had been a great day. This move to Easton Animal Hospital looked like it was going to work out well. He liked all his new employees, especially his assistant, Mary. From her personnel file he knew she was a widow, and that she had four children and one grandchild. Yet there was something very fresh and youthful about her, something that drew him like a magnet. She had a sweet gentleness with the animals that he found touching, so unlike his ex-wife, Gladys, who had disliked anything with fur or feathers.

Easy, old man, Tom warned himself. The lady may already have a serious suitor, or she might just not be interested in an office romance. Tom chuckled. Office romance! They were both beyond that kind of nonsense, but he wouldn't mind spending an evening with Mary . . . maybe dinner and a show, or just a long walk. He had a feeling she would be easy to talk to.

Pushing his chair back, Tom stood up and stretched. The best part of the day was Rickie's progress. He was doing so well lately. Making such great strides.

"I'm going up to my room now, Dr. Warren," his housekeeper said, interrupting his thoughts. "Is there anything you need before I go?"

"No, thank you, Helen," Tom said. "I'll be turning in soon myself."

Helen was another treasure he needed to give thanks for. Without her here taking such excellent care of the house and Rickie, he wouldn't be able to work at all.

"Rickie did well today, didn't he?" Tom asked Helen. "I'm pleased with his progress."

Helen beamed. "He's a joy," she said, her round, wrinkled face shining with pleasure. "How anyone could ever think of him as a burden I'll never know!"

"Well, we don't, and that's all that matters, right?"

"Yes indeed," Helen said. "We'll fix him up good, doctor. You'll see."

Tom nodded, wanting to believe it, but not quite sure. There had been so much pain, so much suffering. Would things ever be right?

On Friday the thirteenth, two weeks after he

95

took over the clinic, Tom asked Mary to go to dinner with him. Nothing fancy, he said. Just someplace quiet where they could get a decent meal and get better acquainted.

Mary was speechless. She could do nothing but nod, and then make some inane excuse to leave the room.

"Dinner," she stammered to Jesse. "He asked me out to dinner!"

Jesse smirked. "I knew it! I can feel the good vibes between you two, or maybe it's the electrical sparks flying back and forth. Wow! This is neat! A love affair right in our own office!"

"Sh," Mary cautioned. "I'm already sorry I told you. And one dinner date does not constitute a love affair, Smarty Pants."

"No, not one dinner date, but I'm sure more will follow. Even though our hunky employer is a bit past his prime, he's still a healthy male animal, and you are definitely a cool lady!"

"Oh, what am I going to do with you?" Mary asked. "This is just what I was afraid of, that you'd make a big deal out of nothing."

"Nothing? Oh, forgive me, but I'm not the one who came staggering into this office in a state of agonizing bliss. Admit it, Mary. You've got the hots for our new doc!"

It was nearly impossible to concentrate on

her work for the rest of the day. By four o'clock Mary was making up and discarding one excuse after another not to go through with the date. She should never have accepted in the first place. Mixing business with pleasure rarely worked, and she liked her job. She didn't want to do anything to jeopardize that. On the other hand, she thought, chewing the tip of an eraser, it was just going to be a casual supper. Tom had made it plain it wouldn't be an elegant, candlelight sort of evening.

And what was wrong with two mature adults sharing a meal and some conversation? She asked Jesse that question just before they closed up.

"Not a thing," Jesse said, her knowing brown eyes deceptively wide and innocent. "I think it's a great idea. Do you think doc would mind if I tagged along?"

"No way!" Mary cried, giving Jesse a push towards the door. "Go on, go home. You're making me crazy!"

"Uh-uh," Jesse taunted. "Something is making you crazy all right, but it sure isn't me. It's him, Dr. Thomas D. Warren. He's the one making you crazy!"

"What's all this about crazy?" Tom asked, entering the room through the side door just as Jesse exited through the front.

"Just one of Jesse's jokes," Mary said, avoiding his eyes. Why did she feel that it would be impossible to lie to this man? That his incredible dark blue eyes would be able to see straight down into her soul?

"Tom, I . . . I'm not sure our going out together is such a hot idea," she said slowly. "I mean, we're employee and employer, and right now we work pretty well together. If we clutter our working relationship with . . ."

Tom walked up to her and put his hands on her shoulders. Mary quivered, realizing it was the first time he had touched her in a purely personal way. Her flesh tingled and she was conscious of an overwhelming urge to snuggle close to his broad chest. Tom stared at her thoughtfully, and she waited to hear what he would say.

"I've had the very same thoughts," he said, his voice deep and strong. "That's why I waited this long. I really wanted to ask you out that first day. You have no idea how many arguments I've had with myself about mixing business with pleasure, because believe me, Mary, going out with you is definitely going to be a pleasure."

"You think we should?"

"I think we have to," Tom said, his voice deepened even more, and his hold on her shoulders tightening. "There's something between us, Mary. Haven't you felt it?"

"Well, yes, but . . ."

"I'm not married, Mary, if that's one of the things you've been worrying about. There are no wives or lovers lurking in the background. I've been divorced for more than three years."

"Oh. I did wonder, but . . ."

"And I know you're a widow from your personnel file," he interrupted. "I suppose I should say I'm sorry, but right now I'm not sorry at all. I'm glad we're both free."

"So am I," Mary said, her tremulous smile widening. "So am I."

Tom picked her up at her place at seven. He met Rascal and pronounced him a fine fellow. Mary offered him wine or a beer, but he declined. He seemed a little nervous.

"Do you have as many butterflies as I have?" she asked, smiling.

"Is that what those things in my belly are?" Tom asked, breaking into a grin. "I have a confession. This is only my second date since my divorce. I haven't had a lot of experience with this sort of thing."

"Good. Then we're starting off even," Mary replied. "I haven't, either."

A half-hour later they were settled in a cozy booth in a small Italian restaurant. "I hope you like Italian," Tom said. "I chose Antonio's because it's quiet and I know they have great food, not to mention that it's close to home."

"Why would you . . . ?"

"Here comes our waiter," Tom said, waving Mary's unasked question aside. "Let's order, shall we? I'm starved."

And suddenly, so was Mary. She hadn't realized how much she had missed having a dinner companion. They feasted on antipasto, fettuccini and tiny shrimp, a huge green salad, and finally, thick, delicious slices of Italian cream cake.

"Oh, I'm stuffed," Mary said when the waiter brought them hot, fragrant cups of coffee.

"Me, too," Tom agreed. He stirred cream into his coffee thoughtfully, then looked directly at Mary. "I'm afraid I wasn't totally honest with you earlier, about being free."

"You're not divorced?"

"Oh, I'm divorced all right," Tom said, a hint of bitterness creeping into his voice. "Gladys couldn't wait to get out of our marriage. No, it's something else, or maybe I should say someone else."

"What is it, Tom?" Mary asked. Her heart had almost ceased to beat when he said he wasn't actually free. Now she took a deep breath and waited.

Tom grimaced and ran his hand through his hair, rumpling it in a deliciously boyish way. "I like you, Mary, and I just don't want to start a relationship on the wrong foot. That's why I think you should know my situation up front." He took a long, slow breath. "I have a child. Actually, he's my grandchild, but with every passing day Rickie seems more like my own, and I have legal custody. He doesn't really know his mother, and he's never even seen his grandmother."

A child. It was the last thing Mary would have expected Tom to say. The room suddenly went dead and still despite the clatter of dishes, the laughter and noise of the customers, and the rich, fragrant odor of food. A child. She'd thought of an ex-wife, an old lover, even an elderly parent, but not a child. That she had never expected.

"Why don't you tell me about it?" she invited quietly, sipping her coffee.

Tom sighed and stared down at his cup. Unlike the time they spent together in the clinic when he was animated and vigorous, he seemed older than Mary knew him to be.

"Kim was a good girl, a sweet child, until she started high school," Tom said. "Then it was like someone flipped a switch and turned her into a monster. She got fresh and flip. She started failing in her schoolwork. She skipped school, stayed out late, and defied Gladys and me." Tom motioned for the waiter to refill their cups and resumed speaking when the man left.

"We tried everything. A psychiatrist, peer counseling, grounding, leniency in the hope that she'd just go ahead and get it out of her system, but she didn't. It just went on and on, getting worse and worse, until our marriage started falling apart. Gladys blamed me. She said I'd been too strict with Kim. I said she was too easy, that she'd let our daughter run wild, and had given her no boundaries. We fought all the time, over Kim, over who got out of bed first in the morning, over who should put the cat out at night . . ."

Mary nodded. She could see this was hard for Tom. Perhaps it was the first time he'd really talked about it. She sensed he needed to get it all out.

"Anyway," Tom said, setting his cup in the saucer. "When Kim announced, at seventeen, that she was pregnant and didn't know who the father was, my wife and I knew the marriage was over. Gladys stated flatly that she was not going to let a spoiled brat ruin the rest of her life. She moved out immediately. I kept Kim with me until her baby was born. It wasn't until the final months of her pregnancy that I realized she was on heavy drugs."

"The baby?" Mary asked, feeling as though her heart was breaking. "Was the baby . . . ?"

"Yes. Rickie was born addicted to cocaine. For a while it was touch and go. We weren't sure he would make it, and God forgive me, there were times I wasn't sure I wanted him to make it." Tom paused, then shook his head. "But he's a tough little guy and we were able to bring him home from the hospital when he was eight weeks old."

"Does your daughter still live with you?"

Tom sighed heavily. "Kim is in a rehab center right now. She's been in and out since Rickie was born, and he just celebrated his third birthday."

"And you're raising the baby?"

Tom shrugged. "I have no choice, Mary. Kim isn't fit to look after him. He's doing great now, but he still needs a lot of attention, and there's no one but me to give it to him."

"What about Gladys?" Mary couldn't help asking. She'd heard of grandmothers taking over the care of their grandchildren, but grandfathers were something else.

"Gladys has never even seen Rickie," Tom

said quietly. "She simply isn't interested. She's washed her hands of all of us."

"Do you . . . isn't there any chance your daughter will get her life straightened out so she can take care of her son?" Her heart ached for Tom, and for the motherless little boy, and for the poor, sick girl, his daughter. But she also knew that what he had just told her spelled the end of any possible relationship between her and Tom. There was just no way she could allow herself to get involved in a situation like this. She'd raised four children. She'd done her stint as a den mother and a car pooler. She had coped with runny noses, measles, and broken arms. She'd lived through temper tantrums and the terrible teens—with broken hearts that needed bolstering. She'd drained herself physically and emotionally, and now she'd finally gotten to a place where there was time for Mary. Freedom and peace and quiet. She couldn't give that up for anyone, not even Tom Warren.

Tom looked deep into Mary's eyes and she shivered, certain he could read her ambivalence.

"I won't lie to you, Mary, or to myself. That's not how I operate. In the beginning I thought Kim would grow up and get herself straightened out. I was prepared to help her, but I honestly thought she would eventually be able to care for her son. It hasn't worked out that way. She's slipping farther away every day. In my heart I don't believe she'll ever be able to be a mother to Rickie."

"So where does that leave you?"

"As a grandpa turned daddy, I guess," Tom said philosophically. "He's my grandson, Mary. My own flesh and blood. What choice do I have?"

None, Mary thought, feeling sick to her stomach. Tom hadn't even kissed her, yet she knew there could have been something special between them. Her newly-awakened dreams washed away, like seeds in a garden during a summer rain.

"I'm sorry, Tom," she said softly. "I really am. I raised four children of my own and at the time I loved every minute of being a mother, but now . . . well, I guess what I'm trying to say is that it would probably be best if we didn't see each other socially again. I don't think I'd make a very good recycled mom."

Tom nodded. "I understand. I don't like it, but I do understand. You're just not up for training pants and PTA, are you?"

"I guess not."

"Well, thanks for being honest with me,

Mary, and for letting me spill my guts. I wish things could be different, but we have to deal with what life hands us, don't we? Sometimes it's really rough being responsible for that little guy at this stage of my life, but when he hugs me, I melt. I just can't let him go into foster care, Mary. He already has too many strikes against him."

With tears stinging her eyes, Mary nodded and stood up, tucking her purse under her arm.

Tom drove her home in silence, a silence filled with the death of dreams for both of them.

When he stopped the car in front of her house, he turned to smile at her. "I have a feeling there could have been something special between us, Mary Jeffrey. I wish you well."

"And I you, Tom Warren," Mary said. "You're a hell of a guy."

"Yeah," Tom said, smiling ruefully. "That's what they all say."

Mary wasn't sure what to expect when she went to work on Monday morning. Would she and Tom be able to work together amicably? Or would their one brief date ruin everything?

But it turned out that she needn't have worried, at least as far as Tom was concerned. He was polite and friendly, and he seemed completely at ease, which was more than Mary could say.

"So, how did it go?" Jesse whispered when Tom and Pete were in the back room checking supplies. "Was it as casual and platonic as you tried to make me think, or did things get hot and steamy?"

"Definitely not hot and steamy," Mary replied sharply. "and that first date was also the last."

"What? Why? What happened?" Jesse was wide-eyed and all ears, and Mary was instantly sorry she'd said anything. But it was too late. Jesse would never rest until she'd dragged every last detail out of her.

"He has a baby," Mary said quietly. "Actually, it's his grandchild, but he's raising the little boy and . . . well, it sounds like it's a long-term thing."

Jesse waited. Then she shook her head in confusion. "So? What does that have to do with the two of you dating? He can afford babysitters, can't he?"

Mary shook her head. "That's not the problem. We . . ." she blushed, sorry she'd ever opened her mouth. "Tom and I . . . well, we were attracted to one another and . . ."

"I knew it!" Jesse squealed, bouncing up and down on her chair. "I knew it the minute he walked into this office!"

Mary frowned. "Well, it's not going to do either of us any good," she said. "Tom is committed to his little grandson, and I am committed to my freedom. I raised four kids of my own, Jesse. I've been through all the highs and lows of parenting. I'm not interested in doing it again."

"Oh wow! Now I understand. Boy, what a bummer!"

Mary nodded silently. Bummer indeed!

Promptly at noon Tom shrugged out of his white coat, washed up, and went home to lunch and his grandson. Mary smiled ruefully. At least she knew he wasn't going home for a quickie. That made her feel a little better. No, damn it, it didn't!

Actually, she felt like hell. Like the lowest of lows. How could a grown-up woman resent a motherless little boy?

Rewrapping her uneaten turkey sandwich, Mary sipped her coffee thoughtfully. It wasn't the child she resented, just the situation, the damnable situation that made a close relationship between her and Tom impossible. What kind of girl was Tom's daughter anyway? Was she a spoiled, bored little princess who turned to drugs and sex in a search for thrills? Didn't she even care about what she was doing to her father, a man who should have been able to kick back and enjoy life a little? And what about her baby? Didn't she want to be with her son and act like a mother? Apparently not, Mary decided, at least not enough to give up drugs.

It was a sad, hopeless situation, and she almost wished she'd never met Tom, never heard the sound of his laughter, never seen the way the lines at the corner of his eyes crinkled when he smiled.

Several days went by and Mary kept her feelings under tight wraps. She did her work efficiently, but she tried to avoid joking with Tom as much as possible. Sharing laughter with him was painful. It made her long for what they might have had.

Then one night, just after she had crawled into bed and Rascal had curled beside her, the telephone rang.

"Mary? It's Tom. I'm sorry if I woke you, and I'm sorry to bother you at home. I've got a problem, and my housekeeper isn't home."

"Tom? What is it? What's wrong?"

"It's Rickie. He's spiking a high fever and he's complaining of a stiff neck. I know you raised four children and I thought . . ."

"Call his pediatrician, Tom," Mary said, swinging her legs over the side of the bed. "I'll drive to your house. It's 723 Beech Tree Drive, isn't it? I think you may have to take Rickie to the hospital. It may be serious."

Mary was shaking as she hastily pulled on jeans and an old cotton shirt. Meningitis! The very word struck cold fear in her heart. Of course, it could be something else, but she didn't like the sound of it . . . a stiff neck and high fever.

Tom didn't know that she'd already been to his house once before. She'd driven there one day just to see what his home looked like. It was a pleasant, homey frame house with a large fenced back yard. She'd parked across the street and listened to the sound of a woman's motherly voice and a child's laughter. And then she'd seen the little boy. He'd looked like something from a movie ad, with huge dark eyes and a mop of curly dark hair. For a minute her heart had melted and she'd wondered . . . but she quickly came to her senses. It wouldn't work. She was just too old to do it all again.

But now, now Tom and the little boy needed her. And she could no more have ignored Tom's plea for help than she could fly to the moon.

She parked in front of the house, noting that every light in the place was on. Poor Tom. He must be frantic.

He met her at the door, the boy in his arms, the child's flushed cheek pressed against his shoulder.

"Thank you for coming," he said. "I feel terrible about getting you out like this, but I just didn't know who else to call. Of all the times for Helen to be away visiting her sister."

"Did you call the doctor?" Mary asked, gently lifting Rickie's eyelids. The child was limp and unresponsive, and that was not a good sign.

"Yes," Tom said. "He'll meet us at the emergency room. Could you, would you mind keeping an eye on Rickie while I grab a pair of pants and a shirt?"

For the first time Mary realized that Tom was in his pajamas, but then he was handing the boy over to her and there were other, more important, things to worry about.

The warm, feverish weight was frighteningly familiar. She'd played this same scene with her own children on more than one occasion. But except for the usual childhood illnesses and broken arms and such, her kids had all been remarkably healthy. With this little guy it was different. He'd come into the world with several strikes against him. Father unknown, mother a teenage drug abuser, a cold, uncaring grandmother, and his own innocent addiction. The only thing he had going for him was Tom.

"It's okay, sweetie," she crooned softly, smoothing the dark curls off the boy's forehead. He really was a beautiful child. How could Tom's wife have turned her back on him?

You did, Mary, her conscience prodded. You weren't even interested in getting to know the child. You rejected him before you even saw him.

But that was different, Mary reminded herself. She had no ties to this child, legal or otherwise, and therefore no responsibility to him. And she had been a damn good mother to her own four kids. They were all responsible citizens now, and largely because of her nurturing. But loving and caring for a child took a lot of time and effort and emotion. It ate up huge chunks of your life. One minute you were a young mother, proudly coming home from the hospital with your first baby, and then one morning you woke up and you were a middle-aged woman. The kids were all grown and gone, and there was gray hair, wrinkles, and crow's feet to show for all your trouble.

Mary patted Rickie's back gently and smiled ruefully. There was a little more to it than that. There was the pride of accomplishment at a job well done, the joy of knowing that the young people who stood so bravely on the threshold of their lives had come from her body and her heart.

Mary's eyes misted as Tom raced back into the room, car keys dangling from his hand. "Come on," he said nervously. "Let's get going!"

By unspoken agreement, Mary climbed in the back seat with Rickie where they had plenty of room to stretch out. She could feel Tom monitoring them in the rearview mirror, but he seemed too terrified to speak.

"Kids often seem sicker than they are, Tom," she said softly. "Rickie's temperature could go down just as quickly as it came up."

"Yeah, I remember that happening when Kim was a toddler. Her fever shot up to almost a hundred and four, and a couple of hours later it was almost down to normal. But it scared the hell out of me."

"I know," Mary agreed sympathetically.

"We're here, thank God," Tom announced a few minutes later. He braked to a stop, jumped out, and opened the door to help Mary out with Rickie. Mary relinquished the boy to his grandfather and was surprised at the sudden emptiness she felt. Then there was no time to think as she hurried after Tom into the emergency room.

The nurses whisked Rickie away immediately, and Mary sat down on a plastic chair while Tom filled out the necessary papers.

By the time he was finished, she'd gotten two paper cups of steaming coffee from a machine. She handed one to him and he nodded gratefully.

"I don't know how to thank you, Mary. I know you didn't want to get involved with . . . us, but I honestly don't know how I would have managed on my own." He held out his free hand so Mary could see the way it trembled.

"Come on, sit down," Mary said. "It will probably be a while before the doctor comes out and tells us anything."

Tom sat down beside her, and reached over to clasp her hand. "Do you mind?" he asked, almost shyly. "I need someone to hold on to."

Mary squeezed as hard as she could. It was the middle of the night. The coffee was the worst, and she knew she looked like hell, but suddenly she knew there was nowhere else she'd rather be. It was crazy, and it went against everything she'd been telling herself for days, but it was true. She cared about Tom and his little grandson.

It was almost four a.m. before they got any news, and then it was only because Tom practically threatened the nurse with bodily harm if she didn't find out how Rickie was doing.

A tired, haggard-looking doctor appeared a few minutes later. "Mr. and Mrs. Warren?"

"No, I . . ."

"I'm Mr. Warren," Tom said quickly. "How is my grandson? Is he going to be okay?"

"We're running some tests and probably won't have all the results until sometime later this morning. You may as well go home and try to get some rest. There's nothing you can do for him now."

Tom swallowed. "Is he awake? He'll be frightened."

"He's drifting in and out with the fever, Mr. Warren. Even if you stay he won't know it. If you leave your phone number at the desk we'll call you as soon as we know anything definite."

Tom's jaw hardened. "What's your best guess?"

The doctor shrugged. "Meningitis, and I sure as hell hope I'm wrong."

They were allowed to see Rickie for just a minute. The child lying there flushed and restless looked nothing like the handsome little boy Mary had seen playing in the yard.

"He's so small," she whispered, unable to resist touching his feverish cheek. "So helpless."

"Yes," Tom agreed. "That's why I can't abandon him."

They drove back to Tom's house in silence. What was there to say? Tom was badly frightened, and Mary was filled with sympathy.

"Will you come in and have some coffee?" Tom asked.

Mary rolled her eyes toward the lightening sky. She smiled and shrugged. "Why not? It's almost daylight. How about some breakfast, Doc? I make a mean omelet."

While Tom went to take a quick shower, Mary bustled around his modern, compact kitchen. His housekeeper apparently did a good job, she decided. The cabinets were neat and well stocked, and the refrigerator was full of fresh, healthy food.

Mary beat eggs, chopped fresh mushrooms, green pepper, and cheese. Then she set out two plates, two juice glasses, and started a pot of coffee. As the pungent aroma filled the kitchen things started to look a little brighter. Rickie was in good hands, she told herself. The

116

nurses and the doctor attending him had seemed competent and caring, and Tom had said that he was basically a strong, healthy child. He would be all right, and in a few days she and Tom would laugh about their midnight ride.

"Mm, smells like heaven in here," Tom said, entering the kitchen with his snowy hair still damp. He came up to Mary and stood just behind her, the warmth of his body penetrating her thin cotton shirt and jeans.

"What an omelet," he said admiringly. "I do like a woman who knows her way around the kitchen."

"After twenty-eight years with a husband and four children I better know a can opener from a kitchen knife," Mary said, laughing.

They sat across from one another and ate hungrily. Mary had toasted muffins to go with the omelets and the coffee was hot and rich. For a few minutes there was a contented silence.

Then Tom pushed his empty plate away and refilled their coffee cups. "Tell me about your marriage, Mary," he asked. "Was it a good one?"

Mary hesitated just a moment. It had been good, at least in the beginning, but now, looking back, she could see there had been signs of unhappiness and discontent in Raymond for a long time before his suicide.

"Well, I thought so at the time," she said, "but I guess it wasn't as good for Raymond as it was for me. I had the children and I think I was a pretty good mother, but Raymond never seemed to get where he wanted to be in his career. I guess it was that feeling of failure that made him take his life."

"Your husband committed suicide? I didn't know," Tom said. "I'm sorry, Mary. I shouldn't have asked."

"No, it's all right. I can talk about it now. I've come to terms with it. At first I blamed myself, but now I realize that each of us is responsible for our own actions. Raymond made his choice, and now I must make mine."

"And your choice is freedom," Tom said quietly, setting down his coffee cup.

"Yes," Mary said, hating the way her eyes started to sting. She stood up. "I'll help you clear up and then I better get going. You won't be in the clinic today, will you?"

Tom shook his head. "I'm going back to the hospital, and I'll stay there until I'm sure Rickie is out of danger."

Mary nodded. "Will you let me know?"

"Of course, and thanks again for everything. I wouldn't have survived this night without you, Mary."

"What a shame!" Jesse said when Mary called and told her what had happened. "Look, how about if I go in and just answer the phone and catch up on my filing? Shall I call Pete and tell him to stay home, too?"

"You may as well. There wouldn't be anything for him to do."

"Okay. I'll take care of it. And you better climb into bed and get some sleep. You sound like you're dead on your feet."

Sleep sounded wonderful, but once Mary lay down, her eyes stubbornly refused to close and she kept seeing Rickie's flushed face and his incredibly long, thick eyelashes. She kept remembering the weight of him in her arms. Finally she sat up and threw off the blanket. It was ridiculous. Couldn't a mother ever stop having motherly feelings? Wasn't there some way to turn the other cheek when a needy child came along? Some way of protecting oneself from caring too much? Mother Nature sure had a weird sense of humor, Mary decided. She brought little girls into the world, let them grow up, and then turned them into mothers — but somehow she forgot to turn them back when the job was done. She forgot to set them free.

Disgusted with herself and the way her mind was working, Mary staggered wearily into the bathroom and pulled off her nightgown. A shower. That's what she needed, something to clear the cobwebs from her brain.

A half-hour later, hair still curling in damp ringlets around her ears, Mary was dressed in light blue slacks and a white blouse. On impulse she went to the spare bedroom and picked up the stuffed bear she'd bought for her granddaughter.

"Sorry, Mindy," she said, tucking the bear under her arm, "but there's a little boy who needs this more than you do."

A half-hour after that she pulled into the hospital parking lot. She started to get out of the car, then fell back in the seat.

"What am I doing?" she moaned. "This is not what I want!"

But a moment later she knew she no longer had any choice in the matter. Inside the hospital was a frightened man and a sick little boy. They needed her, and there was no way she could ignore them.

She found Tom almost asleep in a chair outside the ICU. She shook his shoulder gently, careful not to startle him.

"Tom? It's Mary. Any news?"

"Mary? What are you doing here? I thought

120

you would be home in bed."

"That's what I thought, too, but I couldn't sleep, and I had to know how Rickie was doing. Has there been any change? Did the test results come back?"

"A couple of them have, but they're still waiting for the last one, the one that will definitely tell if he has meningitis or not. But the doctor seems pretty sure that's what it is."

Mary sat down on the chair next to Tom. She reached out and pressed his hand. "Well, even if it is meningitis, they have all kinds of wonder drugs these days."

"Yeah, that's what I keep telling myself. But why are you here, Mary? I thought . . ."

She shook her head and smiled ruefully. "So did I, Tom, but I guess I was wrong. That little turkey got to me."

"But . . ."

"Not now, Tom," Mary said gently. "Let's just get Rickie well. Then we'll see."

It was meningitis, and for a few days it was pretty tense. The clinic was closed for almost a week while Tom practically lived at the hospital. During the day, Mary went over and made him go home and rest while she kept a vigil at Rickie's bedside. She tried to fight her growing feelings for the little boy. It was one thing to help a friend through a crisis, she told herself, another to take on a life sentence, and that's what she would be doing if she became romantically involved with Tom. Because he was not the kind of man to want a brief, meaningless affair. With Tom it would be all or nothing. She sensed that was why he had told her about Rickie in the beginning.

But as Rickie began to improve, his bright, bubbly personality made itself known and she found herself falling in love. Who could resist a child who pursed his lips, squeezed his eyes tight shut, but never uttered a sound when lab technicians poked and prodded him? Who could help loving a little boy who looked at you with trust and confidence, believing that you could make everything all right? Who could turn away from a child who held his stuffed bear tight as he fell into a restless sleep? Not Mary, and by the time Rickie was released from the hospital she knew she was trapped.

Trapped. What a horrible, ugly word. How could she continue seeing Tom and Rickie when deep in her heart she felt trapped?

She tried to explain her feelings to Jesse one day, but the younger girl seemed thoroughly confused. "But if you love the little boy . . ."

"I do . . . or at least I could, but I don't

want to, Jesse. Look, right now, for the first time in my life I have total freedom. There is absolutely no one I have to answer to, no one who depends on me, except Rascal. And I like it that way. I can come and go as I please. If I don't feel like cooking I don't have to. If I want to sleep until noon on Sunday I can. You can't do that kind of thing with a small child."

"But Tom has a wonderful housekeeper. You told me so yourself. It's not like you would have to sit home and play mama all the time."

"But I would be his mama if . . . oh, God, what am I doing? I've never even kissed Tom and here I am thinking about marrying him. I'm definitely losing it, Jesse."

"You've never even kissed?" Jesse asked, shaking her head in amazement. "Never?"

"Never," Mary answered. "Not even a peck."

"Wow!" Jesse said, her eyes going all dreamy. "I wonder what it would be like to be in love when you've never even kissed?"

"It's hell," Mary snapped, "and I'm almost sorry I ever laid eyes on Tom or his grandson!"

She turned away from Jesse's desk and felt the blood slowly drain out of her face. For standing in the doorway, a stricken look on his handsome face, was Tom.

* * *

"Mary, can you give me a hand in here?" he asked, his jaw tight and his eyes deliberately not meeting hers. "Mrs. Jennings' kittens are a real handful."

"Certainly," Mary said, jumping up from her perch on the corner of Jesse's desk. "I . . . I'll be right there."

"Oh my gosh!" Jesse said. "What a mess this is turning out to be!"

"You can say that again," Mary muttered. "Me and my big mouth!"

It was agony to stand next to Tom and restrain the kittens while he administered the shots. She was so close she could smell him — the rich, slightly spicy scent of his aftershave, his warm, male essence. And when his arm brushed hers she shivered. The words Tom had overheard must have sounded incredibly cruel and heartless, but she couldn't help the way she felt and she couldn't rid herself of her ambivalent feelings towards him and Rickie. Deep down, a part of her longed to mother the little boy, to give him all the maternal softness and caring he could handle. And she ached to love Tom in the way a woman loves a man, but she was scared — afraid that if she gave in to her feelings now, she would regret it later, and what would that do to both of them? Could little Rickie handle yet another rejection?

"Thanks for your help," Tom said, startling Mary. Her scattered thoughts had wandered and she'd done her job mechanically. Now she looked up at him, and the ache inside her swelled until she thought it would burst out of her chest.

"Tom, I . . ."

"Not now, Mrs. Jeffrey. I believe there are patients still waiting outside."

Mary was stung. *Mrs. Jeffrey!* Well, maybe it was better this way. Or maybe it was time she started looking for a new job.

"Are you really thinking of leaving?" Jesse asked, wide-eyed with disbelief. "Gee, Mary, I can't imagine what it will be like around here without you. And the location is so convenient for you and all."

Mary nodded. Tom was home having lunch with Rickie and Helen, and Pete had gone out for a sandwich, so the two women were alone.

"I've always loved working here, Jesse," Mary admitted, "but everything is different now. Seeing Tom every day, wondering and worrying about how little Rickie is doing . . ."

"If you care that much for the little boy maybe you're kidding yourself about not wanting to be a mother again, Mary."

Mary nodded and sipped her coffee thoughtfully. "I thought about that, and I guess a small part of me does kind of miss all that mothering stuff, but once you have a child you can't turn it off and on, you know? It's a small person and it's there for the duration, and besides, do you know what the odds are of either Tom or me living long enough even to see this boy through high school? In a little over fifteen years I'll be sixty-five years old! Tom will be seventy. Do you have any idea how devastating it would be for a teenager to lose one or both parents at such a vulnerable age?"

"But wouldn't it be better for Rickie to have loving caretakers for at least part of his life?" Jesse argued. "And what about you and Tom? If you really love each other, how can you deny yourself this time together?"

"I don't even know if I love him, Jesse. How can I? We've spent hardly any time together, and he's never even kissed me."

"I'll bet he would if you gave him half a chance," Jesse said teasingly. "Why don't you take a chance and go for it, Mary? Get to know Tom and see where it leads. You might not even like him once you get better acquainted, and then none of this will matter."

Not like Tom? Mary couldn't imagine it, but maybe Jesse had a point. Maybe she was making a big deal out of nothing. And maybe Tom wouldn't even want to get married. He had a perfectly competent housekeeper. Maybe all he was interested in was a few pleasant evenings, some laughs, a little diversion.

"You've given me something to think about, Jesse," she said seriously. "I may have been missing the whole point here."

That night, after eating a sinfully delicious hero sandwich she'd picked up on the way home from work, Mary stretched out on the sofa with her new paperback novel.

"Okay, Rascal, what do you think?" she asked her slumbering canine. "Should I just take a chance and have some fun? After all, who says a few dates have to lead to a marriage proposal? That kind of thinking went out with the dinosaurs, didn't it?"

The telephone rang, interrupting Mary's musings, and she was pleasantly surprised to hear Sunny's voice.

"Honey, how are you? Is everything okay at school?"

"Everything is great," Sunny replied, "except that I've fallen hopelessly in love, and there's nothing I can do about it."

Join the club, Mary thought. Then her mind clicked into gear. Sunny? In love? Hopelessly? That could only mean that she was involved with a man she couldn't have. Who was it, a professor, a married man? Someone who didn't return her feelings?

"Oh, honey, what is it? Is there any way I can help?"

For a moment there was silence, then the sound of Sunny's bubbly laughter. "Oh, Mom! Not in love like that! I'm talking about a child, one of the handicapped students I've been working with."

"Oh." Mary sighing with relief. As part of her student training, Sunny spent several hours each week working with children with various handicaps. She'd been doing so for several weeks.

"Do you want to hear about him?" Sunny asked eagerly. "Oh, Mom, you would adore him! He's precious. His name is Anthony and he's two years old. He was born with all kinds of problems. He has a congenital heart defect as well as cerebral palsy, and just recently they discovered that he has a partial hearing loss. But you'd never know it. He's bright and happy and so loving. I just wish I were old enough to adopt him."

"Oh, honey, adoption is a big step, and a handicapped child can bring problems you can't even imagine."

Sunny had always had a tender heart, reaching out to anyone in need. Mary loved her for her unselfishness, but in all honesty she couldn't endorse such a step.

"Mom, you would have to spend time with these kids to know what I'm talking about," Sunny said. "They're regular kids, and yet they're not. They're something special."

"And so are you, sweetheart," Mary said, "but just remember that you're only one person and you can't fix all the world's ills."

"I know," Sunny replied. "But I still wish you could meet Anthony. Any chance of your coming up for a long weekend? Do you think your new boss would let you off some Friday?"

"Oh, I don't . . ." Mary started to protest, then abruptly changed her mind. Maybe a change of scenery would do her good. Maybe it would help her put things in their proper perspective.

She broached the subject to Tom the next morning.

"I'd really like to spend a couple of days with my daughter, and she wants me to meet one of the children she's working with." She lowered her eyes, unable to look at him. "And when I come back I want us to talk."

Tom nodded. "No problem. Fridays are normally slow anyway, and if necessary, Jesse can assist me."

He'd been stiff ever since he overheard Mary's remark about wishing she'd never met him or Rickie. She couldn't blame him, but she knew that things couldn't go on as they were. She was seriously considering Jesse's advice to get to know Tom before she wrote him off, but maybe she needed this time with Sunny first, to get everything all sorted out.

She looked at Tom's set profile and suddenly found herself wondering if it would even matter. Maybe by the time she figured out what it was she wanted, Tom wouldn't even be interested.

Mary made arrangements to visit Sunny the following weekend. The Thursday before she was due to leave she asked Tom if she could go home with him at lunch to see Rickie.

"I think about him a lot," she said truthfully, "and I really would like to see him again."

Tom looked as though he might refuse, then he seemed to reconsider. "Sure. Why not? Rickie has asked about you several times. He calls you the pretty lady."

"Smart boy," Mary said in an attempt to lighten the mood, but Tom wasn't smiling. A few minutes later, as she slid into the passenger's seat beside him, she was almost sorry she'd asked to come.

Tom obviously wanted nothing to do with her. Apparently he wasn't interested in a woman who couldn't find room in her heart for a motherless little boy. And she didn't blame him. She felt every bit as selfish and self-centered as he undoubtedly thought she was. But she couldn't help the way she felt, the actual fear that gripped her when she thought of crying babies and sickness, of interrupted sleep, and plans that had to be canceled. She'd done it all before. She wasn't sure she had the stamina to do it all again.

"So how is Rickie doing? Is he completely back to normal?"

Tom nodded. He took his eyes off the road just long enough to glance at Mary. "Pretty much. He still hasn't regained all the weight he lost, but Helen and I are working on it."

"Helen sounds like a jewel beyond price," Mary mused, smiling.

"She is that. I don't know how I'd have managed without her all this time. I think she loves Rickie almost as much as I do."

"That's good," Mary said softly, picturing the motherly woman cuddling Rickie in her arms.

"How is your daughter?"

Tom sighed heavily, and this time he deliberately kept his eyes focused on the road. "Kimmie's just about the same. Up one day, down the next. Whenever I visit her she swears she'll never use again, but the minute she gets out, it's the same old story. The doctor working with her thinks she needs a complete change of environment."

"You mean get her away from her old friends?"

"Something like that. I don't know, Mary. Sometimes I wonder if there's any point in even trying. And yet I can't bear to see such a young life go down the drain. And why? For what? What did I do wrong?"

Pain so sharp it could have sliced her heart to ribbons rocketed through Mary's body. Poor Tom. He was such a nice man, such a good person, but he couldn't solve this one all-important problem.

"Well, here we are," he said, his voice taking on a cheerful tone. "Time to see my little buddy."

Rickie must have been waiting just inside the door, because before they even made it to the front steps he was running down the path.

"Grandpa! And pretty lady! You came to see me?"

Tom bent and scooped Rickie up in his arms. Mary was struck by how natural he looked holding the little boy. And the smile that lit his face was genuine.

"Hi, Rickie," she said, holding out the plastic Disney character she'd brought him. "I brought someone to play with you."

"Goofy!" Rickie squealed gleefully, reaching for the toy.

Over the top of Rickie's head Tom smiled at her, the first smile he'd sent her way all week. Mary smiled back. This man would be so easy to love, and Rickie, too. All she had to do was open her heart and stop dwelling on the down side of parenting.

"Come on," Tom said. "Let's go have some lunch, partner. I'm as hungry as a bear!"

"Me, too, partner," Rickie cried, clapping his hands. "You come too, pretty lady," he insisted, stretching himself towards Mary. "Please?"

Mary smiled and patted Rickie's cheek. "I wouldn't miss it."

"So what's bugging you, Mom? You're not yourself," Sunny remarked, studying Mary's expression.

"I should have known I couldn't fool you," Mary said, trying to laugh. But the laugh ended on a sob, and without even knowing how it happened, Mary found herself in her daughter's arms. Sunny patted her back while she cried and murmured soothing noises.

Talk about role reversal, Mary thought. This was the ultimate!

"I'm sorry," she murmured a few minutes later, sniffing into the tissue Sunny handed her. "I guess I've been needing this for a long time."

"Then I'm glad you came up this weekend," Sunny said. "Now give, Mom. What's going on? You're not sick, are you?"

Her young face was frightened and Mary hastily reassured her daughter.

"No. I'm fine, at least physically. Emotionally is another story. It's my boss, or rather his grandson . . . oh, Sunny, I'm so confused!"

"Whoa, Mom, now I'm confused. You're upset about your boss's grandson? Why?"

"Because Tom is raising him, and his daughter's a drug abuser and I don't want to be a mother again, not now at this time of my life!"

Finally, bit by bit, Sunny managed to pull enough information out of Mary to understand the situation.

"Wow, Mom, this is heavy. I know all of us kids encouraged you to date after Daddy's death, but . . . well, I never imagined anything like this cropping up. Just think, if you marry

134

this guy, I'll have a baby stepbrother."

"I can't expect you to understand," Mary said. "You're so young. You've never been a mother. You don't know what it's like."

"I guess not," Sunny replied, hopping up from her narrow twin bed. "Come on, let's get out of this stuffy little room. A dorm is no place to be on a beautiful day like this. How about coming to the hospital with me to meet Anthony?"

Mary hesitated. She did feel a need to get out of the tiny, boxy room, but was this a ploy? An attempt on Sunny's part to make her see how sweet and adorable babies could be? But how could it be? Sunny hadn't known anything about Tom or Rickie until just a few minutes earlier.

"I'm not sure . . ."

"Anthony really is something special, Mom," Sunny said. "Please come to the hospital with me. I'm sure you won't regret it."

"All right. But on the way back I want a pizza, a thick juicy pizza smothered with pepperoni and mushrooms. Deal?"

"Deal," Sunny agreed happily.

The hospital was only a few blocks from the college campus, so they walked. The air was fresh and crisp, and as she walked, Mary felt her spirits lift.

"I always loved Boston," she told Sunny. "Your campus is beautiful."

"It *is* great," Sunny said, "but honestly, Mom, what I love best are the kids. I don't know, maybe I'm the kind of person who needs to be needed, but when I'm with those kids something happens to me. I'm bigger than life, you know? I feel twenty feet tall, like I can do anything."

Mary nodded. She'd had the same feelings as a young mother, when she held her babies in her arms. They were so little and helpless and they depended on her for everything. She had felt strong and powerful in those days, as though nothing could defeat her, but through the years life taught her differently. She lost her parents, and then her husband, her life's partner. And suddenly she wasn't young anymore. She'd lost her strength and power. She was a vulnerable, middle-aged woman and she couldn't view life quite so fearlessly.

They entered the hospital and went up to the third floor to the pediatric ward. Mary was gratified to see how eagerly the nurses greeted Sunny.

"Hey, Sunny, didn't expect you here today. What's up?"

Sunny beamed proudly. "This is my mother, Mary Jeffrey. I wanted you all to meet her, and I want her to meet Anthony."

"Oh, Anthony." A dark-skinned young nurse stepped close to Sunny and laid her hand on her arm. "Anthony's not so good today, hon. I don't know if you should go in."

Sunny lost all her glowing color and her eyes looked stricken.

"What happened? He was fine earlier this week."

"Yeah, well, you know how these things go, Sunny. His heart, you know? It's not real strong."

"Then I definitely have to see him," Sunny insisted. "He trusts me, Heather."

"I know hon, but . . ."

"I'm going in," Sunny said firmly. "Do I need a mask?"

Mary watched helplessly as Sunny struggled with a face mask and tried to hold back her tears. This was the kind of hurt mothers hoped to spare their children.

She followed Sunny down the hall, praying silently for a little boy she didn't even know. And then the dark-skinned nurse stopped and opened a door.

"Just a few minutes, okay? He needs to rest as much as possible."

Sunny stepped inside and Mary heard her gasp as she saw the tiny child hooked up to all

137

the machinery. The boy's little face was as white as flour and his hands lay lifelessly on the sheet.

"Oh, Anthony," Sunny whispered sadly. "What's happening to you?"

Mary stood in the doorway, not wanting to intrude. This was Sunny's child, Sunny's grief. She wasn't, couldn't be, a part of it.

She saw her daughter gently stroke the tiny hands and ever so tenderly kiss the pale cheek. She saw the tears that slipped silently down Sunny's face and the agony in her daughter's eyes, and she was helpless. There was nothing she could do.

She had to hold Sunny up as they left the hospital.

"Why?" Sunny cried. "Why Anthony? It isn't fair! He was so sweet, and he had no one. No one to care if he lived or died. His mother abandoned him at birth, and no one knew who his father was. The social worker told me his grandparents never once visited him. Why, Mom? How can people be so cruel and heartless?"

Mary winced as each of Sunny's words struck a blow to her heart. Anthony's story could have been Rickie's, except for Tom, a warm, wonderful man who was willing to put aside his own pleasures to love a child. She thought of her precious freedom, the freedom she'd guarded so jealously since Raymond's death. What did it mean when stacked against the feel of a child's arms around your neck, a baby's tiny lips pressed against your cheek, a child's blind trust?

She settled Sunny in her room and ordered take-out; then, while her daughter slept, Mary made plans. The first thing she had to do was go home and ask Tom to give her another chance. Somehow she had the feeling he would understand and forgive. He was just that kind of man. Then she needed to get to know both Tom and Rickie, to let them learn to trust and depend on her. And then . . . Mary stopped and shook her head. The future would take care of itself. All she had to do was be true to her own heart and mind. Sure, freedom was nice, but love and being loved was nicer.

When Sunny woke up she wanted to talk. Mary listened quietly, aching with her daughter's pain.

Finally, when Sunny grew quiet, Mary began to speak.

"Don't ever be sorry you loved that child, honey," she said, "because Anthony will carry that love wherever he goes."

"I know, but I wish things could have been different. I wish he could have grown up the way I did, Mom, with two loving parents. With brothers and sisters and pets and a nice home. He had so little, and so much pain. It just isn't fair!"

"No, it isn't," Mary said, "but sometimes life deals us a bad hand and we just have to work with it."

Sunny looked up, her eyes shining with tears. "Are you thinking about Daddy? I know it was hard on you, Mom, but you shouldn't blame yourself. I don't think Daddy would want you to."

Mary smiled through her own tears. "I don't think so either. Looking back I realize Daddy was unhappy for a long time, but I don't know what I could have done to change things. I just hope he's found peace."

"He has, Mom," Sunny said softly. "I know he has."

"And now I have to get on with my own life," Mary said. "Do you think I can be a good mom at my age?"

Sunny grinned. "You'll be the best ever. Whoever this Rickie kid is, he'll be lucky to get you. And as soon as I meet him I'll tell him so."

Mary told Sunny all about Rickie then, and about Kimmie.

Sunny was full of sympathy for the little

boy, and for his mother as well.

"How terrible not to be able to be a good parent to your baby," she said. "She must be suffering a great deal."

Mary thought about Sunny's words. She'd never really thought much about Kimmie, except to label her a selfish little brat. But what if she was suffering?

"I'm going to go see her," Mary said, suddenly making up her mind. "I'm going to talk to her, one woman to another. I have a feeling she may need some mothering herself."

Sunny grinned. "Go for it, Mom!"

"Are you sure you want to do this?" Tom asked, squeezing Mary's hand. They'd grown amazingly close in just a few weeks, and there was no longer any doubt in Mary's mind that Tom was the man she wanted to spend the remaining years of her life with.

"I'm positive," she said. "You know what they say, once a mother, always a mother. Maybe I can get through to her. At least I want to try."

"Then . . . thank you," Tom said, "for loving me enough to accept my daughter and my grandson."

Mary smiled. "It's my pleasure." And it was. The weeks since her visit to Sunny had been wonderful. It seemed she and Tom had been destined to be together. It was as if they fell in love overnight. One kiss and their fates were sealed.

Kimmie was in a private room, and Mary was surprised at how pretty she was. Her long, blond hair was clean and sweet-smelling and although her face was thin, her skin had a healthy glow.

"Honey," Tom said huskily as he took his daughter in his arms. "How are you? You look wonderful."

"Thanks, Daddy. So do you. How's Rickie? Is he all over that cold?"

Mary didn't wait for an introduction. She stepped forward and held out her hand. "I'm Mary Jeffrey," she said. "I work for your father and I . . . that is, we . . ."

"I know. You're going to be married. Dad told me on the phone. I'm glad." She turned to her father. "You're too nice to be alone."

"Ah, but I haven't been alone. I've had Rickie and Helen," Tom reminded her. He pulled a piece of paper from his pocket. "Rickie made this for you. It's a Mother's Day card. It's a little early, but he was anxious."

"Mother's Day? For me?" Kimmie's eyes filled with tears. She looked at the crumpled piece of construction paper and the crudely-drawn red heart and sobbed. "Oh, Daddy, I've made such a mess of things! I ruined everything! My own life, and maybe even Rickie's, too. I'm his mother and he doesn't even know me!"

"But he can," Mary said softly, laying her hand on Kimmie's arm. "It's not too late, Kimmie. It's never too late to start over, and your Dad and I will help you in any way we can."

"You mean it?" Kimmie looked surprised as she turned to Tom. "I thought . . . well, I was afraid you'd given up on me, Daddy."

"Never, baby," Tom said, hugging his daughter close to his heart. "You'll always be my little girl, and I'll always, always love you."

"Mom doesn't," Kimmie said. "She's washed her hands of all of us. She never comes to see me. She probably wouldn't care if I died tomorrow."

Tom started to protest, but then he caught Mary's eye, and saw her shake her head ever so slightly. It was time for the truth.

"Your mother has her own problems, honey, but you can't let that stop you from doing what you know is right. Try to get well this time, for Rickie's sake, and for your own. Your mother may not be able to help you, but Mary and I will. We'll be here for you."

A few weeks after Mary and Tom's visit to Kimmie, they sat on the floor of Tom's family room trying to figure out how to put together a tricycle for Rickie.

"He's been wanting this thing for months," Tom said, grinning, "but I was afraid he'd fall off and hurt himself."

Mary laughed. "I know. We'll worry ourselves sick, but kids have to take some risks, Tom, or they grow up afraid of their own shadows."

"You're right," he said, putting down his tools and pulling her into his arms. "Do you think we could forget this blasted toy for just a few minutes and take a smooch break?"

Laughter bubbled up in Mary's throat and suddenly she felt young and carefree again. "I'm game if you are." She closed her eyes and waited.

And it was everything she'd hoped it would be the very first time she laid eyes on Dr. Thomas Warren. It was warm, sexy, protective, and very, very inviting. Definitely worth waiting for.

"Whew!" Tom said a moment later. "I still can't believe we wasted all those weeks fencing with each other when we could have been doing this." He ran his hand down Mary's arm, then boldly cupped her full breast. "And this."

"Um," Mary said, leaning close to whisper in his ear. "Are you sure Helen is in bed?"

"Positive," Tom said, "But if you're worried about being caught in a compromising position, why don't you just say you'll marry me? I'll make an honest woman out of you, and we can relax."

Mary laughed, running a perfectly-manicured finger beneath the collar of Tom's shirt and making him squirm. "All in due time, doctor," she said. "Right now I'm enjoying this rather illicit courtship. I've never been this naughty before."

"Me either," he confessed, his breath warm against her neck as he pushed her back against the sofa cushions. "Um, I do like a softly padded woman."

Mary pushed herself against Tom, enjoying the way he caught his breath. And to think she'd almost missed this. Oh, despite her growing love and devotion to Rickie, she still had a few lingering doubts, but she and Tom had talked long and seriously about what they expected from each other when they married. It was understood that Helen would stay on to take care of Rickie so Mary could retain a measure of her former freedom, but she knew that once she married Tom and officially became Rickie's guardian, her life would never be the same. No, it wouldn't be the same, it would be better. She would be better.

She already felt years younger. There was something about sitting in a doctor's waiting room with a toddler, surrounded by young parents, that made you feel a part of it all. And at night, when she kissed Rickie and tucked him in, she had a hard time remembering why she'd been so afraid of doing all this over again. The best years of her life, that's what they'd been, and now she was lucky enough to have a repeat performance. She leaned back and smiled up at Tom. And then she closed her eyes and waited.

Jesse and Pete attended the simple wedding ceremony, along with Sunny and Kimmie. Just released from rehab, Kimmie was pale and thin, but Tom swore there was a new strength and determination in her eyes, and as soon as the small party was over, she was off to a fresh start in a halfway house in a new city.

"Maybe this time she really will make it," Mary whispered to Tom as they danced.

"I hope so," he replied, "But if she doesn't . . ."

"If she doesn't we'll manage just fine, you

146

and me and Rickie. Look! Helen has her hands full keeping him out of the cake, hasn't she?"

Rickie was the star of the show. Sunny had fallen in love with him on sight, and had promised to babysit whenever she was in town. And according to Tom, Kimmie had shown more interest in Rickie than she ever had before. Maybe things really would work out. But no matter what happened, Mary knew she and Tom could cope. When there was love and trust anything was possible.

"Happy wedding day, Doctor Tom," Mary whispered against his neck.

"Same to you, darling," Tom whispered back. "And Happy Mother's Day as well."

Mary smiled. Married on Mother's Day. It must be a good omen.

Listen To Your Mother

by Martha Gross

They poured onto the open boat deck like
so many orange ducks, bumping each other
awkwardly in their bulky life jackets. Just as
Maggie stepped through the doors, her mother
and her daughter, Libby, close behind her, she
thought she saw him. Down the deck. Just a
glimpse. The guy who was always delivering
things to the school library when she was
working as a volunteer there, Jeb Dalton. Bad
enough she kept thinking about him. Bad
enough that every time he delivered something
and she had to talk to him, she got all self-
conscious and could barely speak coherently.
Now, was she imagining she was seeing him,
too?

When he carried in those computers that
first time, she hardly noticed him, until he
started explaining the keyboard to her. Stand-

ing right next to her, so tall and lean, he smelled like soap. Two days later, he came by with a box of floppy disks and software. This time she noticed him right away. He looked right into her eyes when he was explaining the software, and she felt something grab her inside. Not mystical. Physical. A kind of sensual charge.

And since then, it was like that every time he came. Worse—she kept thinking about him, and trying not to. What was she—some dotty teenager? Besides, he was always such a mess—shoelaces untied, socks mismatched, pants or shirt torn. Twice he'd been out in the parking lot when she left the school and they had talked for a bit. He seemed to like her. But Maggie didn't care what her mother and her daughter said, she was *not* interested in that stupid dating scene. And certainly not with a delivery man who didn't even own a pair of matching socks.

Yet she kept thinking of him. Maybe there was something in this pheromones business after all.

She peered down the deck again. Nothing. Just blurry swarms of people staring up at the lifeboats and trying to find their stations. And crew members with lists herding them into lumpy orange rows against the wall.

"Mom!" cried Libby, right behind her. "Move it. You can't just stop like that. You're in everyone's way." Maggie blinked and scrambled ahead to where the crewman was pointing, her mother and Libby following.

She had to get that man out of her mind! "Sorry, honey," she said. "I just thought I saw someone I knew." She leaned forward and scanned the crowd once more. Was that he, that tall one, way down? Damn. Her eyesight was so bad. It could be Santa Claus for all she could tell.

"Who'd you think you saw, Maggie?" asked her mother, Ivy Fines.

"Oh, uh, just someone from the school."

"There's probably lots of people you know on board," Ivy said with a shrug. "All those Agency On Aging people. You'll probably see them all tomorrow tucked under blankets in the deck chairs, shivering."

"Oh, Mother! Everyone over seventy can't look like you. Only so many Peter Pans are allowed on this earth at once."

"Well, listen to Grammy, Mom," said Libby. "And don't spend any time with those decrepit old farts. You're here to have fun, and maybe find some lively, hip guys to dance with."

"Dance!" snorted Maggie. "I can hardly walk. You and your darn aerobics. I feel like a cripple. I'm too old for that stuff."

"If I'm not too old, you're not too old," countered Ivy. "Listen to your mother, Maggie. Keep at it and all the pain will go away and you'll feel so great you'll want to take trapeze lessons."

"Don't hold your breath," Maggie sniffed.

"Oh, Mom," cried Libby, "chill out. Go with the flow. This is going to be such fun. This ship has everything. A great gym and workout room, and hot tubs, dance lessons, a Turkish disco. And I've already spotted some really sexy hunks giving me looks. Wheee! Am I going to have a whizbang time."

"Yeah, especially with these marvelous orange jackets to waddle around in," grumbled Maggie. "What fun!"

"Don't be a poor sport, daughter. You were the one who was selling chances on this cruise."

"It was benefiting the Agency on Aging," said Maggie. "Of course I was selling tickets. But I didn't expect Libby to buy one. And I sure didn't expect her to win."

"Well, I think it was terribly sweet of her to use it for us for Mother's Day. She could have just taken her friends."

The crewmen began calling roll at the various stations up and down the deck. Libby crowed when a couple of handsome studs answered. Finally their crewman called his final name. "You may return to your cabins now, and put your life jackets away," he said.

"Let's go check out the gym, Grammy," said Libby as they filed out with the rest of the crowd, back through the doors and down the stairs toward their cabin on the deck below. "I hear they've got great machines."

"You go ahead," said Maggie.

"What time's dinner, Mom?" asked Libby, struggling out of her life jacket. "God, this thing is worse than a chastity belt."

"Not until 8:30. But remember, there'll be three of us trying to use that one tiny bathroom," she warned.

"I'll meet you in the gym, dear," said Ivy. "Give me your jacket and I'll put it in the cabin with mine. Three are too much for your mother to carry."

"OK," said Libby, handing hers over. "You'll find this little virgin over by the weights."

"Little virgin?" Ivy repeated, looking over her glasses at her retreating granddaughter.

"That's her newest thing," sighed Maggie. "She has refrained from sex for a whole year, she tells me. Because I scared her witless carping about AIDS. She says a year without sex re-qualifies you as a virgin."

Ivy hooted. "Well, I never intend to try for that rating anymore," she said. "Life is too short. Especially at my age. But I guess you qualify."

"I—I—" Maggie hated to lie to her mother.

"Wait a minute. You've been a hermit since Roy died, except for your volunteer work. Kissing and shaking hands don't count."

"Well, I did more than that, once," she admitted.

"You did? For heaven sakes. Maybe there's hope for you yet."

"No. That's exactly why I'm not interested in this stupid dating scene, Mom. You and Libby are wasting your time."

"It was that bad?"

"Terrible. He just jumped on me and began banging away. I didn't feel like I was taking part. I was just being used."

"Well, you should have said, 'Excuse me, I'm here, too. You're not the only one doing this, buddy.' That's what I said to your father when he tried that a couple of times, when he was younger."

"He didn't even take me anywhere. A couch. In his office. He said he had to stop and check his calls. He said we'd go to dinner after. But I just went home."

"That happened to me on a date once, too,"

said Ivy. "I'd gone with him for three months, and never guessed he was such a selfish jerk. But I fixed him. I called him three days later and told him my doctor just discovered I had four sexually transmitted diseases and I must have caught them from him. And that if he ever called me again, I'd get the police after him. This was before AIDS. But I bet he was being tested for *months* after, for everything from warts to cholera."

"Well, I don't need it. They all want something. They buy dinner, they want to be paid. And there's nobody out there I could be really interested in. Jerks. I need someone like Eric Sevareid. Or Gary Cooper. Lean, wise, perceptive."

"And dead. Well, here's our cabin." Maggie unlocked the door, and Ivy tossed the jackets in. "Put them away for us, will you, Mag? Libby's waiting. And let me tell you something, daughter. Not all of them are jerks. But you have to take a closer look to tell the difference." And she hurried off down the hall.

Maggie hadn't picked up the dice for two years. She never had been crazy about gambling; it had been one of her wifely chores. Roy had liked her to gamble with him. To him, a crap table was a bit of heaven on earth. But not to Maggie.

Oh, well, it would be distracting. Anything to get this weekend over with. It beat visiting the gym with her mother and Libby, who never knew when to quit. It's a wonder they both didn't look like Arnold Schwarzenegger.

Two tables were open. She picked the one that was half-full. A small, Spanish-looking fellow was rolling and hissing "Hai!" as he threw the dice. She put two hundred-dollar bills on the table, and the croupier pushed four stacks of five-dollar chips toward her. The Spanish fellow rolled a seven.

His wife or girlfriend rolled next, flinging the dice almost angrily. One skipped over the table's edge and fell on the floor and she had to roll again. The Spanish man laughed and held her arm up as if she were a champion boxer. Maggie played the field and bet all the hard ways. She had a feeling the lady wouldn't last long. She was right. Double fives, double threes, double sixes, snake eyes, and a seven. And Maggie had picked up twenty more chips.

Something made her look up. And there he was, the delivery man, Jeb Dalton, in a red shirt, standing next to the Spanish woman at the other end of the table. Looking surprised—right at her. He grinned and ambled around to her end of the table and placed his chips on the rack next to hers. "What a nice surprise," he said. "You're Maggie Bliss. From the college. Remember me? Jeb Dalton?" She nodded, afraid to trust her voice. "OK if I play here?"

She nodded again. When he stood this close, she could almost *feel* a current between them. Much stronger than those vibes she kept getting at school. Did he feel them, too?

"Are you playing?" asked the croupier, impatiently.

"Oh, yes," they both answered at once. Maggie put two chips on the pass line. He did the same. The next roller, the man next to Jeb, threw a four. Maggie put two chips below the pass line. Jeb did the same. The man rolled a seven, and the dealer swept away their chips. Jeb looked puzzled. It was his roll. "Just throw the dice to the other side of the table?" he asked Maggie.

"Yes," she said. "All the way." A novice. Then what was he doing here, throwing his money away?

He began an incredibly long roll. He watched the board intently, bet exactly as she bet, said little, and tried to follow the other

157

players, too. Maggie increased her bets—he did the same. When she threw a chip on the field, he threw one, too. It was suddenly a hot table. The spaces filled. The cloth was covered with chips.

He hit elevens three times on one new roll, sevens twice on two others. He looked surprised when the croupier pushed chips at him. He made number after number. And when he finally crapped out, everyone at the table clapped.

He looked at her expectantly. "How'd I do?"

"Beginner's luck," she replied. "You made everyone rich."

Maggie was next. Her roll wasn't half as good as Jeb's, but she made five numbers before tossing a fatal seven. Then the table went cold. She pushed her chips toward the croupier. Jeb looked at her, puzzled. "I'm cashing them in," she explained. "Even if I play later, and I probably will, who wants to carry them around? They're heavy."

"Makes sense," he said and pushed his forward, too.

"I have to go down and check on my mother and my daughter. I'm here with them," she said, heading out of the casino.

He stayed right beside her. He seemed to

want to talk. "Your mother and daughter?" he repeated.

"This trip was a Mother's Day present to my mother and me from my daughter," she explained. "She won it at a raffle."

"Does your daughter have red hair like you?"

Maggie nodded. "Mom, too. Together we're blinding. With more freckles, Mom always says, than there are stars in the Milky Way."

"I think I saw you at the lifeboat drill. There were three redheads down the deck from me and one, I think, looked like you. But I don't see very well more than a few feet away."

"Me, either."

"You know, you're a pretty good gambler."

"Well, I did it for sixteen years."

"You must really like it."

Maggie shrugged. "Not really. My husband loved it. And liked to have me standing with him while he played. He'd keep feeding me chips. I could never lose. It was sort of a wifely duty. This is my first time at a table since he died two years ago. And I'm only here now to give me an excuse so my daughter and my mother can't drag me off to the gym, like they've been doing the last couple of weeks. They're into aerobics."

"And in great condition?"

"Like Charles Atlas. And they've been putting me through torture lately trying to make me fit. I hate it. I hurt all over."

He laughed at that, then said, "Listen, could I just watch you when you play? Like I did tonight. I want to learn a little bit about this game. I don't know anything. I got that booklet they give you, but it doesn't mean much until you watch the play."

"Sure, you can watch. But do you really want to learn? You can lose a lot of money playing craps. Maybe more than you can afford. You don't always rake it in like tonight. Usually it goes the other way. Everyone loses sooner or later."

"Well, it's kind of academic. I've got an idea about doing something on a computer."

"But people get wiped out at craps. I mean — well, as a delivery man, it's none of my business, but how much money can you make?"

He looked down at her and grinned. "I'm very good at my job," he said. "And I've budgeted money for this. Oh, and by the way, what sitting are you at? What table?"

"Second sitting. My daughter insisted. She said the best-looking hunks take that one. I don't remember what table."

"I could find you," he offered. "If you wanted to go to the show after dinner, I could get us a good table. For your mother and daughter, too, of course, if they'd like."

The had reached the elevators and stairwell. Just then, a tall brunette wearing enormous pink earrings slithered up, wrapped her arms around him, and cried, "Jeb Dalton! Is that you? Oh, how fun!"

He looked puzzled. "You remember me. I'm Hedy Halperin, the receptionist at your dentist, Dr. Wibbrinsky. What a coincidence!"

"Ah, yes. Wibbrinsky. Nice to see you," said Jeb, clearly very uncomfortable. "Uh, Miss Halperin, this is Mrs. Bliss. Maggie Bliss. Hedy Halperin."

The brunette gave Maggie a quick once-over and a chilly smile, then flashed her teeth invitingly at Jeb again, taking his arm. "Jeb, let's do the show together tonight. What sitting are you?"

"The second, but I'm sorry — I'm busy. I'm attending that with a group. Including Mrs. Bliss."

"Oh, that's OK," Halperin said airily. "Maybe we can all sit together. Anyway, we'll find you later, my roommate and me."

He pulled his arm free and turned around to Maggie. Only she was gone.

A loud, insistent knocking on his office door tore Maitre d' Emanuel Russo's attention away from his seating diagrams. He called out crossly, "Who is it?"

The door opened and the purser, Gola Pendeka, stepped in. "Manny, we got a couple last-minute requests."

"When *don't* we have a couple of last-minute requests? When don't we have last-minute problems? The bananas they delivered are too ripe. They'll never make it. We'll have to pick some up in Nassau and get robbed. The shrimp are too big — we'll have to limit cocktails to four. Not enough swordfish. We'll push the dolphin. And one of the laundry women didn't show and she's got the key to the table linens. All I need is a few last-minute requests to push me over the line altogether. So what are they this time?"

"First of all, Manny, that guy that's setting up the new electronic stuff on board, that's going to make running this ship so easy they'll probably fire half of us — Jeb Dalton's his name — he wants to sit at the same table as one Margaret Bliss, her daughter, and mother. Three redheads, he said. He thinks they're at the second sitting."

Manny grabbed his toupee dramatically. "Jesus, doesn't he realize how impossible these last-minute changes are? We're already set in concrete. Allow one change, you gotta allow fifty more and you're starting all over again. I gotta be there for the first seating in fifteen minutes! What does he think I am? A fucking magician? Oh, God! My stomach's beginning to churn!"

"I know, Manny," soothed the purser. "But I think you'd better see to this one. He's Captain Woodard's guest. Very important. He looks like someone who lives under a bridge. Messy. But he's the one doing all those new automatic programs for us. Pretty soon this whole tub will be run by his computer tricks."

Manny groaned again. "What we should probably do instead of changing his seat is push him overboard. You know how fucking hard it is to learn a new system." He checked his second sitting lists, found Dalton's name and the Blisses, and made a switch. "Walsors from 59 to 36. Bliss from 36 to 59. Dalton from 22 to 59. OK, done. Now what next, Penny?"

"This one's funny, Manny. There's this lady, Hedy Halperin—real dishy broad—who corners me ten minutes ago and says she and her roommate—they're in S12—want to sit with Dalton. The plot thickens. But they're in a sundeck suite, too, so she may have some clout. We probably better try and do what she wants."

Russo pored over his papers for a moment more and then made another switch. "Yeah, OK. The Peteroids don't care where they sit. He's about 110 and they'll get fed in their room most of the time, anyway. OK, done. How much did this Halperin chaser pay you?" Pendeka pulled twenty-five dollars from his pocket and handed it over.

"She paid me fifty dollars; here's your half."

"Now, that's it? I hope?"

Pendeka smiled sheepishly. "Well, not quite."

"OK, give me the rest. Nothing can help my ulcer now, anyway. Farina again for dinner tonight."

"Well," the purser said, "the mother of this Maggie Bliss—she's a flaming redhead, too, just like Bliss and her daughter—she told me she'd appreciate it if I'd put them at a big table and seat some single men there, too. Not for her granddaughter, but for Bliss! Fiftyish, sixtyish guys would be suitable, she says, but no decrepit old farts." Russo guffawed at that.

"And if there was anybody a little older for *her,* again no decrepit old farts. She'd appreciate that, too."

164

Russo roared and slapped his knee. "Damn, this is too much. We're matchmakers now?"

"Well, she's seventyish, I'd say, but wait 'til you see her. Trim. Bouncy. You know. What seventyish guy could keep up with her?"

Russo slid his glasses down on his nose and pored over his charts. "Well, why not? We got the Bornens for the mother. He's old enough and he knows which end is up. And let's see. Yeah, I got a couple of businessmen for Bliss. Hah! Now stir the pot and watch it explode. This is too good to pass up. How much did she give you?"

"Only ten bucks."

"Keep my half. We try to please everyone. Especially friends of Captain Woodard's. No wonder I've got an ulcer."

"How do they expect three people to dress at one time in this tiny cabin?" grumbled Maggie, when she had to wait until Libby moved out of the way before she could open the closet.

"Easy," said Libby. "One in the bathroom. One on the floor. One standing on a bed. You could dress four if you had to. You have to think outside the lines, Mom."

"It's so great having a genius in the family," said Maggie.

"Besides, all this closeness is bonding."

"That's all I need," grumbled Maggie. "If we get any more bonded they'll take us for Siamese triplets."

"That's why we took you on this cruise, Mom. To find you a man and get us a little less bonded."

"How was the gambling, dear?" asked Ivy, poking her head out of the bathroom.

"Great. I've never yet pulled a tendon throwing dice."

"Let's get down to the important part," Ivy replied, stepping back into the room wrapped in a towel. "Meet anyone?"

"Well, as a matter of fact, I did."

"Oh, Mommy, who? What happened?" cried Libby, dancing with glee.

"Nothing so wonderful. This delivery man who keeps bringing stuff to the school when I'm working in the library."

"I meant to talk to you about that, Mom. Couldn't you do volunteer work somewhere else? It's like you're still trying to keep an eye on me. Hovering over me like I'm a six-year-old."

"Be still, Libby. You can fight that round later," said her grandmother. "Let's get your mother's story."

"Well, he's tall and thin and he dresses so

badly he looks like the scarecrow in *The Wizard of Oz*. Buttons missing, shoelaces untied, socks that don't match. But otherwise nice-looking. Pleasant. He's really tried to be friendly at school. Twice he was waiting in the lot when I left and we talked."

"Mom! And you never told me. What's his name?"

"Jeb something. And I think he likes computers. A delivery man with an expensive hobby—what a great prospect."

"You don't have to marry him," said Libby. "But if he's nice, if you can talk to him, that's what counts. You don't find Clark Gable on the first shot. And you need practice flirting. And you have to start somewhere."

"No, he's not Clark Gable. Not that I was that crazy about Gable, anyway. I hear he had terrible breath."

"So what happened?" asked Ivy, pulling a dress over her head.

"Well, I was just getting started and there he is, right across from me, looking as surprised to see me as I was to see him. And he comes around and plays next to me. But he hasn't the vaguest idea what he's doing. So he copies me. Exactly. He has a roll that would have put Roy on cloud nine—on and on. We made a bundle. And when I cashed in, he did, too."

"Does he like you?" asked Libby.

"I think so. And I like him. But a delivery man? By his age, I just expect a man to have gotten into something a little deeper."

"Well, he might be into something else, for all you know. Listen to your mother, Maggie. You don't learn everything about a man in the first ten minutes. Give him a chance. There may be more to him than you realize now. And you need somebody."

"Wait a minute. That's your idea. And Libby's. Not mine. I think I'm fine all by myself. And besides, this man has some kind of appeal. I might really get to like him. And then what would I have? Probably someone I can't even talk to about anything I'm interested in. And he's the last person who should be taking up gambling. On a delivery man's salary?"

"OK, so he's not Eric Sevareid. Who is? Give him a chance. Wait and see."

"Anyway, he wanted to take us all to the show. We'd sit at the same table. He said he'd try to find us during dinner. But that was before this woman came up and wrapped her arms around him and asked him to sit with her and her roommate. He said he was sitting with us but she didn't give up. So I just slipped off and came back here. I didn't want to make it awkward for him."

Libby groaned. "Mom, sometimes you're so dumb, I can't believe it. You should have stayed. Why can't you give anything a chance? I don't mean you have to hop into bed with him or pledge your life right away. But flirt a little. Don't you want something more in your life besides coming home and getting out your sketch pad? All alone? And telling Grammy and me what to do?

"You've just got to get interested in something or somebody else and get out of my school and off my back and Grammy's, Mom. Give us a little space. And have a life yourself. A guy would help. I don't need constant mothering anymore. I just need you as my friend."

"Well, tough, darling," said Maggie. "Because I'll always be a mother to you. You don't get over that. Just like Grammy is always a mother to me. And if anyone's on anyone's back all the time here, it's Grammy on mine."

"Me?" said Ivy.

"Yes. Now that we're letting it all hang out — you can't stop telling me what to do anymore than I can stop telling Libby. You keep saying 'Listen to your mother. Listen to your mother.' You want me to start dating around whether I want to or not."

"I just want you to be happy and not screw up the rest of your life," said Ivy innocently. "But I also absolutely refuse to sit for another sketch. You draw in all my wrinkles."

"OK," said Libby. "Then the consensus is, mothering is a habit that's hard to break. But both of you could try."

"Us? What about you, you bossy child. And you're not even a mother yet. Say, maybe that's this guy's appeal," giggled Maggie. "Boy, does he need mothering! My instincts are turned on. But I'm fighting them."

"Mom," said Libby. "Open up that blouse another button. You look too chaste with it that way. Oh, and listen, you have to try out this gym. You could end up looking like Raquel Welch."

"You're mothering me again, Libby," teased Maggie.

Libby laughed. "God, we're all incurable."

"Well, are we all ready?" asked Ivy. "Then let's go."

"Are you crazy?" cried Libby. "We have to wait another ten, fifteen minutes, and make an entrance. Three redheads strolling in together. If there's anyone there, that'll get his attention."

Libby was right. Maggie was often amazed at her daughter's perception.

Most of the guests were already seated when they swept into the Marmaris dining room. A waiter led them to their table — a large, round ten-seater at which just three seats were empty. "At least they're together," whispered Ivy. But Maggie didn't answer. She was staring at the seat to the right of the empties where Jeb Dalton was sitting, grinning back at her. And next to him, Hedy Halperin, the woman who had latched onto him at the elevator.

"Good. Now you're here we can all introduce ourselves," he said, standing up. "Everyone, this is Maggie Bliss."

"And this is my mother, Ivy Fines. And my daughter Libby," said Maggie, taking the chair that Jeb held out — the one next to him. He then seated Libby next to her and her mother in the third chair. The man next to Ivy stood up. "I'm Thor Bornen, and this is my sister, Asa Bornen." The portly man next to his sister said, "I'm Doug Pintner." The next man stood only half-way up and mumbled. "Jack Teidel."

Next to him was a 45-ish, bone-thin blonde with a mane like a lion's. "Dawn Garland," she said. "So glad to meet you all." And next

171

to her, Hedy Halperin said, "I'm delighted to meet all of you, too. I'm sure we'll have a marvelous time together. Especially with Jeb Dalton at our table. Jeb—"

"Oh, excuse me a minute, Miss Halperin," Jeb interrupted. "Mrs. Bliss and I have a friend over there waving at us. He stood up, pulled out Maggie's chair, and led her over to the other side of the dining room.

"Who is it?" asked Maggie, puzzled. "Someone from school?"

"Nobody. I just wanted to check with you about the show. And I want to have it all set before I make my excuses to that Halperin woman again. They'll hold a table for us if you want to see the show. One just big enough for us and your mother and daughter. Or we can include anyone else you like."

"How can you reserve a table?" asked Maggie. "I didn't know they let anyone do that."

"I have a friend or two on the staff. That's how I got to your table. Is that OK?"

"Did you have your lady friend put there, too?"

"You mean Hedy Halperin? Hell, no."

"Maybe she's got a friend on the staff, too."

"I don't know. I barely know her. And I didn't ask to have her and her friend at my table for dinner. And I don't intend to ask them to join us for the show."

"Well, I don't want to cause you any bother—"

"No bother. We can have any size table we want."

Maggie was puzzled. He really seemed to want to spend time with her. Well, if he could get them seated at the shows, if he knew a couple of crewmen who could pull a few strings, why not let him do it? "I guess just the four of us," she said, smiling up at him.

"Great. And—uh—thanks," He gave her arm a small squeeze, and led her back to their table.

"So who did you run into, Jeb?" asked Hedy. He looked at her blankly.

"Oh, it wasn't the person we thought it was," said Maggie smoothly. And Jeb's foot gently nudged hers under the table.

Dinner was one of those probing, sparring talkfests—everyone trying to find out something about the others while making their tablemates aware that they were worth knowing. Hedy was still trying to ignite some spark of interest in Jeb. Dawn and Hedy were also trying to do the same with Doug Pintner and Jack Teidel. Ivy and Libby were fascinated by Thor Bornen and his sister, who was a tad pompous but very funny, too, Jeb noticed.

173

"Should we invite them to sit with us at the show?" he whispered. "Would your mother and daughter like that?"

Maggie nodded. "But how do we invite them without inviting the rest?"

"I'll think of something."

Just then an officer tapped Jeb on the shoulder. He excused himself, left the table with the officer, and returned a few moments later. Maggie knew he must be making arrangements for the show. After trying several conversational gambits on Jeb, with only polite response and no encouragement, Hedy switched her attention back to Doug and Jack. They ate it up. When the dessert was served, Doug said, "Well, we four are heading up to the Bodrum Disco instead of doing the show. Too hard to get a good table down front unless you have someone leave half-way through dinner and save it. If you want to join us, come on up."

After the four of them left, Jeb said, "Listen," to the Bornens. "We're going to the show and someone is saving us a good table. We'd really like to have you join us if you don't have other plans."

"Oh, my, that would be lovely," said Asa. "I adore VIP treatment. It always feels so right, I'm sure I must have been at least a duchess in some former life."

"Come, your highness," said her brother. "Let's not keep our hosts waiting. They might change their minds and we'll have to sit with the peasants."

In the ladies' room on the Aegean deck, Dawn and Hedy repaired their makeup. "I don't know about these two," said Hedy. "Did you see all the broken veins on Doug's face? And the size of his nose? A drinker. I bet he passes out before midnight."

"So what? Then you don't have to worry about what comes later. Besides, who else is there? That Bornen guy must be 70 or older. And he's got his sister to babysit. And you sure weren't getting anywhere with Dalton. Me neither."

"Not yet. But I will," said Hedy. "I just have to figure out exactly what gets to him."

"Well, meanwhile, a bird in hand. Let's not keep our dates waiting."

Hedy and Dawn weren't gone five minutes when Ivy and Maggie opened the door. "Didn't Libby want to come with us?" asked Ivy.

"Mom, you know that kid is a camel. She must take after Roy's side. I'm like you. I need a ladies' room every ten minutes."

"So tell me what's going on."

"He got his table changed to sit next to us. Don't ask me how that Hedy person and her friend got to our table, but I'm sure it was to be near him, not us. When he said we saw someone we knew, that was when he asked if we could all sit together for the show. He knows someone on the crew who saved the table. And he liked the Bornens so he asked them, too."

"Well, that was really nice of him. I like this Thor, too. His sister is funny as can be. He's a real gentleman. Probably too much so. But kind of fun. He plays backgammon, and they live in Boca Grove—she said something about a Backgammon Club he belongs to. I think he's going to ask me to go with him there when we get back, but he hasn't yet. Did you find out who Jeb knows that got him such a good table?"

"No idea. I'm going up to the casino later and he wants to come along. I'll explain some of it to him first, although I think he's making a big mistake. He'll end up in the poorhouse."

Two minutes later Asa Bornen came into the ladies' room, alone. She looked in the booths. In one she found an unopened roll of toilet paper on a shelf. She slipped it into her purse, grinned gleefully, patted her hair in the mirror, and left.

Bouncy calypso. Splashy Junkanoo. Great vocalists belting their songs to the stratosphere. A laugh-a-minute comedian—even a magic act. Vegas quality, Maggie had to admit. The Bornens were delightful, if a bit old and creaky. He, the perfect gentleman. She, the perfect lady, her white hair piled high in elaborate scrolls. Just a bit sniffy, but charming them all with naughty, outrageous comments in her tremulous voice.

Maggie was flabbergasted. How did Jeb get this perfect table, with exactly six chairs and waiters hovering? And what lavish service! Nobody could finish a drink before it was refilled.

At the end, amid a storm of applause, a waiter presented Jeb with a check. How could he afford to pay for all that? "No," she cried aloud. "We've had so many drinks. There are too many of us. We'll all go Dutch, right, everyone?" They all nodded.

"No, I asked you to sit with me—you're my guests—" countered Jeb.

But Maggie grabbed the check and handed it to Libby. "Honey, figure that out, will you?" And then to Jeb, she scolded, "I don't know why you're so determined to put yourself in the poorhouse."

Libby tried to read the check, dodging Jeb's attempts to grab it back. "It's too dark in here. Is it OK if I just divide the bottom line by six? Let's see. If we just add a tip . . . carry the two . . . that makes . . ."

But at that point, Thor Bornen deftly lifted it from her grasp, put it in the waiter's hand with some bills, and said, "That change is yours if you get out of here right now." The waiter practically sprinted off.

"It's taken care of," said Thor.

"Well, then, we can all pay you," replied Maggie.

"No, you can't," said Thor. "All that arithmetic and bookkeeping will give me a terrible headache. I'm allergic to arithmetic."

As they all stood up and thanked him, Hedy and Dawn swooped by. "We're over in the Bodrum Disco on the other side of the lounge," gushed Hedy. "Come on over. You won't believe that place. We're having so much fun. The music is to die for!"

"Grammy and I will," said Libby. "Any cute guys to dance with?"

"We'll take a look, too. Though it's past my bedtime," said Asa.

Hedy nodded impatiently and looked expectantly at Jeb. "Maggie and I would love to," he said. "But we've made other plans."

Hedy's smile vanished for an instant and she shot Maggie a look that could kill.

"We'll be there for a while," coaxed Dawn. "Check it out later. If not, we'll see you at the midnight buffet."

"Ugh. You could eat anything more after that dinner?" cried Asa. "Where do you put it—in your ear? That's the only thing wrong with these cruises. They're always stuffing you like cattle before the slaughter."

"Well, listen, we better get back," said Dawn. "We told the guys we were heading for the loo again. That crazy Jack said to go for him, too. He's so funny."

"Oh, just a scream," said Asa, giving her brother a look.

"Let's sit out here for a minute before going in," suggested Maggie, pointing to one of the tables outside the casino. "Are you sure you want to do this? I know we made money this afternoon, but we might not tonight, Jeb. It's really a terrible habit. Sometimes once people get into it, they find they're out of control."

"For someone who gambles, you're pretty

down on it."

"Well, it's not my favorite thing, as I've explained. But I can afford it. I mean, if I play once in a while and lose a couple of hundred dollars, I won't be out in the street. My husband left us a little income. The way Roy gambled, I was sure there'd be nothing left. I worried about taking care of Libby. But you—on a delivery man's salary—well, you don't want to get into a mess."

Jeb stared at his hands, then seemed to choose his words carefully. "Well, I appreciate your concern. I don't plan to do this very often. I told you I'm interested in writing a computer program, maybe for guessing what move to make when. Looking up odds and stuff, I'm not sure. I know probabilities and all that, but there's so much I don't know yet."

He handed her the booklet that the casino gave to beginners. Page by page, line by line, Maggie went through it with him, answering his questions. But her arms hurt and she kept stopping to rub them. "That's from the exercises you mentioned—with your mother and daughter?" he asked.

"Yes. I should have started easier. But sometimes with those two pushing, the only way to shut them up is to give in and get it over with. Like this dating business. They keep pushing me. I'm really not interested. I see widowed friends, what they've gone through trying to find someone to have dinner with at their clubs on Saturday nights. It gets to be the focus of their whole lives. Plotting and subterfuge by so-called friends, trying to latch on to each other's dates. Who needs all that? There are more important things I still want to do with my life. I want to make a little difference. I try to help some causes I think are important. The school library. The literacy program. The Agency on Aging. And I like to do sketches. I don't need to be around crowds of people all the time. But my mother and Libby keep pushing me."

He nodded sympathetically. "I know. After my wife died six years ago, I was constantly pestered by women. Amy was a juvenile diabetic. I was thirty-two when we got married. After a couple of really great years she started falling apart. It was such a long, long ordeal—fourteen years. She died by inches. Sometimes, she'd be so discouraged she'd start drinking. She was a different person then. Angry. And it made her sicker. But she couldn't be strong and careful all the time. Oh, listen to me. I don't know why I'm telling you all this."

"I just unloaded to you. Tell me."

"The last years, she had operations. Amputations near the end. Anyway, for a couple of months after she died—all those women hanging around—I slept with a great many. Drank a lot. But it disgusted me. I think I resented the fact that they were there and Amy wasn't. She was so sweet and some of them were so tough and hard. Maybe I felt guilty. Everyone was pushing me to meet this woman and that. I finally just stopped seeing anybody.

"I became a kind of recluse. I saw how short life can be and I decided not to spend it with anyone I didn't really like. I'm not doing anything anymore I don't damn well want to. Funny thing you mention sketching. I do that, too. Nothing fancy. Just a pencil and any handy tablet. I always did a little here and there, but after Amy died it's been a kind of release for me. And I sure needed one."

Maggie nodded. "That's how it is for me, too."

"I decided to go to college. At my age. I had to work. I'd run up a lot of debts with Amy. I put in twenty-hour days, sometimes. There was no time for dating. I got a degree in computer science at Nova University. It took me five years. But I've been deeply into it, enjoying it from the start. And with this

AIDS thing, I decided to forget women. I know how the probabilities work. They're appalling. Messing around with one of those free-and-eager types today is Russian Roulette."

"You're right," Maggie nodded emphatically. "So, sure I get a little lonely sometimes. A lot lonely. But then I think of the risk. The hassle. And it's just too much to handle."

"Me, too. Unless I find someone nice, who kind of thinks the same way I do." He stood up, took her hand, and pulled her to her feet. "Come on, teacher. Lesson time." Maggie winced. "Your arm hurts that much?"

She nodded. "Sometimes. Both arms, in different places. And my left leg. And the heels of both feet."

"Maybe you ought to try acupressure."

"Acupressure?"

"I forget who told me to try it. The guy at the gym, maybe. So I got a couple of books and made up a little computer program. You just tell it where you hurt and how from a long list of descriptions, and it tells you the acupressure points and what to do to them. I can probably remember some of them. Want to go up to the gym and I could show you what I remember?"

Maggie looked at him and the concern written on his face. She was tempted to agree. "I—uh—I'll think about it. I mean, thank you. Maybe later. After we hit the tables." But as they entered the casino and looked for empty places at the crap tables, and even after they started playing, she kept thinking of his offer, wondering what it would be like to have him touching her. Therapeutically, of course. And at one point she thought that since Eric Sevareid spent so much time in all those Oriental countries, perhaps he'd learned something about acupressure.

The Bodrum Disco, revealed a plaque at the entrance, imitated the famous Halicarnas Disco in Bodrum, Turkey. Inside, pillars lined the walls, fountains spurted, and colorful laser beams darted and danced in a frenzy. The walls depicted cauldrons of fire flaming high before the shores of the Aegean. The music was good, compelling. Not all rock and not too loud. You could talk, too.

Grammy was dancing with Thor again. He was a neat dancer. He could do any step well, but not too fancy, like a dance instructor. Dawn was dancing down-and-dirty with Jack, or rather *against* Jack. Some people's idea of dancing, thought Libby, looked more like foreplay. Hedy was listening glassy-eyed as Doug Pintner went on and on about what was wrong with the real-estate industry and how he would fix it. When he finally headed for the men's room, she turned quickly to Libby. "Your grandmother has a lot of zip for her age."

"Correction. My grandmother has a lot of zip, period. Nobody can keep up with her."

"You know, I was wondering," Hedy said in a syrupy tone. "Has your mother known Mr. Dalton very long?"

"That depends on what you consider a long time," answered Libby, sidestepping the question. "How long have you known him?"

"Well, he's been coming to the dentist I work for for several years—" Just then one of the four good-looking young men from the back table came over to ask Libby to dance. Libby nodded quickly, rising. "Talk to you later, Hedy," she said sweetly. "My feet are twitching."

"You rescued me just in time," she told the young man. "My name is Libby Bliss."

"I'm Ted Ivanos, and I know your name. Your grandmother told me. She's pretty neat."

"Yeah."

"I asked her to dance first because I didn't know if you'd say yes or not. And that real ancient guy she was dancing with before looked like he was ready to conk out."

"She wears anybody out. But say, if you guys really want to have some fun, you should ask those other two. Not the older one. That's the old fellow's sister. She can barely walk. But those other two — Hedy and Dawn. They're a couple of wild women. If you come over to the table one at a time and tell me your names, I'll introduce you."

Ted Ivanos laughed. "I'll ask the guys. You can introduce me. Might be fun. But then you gotta dance with me some more, too. You going around in Nassau tomorrow?"

"I guess so."

"Well, if you want to go, come with us. Those girls at the table are going. Think about it and let me know."

"What's your cabin number? I'll call after I talk to my mom."

"It's 422."

"Gotcha."

When Ted brought her back to the table, she introduced him. "Hedy, you've got to dance with Ted. He's a great dancer," she urged. Ted reached for Hedy's hand and pulled her to the floor and began a sensuous rock.

Asa Bornen had had enough. "My dears,

it's time for this princess to call it a night," she said, "before I turn into a pumpkin."

Her brother nodded, caught a waiter's eye, and beckoned for the check. As the waiter hurried over, Ivy saw Asa take a disco ashtray and slip it into her purse! The waiter said to Thor, "Sorry, but Mr. Teidel is paying for this, sir. He insisted."

"Well, thank you for everything," said Bornen, handing the man a few dollars. He helped his sister to her feet, then turned to Ivy. "My dear, it's been a wild and wonderful evening. I'm taking Asa to her cabin, and I'm ready to turn in myself."

"I think I'll do the same," said Ivy. "You're a marvelous dancer. It's been fun."

After watching the Bornens depart, she turned to find Libby, who was over at the table where the young people were sitting. She went over, too. "Excuse me, everyone. Libby dear, the Bornens left. Dawn and Jack look like they'll be dancing all night. Did you want to stay?"

"I'm not danced out yet, Grammy."

"Neither are you, Ivy," said the one they called Rags.

"And I haven't danced with you yet, either, Gramma Ivy. I'm Chuck. And this is Lola and Barbara." He took Ivy's hand and swung her out onto the floor, just as Rags did with Libby.

Gosh, they were good dancers, thought Libby. Oh, well. Might as well stay a little longer, as long as Grammy wanted to. Grammy didn't look like she was ready to wind down anytime soon. She was glad everyone kept Hedy busy dancing so she couldn't start asking any more questions.

The gym was deserted. The inner room with its fancy machines was locked, but the outer room was open. Two mats on the floor, a bar, a mirrored wall, tables, chairs, benches. They sat on a bench. "There's a whole lot more to this acupressure business than just finding spots and poking them," said Jeb. "They have this whole Yin and Yang theory. It's complicated. So I just looked up what you do for which problem. Muscle aches are only one of many it's supposed to help. There are points all over your body. Now, for your arms," he took her wrist in his hand, his long, bony fingers surprisingly gentle. "Here's a couple that help your muscles." He pulled her arm a little closer. Maggie tried to keep her mind on what he was saying. But his touch — warm, firm, gentle — was sending currents through her. Oh, God, she was melting!

"Now, here on your wrist, for instance," he said, "two fingers' width below where your hand joins it. On the palm side, in the middle between those two bones. See if you can find it."

She measured two fingers' width and found the spot. "That's it," he said. "And now, hold your hand up and spread your fingers wide. Here. See this little web between your thumb and index finger? That's another. Now we have to kind of gently pinch the web, then push into the other spot. Try that and see if it helps."

He was talking so quietly, but his voice was swallowing her up. A husky, hungry sound. Growing huskier. She was afraid to look up at his face, but she couldn't stop herself. Their eyes met. And locked. "You want to try it?" he asked.

Try what? she thought. A kiss? Oh, yes, the pressure points.

"No. You do it," she whispered. "Please." And never taking his gaze from hers, he began gently to squeeze the web on her right hand. No, not quite squeezing. It was more of a caress. He might as well have been touching her breast. She felt goosebumps rising. She felt his touch all through her body. He groped for the other hand and touched the web there, too, pulling her ever so slowly toward him, into his arms, for the softest, most tentative of kisses. And then, pulling her head onto his shoulder and holding her as tightly as she suddenly needed to be held.

"Oh, Maggie, I don't know what this is, what's happened to me. I thought I didn't need any part of this stuff anymore. But I've been wanting to kiss you ever since that first time we talked in the library. Sometimes it's all I can think of."

She nodded. "I know. You keep popping into my mind at the oddest times. And now— But, please, Jeb, let's be rational. Let's think about what we're doing. Playing with fire. Asking to be hurt, maybe."

"Whatever it is, it's sooo good," he said. And this time he kissed her the way a man kisses a woman he's going to make love to. Hard, sensuously. His mouth tasted good. She couldn't get enough. But she managed to break away.

"Oh, Jeb, no. Please don't do that. It feels too good. You're waking up everything inside me." She clung to him tightly for a moment, then pulled back abruptly and stood up. "Please. I—can't. I—I've got to go to my cabin." A tear slipped down her cheek.

"Maggie, please. Oh, Maggie, don't cry. I

wouldn't do anything to hurt you. Honey, I don't know what all this means, either. But I just thought maybe we should try to find out. Together."

He stood up, too. "Let me walk you to your cabin." He led her from the gym toward the stairs, walking silently, holding her hand tightly.

At her door, he whispered, "Bliss. A good name for you. I knew there was something about you from the beginning. I'm not sure exactly what it was, but it's still there. I don't want to lose you, Maggie. I want us to be friends. Maybe a lot more." He took her in his arms. She stood on tiptoe and he kissed her good night with passion. His body felt so good pressed against hers. When he finally let her go, he shook his head, "I'd better not kiss you again or I'll carry you off to my cabin." He brushed his lips to her forehead and then stepped back. "Open your door. I want to see you safely inside. I won't try to come in."

Maggie fumbled for her key, found it, and let herself in. She closed the door behind her and leaned against it, weak but gloriously elated. The cabin was empty. They must still be dancing, she thought. Those two busy-bodies. Now look what they'd pushed her into.

She undressed slowly, remembering the feel of his arms around her. She was just going to step into the shower when the phone rang. It was Jeb.

"Listen, Maggie. Tomorrow, when we get into Nassau, want to do it together? I don't care who else you'd like to have with us. Take the Bornens and your mother and Libby if you like. I'll get a van so there's room. But you and me, at least. OK?"

"OK," said Maggie.

"If we miss each other at breakfast, I'll have the van waiting right at the bottom of the ramp where we get off. As soon as they let us go. OK?"

"OK."

"Get a good night's sleep."

"You, too."

"I know what I'm going to be dreaming about."

"Well, it's your own fault," she teased. "And don't think I'll be dreaming of anything different."

She put down the phone and shook her head. What was she getting into here? Was it all her imagination? He made it clear that he didn't really want to get involved, either. Was that a hint that this was just a shipboard romance?

Well, she'd worry about that in the morning. Before she crawled in bed she grabbed the pencil and message pad by the phone and quickly sketched his face. Easy to remember that long, straight nose, strong jaw, furrowed brow. She tore the page off, kissed it, and tucked it under her pillow. There was something very nice about knowing that tonight, they'd both be feeling each other's touch, if only in their dreams.

The phone shattered the quiet of the cabin. Who had turned that damn ringer up? Russo picked up the receiver quickly so it couldn't ring again. It was Gola Pendeka. "I just had to tell you this one, Manny. That table where you put Dalton and Bliss and that other pair of women? I've got three more that came to me — individually, mind you. One last night and two calls this morning at the very crack of dawn. They want to be at that same dinner table. Would you believe it? Two tried bribes and one was hinting she could get us all in hot water because she's connected."

"I wouldn't worry. When they're really connected they don't threaten, Penny. They talk real nice."

"And there's another pair who want a table

nearby. What is it with this guy? He looks like some poor bugger who couldn't even afford this cruise. But he must have money. That's all I can figure. These broads sure aren't attracted to his clothes."

"Just tell them we can't change anything anymore. Too late. Ship's policy. Hell, the cruise is almost over. These weekend things are done before they start."

"Wait. There's more. I also got a call from that Halperin woman, ten minutes ago, bawling me out for putting Bliss and her family at Dalton's table, and wanting us to move them somewhere else."

"You give in once, they think they can get you to do anything. Tell her to go suck an egg. But put it tactfully, of course."

Pendeka sighed. "Of course."

She missed him at breakfast. She missed everyone at breakfast. She didn't awaken until she heard her mother and Libby come back. "Oh, I'm glad you're up, Mom," said Libby. "I won't have to leave a note. I'm going with that bunch of guys from the table near us in the dining room. We're doing the straw market and the Crystal Palace. Rags says it's something else. He has a friend who works there who's got a car."

"You and four young men?" cried Maggie.

"No. Those two girls will be there, too."

"But you don't know them. What if something happens?"

"What's gonna happen, Mom? Simmer down."

"Simmer down, my foot! You listen to your mother, young lady. Plenty can happen when a girl is outnumbered."

"Only four to three. And I'm too strong to mess with. I'll have my passport in my bag and $30 in my shoe. Don't worry, Mom. They're OK. You learn a lot about guys when you dance with them."

"Let her go, Maggie," said Ivy. "Kids have to learn everything the hard way. Besides, I danced with three of those young men last night. They seemed harmless. Not too bright, but harmless. I'm going to the casino, too, with the Bornens. If I don't find Libby there, I'll call the police. You're invited, too if you want to come."

"Or are you spending the day with Jeb, Mom?" asked Libby.

"Yes, I think I am. You're both invited with us, too, if you'd like."

"So many invitations," said Ivy. "I feel like Marylou Whitney. Too bad I don't look like her, too. Anyway, Libby and I are going to work out a little in the gym before we hit Nassau."

"I'm table 59," Maggie told the captain at the dining room door.

"Oh, no, madame. It's all open seating for breakfast. We have a nice place for you." He led her to a large table where four other women were already eating. "Would you like some coffee or decaf to start?" asked the captain, handing her a menu.

"I know what I want. Cantaloupe, decaf, oatmeal with skim milk, and a bagel or English muffin with diet jelly. No butter."

"You'll never get fat on that," said the lady sitting next to her, a woman about Maggie's age, dressed in a white sailor outfit. In fact, all four women were dressed in blue and white nautical outfits.

"I hope not. I'm going to have to order a few more meals like that or there'll be five pounds more of me when we get back home."

"I'll be lucky if I don't make that ten," said the woman, taking another huge bite of syrupy, buttered pancakes. "On just a little weekend cruise. But I can never resist the food. No matter how much you eat it costs the same. And I don't have to fix it. So I always get my money's worth."

"My name is Maggie Bliss," she said. "I live in Deerfield Beach."

"I'm Belle Whitaker," said the woman. "I live in Miami, but my brother lives in Boca. I have friends in Deerfield."

The waiter brought Maggie's melon, then her oatmeal in a covered bowl and a bagel and an English muffin, toasted dry. He returned two seconds later with an individual pot of decaf.

"Well, that's pretty fast," said Maggie, attacking her melon with gusto. "Gosh, this is great. Sweet as sugar."

Belle Whitaker was staring at her. "Wait a minute," she said. "I know who you are. Bliss. You're the woman who was sitting at that guy's table. Jeb Dalton's."

Maggie looked up. "How did you know that?"

"My friend here, Sally—Sally, say hello to Maggie Bliss—Sally and I tried to sit at his table, but we were too late. He's supposed to be some catch. How'd you do it?"

"I don't know. I didn't do anything," said Maggie, shoveling down her oatmeal as fast as she could so she could finish and run.

"No kidding. Just luck? Go play the lottery the minute you get off this damn boat."

"Why were you trying to get to sit there?

Do you know him?" Maggie asked.

"Well, not exactly. We know someone who knows him." Maggie saw Sally poke Belle's arm.

"Did you know him before the cruise?" asked Sally sweetly, and both women leaned forward with rapt attention as if her answer were incredibly important.

Maggie shrugged. Why were they so interested? What did they know that she didn't? And why should she tell them anything? In fact, why not just stretch the truth a little. "Well, of course, I know him much better now than I did before," she said in what she hoped was a suggestive tone. "He's such a delight. But then I'm sure there's nothing I could tell you about him that you don't already know. Well, almost nothing. How did you like the show last night?"

The women sat back. "The show?" repeated Sally.

"Did you see it with him?" asked Belle.

"Oh, it was great," cried Maggie, downing the last of her oatmeal. She'd better get out of here. Jeb might not want them to know anything about him. But why were they so fascinated? Maybe he looked more like Eric Sevareid than she realized.

She drained her coffee cup and gathered up

her bagel, muffin, and diet jam in a napkin and stood up. "Sorry to eat and run," she said, "but I must." And she fled the dining room.

Hundreds of people were waiting in the stairwell when the crew finally started letting passengers off. It took more than ten minutes before Maggie, too, stepped down the gangplank amid a blaze of camera flashes. Ship's photographers. She could understand their zeal, however annoying it was. The more they shot, the more they sold. So they never stopped.

About a hundred feet away, she saw him standing next to a large green van with a taxi sign on top. He spotted her and hurried over. "Are your mother and daughter coming?" he asked, taking her hand.

"No. Mom's going with the Bornens. Libby's going off with some young people. Just us."

He groaned. "Not quite. Jack and Doug and the girls just invited themselves along and climbed in. I told them I was expecting some other passengers who had first choice of the seats. But now I think we're stuck with them."

"Oh, dear. Well, why didn't you just tell them no?"

"It happened too fast."

As they approached the van, Maggie could see that Dawn and Hedy had taken the second seat. The men sat behind them. What was she supposed to do, sit alone in the last seat? She'd show them. When Jeb helped her in, she squeezed between Jack and Doug who quickly moved to make room. "Isn't this cozy?" leered Doug, rubbing her shoulder with his. Jeb frowned and climbed into the front seat next to the driver.

Maggie was furious. All she needed was a whole day with these four. It was a plot. Hedy was so determined to score points with Jeb, she grabbed at every chance. Maggie gritted her teeth. She'd give that woman a dose of her own medicine.

"This was so clever of you, Jeb," Hedy cooed. "Getting this big van. It's always more fun to do things with people you really like," she said, reaching to pat him seductively on the shoulder.

"Oh, no, it's Doug and Jack who've been so clever," Maggie cried. "They got their transportation taken care of and Jeb did all the work. And I'm the cleverest of all because I've been dying for a chance to flirt with these two handsome guys and here I am practically sitting in their laps!"

Jack and Doug roared. "And I'll bet if I promise to be very, very good," she added with a dirty little chuckle, "they'll dance with me tonight again and again. If I'm very, very good."

"You don't have to be that good," laughed Doug, giving her arm another squeeze.

"I'd rather you be a little bad," cried Jack and the three of them giggled.

"OK, let's get out of here," Jeb said tersely to the driver. But just as he turned on the ignition they heard a cry, "Oh, Maggie! Maggie Bliss! Remember us? From breakfast? Belle and Sally and Barbara and Joan?" Running up to the van were the four women she'd met over her oatmeal.

"Listen," said Belle breathlessly. "Do you have room to give us a lift to the straw market? We could all fit in that back seat. We'll sit on laps."

"Why not?" said Maggie. "The more the merrier."

Belle yanked the door open, and all four scrambled in. Sally sat on Joan's lap. "Oh, this is so nice of you," said Belle as the driver pulled away.

"We do anything for the U.S. Navy," said Doug, eyeing their sailor outfits. "You might outrank us. So why don't we just call out our

201

names, in turn. Starting with you," he added, pointing at Belle.

"Belle Whitaker."

"Barbara Jamison."

"Sally Sembrace."

"Joan Du Bois."

"Doug Pintner . . ."

Jeb was last. When he called, "Jeb Dalton," Belle and Barbara exchanged a look.

"So what are you guys doing today?" Belle asked innocently.

"I'm not sure what we're doing but Maggie here has promised to be very, very good," replied Doug, giving her arm a squeeze.

"Or maybe very bad," leered Jack with an obscene chuckle.

Within a few moments the van pulled over to one of the many straw market entrances. Jeb jumped out and came back to open the back door. "Here you are, ladies. The straw market."

"So soon?" cried Sally, disappointed. "Sure you don't want more company wherever you're going?" she asked, stalling.

"We'd love it but we won't have the space," ad-libbed Maggie. "We've got to pick up a load of packages and deliver them."

The four women reluctantly climbed down. "Well, see you all later," Belle cried as the van sped off.

Hedy and Dawn flirted with Jeb all the way to the Crystal Palace while Maggie did her best to keep up a light, sexy banter with Doug and Jack. She thought the ride would never end.

When they arrived at the Crystal Palace, Jeb announced, "OK, the van will be back here at 2:30. Those who aren't here on time will have to get their own cab back."

"You wanna come around with us, inside?" Jack whispered to Maggie as they crawled out of the van.

"I'd be a fifth wheel," she whispered back. "You all go ahead. We'll find you in there."

Jeb watched them head for the entrance, then turned to Maggie. "Why the hell did you invite those four women?" he asked, irritated.

"Same reason you invited our tablemates, I guess. Now you've got four more dying to pester you. They were at my table at breakfast, asking about you. Why do they know so much about you? All this strategy and plotting. That's exactly what I wasn't looking for."

"Well, I certainly don't need another bunch of predatory women chasing me, either."

"And I don't need to get involved with someone who can't shoo them away," countered Maggie. "I said I'd go with you to this casino, and watch you and answer any questions. And I'll do it. And then that's it. No hard feelings. But I think we both see why we want to avoid this whole messy dating business."

Jeb frowned at her for a minute and then sighed. And nodded. "You're right," he said. "That's what we'll do."

For a full half-hour they simply walked around while Jeb explored the colorful complex. As she cooled off, Maggie had to admit there was something so nice about walking with him. Their strides didn't match at all. But when he took her arm to guide her past the crowds, it was a firm grip. And he still smelled faintly of soap. It was a good smell.

"I've never seen anything quite like this place," he said, staring up at the ornate pinks and purples. "The walls and ceilings look like they were squirted on with pink and purple caulking." She was just thinking the same thing. Funny, how they thought alike on so many things.

Back in the casino, he played. Maggie just watched, answering his questions, trying to explain how much superstition and hunches affected the bettors, repeating herself when he wanted to take notes. He lost steadily at first. He must have fed in over three hundred dollars. Then he began breaking even and kept scribbling in his notebook. After an hour, he asked her to play. "Use these chips," he said, "and I'll just watch and take notes."

She played until she lost about eighty dollars and it was time to head back to the van. They had hardly exchanged two words that didn't have to do with his research. They both looked decidedly unhappy.

Libby and Ivy were in the cabin when Maggie got back. "See, Mom? I didn't get kidnapped, mugged, or raped. How'd it go for you? How's the big romance?"

"Well, if there ever was one, I guess it's over."

"Oh, no!" cried Libby. "And I thought I'd finally gotten you out of my hair."

"What happened?" asked Ivy.

"Well, I got down there and he had Hedy, Dawn, Jack and Doug in the van with him. Hedy flirted like crazy."

"But I don't think he likes her, Maggie," said Ivy.

"I didn't either, but why did he let them come along?"

"They're very pushy. Sometimes it's not easy to say no."

"So I fixed him. First I started flirting with Doug and Jack. What a couple of jerks, Mom. Then there were four women I met at breakfast who are dying to meet Jeb, and when they came by the van just as we were pulling out and asked for a lift to the Straw Market, I told them sure, hop aboard."

"But the straw market's so close. Why did they need a ride?"

"I guess they didn't know. But until we let them out, they were flirting with him, too. It served him right."

Ivy looked at her daughter in dismay. "Darling, that was a terrible tactic. Vengeful. That's not like you. I think you really like this guy. That's why you're letting things get to you."

"Well, I'm afraid it's too late now," shrugged Maggie. "He didn't say anything about cocktails together tonight before the captain's dinner. He hardly said anything. So how was your day?"

"Oh, the Bornens and I went to that living reef place. You go down in this tower with its bottom right down in the reef, and that part is all glass walls. You watch the living reef. It's fascinating. It pulses. But—"

"But what, Mom?"

"Well, something's peculiar there. Oh,

Thor's a darling, and I get the distinct impression that there's life in the old boy yet. Especially when we're dancing. And she's so funny. But sometimes she says the same funny things over again. Or things that don't quite fit the thread. And at the living reef, I saw her slip a salt shaker into her purse. Thor saw it, too. He didn't say a word. He just excused himself for a minute and went to talk to the cashier. I think he paid for it, and then he came back."

"Oh, I'm sure there's an explanation," said Maggie. "So what do you want to do now, stop at the Straw Market? It's still about two hours until the ship leaves."

"I think we should hit the gym, Mom," Libby replied. "Come on, throw on your leotard and I'll tell you all about my day."

Gola Pendeka called the dining room first. Russo wasn't there. He tried his office. Not there. He tried his cabin. "Trust you to see I can't sneak forty winks no matter how hard I try," Russo said when he answered. "Now, what emergency is upon us?"

"Woodard's private cocktail party. Before the second sitting. Dalton, the one all the women want to sit by? He wants his whole table invited, too. Woodard said yes. The Bornens had already been invited, anyway. How do we work this? Shall I have them all meet in a certain place and one of the officers escort them to the club room just like we do for the others, Manny?"

"Of course. They'll never find it otherwise. Eight o'clock, and Woodard'll duck in about 8:30 for a few minutes. You want me to call them?"

"Do cards under their doors. Like they were real VIPs."

"You got it. Send the cards and arrange for their officer. I'll put them on the list and order more shrimp. Ten more, right?"

"No, Dalton and the Bornens were already on the list. Only seven more."

"*Only*, he says. OK. It's a done deal."

The gym was almost empty. "Mom, Grammy, look! They've got machines I've never seen before. Come on, let's try them."

"I'll just watch, dear," said Ivy. "I'm meeting Thor in about ten minutes for a fruit juice cooler while his sister is napping."

Maggie grabbed the handles on one machine apparently designed so you could pull them sideways only and gave a yank. Ouch, her arm! She tried it again, wishing Hedy's face were in front of her. She'd mash it into a

208

pulp. She slammed the machine's handles like she was trying to break something.

"Mom, what are you doing there?" cried Libby.

"Trying out this new machine, like you said."

"Well, don't slam it like that. Who are you mad at? You'll hurt something."

Maggie stopped. "You're right. I could hurt myself." She winced as she grabbed the handle of another machine. "Maybe I already have. I'm going back to the cabin." It wasn't just her arms that were aching. Her heart, too. What had she done? Just turned away from the only person who had really gotten to her in two years. A person she couldn't even walk next to without getting goosebumps. Without wishing he would sweep her up in his arms and hold her tight. OK, so he was a delivery man. But what difference did that make? He wasn't stupid. A degree in computers. And he apparently wrote software about everything. He was kind. And he loved to do pencil sketches, just like she did.

Dating wouldn't be so bad with someone like him, maybe. It would probably be kind of wonderful. She should have listened to her mother. But too late now. She wanted to cry.

Maggie found the invitation on the floor

when she came back to their cabin. It had been slipped under the door. The Captain's private party. They were supposed to meet near the casino entrance at 8 pm. Well. OK. She would wear her slinky new black crepe pant suit with the low, low beaded neckline. She would do her hair just so. And her makeup. And hopefully, Jeb Dalton would take one look and forget this morning and this afternoon. Hopefully.

Or would he just shrug and ask Hedy to dance? Damn him. She would probably go on thinking of him and being sorry for the rest of her life.

Thor was waiting at the juice bar. As he stood to help Ivy onto a stool, the attendant placed two large Orange Slush coolers in front of them. "If we finish these, we'll slosh as we walk," she said. "And we won't be able to eat a bite at the Captain's dinner."

"But we'll. make a valiant effort, I'm sure," chuckled Thor.

"Asa got off to sleep all right?" asked Ivy.

"Oh, yes. She needs an inordinate amount of sleep these days. But that's what I wanted to talk about. In confidence, of course."

"Of course," said Ivy. He looked troubled.

"What is it, Thor?"

"My sister is a wonderful, witty, wise woman, but she's having problems lately. Early Alzheimer's, dementia, too soon to tell exactly what, they say. She's bright and funny sometimes, then sometimes she suddenly has no idea what anyone's talking about. She needs to sleep a lot—twelve hours or more. She used to sleep four hours a night. And then there's another twist."

"The salt shaker," asked Ivy. "The ashtray?"

"Yes. And full rolls of toilet paper. She's not a real kleptomaniac. She's never taken anything from a store or anyone's purse or anything like that. But she takes whole unopened rolls of toilet paper from any public bathroom. That's why she always carries big purses. And ashtrays. Salt and peppers. Mustard jars."

"But what if someone catches her and makes a scene?"

"As soon as I see her take anything, I go right to the proprietor and pay for it. In the care center where she lives in Jupiter, it's no problem. The maids just keep recycling. Taking the toilet paper rolls from her drawers and putting them back on the maid's cart. Putting ashtrays back on the tables in the public rooms."

"It's so sad," said Ivy. "You're a good brother, Thor."

"I just wanted you to know that we're not some kind of petty thieves or such. You're a very nice person. Sometimes I have occasion to attend events where I can take a lady-friend with me. And I would hope that long after this little cruise is over, we'll still be friends and I could call on you to join me."

Ivy nodded. "Of course you can. I'd be delighted. And I think your sister is a delight, no matter what wires have gotten crossed. She can't help it. It could happen to any of us."

As Thor reached over to help Ivy from her stool, suddenly Jeb was standing there. His tee shirt, she noted, was inside out. He took the stool next to hers. "I've been looking for you. I checked the gym and Libby told me you might be here. I—I wasn't sure if I should call your cabin, Ivy. I need to talk to you."

"I'm just leaving," said Thor. "We've about covered everything we wanted to discuss. I've got to get back and check on Asa."

As soon as Thor was gone, Jeb eyed the half-empty glass before her and asked, "What's that you're drinking?"

"An Orange Slush. It's enough for a family of six. It's sort of like a milkshake made of orange juice and orange sherbet, I think.

212

You're wired with vitamin C after drinking one."

"Give me one of those and give her a refill," Jeb told the fountain attendant. Then he turned to Ivy. "Look, can I talk to you sort of confidentially about something?"

"Of course. Everyone does. I have that kind of face," she replied with a grin. The waiter placed two more of the oversized glasses in front of them.

"Well, it's about Maggie. I don't know quite how to handle this. I cut out of the dating scene a few years ago, and I never wanted to get back in it. I have a software company—"

"I thought you were a delivery man."

"That's what Maggie thinks because she always sees me delivering things to Randell—the Junior College." Jeb took a long swallow of his drink, then shook his head and made a face. "God, that's sweet. And sour, too!"

"Why are you at the school so much then?"

"I give stuff to a few school libraries all the time—computers, software, printers, books, tapes. Maggie's almost funny about it, worrying that I'm spending too much money for a delivery man. Well, I was one once. Or I had a delivery company. I took it over when my father died and made a living from it for about fifteen years while I was married. I

213

wanted to do something else, but couldn't chance it then. I needed the money. I sold it but still own a part of it. No, I started this thing about five years ago and it's just going public. I'm not hurting. But I don't know what to do about Maggie." He pushed the Orange Slush away. Ivy nodded in agreement and pushed hers away, too.

"I think I've finally met someone I'd really like to be involved with," he said, "and I think she feels the same way. We click. It's amazing. We think the same way. We both like to do pencil sketches. This kind of thing doesn't happen very often, but she's so sure it'll just be a grind. The dating thing. She's as uninterested in that social merry-go-round as I am. So she's not easy to corral."

"I'll say!" Ivy chuckled. "Libby and I have been trying to push her out of the nest for over a year now, but she won't push. It's time she did. Life is better with someone you enjoy by your side. What can I do to help?"

"I'm not sure. Except maybe tell her I mean well. When Dawn and Hedy came with us today, I sure as hell didn't want them there. I didn't ask them. I just wanted Maggie. But maybe that's why she got so pissed. I mean, upset."

"No, I think you could accurately say

'pissed.' "

The waiter brought a check and Jeb quickly signed it. "Maybe because she likes me a little and didn't want to share the day?" he suggested, throwing a dollar on the bar. "I hope so. But the thing is, I didn't know how to get rid of them. I'm not good at these social tricks. It's been too long. I'm a loner. I don't worry about what I wear or where I eat or anything. I just like to help the schools a little, do my computer things, and go fishing once in a while."

Ivy sat back and stared frankly at this badly dressed, concerned, and puzzled man on the next stool. He looked like those statues of this country's early settlers always looked—kind of rawboned and strong and sincere.

"Well, I wouldn't stew over this morning's debacle," she said. "If Maggie didn't care, if she wasn't really interested, she wouldn't have gotten so 'pissed' and difficult. But let me think about this a little. Maybe the next time your name comes up in conversation, I can say something that might help. Not often, but once in a while, she listens to her mother."

"Thanks, Ivy. Listen, I'll see you and Libby and Maggie at the Captain's private cocktail party tonight."

"You mean the Captain's dinner?"

"No, he has a small private party, too. He only ducks in and out. He's got to be at the Captain's dinner cocktail parties for the masses, too, but his is first class. I had the whole table invited. I was afraid to ask just Maggie and you after this afternoon."

"Have you that much clout?"

"Well, I'm automating some procedures here. The software will probably be used on other cruise ships. That's what does it."

"Interesting. You know, I suggest you wear a tux tonight. Is that possible?"

"Yeah. Captain Woodard insists. I came to the first one of these two months ago in a pair of slacks with a tear in the pocket and he read me the riot act. I bought a tux as soon as I got home."

Ivy nodded. With that tall, lean frame, and that shock of greying hair, she was sure he'd look as handsome as all get out.

"And Jeb," she said, "try to make sure your socks match?"

Everyone else was already waiting outside the casino, dressed to the nines, when Libby, Ivy, and Maggie got off the elevator. People turned for a double take. Three pretty redheads. Three generations. All built alike, small and wiry. Ivy wore a snaky, long-sleeved, red beaded shift with a slit that revealed one leg up to her thigh. Libby was in royal blue—a tiny-sequined, figure-hugging skimp of a dress. And Maggie's black pant suit with the low-cut neck revealed the firm swell of her bosom.

"Gorgeous, gorgeous, gorgeous," cried Doug, shaking his head. "I don't know which one of you to grab first."

"And will you look at this kid?" said Jack, pointing to Libby. "Honey, you can not only see every line and muscle in that thing, you can see every cell. It must run in the family."

Hedy and Dawn looked over with irritation, then forced smiles to greet the trio. Hedy kissed them all on the cheek.

Jeb watched them from across the room for a moment. Then he came over to Maggie.

She stared, open-mouthed. Was that Jeb? In a tux? With matching socks? She smiled at him. "Well, who'd have thought it," she murmured. "You look absolutely smashing."

"Funny how our minds work alike. I was just going to say the same thing about you."

"I guess I just didn't think you'd have—"

"A tux. I know. Delivery men don't have tuxes. Listen, can we have a truce tonight?"

She grinned. "You can have anything you want tonight, looking like that. Actually, I was just going to suggest the same thing." Maybe this relationship would evaporate once the cruise was over, but for tonight, she wanted to enjoy the fantasy. My God, it was amazing. In a tux, he looked so much more like Eric Sevareid. Only more handsome.

All evening, the vibes between them never stopped. She noticed that during the cocktail party, he hardly talked to Hedy and Dawn. And when they approached him, he'd move somewhere else. Why had she been so difficult this morning? In case she did want to be involved with him, it was about the worst thing she could have done. Pouting and acting snippy, like she had the right to tell him who he could take along and who he couldn't. Just because those pushy girls had horned in. What difference did it make if other women wanted him, so long as the one he wanted was her? Oh, if only she could get him alone. Tonight, before the cruise was over. But how?

Halfway through dinner, Jeb said to her, "Maggie, I can get a table again for the show tonight. I can ask everybody or nobody. What do you think?"

That was it! The opening she needed. "Well, that would be nice," she said. "But I don't know if I can last the whole show. My arms are hurting so. I've got to find some Ibuprofen, somewhere."

"I've got some in my cabin. I'll get it for you." He started to get up, but she stopped him quickly.

"Oh, after dinner is fine. I hope I can remember those acupressure points you told me about. Where is one for your leg?"

Jeb swallowed his bite of hard roll whole. "Well, actually, I'd have to show you. You can't just describe it. You have to—uh—feel around to find the point. And some of them—uh—take two people. One has to kind of knee the spot on the other."

Maggie could hear the huskiness in his voice again. "That sounds wonderful. I mean, it's worth a try."

"Oh, yeah. But—uh—if you'd like me to, you can come with me to get the Ibuprofen and I'll show you in my cabin. I've got plenty of room. And—uh—it's more private. You know, right after dinner."

"But you were going to get a table for the others—"

"No problem. I'll arrange it and let Bornen look after everyone. No one will miss us. I'll leave first. I'm in cabin S-19 up on the sun deck. That's three decks up. And then forward. Got it? You leave a couple of minutes later. No point in letting the whole table

219

know. They'll be sure we're—up to something."

"And we can go to the show room and find the bunch when my leg and my arm feel better," Maggie said, thinking at the same time, *Fat chance!*

Jeb nodded. Good God, it was all happening. Instead of running away, she was falling right into his arms. If he just didn't blow it.

Maggie nodded back. It worked! In twenty minutes or so they'd be in his cabin together. Alone. And he'd be touching her like he had last night. She could hardly breathe.

Soft music was playing on the radio.

"I—guess I'd better get out of this pantsuit," Maggie said.

"There's a robe in the bathroom, right off the bedroom through that door," he said. "I'll put one on, too. You have to get down on the floor for this. We don't want to mess up our fancy duds. And the Ibuprofen's in there, too."

"This isn't a cabin; it's a suite," she said as she stepped into his bedroom and closed the door behind her. She started for the bathroom but stopped when she noticed, on the table just to the right, a message pad with a pencil sketch of herself on the front page! She picked up the pad and leafed through it. More sketches. All of her. Different angles, different expressions. Seven in all! She put the pad back on the table.

Inside the bathroom she found a large terry robe in a clear plastic bag. She undressed down to her panties and bra and put it on, moving as if in a trance. But then she thought of the sketches. She smiled, took off the robe, removed her panties and bra, and donned the robe once more. The Ibuprofen was right there on the counter, but she didn't take any. She didn't want to miss any sensations tonight.

Back in the sitting room, she found Jeb in a robe, too. In a horrible orange color, and the pocket was torn. He had spread a blanket on the floor. "I think you remember the arm things we tried before," he said. His voice was so husky he was almost whispering. She nodded. He took each of her hands in turn and touched the webs and the pressure points on her wrists. Each touch was like a kiss. "So let's try this — leg thing," he said. "Uh — you lie down on the floor on your stomach. And I have to put my knee on the back of your leg first — "

"Like this?" she asked, quickly dropping to the floor and lying on her stomach. He knelt beside her and put his knee lightly on the

221

back of her leg. "And then—"

"And then," Maggie interrupted, "I think you'd better kiss me, Jeb." She slipped from under his knee and rolled onto her back, her robe opening as she turned.

"Oh, Maggie," he breathed, quickly stretching beside her and pulling her close. "Come to me, Maggie, Maggie, Maggie."

They kissed, murmuring. He kissed her neck. "Mmmmm, I knew you'd taste like that," he said. He rolled halfway on top of her to kiss her breasts, and she could feel the sinewy muscles of his long, lean body.

"Oh, I want you so much," she cried, reaching for him, pressing toward him, wrapping her legs tightly around him, coaxing him to enter her quickly.

"It'll be too fast for you—"

"You couldn't be too fast for me now—" she cried. And there on the floor, in a frenzied feast of touching, tasting, pushing, grinding, straining to climb higher and higher—they crashed through to that fervent deliverance that Maggie had somehow known was waiting for them.

Afterward they lay there, gasping, purring, groaning with delight, unable at first to find words to express their joy.

"I meant to get you into my bed," he said

finally in a groggy voice. "It's softer."

"You didn't have a prayer," she said. "You're lucky we didn't do it in the hallway."

"I guessed it would be like that," he said. "Only how could anyone expect anything to be like that? Oh, Maggie." And then he remembered her muscle pains. "Oh my gosh, how's your poor leg? Your arms?"

"They feel divine. Nothing would dare hurt me now."

"Did you take some Ibuprofen?"

"No, I didn't want to miss anything."

He hugged her. "Listen, know what let's do?"

"Whatever you say."

"Let's crawl into my bed. My bony limbs are noticing the hard floor now that we're through."

"We're through?" she repeated.

"Until we get into my bed."

They did. The room was cool. They snuggled under the covers and drowsed for a short time. Then Jeb began kissing her gently here, licking her there, touching her everywhere, exploring her body as she dreamily explored his. For the next hour, they floated through the most delightful research that any two people in love can do. And when he brought her to that magical peak again, as she slipped over the other side, she cried out, "Oh, Jeb, thank you, thank you, thank you." He held her trembling body tight and whispered in her ear, "Honey, my pleasure."

At midnight, she reluctantly slipped back into her pantsuit, and Jeb into his tux, so he could walk her back to her cabin. They were supposed to pack and put out their luggage by one a.m.

"It's OK. There'll be other nights," he said. "And longer nights. Remember, if we don't see each other in the morning, I'll call as soon as I can. I get tied up here sometimes."

He walked her back to her cabin. "Just squeeze my hand and kiss my cheek," she ordered. "Don't really kiss me or the first thing you know we'll be on the floor right here in the hallway."

The seas felt a little choppy, Maggie noticed as she undressed, packed, and put her luggage out. Darn. They hadn't brought the dramamine. By the time her mother came in, twenty minutes later, she knew she was seasick.

"It's getting rough out there," Ivy said. "Asa Bornen just got so sick in the lounge, they called the ship's doctor."

Libby came in a few minutes later and the

two of them had their luggage packed and outside their door in no time at all. Libby never got seasick.

Maggie slept fitfully. She woke at five and again at six, feeling even sicker. By seven the seas were quieter and a half-hour later they were docked, but her head and stomach were still rocking. "You two go up to breakfast," she gasped. "I can't."

"We might as well," said Ivy. "It always takes a little time before they let you off."

At eight, Maggie called Jeb's cabin. The phone rang a long time. No answer. Was he in the shower?

She managed to fumble her way into her clothes and shove everything else in her tote. But then she had to flop on her bed while the room danced around her. She was seeing double. At 8:30 she called Jeb again. No answer.

When Libby and Ivy came back, they grabbed the hand luggage, helped her to her feet, and half-dragged, half-pushed her up to the Izmir Promenade deck for the immigration procedures. Libby's new friends came over and Libby explained that her mother was ill. "Gee, anything we can do?" asked Rags and Chuck. Jack Teidel came over to hand Maggie his card. "You're looking a little green there, kid," he said.

"Only—because I—feel—a little green," she gasped.

When they were finally allowed to debark, one of the crew helped her down the escalator and out to the curb. Libby went for the car while Ivy claimed their luggage. Maggie clung to a pole because she could hardly stand up. Jeb was nowhere to be seen.

By the time they pulled into their driveway, Maggie was feeling much better. The sickness never lasted too long after the rocking stopped. "Just take it easy, love," said Ivy. "Libby and I'll get everything in and unpacked."

"I don't know if I'm seasick anymore, Mom, or just terminally disappointed. He wasn't there this morning. That says a lot."

"Don't be silly, Maggie. There could be lots of reasons why."

"Name one."

"Well, uh, I can't think of one at the moment. But I'm sure he had one. I think he really cares about you, Maggie."

"Well, I care about him, too, I've decided. We went to his room last night. In fact, I sort of engineered it."

"Well, what's wrong with that? Don't look so guilty."

"If this was just a shipboard romance to

226

him—"

"I'm sure it wasn't, dear. He looks a bit grubby, but he's for real."

"Grubby?" Maggie rushed to his defense. "The reason, Mom, is that he's color blind. He can't help that. And he just doesn't care about clothes much. His wife used to pick them out for him."

"A lot of wives do that."

"He has more important things to think of. But why hasn't he called? He said if he missed me debarking, he'd call."

"Well, give him a chance. He surely will. And when he does—"

"*If* he does—"

"Don't be upset right away. Let him explain. Don't be touchy."

When Libby finished unpacking she joined them in the kitchen. Ivy was mixing pancake batter. Maggie was staring at the phone. "He didn't call yet, Mom?"

She forced a cheery smile. "No, but he will. I think. And darling, Grammy and I thank you for a wonderful weekend."

"A perfect Mother's Day present," said Ivy. "With bonuses. I've met a delightful person. Thor is so nice. And your mother's met someone very special, too."

"Are you going to see them again?" asked

Libby. "Any plans in the works?"

"Oh, I'm sure we will. The Bornens weren't there at checkout, either, did you notice? But she was so sick last night. I expect we'll hear from them any time."

It was eleven a.m. and Jeb had still not called. By then Ivy was eyeing the phone, too.

When it rang exactly twenty-seven minutes later, they both lunged for it. Maggie won.

"Hello, Maggie?" Grinning gleefully, she mouthed the words to her mother, *It's Jeb!*

"Oh, Jeb," she said as if she hadn't a care in the world, "I'm so glad you called. I missed you this morning at checkout."

"Yeah. Two things. First, Captain Woodard calls me at seven am. to go over some details on the disembarking software. And right after I finished and got back to my cabin, Bornen called. His sister was really sick and the ship's doctor was there and they'd called an ambulance and he needed my help. I went over — it's just three cabins down from mine — and the doctor had set it up so we could just leave the minute the ambulance came. We didn't even pick up our luggage. When the ambulance guys came we were right behind the stretcher. We went to Northridge Hospital, got her settled, and he stayed there. I cabbed back to the port for my car and the luggage. I had a little trouble with them at first until I had them call Captain Woodard. Then back to the hospital. She was a little better so I drove him home to pick up his car and we dropped their luggage off. What a morning!"

"Will Asa be OK?"

"They think so. Some kind of mild heart failure, I gather. And Bornen said if I talked to your mother, to please explain what happened. They were both sorry they didn't get to say good-bye."

"Wait, let me tell my mother," said Maggie, giving Ivy a quick rundown on everything Jeb had just told her. "But you're OK?"

"Yeah, I'm fine. I just need some breakfast, or lunch. Are you free?"

"Yes. Whenever you like. Tell me where and I'll meet you."

"Did you get off the boat OK? No problems?"

"Oh, I got seasick last night. But I'm OK for lunch."

"Good. We can talk. Are you ready to explore the possibilities of you and me? Or would you rather I just got lost?"

"No, don't get lost," said Maggie quickly. She waved at her mother, who ran out of the kitchen so her daughter could talk. "After last night, I—I'd like to explore the possibilities. If you would, I mean."

"Don't you know I want to? Oh, Maggie, I'm so glad you're willing to give it a try."

She kissed him over the phone. "I had to, whether I wanted to or not. My mother gave me this long lecture and pep talk. She said you're really very nice. And that I could pick our your socks and clothes for you and you'd look smashing."

He laughed.

"And when you weren't there this morning, she said that there had to be a reason. That you didn't play games. You were for real. And I was very lucky to have met you."

Jeb chuckled again. "And you believed all that?"

Maggie laughed, too, and said, "Of course. I always listen to my mother."

Lost . . . and Found

by Marian Oaks

Celia Hamlin returned to work from her annual one-day retreat feeling decades older than her fifty-six years and wondering how something that had happened almost four decades ago could still hurt so much.

She'd begun the retreat as a combination of penance and remembrance, a self-imposed martyrdom to ease her conscience, but over the years it had become an almost unbearable ordeal. And it was no longer just her conscience that hurt, but her heart.

Maybe it was time to give it up, pretend that April sixteenth was just another day on the calendar, and try to be what everyone thought she was: a woman who'd had it all — good marriage, successful career, loving son.

She smiled wryly. She still had the loving

son, thank God, but James had died three years ago, leaving her to deal with that other grief alone, and as for the career—

She stared down at the memo on her desk. What it said was simple enough. What it *meant* was equally clear. She felt a twinge of contempt for the writer. Did he think she was so stupid she wouldn't realize he was trying to ease her out to make room for a younger woman? Or so helpless that she couldn't do anything about it?

The question was, did she want to do anything?

Her work as assistant editor of a small, regional magazine had given her at least the illusion of being useful, even necessary, but now . . . She wasn't sure it was enough anymore, or that it was worth fighting over, or that anything was, for that matter.

James had left her well off; she could afford to retire, if she wanted to, or take the risk of plunging into something more difficult, more challenging. She made up her mind abruptly. If a younger, less experienced woman could handle the job, then Celia no longer wanted it.

She reached for pen and paper and began to draft her letter of resignation.

A few moments later she glanced up as the door opened and sounds from the outer office drifted in. "Yes, Angie. What is it?"

"Celia, there's a Mr. Ross McClain to see you."

She didn't recognize the name. "Did he say what it's about?"

Angie shook her head. "Only that it's extremely important . . . and personal."

Personal? Celia hesitated, then shrugged. The letter could wait. "Bring him in." She pushed her chair back and stood up, knowing that if Ross McClain turned out to be someone she didn't want to waste time on, it would be easier to get rid of him If they were both standing.

Angie returned almost immediately with a tall, well-dressed man, parked him in the center of the moss-green carpet, and stepped back, as if to admire the effect.

There was plenty of effect to admire, Celia had to admit. Ross McClain appeared to be in his middle sixties, broad-shouldered, slim-hipped, an eye-filling, pulse-quickening package of muscle and sinew that would have done credit to a much younger man. His eyes were dark brown, his chin firm, bordering on stubborn, and the unruly lock of hair that tumbled over a broad, smooth forehead made Celia ache to reach out and brush it back.

She realized she was gawking like a school-girl and felt her cheeks grow warm, then realized he was studying her, too — not in the same way, but with a kind of fierce yearning, and as if he couldn't quite believe what he was seeing. "I expected a resemblance," he said softly, "but you look just like her. Or as she would have looked in a few years."

"Like who, Mr. McClain?"

He set his briefcase on the floor near her desk and ran his fingers through his hair in a gesture of frustration. "Damn. This is turning out to be harder than I thought it would be. I'm afraid I don't know any way to go about this except to plunge right in."

"By all means," she said. "Plunge."

He took a deep breath. "Mrs. Hamlin, I want to talk to you about the baby girl you gave birth to thirty-seven years ago yesterday."

Celia's legs gave way beneath her abruptly and she sank into her chair. "How do . . . How do you . . ."

"My wife and I were the ones who adopted her." His voice was gentle, as if to make up for the bluntness of his first statement.

She stared at him while the shock began to

wear off and the pain crept in. "I don't believe you," she said finally. "Why are you here? What do you want?"

He picked up his briefcase and set it on her desk, opened it, and took out a manila envelope and a folder filled with papers. "I thought you might not accept my word, so I brought these. The papers in the folder are my daughter's birth certificate and a step-by-step record of my search for you. The envelope contains photographs."

She ignored the envelope and repeated, "What do you want? What kind of scam is this?"

He shook his head. "No scam. And as for what I want—Look, this is going to take some explaining. Do you mind if I sit down?" Without waiting for an answer, he sank into the chair nearest her desk.

Celia's brain still hadn't kicked back into gear, but instinct took over. "If you're telling the truth, where is my daughter? I want to see her."

"I'm sorry," he said. "That isn't possible. She was killed in a car accident last year."

"I don't believe you," she said again. "My daughter is still alive. If anything had happened to her, I'd know it. I'd have felt it.

235

You're lying."

"I wish I were. Mrs. Hamlin, please, just listen to me for a few minutes. I know this is difficult for you, but it isn't easy for me, either. I also lost my wife in that accident, and my son-in-law."

"I'm sorry." Her words were automatic; her mind was still trying to focus on the idea that this man claimed to have known and loved the daughter whose loss she mourned every day of her life. Another pain, sharper, more insistent, pushed that one aside. "You said . . ." She paused and swallowed painfully. "You said my daughter was killed. In an accident."

He didn't answer at first, and she realized he, too, was dealing with pain. "That's right," he said finally.

"In that case, what can you possibly want with me?" She winced at the sound of her voice. She hadn't meant to speak so sharply, or sound so shrewish.

Her tone seemed to irritate him, too. His voice was equally sharp as he exclaimed, "Let's get one thing straight right now. *I* don't want a damned thing from you. If it had been up to me, I'd never have bothered to find you. But there's someone else involved. My granddaughter. *Your* granddaughter."

Celia stared at him, too stunned to speak. In all the years she'd dreamed that someday, somehow, her child would manage to find her and they'd be reunited, it had never occurred to her that someone else — Ross McClain — would come looking for her, to tell her that her daughter was dead, but that she'd left behind a daughter of her own. Celia's granddaughter.

How could she be a grandmother and not even know it? The same way, she decided, that she hadn't known her daughter was dead. The psychic bond she'd always felt between them hadn't been real, but only a figment of her imagination.

She came out of her fog enough to realize that McClain was speaking to her.

"Mrs. Hamlin? Mrs. Hamlin! Are you all right?" He stood up and opened doors on the far side of the room until he'd found her small lavatory, stepped inside, and returned a moment later carrying a cup of water. He stood beside her while she sipped it, asked if she wanted more, then sat back down when she shook her head.

"I'm sorry to keep shaking you up like this," he said, "but Jennifer needs you."

"Jennifer?" Her voice was a harsh croak.

"That's your granddaughter?"

He nodded. "And she's the reason I'm here. The *only* reason. May I tell you about her?"

Celia nodded. "Please."

He leaned back in the chair and pressed his fingertips together, staring at them as if he were holding the words he needed between them. "Jennie was badly injured in the accident that killed her parents and grandmother. Both her parents were only children, and her paternal grandparents died years ago, so . . ."

He shrugged. "She and I are all that's left. I guess we've both been pretty lonely, Jennie particularly, because while I've been busy taking care of her, she's had nothing to do but lie in bed grieving. You have to understand. She and her mother and grandmother were extremely close. I think she suffered more from their loss than from her physical injuries.

"And one day she shocked the hell out of me by asking if I'd try to find you, her natural grandmother. I didn't want to at first, couldn't see how any good would come out of it, but she's been in frail health since the accident. The truth is, she's already lost so much I just can't bring myself to deny her anything it's within my power to give her."

He grinned a little. "And you really weren't

all that hard to find, you know. It's almost as if you wanted to be found."

She ignored that and zeroed in on the other thing he'd said. "Frail health," she repeated. "How frail?"

"She's in a wheelchair. She's going to need extensive therapy if she's ever going to walk again."

There it was, she thought. The scam. She'd been expecting it, but it hurt just the same. She had no idea whether the mysterious Jennie really was her grandchild or not, but she had no intention of throwing a fortune away on Ross McClain's say-so. She drew a deep breath. "Therapy," she said. "Extensive therapy. *Expensive* therapy. That's why you're here, then. You want me to—"

She cringed in sudden fear as he lunged out of his chair and braced himself with clenched fists against her desk. "Don't say another word. Don't even think it. I told you, I don't want a thing from you. Not one red cent."

Some of the anger went out of him as he drew a deep breath and exhaled slowly. "Do you know what Jennie said when she asked me to find you? She said, 'You always told Mother that her mother gave her up because she knew it would be best for her, but that she really loved her and wanted to keep her. Well then, wouldn't she love me and want me, too? She's my grandmother.'

"What a laugh! I should have known you wouldn't want to jeopardize your reputation and social standing by admitting you had an illegitimate child. I should have known you wouldn't care that your grandchild is ill and needs you."

Celia leaped to her feet and leaned across the desk, bringing her face close to McClain's as she cried, "Shut up! Just shut up! You don't know anything about it. I'm not ashamed because I bore a child out of wedlock. I loved her father, and I loved her. And I did want to keep her, but there was no way I could. It's tough enough to be a nineteen-year-old unwed mother today, but back then, it was almost impossible. I had no job, no resources, no way to care for a child. But I've spent every day of my life since then grieving because I gave her up.

"That's what I'm ashamed of — that I wasn't strong enough to stand up to the people who said I shouldn't keep her. So shut up, because you don't know. You just don't know." She dropped back into her chair and buried her face in her hands, fighting to get

240

herself under control.

"I'm sorry," McClain said. They were both quiet for a while, and then he added, "Look, I didn't mean to just come in here and dump all this on you. I certainly didn't come in to make any demands or ask for anything. I just wanted you to know that the child you gave up had a child who needs you and wants you. Anything else is up to you."

He slid the folder and envelope toward her. "Take a look at these, especially the pictures. If you still have any doubts that I'm who I say I am, or that Jennie is your granddaughter, throw everything in the trash and forget I was ever here. If you decide you can give her the love and caring she wants and truly be her grandmother, you can call me. Either way, it's up to you now. I won't be back without an invitation."

He picked up his briefcase and started to leave, then turned back. "We're in town to get her therapy started. You can reach me at the hotel until the end of the week, but don't call unless you're very, very sure. She's been hurt enough. I don't intend to let anything or anyone ever hurt her again, and that includes you." His tone left no doubt that he meant what he said.

She watched the door close behind him, then buried her head in her arms and wept.

Celia sat at her kitchen table, her fourth cup of coffee growing cold while she stared at the unopened manila envelope and file folder. At the sound of a car in the driveway, she drew in a deep breath and transferred her stare to the back door.

In a moment, the door opened and her son—tall, dark-haired, so much like his father—came in. "Mom? Are you all right? You sounded terribly upset on the phone."

She'd been rehearsing what to say to him, but now the words turned sour in her mouth. She sipped at her coffee for courage, grimaced when she found it cold, and held it out to him. "Heat it up for me, would you please, John? Then pour yourself some and sit down. There's something I have to tell you."

He obeyed, moving quietly and competently and not asking questions until he was seated across the table. "Okay, I'm ready to listen. What is it?"

She cradled the cup between her hands, trying to ease the chill inside her with its warmth. "John, there isn't any easy way for me to say this, but . . . You know I loved your father very much."

"Yes, I know." He studied her soberly. "Mom, if you're trying to tell me you've found someone else—"

Hot coffee splashed from her cup as her hand jerked. "No! That isn't it at all!" She slid the envelope and folder out of the way, then grabbed a napkin and blotted up the spilled coffee. "I'm doing this very badly. Maybe what I should have said was that I loved your father with all my heart, but . . . He wasn't the first man I ever loved." She rolled the wet napkin in her hand and squeezed it into a little ball.

He took it away from her and dropped it into the trash. "I never thought he was."

She drew a deep breath and forced herself to add, "And your father was not the first man by whom I had a child." She paused, giving him a chance to react, but he only watched her silently and waited for her to go on.

"I was very young, and very much in love. He loved me, too, but there were . . . problems. A permanent relationship—marriage— was simply out of the question. It wasn't until a few weeks after we went our separate ways that I found out I was pregnant."

"And you had the baby." It wasn't a question, but a simple statement of fact.

She felt a surge of gratitude for his understanding. "Of course. Abortion wasn't a viable option then, and I couldn't have gone through with one anyway. I loved that baby, just as I loved her father." She sipped her coffee again and felt a stab of pain as she confessed, "But I did something almost as terrible. I gave her up for adoption." Her voice broke on the last word.

John caught her hand in his and squeezed it gently. "Did you have a choice?"

"I didn't think so, at the time. Now . . ."

"Never mind *now*," he said firmly. "You did what you thought was best then. You can't ask more of yourself than that." He hesitated, then asked, "Did Dad know?"

"Yes."

"But you never told me."

"No. Perhaps we should have, but . . ." She managed a shaky grin. "Somehow, it just never came up."

"I can see where it wouldn't." He grinned, then sobered. "You must have some reason for telling me now."

"Yes, I do." She picked up another napkin and crumpled it, smoothed it out, then crumpled it again. "John, I had a visitor today—a man who claimed he and his wife adopted the baby I gave up." The words came more freely now that the big secret was out. She described Ross McClain's visit, calling on her skills as an editor to make her account coherent and concise.

When she finished, John was silent for a while, then gave her the quirky grin that reminded her so much of his father. "You mean, I'm an uncle?"

She tried to grin back and couldn't. "I don't know. He may be telling the truth, but suppose it's a scam? He said he didn't want anything from me, but . . . How can I be sure? If she really is my granddaughter . . ." She blinked hard as tears stung her eyes. "I want her to be, so badly. I don't think I can stand it if he's lying."

"Did he have anything to back up his claim?"

She touched the envelope and folder, then pulled her hand back as if it had been burned. "Records of his search for me. Photographs."

"Well?"

"I've been afraid to look at them," she admitted.

"Don't you think you should?"

"Yes, but . . ." She shrugged helplessly.

"Do you want me to look?"

She nodded. "Would you? Please."

He reached for the folder, then pushed it aside and opened the envelope instead. He pulled out a sheaf of photos and riffled through them, his expression neutral and controlled, giving no indication of what he was seeing or thinking. After a minute, he pushed his chair back and left the room.

He was back seconds later, carrying a photo album which he opened and laid in front of Celia. Then he spread the other photos out beside it. "You told me he said you looked just like her. He was right. Flip back twenty or so years, and the resemblance is even stronger. And here, go back a little more, and compare these early pictures of you with the ones of his granddaughter. *Your* granddaughter. My *niece*." He grabbed the napkin she had crumpled earlier and handed it to her as tears began to roll down her cheeks.

Obediently, she blotted until the napkin was a sodden mass and he handed her another one. "It's true, isn't it?" she said. "It's really true."

"It really is," he agreed.

Celia blotted once more, blew her nose, then pushed her chair back abruptly and stood up.

"What are you going to do?"

"I'm going to see my granddaughter." She started for the door, came back and picked up her purse, fumbled for her car keys, and dropped them on the floor. He picked them up and offered them to her. She stared at them as if she couldn't remember what they were, then asked him hesitantly, "Please, John, will you come with me?"

He grinned and dropped the keys back into her purse. "I thought you'd never ask."

Celia stood in front of the door to Ross McClain's hotel suite and swallowed hard. Twice, she lifted her hand to knock on the door, and twice, she let the hand fall to her side again. John finally reached past her, knocked firmly, and stepped back out of the way.

When the door swung open, it was the wheelchair Celia saw first, and the legs, their thinness painfully obvious even under the heavy denim of jeans. She looked higher, into blue eyes and a slender face surrounded by a cloud of auburn hair.

Celia tried to speak and couldn't. She tried to breathe, and couldn't do that either. For a minute, she wondered if her heart had stopped beating, too.

Then the girl's eyes, so much like John's, widened. She drew in a ragged, shallow breath and whispered, "Grandmother! You're my grandmother!" She gave the wheelchair a quick half-turn and called over her shoulder, "Grandpa, come quick. It's my grandmother. She's here."

She spun her chair back to face Celia, tears streaming down her face, and held out her arms. Celia dropped to her knees and caught the frail young body in a warm embrace. "Jennie. My Jennie. My grandchild."

Jennie pressed her face into Celia's shoulder and exclaimed fiercely, "I knew you'd come. I knew you'd come."

When they finally separated, Celia glanced up and found Ross McClain watching them, his lips curved into a satisfied smile. He held out a hand to help her to her feet. "I knew it, too," he said. "You couldn't be Leslie's mother and not come."

Behind her, John cleared his throat, and she suddenly remembered her manners. "Oh, this is—"

But she was too late. John had already dropped to his knees beside the wheelchair to grin at Jennie and take her hand in his. "This is your lucky day, Jennie. You get two for the price of one. I'm your Uncle John."

Jennie wheeled her chair through the dining room and into the kitchen, out into the hall, and then back to the living room where Ross and Celia stood watching her. She stopped with a flourish and grinned up at them. "I like your house a lot, Grandma. My chair fits anywhere I want to go, even into the bathroom." She flushed slightly and admitted, "Bathrooms can be a problem sometimes. Thank you for inviting us to stay with you. I won't mind my therapy nearly as much if we don't have to stay in that stupid hotel."

Celia gave quick but fervent thanks for her old-fashioned, one-story house with the large rooms and wide doorways that seemed made for Jennie's wheelchair. "I should be thanking you," she said. "It gets pretty lonesome here, all by myself."

"It won't be lonesome with me here," Jennie exclaimed. "I can promise you that."

"Amen!" Ross added. "Celia, are you sure

we aren't in your way? I worry that we'll be imposing on you."

"Well, stop worrying. I wouldn't have asked you if I didn't want you. Jennie belongs here now, any time you'll let her come. And you belong with Jennie, so don't argue about it, just make yourselves at home."

"All right," he said softly. "We will." He turned to Jennie. "Don't forget, you promised to go right to bed if we came tonight instead of waiting until tomorrow. You need to be rested for your therapy in the morning."

"Okay," Jennie agreed reluctantly. "I'll rest, but I'll bet I'm too excited to sleep." She caught Celia's hand and pressed it against her cheek. "Will you help me get ready for bed, Grandma?"

Celia glanced at Ross, who smiled and nodded. "Go ahead. Call me when you're ready and I'll come in to say good night."

"Your bedroom is the one in the middle," Celia told Jennie. "Mine is at the front, and your grandfather will have the room that used to be John's." She ushered Jennie into the dainty peach and white room. While John had helped Ross and Jennie pack and bring their things from the hotel, she'd come home to make up the bed and replace the impersonal

250

guest room furnishings with everything she could find that might appeal to an eleven-year-old girl.

Jennie's eyes widened as she rolled her chair around the room, exclaiming at everything from the ruffled spread and embroidered pillow cases on the bed to the cut-glass vanity set and porcelain trinket boxes on the dressing table. "It's even prettier than my room at home," she said.

"If I'd ever been lucky enough to have another daughter," Celia explained, "this would have been her room." She bent to hug Jennie. "Now it's yours."

Jennie returned the hug. "I'm so glad we found you. It's almost like having my mother back."

Celia swallowed hard and blinked fast. "It is for me, too. Now we'd better get you ready for bed, or your grandfather will scold us both."

Jennie sighed, but it was somehow a happy sound. "I guess you're right. We can visit some more tomorrow."

Celia was pleased to find that even if Jennie couldn't walk, she was far from helpless. She supervised the unpacking of her suitcase, undressed herself and slipped into her nightgown with a minimum of help, and needed Celia's assistance only to move from the wheelchair into her bed.

"I'm not paralyzed or anything," she explained, "but it took my legs a long time to heal, and the muscles got weak. That's what the therapy is for—to make the muscles stronger. And I have to do exercises every day, too." She made a face, then hugged Celia again, plumped her pillows, and lay back with a satisfied smile.

"I feel like a long-lost princess who's just returned home to her kingdom," she announced. "Will you call Grandpa to come say good night, please?"

But by the time Celia returned with Ross, Jennie was already asleep.

"I didn't think she'd last very long," he said.

"I hope the excitement hasn't been too much for her."

"It's been good for her. Look, she has color in her cheeks and she's smiling in her sleep. She hasn't been this happy or enthusiastic about anything since . . ." His voice trailed off as if he couldn't bring himself to finish the sentence.

He bent to turn off the lamp and they tiptoed from the room. "Celia, I don't know how to thank you for all you've done for her."

The warmth in his voice flustered her. "All I've done for her? Big deal. I made up the bed in the guest room and helped tuck her in."

"I'm not talking about that, or even about your wonderful hospitality—she does hate that hotel, and I don't blame her. But what I mean is the way you've just opened up and taken her in. When we talked this morning, I was afraid . . ."

"Oh, Ross, I'm so sorry about the way I behaved this morning. I couldn't bear the news that my daughter was lost to me forever, so I told myself you were lying, that you only wanted something from me. Instead, you and Jennie have given me back a part of my life I thought was gone forever."

They'd been moving slowly toward the kitchen as they talked. She inhaled deeply and asked, "Do I smell coffee?"

"I took you at your word. While you were helping Jennie get ready for bed, I made myself at home in your kitchen and brewed us a pot."

"Bless your heart!" She led the way into the kitchen and found that he'd not only made coffee, but set out cups and saucers. "I just realized I haven't had dinner," she said. "I think I'm going to fix myself some scrambled eggs and toast. Would you like some?"

"I haven't had scrambled eggs and toast for any meal but breakfast in a long time. Yes, I'd like some. All of a sudden, I'm ravenously hungry."

He sat at the table, sipping his coffee and watching her while she set the table, dropped bread in the toaster, stirred eggs in the skillet. When the toast popped up, he buttered it without being asked, spreading the butter clear to the edges, the way she liked it.

When she served their plates and slipped into her chair opposite him, he picked up his fork and eyed the eggs with pleasure, then glanced up at her. "I agree with Jennie. I like your house. It has a warm, friendly feel to it."

She'd been thinking the same thing about him, but all she said was, "It's you and Jennie who are making it that way. I'm glad you're here."

Ross watched with amazement as Jennie cleaned her plate. "I haven't seen you eat a breakfast like that in quite a while," he said.

"I haven't *had* a breakfast like that in quite

a while." She broke open another of Celia's homemade biscuits and spread each half with a thick layer of peach butter. "You're the greatest grandpa in the world, but you're not much of a cook."

He grinned at Celia. "I may not be much of a cook, but I'm a whiz at washing dishes. I should have just enough time to clean the kitchen before I take Jennie for her therapy."

Celia shook her head. "Don't be silly. I'm a whiz at washing dishes, too."

He glanced at the wall clock. "Won't you be late for work? Or do you set your own hours?"

"Neither." She hesitated. "The truth is, I handed in my resignation yesterday. No," she added hastily, at his exclamation of dismay. "It had nothing to do with you or Jennie. I'd finished writing it before you came in."

"What kind of job was it, Grandma?" Jennie asked.

"I was the assistant editor of a small magazine."

Jennie's eyes widened. "Gosh, that sounds exciting."

"It was," Celia confirmed.

"Then why did you quit?"

Celia hesitated. How could she tell them she'd quit because she'd been in a bad mood, and because she just didn't care enough about the job anymore to fight for it? She shrugged and answered with deliberate vagueness. "I'm not really sure. It just suddenly seemed like a good time to move on."

"Then it wasn't something you'd been planning to do?" Ross asked.

"No, not consciously. But it must have been in the back of my mind. And I'm not one to fret and stew for a long time over decisions. Once I decide to do something, I generally go ahead and do it."

"So I've noticed." Ross grinned at her, then asked quietly, "What are you going to do now?"

The question startled her. It wasn't something she'd thought about yet—or even realized she would need to think about. She made her voice brisk and positive. "Now? I'm going to clean the kitchen, then go clean out my desk, and after that . . ." Her bravado weakened and she could only say, "I have no idea."

She thought about it while Ross helped her in the kitchen and again as she tackled her desk. When her secretary—correction, she thought—her *former* secretary—asked her the same question, she began to wonder if she'd let her post-retreat depression and anger over the memo on her desk stampede her into making a decision she was likely to regret.

There were few jobs open for someone with her particular experience and expertise, fewer entry-level positions for someone her age, and even though she was in a financial position to retire, she knew she'd go crazy sitting at home doing nothing. She was used to keeping busy, handling responsibilities, making things happen.

She made up her mind abruptly. She hadn't had a real vacation in ages—not since before James had died. She'd take one now and spend the time with Ross and Jennie. She could worry about another job when Jennie was well enough for Ross to take her back home.

But when she stopped at the supermarket to find something special for dinner, she bought a late edition of the morning paper and thumbed through the help wanted ads until Ross and Jennie got back from the clinic.

Jennie returned from her session with the therapist weak, exhausted, and in considerable pain. She refused the lunch Celia had pre-

257

pared. "I just want to rest for a while, but not in bed. Please."

"You'll be terribly uncomfortable in your chair," Ross protested.

"I know, but I want to stay out here with you and Grandma."

"Why don't we make her a nest on the sofa?" Celia suggested, and at Jennie's eager nod, she fetched pillows and her Rose-of-Sharon afghan.

Jennie fingered the afghan, delight mingling with fatigue on her face. "It's so pretty, Grandma. Did you make it?"

Celia nodded. "I made it for you."

"For *me?*"

"Well, for someone special, and you're the most special someone I know."

Jennie leaned back and closed her eyes, her hands still stroking the afghan. "No, *you* are. You and Grandpa."

As they watched, she drifted into a shallow, restless sleep.

"The therapy's hard on her," Ross said.

Celia studied the obvious concern on his face. "It's even harder on you, isn't it?"

He nodded. "And it's going to get harder. Once we learn the routine, we won't have to go to the clinic as often, but she'll still have to do the exercises, and I'm the ogre who'll have to see that she does them."

"I'll help," Celia offered instantly.

He put his arm around her shoulders and held her close for a minute, then leaned toward her and kissed her cheek. "You're quite a woman, Celia Hamlin. I don't know what Jennie and I did to deserve you, but whatever it was, I'm glad we did it." He released her and bent to brush a lock of hair back from Jennie's face, his fingers as gentle as a kitten's paws.

And he was quite a man, Celia thought. Aloud, she said, "Thank you. I've been thinking I was the lucky one. If I could have picked someone to adopt my child, it would have been you."

In typical male fashion, he was embarrassed by the compliment, mumbled what might have been a brief thank you, and glanced back at Jennie. "She'll sleep for several hours and be starved when she wakes, but I'm starved now. What about some of that lunch you mentioned a few minutes ago?"

They ate on trays in the living room, to be near Jennie if she woke, and talked quietly.

"Tell me about my daughter," Celia begged. "You said her name was Leslie?"

"Yes, it was her mother's — that is, my wife's — middle name. What can I tell you, except that she was sunshine and laughter and the joy of our lives? We always believed she came of parents who loved each other, and we thought often of you and how it must have hurt you to give her up."

He hesitated. "Celia, this is none of my business, and you can tell me to shut up if you want to, but . . ."

"You want to know about her father," Celia said. "I think it *is* your business, and Jennie's too, if she ever wants to know. You're right, Ross. Leslie's father and I did love each other, very much."

"But you didn't marry him."

"No.

"His choice, or yours?"

"We didn't really have a choice. We were from different worlds. Literally. He was an exchange student I met at college. We had different backgrounds, different religions, different customs. His family would never have accepted me into their world; he had obligations and duties that wouldn't let him stay in mine."

"Did he know you were pregnant?"

She shook her head. "No. There was a

death in his family and he was called home before I even knew about the baby myself."

"And you never told him."

She sighed, feeling the pain all over again, only a faint echo now, but still remembered, still there. "No. There was nothing he could have done about it, and it seemed kinder never to let him know. But he was a good person, Ross. He'd have loved her very much and been a father she could be proud of."

Jennie stirred and they were quiet for a moment, afraid their voices would disturb her. When her breathing was deep and even again, Ross said quietly, "She'd have been proud of both of you."

As if he realized how deeply he had stirred her, he gave her a few minutes to deal with the tears that filled her eyes, and to get her emotions under control. Then they spent the rest of the afternoon sharing memories of their daughter's childhood. He showed her pictures from the family album he'd brought with him. He had the storyteller's knack of making his accounts vivid and alive, so she could almost believe they were her memories, too. Some of the pain she'd carried for so many years began to ease.

Jennie slept until late in the day and, as

Ross had predicted, was ravenous when she woke.

"Dinner won't be ready for a little while," Celia told her, "but I'm a great believer in between-meal snacks. Do you suppose a couple of leftover biscuits with butter and honey would take the edge off your hunger without spoiling your appetite?"

"I'll bet they would."

"Well, you know where they are. Go help yourself."

Jennie rolled off into the kitchen and Ross stared at Celia with an expression she couldn't identify. "How do you do that?"

"Do what?"

"The right thing. Without even thinking twice. Anybody else would have rushed to get the biscuits for her. You let her do it for herself. And you don't feel sorry for her."

"Oh, yes. I do." Celia blinked back tears. "But I won't let her feel sorry for herself."

Ross drew in a deep breath and let it out slowly. "Celia Hamlin, if I'd had any idea what kind of person you are, we'd have come looking for you years ago."

She found his steady gaze unsettling, and glanced away. "I hear Jennie talking to someone. John must be here."

"Will you look at that?" John exclaimed as they came into the kitchen. "She's taking the food right out of my mouth."

Jennie looked apprehensive but game. "I don't know what you mean."

"You're eating my biscuits, aren't you? You must be. I always get the leftover biscuits, but the way you're going, there won't be any biscuits left over for me to get."

Jennie giggled suddenly. "Well, *these* leftover biscuits aren't yours. Grandma said I could have them. But I'll share them with you. Which one do you want?"

He licked his lips, then rubbed his middle and shook his head sadly. "I guess I'd better let you have them both. I've already eaten too many, and you have a lot of catching up to do."

Jennie grinned at Celia and Ross. "I think I'm going to like having an uncle."

John patted her head. "I think I'm going to like being one. Come on, kid. Let's clear the kitchen so Mom can fix dinner." He sauntered into the living room and settled himself in an easy chair, leaving Jennie to wheel herself after him and park her chair as close to his as she could.

Ross watched them for a minute, then

turned to Celia. "He does it, too—ignores the chair and just sees Jennie. I should have known your son—Leslie's brother—would be pretty special."

"Thank you," Celia said softly. "I think he's almost as pleased to know Jennie as I am. He always wanted a brother or sister, and I felt so guilty, knowing that somewhere, he had one and couldn't know her or be with her."

"How old is he, Celia?"

"Thirty-three. He was born just four years after his sister, and like you and Leslie, he was the joy of our lives. I can't begin to tell you what a comfort he's been to me since James died."

"I can imagine. Leslie wondered, sometimes, if she had brothers or sisters somewhere."

Celia cleared her throat. "Did . . . did it hurt her very much, that I had given her away? Was she ever afraid that . . . that I didn't want her, didn't love her?"

Ross put his arm around her shoulders and squeezed gently, reassuringly. "We would never have let her think that, even if we'd believed it. We made sure she knew she was loved—by all of us."

Celia felt her eyes fill with tears and turned away before Ross could see. "Guess I'd better start dinner, before Jennie's biscuits wear off."

She worked quietly, listening to John's voice from the living room, punctuated by Jennie's frequent giggles. Apparently, they were sharing the comics from the evening paper. She glanced over her shoulder frequently at Ross, still standing in the doorway watching the pair in the living room.

"It's hard to believe that's the same child who was moping around the hotel and feeling so miserable twenty-four hours ago." He shifted his attention to Celia and she turned back to the sink, but not quite soon enough. "What are you smiling at?" he asked.

"I was just thinking that Jennie isn't the only one who's different. It's hard to believe you're the same man who stormed out of my office yesterday."

He gave her a sheepish, lop-sided grin. "Sorry about that. I was pretty uptight when I talked to you."

"Don't apologize. You had every reason to be."

He left his post in the doorway and sat in one of the kitchen chairs, as James had so often done. Leaning back with his long legs stretched out in front of him, he looked as if he belonged there, had always belonged there.

"No, it wasn't you. I'd been uptight for a long time, getting over the loss of my wife, my daughter, and her husband, worrying at first over whether Jennie would survive or not, then knowing she had this blasted therapy to get through."

"And you're not so uptight now?"

He shook his head. "I'm not alone with it anymore. Just finding you, having someone to share the burden, the responsibility—" He broke off abruptly. "Celia, I'm sorry. I really don't intend to dump everything on your shoulders. It's just been damned lonely—and scary—dealing with it by myself. Just having you here to talk to, knowing there's someone else who cares, who'll be there if Jennie needs her . . ."

His voice trailed away and he grinned at her, a warm and somehow intimate expression of pleasure. "And it doesn't hurt that you're the sweetest and prettiest lady I've met in a long time."

Flustered, Celia turned back to the sink and made a fuss over washing lettuce for the salad. After a minute, she managed to say, "I don't feel dumped on. I feel needed and useful. So you see, I'm not the same either, because I haven't felt that way since James died."

She kept her eyes on the lettuce and her face turned toward the sink as she realized that for her, much of the change was in the joy of simply having Ross there, filling some of the emptiness James had left. And it didn't hurt that he was —

She realized suddenly where the thought was heading and cut the rest of it off without finishing it.

Celia relaxed in her favorite chair, taking advantage of a quiet moment to work on her needlepoint. Periodically, she glanced at Jennie, napping on the sofa, and marveled that such a small person could fill such a big space, or turn the world around so completely. She and Ross had settled into Celia's life as if they'd always been there.

Being honest, she had to admit that it wasn't just Jennie who had turned her house into a home again. Ross was a big part of the difference. Having him there helped to ease her loneliness as he filled a little — only a little! — of the emptiness James had left.

She'd made a difference for them, too. She and John. If the four of them had met under other circumstances, she thought, they'd probably have become friends anyway, but with the bond of Jennie between them, they'd become more — much more.

Jennie had summed it up very nicely when she'd said, "We're a family again, aren't we, Grandpa? I mean, you and I were a family, of course, but with Grandma and John, we're a *whole* family."

They certainly were, Celia agreed, and they'd still be, even when Jennie's legs strengthened enough so she could walk again, and she and Ross moved back to their own home. She pushed the thought away as quickly as it had come. She knew it was going to happen. There was no point in fretting over it until it did.

Jennie stirred and opened her eyes. "Grandma? I thought I heard John talking a little while ago. Is he here, or was I just dreaming?"

"He's here," Celia said. "He and your grandfather are outside, putting a new net on the old basketball goal."

Jennie levered herself into a sitting position and stuffed a pillow behind her back.

"Grandpa and John are going to shoot baskets? Great. Maybe I can go out and watch them."

Celia shook her head. "No, I think what they have in mind is for you to go out and *join* them."

Jennie's eyes grew big. "Really? Do you think I can?"

Celia grinned. "I think you'd *better*. You don't know what a beast John can be when he doesn't get his own way."

Jennie giggled. "If he's a beast, does that make me a beauty?"

"It certainly does," John said from the doorway. He scooped her up and carried her out to the paved driveway beside the house while Ross brought her wheelchair and Celia ran ahead to open and close doors.

Ross and John spent the next hour alternately showing off and cheering Jennie and Celia as they took their turns with the basketball.

Watching what she assumed was a prime example of "male bonding," Celia realized for the first time how badly John must have been missing his father. It was one more reason for her to be grateful to Ross.

He was like James in so many ways, she

269

thought. It made him easy to like, comfortable to be with.

A little out of breath, she left the game and sat down on a small wooden bench next to the house. After a minute, Ross joined her, leaving John and Jennie tossing the ball back and forth.

"Look at her," he said. "Roses in her cheeks, a sparkle in her eyes. She's having the time of her life. Remind me to do something special for John sometime."

"I think you already have," she murmured.

"This kid's got a great arm," John told Ross. "Have you ever thought of getting her a newspaper route so you can retire?"

"He's already retired," Jennie said.

John twirled the ball on the tip of one finger. "In that case, we'll still get you a newspaper route, so *I* can retire."

"Ha!" Jennie exclaimed. "In your dreams!" She wheeled her chair close to him and reached for the ball.

"Dreams! Yes!" He held the ball out of her reach and began to sing, "I dream of Jennie, with the strong right arm."

She yanked at his elbow, caught the ball as he dropped it, spun her chair around, and sent the ball flying through the air and into the basket.

Ross laughed and laid his arm lightly around Celia's shoulders. "Couple of great kids we've got here, Grandma."

She settled comfortably into his embrace and grinned up at him. "You know it, Grandpa."

The days slid by, each one more exciting than the last. Jennie blossomed under the care of two loving grandparents, Ross swapped his tense, anxious look for a quick, infectious grin, and Celia found that she had filled not only her house with love and laughter, but her life as well.

"If you had another bedroom," John told her, "I'd be tempted to move back in myself." He watched with approval as she spread custard filling over a layer of sponge cake and topped it with another layer. "I hate to think of you people having all this fun without me."

"Ha! The only thing you hate to think of is that we might have dinner without you." She slapped his hand as he slid his finger around the rim of the custard bowl.

He licked the finger and bent to kiss her

cheek. "Now that's the mother I haven't seen for a while—feisty, sassy, and ready to backtalk. Having Ross and Jennie here has been good for you, hasn't it? Where are they?"

"There's a movie on TV tonight that we want to watch. They went to the store for some corn to pop. And you're right. Having them here has been wonderful. I'll never stop grieving for the little girl I never knew, but finding Jennie has made it a lot easier for me."

"Popcorn, huh? I don't know what movie you're planning to see, but if there's going to be hot chocolate, too, I think I'll stay and watch it with you. And I don't mean to argue, but as cute and sweet as Jennie is, I doubt very much that she's the only reason you were singing to yourself when I came in."

She set the custard bowl aside and reached for a bowl of chocolate icing. "I'm sure I don't know what you mean."

"I mean, maybe Jennie's grandfather has something to do with the spring in your step and the pink in your cheeks."

She piled a spoonful of icing on the top of the cake and began to spread it smoothly toward the edges. "That's ridiculous."

"What's ridiculous about it? In case you haven't noticed, you've made a pretty big change in him, too."

"He's pleased at the progress Jennie's making, that's all. Besides, even if I were having some sort of . . . reaction . . . to him, which I certainly am not, it's only been a few months since he lost his wife. I remember how long it took me to begin caring again about anything after your father's death, and I can tell you Ross isn't any more ready to get involved in a new relationship than I am."

"I don't know about that, Mom. Some people work through grief more quickly than others. Ross looks to me like he's ready to get on with his life." He grinned wickedly and added, "In fact, it looks to me as if he'd like to get it on with *you*." He ducked into the dining room before she could do or say anything more, leaving her with her face flaming, and, for some reason she didn't want to examine too clearly, a more subtle warmth pulsing inside her.

Ross scraped the last few bits of popcorn into the trash while Celia rinsed the cocoa cups at the sink. "That was the worst movie

273

I've seen in ages," he declared, "and I loved every minute of it."

"I enjoyed the whole evening," she told him "especially watching John and Jennie. They've certainly taken to each other quickly, haven't they?"

"That they have. I think he enjoys teasing her almost as much as she enjoys being teased." He caught a strand of her hair and tugged it lightly. "I wonder if it's hereditary."

She grinned and ducked away. "If so, shouldn't I be the one doing the teasing?"

He turned out the light and followed her into the hall. "Either way is fine with me."

They looked in on Jennie and found that she had tossed and turned until her covers had slid into a heap on the floor. As Celia tucked her back in and bent to kiss her cheek gently, she stirred restlessly and muttered something they couldn't understand.

"Poor baby," Celia murmured. "The exercises leave her so stiff and sore, don't they?"

"I'm sure they do," Ross agreed, "but the trouble she has sleeping is more likely emotional distress. I'm worried about her, Celia. She seems so sunny and cheerful most of the time, as if she'd adjusted to the way things are now, but the truth is, she hasn't really dealt with it at all. Until we came here, she'd been having nightmares almost every night. That's one more good thing you've done for her."

They tiptoed back into the hall, but instead of going to their separate bedrooms, they drifted into the living room.

"She couldn't deal with it at first," he went on, "because she needed every ounce of strength she had just to recover from her injuries. There was nothing left over for grief. By the time she was physically well, she'd built a wall around it."

He sat at one end of the sofa, caught her hand, and tugged her down beside him. "Oh, Celia, if you could have known her before the accident! She was so full of joy, so alive . . . almost effervescent."

Celia struggled for words to comfort him and finally suggested, "It usually takes longer to heal emotional wounds than physical ones. Perhaps she's dealing with it better than you realize. I've seen changes in her in just the few days you've been here."

He reached for her hand again and folded his fingers around it. "You're a great comfort to me, Celia. You always know the right thing to do or say."

She relaxed and let her hand linger in his for a minute. She'd quickly learned that Ross was a "toucher." He was the same way with the children, quick to clap John on the shoulder or give Jennie a spontaneous hug. It was a warm and warming gesture that made her realize how much she missed the casual affection she'd taken for granted for so many years.

They sat quietly for a few minutes, enjoying each other's company, sharing an intimacy that came as much from the friendship growing between them as from their concerns over Jennie.

Recalling her earlier conversation with John, Celia asked hesitantly, "Ross? What about you?"

"What do you mean?"

"Well . . . If this is none of my business, just tell me so, but . . . How are *you* dealing with it?"

"Better than I expected to," he said, after a minute. "In a way, I think Jennie's injuries *helped* me get through it. I couldn't just lie down and surrender to self pity. I had to keep moving, to fight for Jennie, be there for her. By the time I was sure she was going to live, I was through the worst of it. And because I still have Jennie, I've faced the fact that life does go on, it *must* go on, and the only choice I have is whether I'll wallow in misery or let myself be happy."

He studied her face for a minute, then smiled. "I choose to be happy."

She felt unexpectedly self-conscious and glanced away.

He caught her chin in one hand and turned her face back toward him. "Celia, are you wondering if I'm ready to begin another relationship? Because if you are—and I hope you are—the answer is, I think—I hope!—I already have. I know it hasn't been very long since Norma died, but it's long enough for me to know I don't like being alone, and I do like being with you. I'm sure Norma wouldn't have wanted me to turn down a chance for happiness because of anything as arbitrary as the calendar."

"She must have been a wonderful person," Celia said, feeling that she ought to change the subject, but not knowing how.

"She was," he agreed. "And so are you. You're like her in many ways—warm, caring, beautiful, and under that very contained exterior of yours, I'll bet you're sexy as hell."

277

"Oh!" Before she could stop herself, she'd jerked away from him. She felt her cheeks burn as he laughed softly.

"Sorry. I didn't mean to startle you, and I'm not trying to push you into anything you feel uncomfortable with, but I think you're as ready as I am to stop being alone and lonely." He leaned forward, tipped her face up to his with one finger under her chin, and brushed her lips lightly with his.

He let her go and leaned back, a faint smile tugging at his lips while she tried to decide whether to smile, frown, or giggle.

The grandfather's clock in the hall came to her rescue as it began to chime the hour. "Goodness," she said. "I had no idea it was so late. Don't you think we'd better be getting to—" She broke off and substituted, "That is, it's time we got some sleep," and wished she hadn't when Ross's smile broadened.

Obediently, he followed her into the hall, but when she paused at her bedroom door to say good night, he told her, "I know Norma and Leslie would be happy that Jennie's found an uncle to tease her and a new grandmother to love her. I think they'd be just as happy that I've found someone to fill some of the empty spaces in my life. Maybe I can fill

278

some of the empty spaces in yours. I'm sure going to try."

He caught her in his arms and kissed her again, not just a mere brushing of lips this time, but a full-length meeting of bodies that left her flustered and breathless.

He gave her a sketchy, two-finger salute and disappeared down the hall into his own bedroom, while she struggled with the disquieting knowledge that the empty spaces she'd thought they were filling weren't the ones he was talking about at all.

Celia set the basket of fresh laundry on the ground under the clothesline and straightened up to fill her eyes and ears and lungs with the clear spring morning. The birds chirped and sang their approval, and although the grass still glittered with moisture from yesterday's showers, the few fluffy white clouds overhead only emphasized the brilliant blue of the sky.

She felt a brief pang of regret for all the mornings like this she'd spent cooped up in her office, then laughed at herself. Somewhere, no doubt, other women were doing just the opposite—regretting the careers they'd given up to be homemakers. Celia—lucky Celia!—had been given the chance to do both.

She reached into the basket and grasped the four corners of a sheet, shook it lightly as she picked it up, and clipped it to the clothesline with three precisely spaced clothespins. The same April-fresh breeze that tumbled her hair around her face and whipped her skirt against her legs caught the sheet and snapped it out in a brief tug-of-war against the clothesline.

She reached for another sheet and shook it out as the back door opened and Ross exclaimed, "Ah, there you are! I wondered where you'd disappeared to." He took in a deep breath and sighed in satisfaction, then asked with mild concern, "Your dryer's not broken, is it?"

She shook her head. "No, it's just too nice a day to dry things indoors. Besides, I thought the wonderful smell of line-dried sheets might soothe Jennie and help her sleep."

"Just knowing that you're thinking of her will help." He crossed the yard and propped himself lazily against the post that held the clotheslines at one end, smiling at her in a way that made her keenly aware that he wasn't just Jennie's grandfather, but an attractive, vital, and altogether virile male.

She was also aware that a subtle change was taking place in their relationship and she wasn't quite sure what to do about it. Ross had begun to treat her not just as Jennie's long-lost grandmother, but as an attractive and desirable woman. He hadn't kissed her again, but only, she was sure, because she'd avoided giving him the chance.

It would be so easy to let their growing friendship, their mutual love for Jennie, and the fact that they found each other attractive trick them into seeing things in the relationship that simply weren't there. Easy, but terribly unwise.

She had to make sure it didn't happen.

"Jennie and I appreciate everything you're doing for us," he said, "but we don't want to become a burden to you. All this extra cooking and cleaning—"

"Don't be silly. I'm loving every minute of it." Then, to make sure he didn't misunderstand, she added, "The truth is, as much as I enjoyed my work, I think I've always been a closet homemaker. If we'd had other children, I'd probably have stayed home with them, but once John started school there just wasn't that much to do."

She picked up a pair of pillowcases and

hung them on the line before adding, "Since John grew up and James died, this house hasn't felt much like a home. But now! Having you here has been like having a whole new family. You and Jennie aren't a burden. You're a blessing."

"Well, I know Jennie is, but I never thought of myself quite that way." He took a handful of clothespins from the holder and held them out to her as she pulled another sheet from the basket. "But you're the real blessing. You and John. Jennie has done more healing these last few days than in all the rest of the time since the accident, and I don't mean physically." He stepped aside as the wind whipped the sheets toward him. "She's inside right now doing her schoolwork—without being told!—because she doesn't want Grandma and Uncle John to think she's stupid."

Celia laughed. "Oh, Ross. You and Jennie have made such a difference in my life."

"It's been great for me, too. I love Jennie dearly, but it's wonderful having another adult to talk to." He grinned at her with a kind of taken-for-granted intimacy that brought an unexpected warmth to her cheeks. "And I'm awfully glad that other adult is you."

She made her voice light and teasing. "I'll

bet you say that to all of Jennie's grand-mothers."

He shook his head. "Only the pretty ones."

"Maybe you'd better go check on Jennie," she told him, trying to sound prim and disapproving, and failing totally.

Obediently, he grinned and went back to the house. He paused on the steps and glanced back at her just as the wind caught her skirt and swirled it around her knees. "By the way," he called to her, "has anyone told you lately that you have great legs?"

He went inside, leaving Celia to face the disquieting knowledge that somehow she was losing control of the situation, and she'd better think of a way to get it back. Soon.

Celia and Jennie put the fresh sheets on the beds, Celia shaking them out from one side of the bed while Jennie tugged them into place and smoothed them on the other side. "I'll bet I sleep well tonight," she said. "I'll probably dream I'm back in my own bedroom. Mama always hung the sheets out to dry, too. She said there wasn't anything in the world that smelled better than sheets dried on the line, unless it was bacon frying in the morning."

The smile left her lips and her voice trembled slightly as she added, "Oh, Grandma, I miss Mama and Daddy and my other grandma so much. Sometimes when I say my prayers at night, I pray that I'll wake up in the morning and everything will be back the way it was."

Celia's eyes stung with sudden tears. She bent swiftly to put her arms around Jennie. "I know, darling. I know."

When Ross and Celia looked in on Jennie before going to bed, she was sleeping quietly, one hand holding a corner of the sheet against her face.

"Look," Celia whispered. "She is sleeping better, isn't she?"

"She's doing everything better," Ross said softly. "She laughs. She's gaining weight. She's working harder at her exercises."

He slipped his arm around Celia as they left the room, and when they were in the hall, he turned her to face him. "I'd be sleeping better, too, except that it's getting harder and harder to say good night out here, and then go down the hall to my own bedroom."

She laughed, and tried to look amused, but the laugh came out sounding like a nervous giggle, and it was Ross who looked amused.

"Celia, you've been walking on eggshells around me lately, and there really isn't any need to. You must be aware that I'm having some pretty strong feelings about you, and I was hoping you'd feel the same way, but if you don't, just tell me so. I'm a grown man. You won't hurt my feelings or destroy my ego."

She swallowed hard. "It isn't that I don't have feelings for you, Ross. It's just that I don't think . . . I don't think they're quite the feelings you're hoping they are. I mean, you're a very attractive man, and I like you a lot, but . . ." Her voice died away as he began to grin.

"But you're afraid you won't respect me in the morning, is that it?"

"No! Of course I'd respect— I mean— Damn it, Ross, don't laugh at me. It isn't funny."

"No," he admitted. "It isn't. But it could be fun." He'd moved closer while he spoke, until they were only inches from each other, almost touching.

Damn! she thought. He'd given her the perfect chance to take back control of the situation, and she'd muffed it, and now she was standing here like a lovesick schoolgirl waiting to be kissed good night.

Well, she wasn't. She was a grown woman, and if he tried to kiss her, she'd—

But she didn't. When he closed the last tiny bit of distance between them and put his arms around her, she realized how lonely she had been, how much she had missed being in a man's arms, and how much she suddenly wanted those arms to be his. Helplessly, she relaxed against him, turned her face up to his, and returned his kiss.

"Aah," he whispered, when their lips parted. "I knew that under that prim and proper exterior there was a very sexy lady."

His words shocked her back to her senses. She pulled away from him, choked out a muffled, "Good night, Ross," and fled to the sanctuary of her bedroom.

His soft, pleased laughter followed her and lingered in her memory as she came face to face with the disquieting knowledge that her sex *life* might have died with James, but her sex *drive* had only been hibernating, and whether she could lull it back to sleep or not was anybody's guess.

An hour later, she admitted that she couldn't even lull herself to sleep. Her lips still throbbed from Ross's kiss and her body tingled from being held against his. That was bad enough, but she knew it would die away eventually.

The thing that was keeping her awake was the emotional conflict he'd stirred inside her. Her grief for James had gradually softened into a vague, general feeling of loss. Ross had reminded her sharply and specifically what a major part of that loss was. Her body craved physical intimacy, but her mind and heart wanted the greater intimacy that went with sex. She might be able to ignore the one, but the other—No. Ross had stirred up a lot more than he'd meant to, and likely a lot more than he realized.

She sat up abruptly, swung her feet over the side of the bed, and was about to go to the kitchen for some warm milk when a thump and a desolate wail from Jennie's room jerked her out of bed and down the hall.

She brushed her hand back and forth across the wall, unable to find the familiar light switch for what seemed like eons, while Jennie's hysterical cries of "Mama! Mama!" lashed at her like strokes from a whip. Her hand hit the switch finally, and the room flooded with light to show Jennie tangled in her covers and lying on the floor.

She dropped to her knees and scooped Jennie into her arms only a fraction of a second before Ross skidded to a stop beside them. Together, they soothed and calmed Jennie until her sobbing slowed to an occasional hiccup. Ross lifted her from the floor and placed her gently back into bed while Celia gathered up the covers and spread them over her.

"What is it, sweetheart?" Ross asked. "Another bad dream?"

She shook her head. "No, it was a good dream. I dreamed I woke up in my own room, and I smelled the clean sheets, and then I smelled bacon cooking for breakfast. And I tried to get up and run in to Mama, but my legs wouldn't work, and I fell and woke up. That was the bad part. Waking up and remembering."

They sat with her, comforting and petting her until she fell asleep again, then slipped quietly from the room. Overcome with guilt, Celia leaned against the wall and brushed tears from her eyes.

"The sheets," she said. "The smell of the sheets caused her nightmare. Oh, Ross, I feel so —"

He laid a hand over her lips. "No. It wasn't your fault, any more than it was mine. And hard as it was on all of us, perhaps it wasn't a bad thing. Maybe now she'll be able to face her grief and deal with it."

When she continued to cry, he pulled her into his arms and held her close until she was quiet again, and beginning to realize that she was dressed only in a short, flimsy nightgown, and Ross was wearing only the bottoms to his pajamas. There was no way she could miss the precise moment when Ross realized it, too.

She tried to ease out of his arms without letting him know that she knew, but he only held her closer. When she started to speak, to ask him to let her go, he kissed her — lightly, at first, then more urgently. For a moment, she was aware of nothing but the warmth of his body and the taste of his lips against hers.

Then he began to move his hands, caressing at first, then exploring, leaving a trail of sparkling warmth as he stroked her face and throat, her shoulders, each vertebra in her spine. He kneaded and massaged her buttocks gently, then spread his fingers wide and pressed her against him briefly.

She fought for the self control to resist him as he eased his hands around to the front of her and slid them slowly up her stomach and over her breasts. When he slipped the straps of her gown off her shoulders and down to her waist so he could stroke her bare breasts with gentle fingers, she made a supreme effort and finally managed to back away.

She pulled her gown back up and left her arms crossed defensively over her breasts. "Ross, please. We have to stop. Now, before it's too late."

He pulled her back against him, his laughter a low, rich chuckle deep in his chest as he captured her hand and guided it through the crisp hair on his chest and down the firm flesh of his abdomen to the even firmer flesh pulsing below. "Oh, my sweet lady, it's already too late."

He slid his own hand under the hem of her short gown to explore the warmth and moisture waiting for him, and as her fingers curled around him of their own accord to caress and explore as his had done, she knew he was right. It was too late.

She shivered, not from the coolness of the night, but in joyous response to his eager and uninhibited caresses. Reluctant to separate, even for a moment, they clung together as they moved into her bedroom, pausing after each step for a kiss, a caress, each one more intimate and stirring than the last.

As they reached the bed, he slipped her nightgown from her shoulders again. She stepped away from him long enough to let it fall to the floor while he shucked off his pajamas, then pressed closer to him, aching with the need to feel his naked flesh against hers, to feel his body moving against hers, entering hers, possessing hers.

When he finally eased her down onto the bed, she expected him to take her immediately. Instead, he lay beside her and rolled her toward him, to explore her breasts with lips and tongue while one hand slid down the flat curve of her belly and dipped between her thighs to tease and fondle her into even greater need.

Her body reacted instantly, thrusting against his hand while she fought to catch her breath. She whispered, "Ross . . . Oh, Ross!" Then he was above her, his eyes glazed with passion as he lowered himself to her and she arched up to meet him.

She couldn't have marked the exact instant their bodies met and joined, only knew suddenly that they had, that they moved together in a single rhythm that pulsed through her until it blotted out everything else.

The world seemed to disappear, until even the bed beneath her was gone and nothing remained but the pounding rhythm and the union of her flesh with Ross's—a focus for time and space and motion that seemed to contract, to pull in on itself, curling into a tight ball, smaller, smaller, until it became a single pulsating point, like the flickering light from a tiny distant star—fragile, tenuous, as if it might be blown out by her quick, astonished intake of breath.

It didn't blow out. It wavered, steadied, and then—fanned by Ross's cry of triumph and her own wordless exclamation of joy—flared up, exploded outward, not flickering or fragile, but blazing, overwhelming, a supernova that expanded and poured through her, shattered her into an infinity of fragments, then caught her up in a swirl of rapture, bringing all the parts of her back together until she was complete and whole as she had never been complete and whole before.

Complete and whole, and yet, part of something greater than herself, part of a single entity that was neither Celia nor Ross, but both of them, and the wonder they had created between them.

For an eternal moment, there was nothing

else.

Then, gradually, the world crept back in — her own body first, joyously alive, taut and quivering with passion, her heart beating a frantic counterpoint to that other, fiercer beat that still rocked her.

Slowly, the beat gentled into a shudder, a ripple, and then the world expanded to bring her the warmth and weight of Ross above her, the touch of his lips against her throat, the soft, quick flow of his passion-slaked breath, the faint moistness of perspiration where his skin touched hers.

She thrust her hips against him one last time, straining to catch the final, vibrant whisper of ecstasy, then fell back, utterly spent but totally satisfied.

Ross pulled away from her slowly, reluctantly, and lowered himself to the bed beside her. She rolled toward him, still needing to be close, to be touching. He made a satisfied, contented sound and pulled her into his arms, settling her against him so that they fit snugly together, bare flesh against bare flesh in a tender intimacy that was as joyous and satisfying, in its own way, as their earlier passion had been.

Her last coherent thought as she drifted into

a light sleep was how strange it was that her first lover and this man beside her now had both been father to the child she had never known.

When she woke, the first light of dawn had begun to turn her bedroom window into a pale gray rectangle tinged with pink. She lay quietly for a few moments, astonished at the buoyant sense of well-being she felt, more astonished when she realized suddenly that she wasn't alone in the bed. She turned her head slowly and saw Ross lying beside her.

Memory returned, not just to her mind and thoughts, but to her whole being. Her body fairly quivered with it. Ross had been as eager and lusty a lover as she'd expected him to be, but he'd also taken care to see to her pleasure as well.

She drew the covers more tightly around herself and propped up on one elbow to study him as he slept.

His eyes opened slowly as her motion woke him. He smiled at her, stretched luxuriously, and reached up to brush her hair back from her face. With one finger, he traced the line of her jaw and chin, then slid his hand to the back of her neck and pulled her face down to his.

His lips were just as warm and persuasive this morning as they'd been last night. She returned his kiss eagerly and welcomed the length of his firm body against hers as he nestled her closer, but when he gently nudged her legs apart with his knee and slid his thigh between hers, she came abruptly to her senses and pulled away from him.

"Celia? What's wrong?"

She rolled toward the edge of the bed, swung her feet to the floor, and realized that she was naked. She fumbled on the floor for her gown and pulled it over her head.

"Celia?" Ross put his hand on her shoulder, tried to turn her to face him. "What's the matter?" he asked again.

"Oh, Ross! How could we have done such a thing? And with Jennie right in the next room!"

He scooted across the bed and sat beside her, one arm around her shoulders. "Celia, it's okay." He turned her face toward his and brushed the tears from her cheeks. "No harm done; we were quiet."

"It doesn't matter. We had no right to—"

"We had every right. And you might as well get used to it; it's going to happen pretty often from now on."

295

His casual assumption shocked her. "No, it isn't. It mustn't. Ross, it's bad enough we got carried away once. That was as much my doing as yours. But it isn't going to happen again, because we absolutely are not going to have an affair, or even a repeat performance, so you might as well—"

She cringed as he burst into sudden laughter. "Hush! You'll wake Jennie. And just what do you find so damned funny?"

"You. My sweet, beautiful Celia. I don't want to have an affair, either. I'm asking you to be my wife, not my mistress."

Of all the things he could have said, that was the one she least expected. He grinned and trailed one finger from the tip of her chin along her jaw and down the side of her throat while she goggled at him.

She jerked away as he reached her breast and cupped it gently. "Your wife! Oh, Ross, that's sweet, but you don't have to ask me to marry you just because we—"

"I'm not."

"Or just because Jennie is so determined for us to be a family. I mean, someday Jennie's going to grow up and not need us anymore. What happens to us then?"

"Great grandchildren," he said promptly.

"But what happened between us last night had nothing whatsoever to do with Jennie."

"No," she admitted. "That happened because we've both been lonely, and . . . and . . ." She couldn't think of a delicate way to say it.

Ross wasn't concerned with delicacy. "And horny?" he suggested with a grin.

Despite her agitation, she had to laugh. "That's one way to put it." Then she sobered. "Truly, Ross, I don't regret what happened last night for an instant, but I'm sure you don't want to get involved in that kind of relationship in Jennie's presence any more than I do."

She drew in a deep breath and let it out in a slow sigh. "And as for marriage, maybe we can consider it someday, when we know each other better and can be sure it's what *we* want, and not just something to please Jennie. For now, it just isn't very practical or reasonable."

He caught her chin in his hand and turned her face toward his. "Oh, Celia. Are you going to let 'practical' and 'reasonable' come between us? I suspect you've spent the last thirty-eight years being practical and reasonable, and what has it done for you?"

She pulled away from him and ducked her head, staring down at her hands clenched in her lap. He was right. Being practical had cost her the first love of her life. Being reasonable had cost her the child she'd wanted so badly.

As if reading her thoughts, Ross added, "We've both lost so much. Must we lose each other, too?"

She looked back up at him, studying his face in the rosy dawn light pouring through the window. She remembered telling him that she wasn't one to fret and stew for a long time over decisions.

She made a decision now as she thought of her yearly "retreat" and the years she'd spent grieving over the child she'd given away.

"You once said that the only choice you had was to wallow in misery or let yourself be happy."

He nodded. "I remember."

"I think," she said carefully, "that I've spent too many years wallowing in misery. But no more. It's time I chose to be happy. With you . . . with Jennie, and John. Not just a family, but . . ." She caught his face between her hands and kissed him in a way that left no doubt what she meant.

"So if you really want a lady who's prim and proper on the outside, but sexy as hell underneath, and who'll definitely respect you in the morning . . ."

He laughed and wrapped his arms around her, but before she surrendered to his renewed passion, she took time to offer up a brief but heartfelt prayer for all that they had both lost . . . and found.

Bermuda Quadrangle

by Garda Parker

"Pack your bags, sweetie, we're off to Bermuda!" Rose Greggs MacAfee burst through the glass doors of Complete Corporate Travel, Inc., and plopped two itineraries on her daughter's desk.

"Mother, please." Maureen Dixon, working after hours as usual, slowly drew her concentration away from the computer monitor, removed her gold wire-rimmed bifocals, rubbed her eyelids, and looked wearily up into her mother's sparkling blue eyes. "I've told you for the last month I can not go on a trip right now. I'm too busy, I—"

"—can't afford it, it's too soon after your divorce, and 'Mother you should be ashamed of yourself for going off on a vacation so soon after Father's death,'" Rose mimicked with good nature. "I know, I know. I've heard you say it all a million times."

With the grace of the dancer she'd once been, Rose lowered her tall, trim body into the burgundy leather chair opposite the desk. Maureen noted how perfectly her mother's ecru fitted linen suit skimmed over her slim waist and hips. Her legs were shapely and well defined, and the above-the-knee skirt over pale buff hose and matching pumps spoke of Rose's fashion sense. At seventy-two, her mother didn't look a day over fifty-five, while she, who'd just turned fifty, looked much older.

"You may have heard, but you haven't been listening," Maureen said. "It's the way I feel, Mother. And what would your friends say about your acting so free and easy, and Father dead barely seven months?"

"I may be free, but I'm not easy," Rose came back brightly. At Maureen's frown, she added, "My real friends would cheer me on. If you're talking about Norman's associates from MacAfee Miami Manufacturing who continue to think of him as the great company god, well, I don't care a rodent's patoot about what they think. They're not my friends, never were." She raked a set of fuchsia enameled fingernails like a comb through one side of her collar-length, perfectly cut and colored ash blond hair, setting one handcrafted silver hoop earring swinging.

"They've always treated you like a queen."

"Yes, while King Norman was alive. He did sign their paychecks, remember. I never wanted to be treated like a queen, simply like a normal, living, breathing woman. Now that he's no longer here, they've forgotten I exist. Which is just fine with me. I hated those silly luncheons with unidentifiable slabs of fish floating in unexplainable sauce and two sprigs of limp asparagus on the side, and weak iced tea. Too, too elegant. Too, too . . ."

"Don't use any of your old show business words," Maureen whispered, swiveling her head around the starkly modern office that was empty except for the two of them. She turned back to Rose. "You deserved to be treated with respect. Father was, after all, founder and chief executive officer of the company."

"And now he's not."

Rose settled back in the leather chair and intertwined her fingers. She regarded her daughter for a long moment. Maureen looked tired and burned out. She'd lost weight and

303

wore severe, plain-vanilla business suits that did nothing for her figure or her spirit. Rose longed to see natural color in her daughter's face again, longed to see her use soft makeup to enhance her gold-specked green eyes. She left her nails untouched and didn't do a thing with her dull and graying chestnut hair except pull it back tightly into a clip.

Classic case of depression, Rose believed. As much as she wanted to burst out of the confinement of her own passionless marriage now that her husband was dead, she wanted excitement to enter her daughter's life, wanted Maureen to make life *happen,* instead of just letting it pass her by.

"There was never another man like him," Maureen said hoarsely. "I wish there could be, at least for me."

Rose saw her daughter's eyes glisten with tears. "I know, dear. He adored you from the moment he first saw you. He couldn't have loved you more if you were his own flesh and blood."

The two fell silent for a moment remembering at the same time, perhaps, when Rose had first told Maureen that Norman MacAfee was not her biological father. She'd explained it as simply as she could, saying that she'd been an unwed pregnant young woman and Norman had proposed to her, knowing that. Norman had been sterile, and he'd been thrilled to be a part of Rose's pregnancy and Maureen's birth. He did, however, stop Rose from talking much about her vaudeville days.

"He was always very good to me," Maureen said at last.

"Yes, he was. And to me, also, in his way. You idolized him. And you married his carbon copy. I wasn't surprised, since those were the only young men he'd let you go out with."

"You liked them, too," Maureen argued.

"There wasn't anything to dislike. They were boring, that's all. Except one. Danny Lonergan. I adored him."

Rose remembered how with boisterous displays of wealth and power, Norman had done his best to scare Danny away. The oldest son of a poor Irish family, Danny was sensitive and loving and creative. Norman always said he'd 'never amount to the sod he's made of,' and pushed Maureen toward the wealthy boys he deemed more worthy of Norman MacAfee's daughter. Rose's argument with him had fallen on deaf ears.

"Remember how he loved taking you for walks along the beach just to feel the 'emotion of the ocean,' as he put it?"

"Mother, please." Maureen rubbed her forehead as a headache gripped her. She didn't need to be reminded of Danny Lonergan. A year hadn't passed since he'd left for college that she hadn't thought about him. She'd heard through friends that soon after she'd married Larry Dixon, Danny decided not to return to Miami to live. She had never understood that.

Danny had nicknamed her Lucky, but called her that only when they were alone. It started the day he'd come upon her in the dense brush along a deserted stretch of beach they'd been strolling. She'd ducked away because she had to relieve herself, and they were a long way from a bathroom. Just as she was pulling up her shorts he'd caught a glimpse of a birthmark on her left buttock, shaped like a four-leaf clover. Ever since that day, he called her Lucky. He was the only one who did, and it remained an intimate episode—the only one they'd ever shared—between them. She warmed just as much now as she recalled the incident as she had when he'd seen the birthmark and teased her.

"I'm sorry, I don't mean to upset you, dear," Rose said with love in her voice. "But I think you're stalled, Mo, stalled right where you've always been, in a sterile life, in a sterile office behind a desk doing a sterile job."

"Father always told me . . ."

"I know what he told you, and you were a dutiful daughter and did as you were told. You went to college, married a successful businessman, built a beautiful home in the suburbs, have a nice safe job as a corporate travel agent. You were a huge success in your father's eyes. The only things that have changed are that you're no longer married to Larry Dixon and Norman MacAfee is dead. Everything else has stayed the same. Maybe I've failed you as a mother. I should have insisted you seek out other things in life. Now I want to make that up to you." She leaned forward. "Maureen, darling, you must make some changes in your life. Start going out with men again. It's not healthy just to work and then lock yourself in your house every night."

"There are no men to go out with. And I suppose you think dragging me to Bermuda will be life-changing?" When her mother nodded and smiled, Maureen continued, "I like things just the way they are."

"Stagnant," Rose pronounced. "You feel safe, secure. And you're not doing anything, meeting anyone. That's why this cruise will be good for both of us."

"Cruise? I hate cruises. They're nothing but excuses to eat and drink and pick up men."

"How do you know? You've never been on one. Now, I've been over to Creative Cruises and Cynthia got us the last first class stateroom on their newest ship, *The Romance on the High Seas.* It's a special Mother's Day tour to Bermuda."

"Romance on the High Seas? That's a bit much."

"There's not enough romance on the high seas or anywhere else, if you ask me."

Maureen raised her eyes heavenward. "I'm not a mother."

"No, but I am, and I expect my daughter to spend a little time with me once in awhile. After all, at my age a little time may be all there is, and I want to live what's left of it before what's left of it isn't worth living."

Rose knew she'd just dumped a load of mother-guilt on her daughter's shoulders, but she wouldn't apologize. Sometimes a good dose of that was just what a kid needed to get her off her duff.

Rose stood up. "So, kid, grab your duffel, stuff in a bikini and a sexy evening dress, and don't forget your toothbrush."

"I wouldn't be caught dead in a bikini, Mother, and you know it. I'm too old." Maureen straightened the already-perfectly-straight stack of computer-printed itineraries on her desk.

"It's thinking like that that ages a woman. You could wear a bikini, or at least a stylish two-piece suit if you got up and exercised once in awhile. You sit entirely too much, and you don't eat properly." Rose felt the sting of the glare Maureen shot at her. Undaunted, she went on, "We leave Friday and we won't be back until the following Thursday, and those are non-refundable tickets. I intend to dance my ever-lovin' buns off, and knowing how much like Norman you are, you'll want to be there just to make sure I don't have too much fun or kick my heels too high. I'm not taking no for an answer. You're my daughter, and you're going to indulge me by going on a cruise with me for Mother's Day. Think of it as not having to buy me a card or send me flowers."

She turned on her expensive eelskin high heels, slung her matching bag over her shoulder, and pushed her willowy body through the glass doors, leaving Maureen holding two cruise itineraries, wondering what Rose had meant about Norman making sure she didn't have too much fun.

And nursing a headache that wouldn't quit.

"Feast your eyes on him!" Rose whispered loudly in Maureen's ear as they started up the gangway toward a uniformed official greeter. His perfectly-cut, jet-black hair and golden tan were sharply set off by a white, stiff-collared jacket that matched his dazzling smile. He turned to pick up something dropped by an elderly passenger, and his white pants stretched over muscular buttocks. "Buns to die for," Rose added.

"Mother, he can't be half your age," Maureen muttered.

The man turned and shook Rose's hand, flashing the smile Maureen knew he'd practiced enough to turn on and off like a light bulb. He took Rose's luggage and lent her his arm to assist her onto the ship. Maureen lifted her own carry-on bag and followed them. The man called an older steward over, and Maureen heard him give orders to "take good care of the lovely lady." Then he lifted Rose's hand and kissed the back of it.

"If I may be of further service, madame, simply inquire after Reuben Smythe. I shall appear at your side before you know it. I hope your cruise with us is all you hope it will be."

Maureen shook her head. This would not be a vacation for her; obviously, she'd have to be a chaperon. Her mother had suddenly become the biggest flirt in North America.

In their stateroom, tastefully furnished and complete with a bouquet of flowers and a bottle of good champagne chilling in a chrome bucket, their luggage had been delivered earlier and was waiting. Rose quickly unpacked her suitcases, arranging her things in one of the bureau drawers. Maureen sat down on the bed nearest the door. Along with the hum of power vibrating through her legs from the engine room, she also felt the dull threat of another headache.

"I wonder if I should have picked up some of those anti-seasickness patches I see so many people wearing," she thought out loud.

"Dulls your senses, I hear," Rose came back. "As many times as I crossed the Atlantic on the *Queen,* I never needed medication

311

no matter how choppy the seas became."

"I think I'd rather have dull senses than be seasick," Maureen said glumly.

Rose thought her daughter's senses had long been dulled by the way she'd lived her life up to now, but she wasn't about to bring that up again. "Let's go up on deck and watch the harbor slip away."

Maureen watched Rose change into a pair of flattering royal blue pleated silk shorts and matching tank top, and slip into a pair of red high-heeled leather sandals. She drew back her hair and secured it and in less than five minutes she looked like a classic cruise vacationer. Yet, Maureen noted, there was a unique softness about her style. As usual, she envied her mother's grace and polish. She wished she could at least *look* like her. She knew she didn't have the boundless energy it took to *be* like Rose.

By the time Maureen made it up on deck, the shoreline was already slipping away and the prow of the ship was pointed toward open water. She sniffed the salty air, then allowed herself a full deep breath. For a fleeting second she felt something else inside her expand along with her lungs. Seagulls flew along the deck, already squawking for handouts. Maureen wished for the briefest of moments that she was all alone somewhere on a beach. No. That would mean everything she'd been storing in the back of her mind would come rattling sharply to the front, and she'd be forced to really think about where she'd been in her life and where she was going, if anywhere.

Lining the rail were crowds of people dressed in the latest cruisewear. They sipped cocktails with heart-shaped stirrers jutting out of glasses that sported the word *Romance* emblazoned across the red and blue logo of the Majestic Line. When she found Rose, Maureen stood back a moment and watched her mother chatting with dozens of people, most of them men, in one of her most animated and charming performances. A trickle of jealousy pricked at her.

"Here's my daughter," Rose said brightly, motioning for Maureen to join the group.

"Hello," Maureen almost whispered as she moved nearer.

"Honey, I'd like you to meet some new friends." She slipped one arm around Maureen's waist, and with the other graceful bejeweled hand touched the arm of every person she introduced. "This is Victor, his wife Evelyn, Jared, Matt, Rich, Aaron, his wife Jody,

Bob, George, Mick, and Roy."

They all applauded when Rose finished the introductions, not missing a single name. Maureen nodded to each, and noticed how it appeared they'd all shopped at the same cruisewear store.

The short man named Roy stuck out his right hand. "And did Rose say your name was Honey?" A chuckle skittered through the group and the portly one named George elbowed Roy in the ribs.

"Maureen Dixon," she said, reluctantly grasping Roy's hand.

"Nice," Roy said, shifting his squinty gaze from her feet to her hair. "But I'll just call you Honey. I like the sound of it better, don't you?"

Maureen was in the midst of a speechless slow burn when Rose spoke up in a serious, yet good-natured tone. "No, Roy, she doesn't like that better. She much prefers her own name, but she's too polite to correct you. I'm her mother, so I will!"

After another laugh and a round of good-byes, Maureen and Rose stepped down the deck and entered a cocktail lounge.

"Now you know why I don't date. I can't abide men like that Roy," Maureen said, sipping Perrier from a tall frosted glass that sported a wedge of lime stuck to the heart-shaped stirrer. She and Rose sat on tall stools at the highly polished mahogany and mirror-backed bar.

"They're not all like him," Rose said gently, stirring a Bloody Maria—she preferred tequila to the usual vodka—with an identical speared lime wedge. "You have to be open to people first before you'll meet the right man."

"Is that what you're doing, opening yourself to new men?" Maureen glared at her mother.

Rose took a long and thoughtful sip, savoring the tequila, tomato juice, spices, and lime before answering. "As a matter of fact it is, dear."

"Mother!" Maureen turned on the barstool and stared at her.

"Yes, I'm your mother," Rose said softly. "But I'm also a woman, a *single* woman who wants to be with a man again, a man who's fun—and physical."

"You don't miss Father one bit, do you?" Maureen's accusing voice held a biting edge to it.

"I miss what he was when I first met him, but I missed that for more than half my married life. I don't miss what he became," she said quietly.

"Well, you couldn't expect Father to be . . . he was older . . . busy . . . he . . ."

". . . Wasn't a physical person after he became successful. Just because I haven't had that in almost five decades doesn't mean I haven't thought about it. I'm ready for romance again. I want a nice man in my life, I want to love and be loved. And I want a satisfying physical relationship, too. I'm sorry if that shocks you, dear."

By the time they'd finished their drinks, walked the promenade, and returned to their stateroom to change for dinner, Maureen's head was throbbing. She gulped a couple of headache tablets and lay back on the bed.

"I feel awful," she said, and flung her forearm over her head.

"You're probably experiencing withdrawal symptoms," Rose replied as she emerged from the bathroom with a washcloth rinsed in cold water. She folded it into a rectangle and placed it over Maureen's forehead. "And you haven't eaten much today. A good dinner should perk you up."

Maureen lay still, listening to the dull hum from the engine room as her mother freshened up in the bathroom. Rose sang a lilting old show tune. Maureen managed a weak smile—she did love the sound of Rose being happy. Why had she never had the capacity to brighten her own day the way her mother could?

"What are you going to wear?" Rose asked, emerging from the bathroom in a black satin bra and lace-waisted sheer black panty hose that showed merely a hint of a belly. "I'm wearing those dressy black shorts and black lace bodysuit."

Maureen rolled her head and took the washcloth away. "How do you ever go to the bathroom with that bodysuit on?"

"Carefully." Rose winked. "Feeling better?"

"I think so," Maureen answered. "Just very tired. I'm going to bed early tonight." She sat up and dropped her feet on the floor, then stood. "Ooo." She clamped a hand over her forehead.

"What's wrong?" Rose asked, stepping closer.

"I guess I sat up too quickly."

"You do need to eat. Let's go down to the Jolly Roger cocktail lounge and get some crackers or something. It won't be too long before we can go to the dining room."

"I suppose you're right. I'll go freshen up

and change into something suitable."

Rose grimaced at the *suit* part of the word. She hoped Maureen had packed a pretty cocktail dress. If she hadn't, that was the first thing she was going to purchase for her when they landed on Bermuda soil.

When Maureen and Rose stepped into the dark cocktail lounge, the Jolly Roger was already hopping with people in a party mood. Squat candles in amber glass hurricane lamps on the bar and tables sent up a flickering golden light over heavy netting hung from the ceiling. Anchors, replicas of ancient mastheads, harpoons, and ship instruments decorated the walls. Raucous laughter cut through upbeat music performed by a quintet of musicians in nautical dress seated on a raised platform at the end of the bar.

Maureen's out-of-date, full-skirted outfit didn't stand out in the over-dressed crowd. They were already a little the less keen-eyed for the cocktails than they would have been a few hours earlier.

It took a few moments for Rose's eyes to adjust to the darkness before she spotted a couple of empty stools at the bar. She grabbed

Maureen by the hand and made a beeline toward them. Three bartenders frantically mixed cocktails, shouting over the music and voices of the crowd. Two were tall, well-built young blond women in white shorts and cropped white sailor tops. The other was a smallish man. He wore a black and silver pirate's costume with an appropriate wide-brimmed black hat and eyepatch.

"Ahoy there, Long John Silver!" Rose shouted gaily. "How about a couple of grogs for me and me mate, here, to wet our whistles?" He ignored them and turned his back. Rose tried again. Still no response. Then she shouted, "There'll be two thirsty women on a dead man's chest if you don't yo-ho-ho over here with a bottle of rum!"

The pirate took his time turning around, then sidled over to them. "Stop shiverin' me timbers, ya' landlubbers," he groused, wiping the top of the bar with a white rag. "What'll it be for ye pair of impatient wenches?" He knitted his heavy black eyebrows and his long black moustache wiggled as if it had been drawn for an animated cartoon as he spoke.

"Don't be impudent, young—" Rose shouted over the din. She leaned closer to the pirate's face and scrutinized him through the flickering

319

lamp lights on the bar. Maureen placed a re-
straining hand on her arm, but Rose didn't
back down. "Excuse me, *not* so young man,"
she finished.

"No need to use yer barbs," the pirate
grunted, leaning into Rose's face. "Yer hooks
are sharp enough."

He stared hard at Rose. She stared even
harder at him. Suddenly she reached out and,
in a flash, ripped off his fake mustache and
held it dangling over the bar.

"Yow!" The pirate screeched in pain and
stepped back against the row of bottles, the
fingers of both hands plastered against the
newly naked space between his nose and upper
lip.

"Mother!" Maureen's mouth dropped open
in shock, and she clamped a hand over it.

"Buddy?" Rose asked tentatively.

"Rosie?" the pirate returned.

"Buddy Beers?"

"Rosie Greggs?"

The pirate swiped the big black hat off his
head and smoothed a long side chunk of his
thin gray hair over a bald spot. He grinned so
widely his black eyepatch shifted up and stuck
at an angle over his fake eyebrow.

"Buddy Beers, you old son of a—!" Rose

320

leaned over the bar and threw her arms around his neck.

Buddy clasped her around the back, and Maureen was positive he would have dragged Rose over the bar if she hadn't grabbed her mother's waist. Buddy leaned back and stared at Rose, and there were tears glistening in his small eyes.

"My God, Rosie, is it really you?" When she nodded her response, tears in her eyes as well, Buddy said, "Look at you. You're all grown up. Boy, have you grown up!"

"Try as we may to avoid it, it's bound to happen to the best of us. I want you to meet my grown-up daughter, Maureen Dixon. Honey, this is Buddy Beers, man of a hundred faces, and personalities to match! Buddy and I used to travel the vaudeville circuit together." Warmly, Rose scrutinized the pirate's face as if she couldn't believe he existed after almost a lifetime had passed.

Buddy thrust out his pudgy hand to Maureen who nodded and took it. He smiled into her face. "Ah Rosie, she's pretty as you, like seeing you all over again forty, no," his eyes went heavenward as he mentally added the years, "almost *fifty-one* years ago. It's a great honor to meet you, Miss Maureen. Your mother was . . . is a very special lady."

"Thank you, Mister . . . Beers, is it?" Maureen thought the name appropriate for a bartender. "It's a pleasure to meet one of Mother's old friends."

"I'm not as old as you think," he laughed, "at least not in mind. Just call me Buddy." He turned to Rose. "Rosie. My God, it's really you." Suddenly he leaped up onto the barman's stool. "Hey, everybody!" he shouted. "Listen up! We got a celebrity in the place!"

"Buddy!" Rose said, grabbing his pantleg, but she could not stop him nor keep from laughing herself.

The band stopped playing and the din died a little. Buddy waved his hands. "Right here in front of me is a little lady I'm proud to say I spent some of the best years of my life with on the vaudeville circuit. We slept in the worst places . . ."

"Buddy!"

Buddy looked down from his lofty perch, as several among the gathering laughed. He scanned the crowd. All eyes around the bar were fixed upon him. "Anyway, put down your glasses and put your hands together to welcome the best lookin', the best singin', the best high-falutin', high-kickin' showgirl in the

322

history of the Keith circuit. The one, the only, and the only one billed as . . . Miss Rosie Greggs and her Fabulous Legs!"

He motioned for Rose to stand up. She did and sent a jaunty wave to the crowd as many of them applauded. Rose knew they'd never heard of her, but she also knew that in a crowd of revelers almost everybody got caught up in the spirit of anyone who cheered them on.

Rose's stomach clutched. Some things hadn't changed in over fifty years. Buddy Beers still had the power to tug at her heartstrings and make her hear music like no one ever could. The memory of one night in particular flashed into her mind. She forced it away, something she'd become almost good at over the years.

"Show 'em your stuff, Rosie girl!" Buddy commanded, extending his arms in her direction.

Rose sucked in a deep breath. "Only if you'll be my partner like in the old days," she came back, caught up as she once was in the spirit that moved Buddy.

"With pleasure!" Buddy plopped both hands on the bar and hoisted his body over it. He dropped down in front of Rose and gave her a big kiss. "Didn't think I could do that anymore, did you?" he whispered, a big grin plastered on his face.

He could still do it, all right, Rose thought. "Do what, you big ape?"

"Leap over the bar, of course," he whispered back. He signaled the band. "Could I have a drum roll, please?"

The drummer complied. Rose flung out her arms and backed toward the band. The crowd gave way to her as the drum rolled louder. Rose turned toward it, gave a mighty kick of one long leg over her head and connected her red high-heeled shoe with the brass cymbals, then did the same with the other leg. Through the tinny clang of the rattling cymbals, applause burst around her.

Rose signaled the drummer to set another roll. She snapped her arms overhead, made a small leap, and cart-wheeled to land in a leg-split right into Buddy's open arms.

Applause, whistles, shouts surrounded the laughing performers. Rose breathed hard and laughed uproariously. Buddy let her down and kissed her again. The elastic fell from the back of her head, and Rose shook her head to loosen her hair. As it tumbled around her shoulders, the intervening years since she'd last been on the stage with Buddy tumbled around her, too. Her heart pounded with excitement. She hadn't felt this good in a month of Sundays.

And then she saw her daughter's face.

Buddy waved his arms and shouted again. "The fabulous Rosie has brought her little girl with her tonight. Everybody, welcome Maureen, too!"

Again a wave of applause went up with a chorus of "Maureen!" Rose watched her daughter's face turn ashen.

Maureen tried to imagine what her father would have done in this situation.

"You okay, hon?" Rose patted Maureen's arm.

Maureen breathed deeply. "Fine," she lied. Her headache had taken hold like a vise grip. She wanted to crouch down, slip through the legs of the crowd, and slink back to their room.

"We're just having some fun, that's all. I hope I didn't embarrass you."

Gingerly Maureen lowered herself from the barstool. "No, no. I'm just tired. Actually, I think I'll just head back to the room for awhile."

"I'll go with you," Rose said, picking up her bag.

"No, no. You stay here. I'll meet you in the dining room later."

"You feelin' a bit on the scurvy side, Maureen?" Buddy asked.

"Just tired," Maureen said wanly.

"Why don't you stop off at ship's hospital on your way back?" he suggested. "You may be on the verge of the green-around-the-gills syndrome. They'll give you something to stop it if you've caught it in time." Buddy pointed out the door. "Go down the stairwell to the right, then all the way to the end of that corridor. There's signs. They'll make you feel better, dearie."

"Thanks. I'll see you later, Mother."

Rose kissed her on the cheek, then walked through the crowd with her to the open door. "I'll see you for dinner, honey. Around eight-thirty?"

Maureen nodded and started toward the stairwell.

"One of the doctors will be right with you, Ms. Dixon," said a gray-haired woman in a white nurse's uniform so crisp it looked like cardboard. When she entered, Maureen had noted the plastic name badge pinned to a pocket over the woman's imposing breasts, *Stella Lawton, Aide,* and thought it curious that a woman obviously somewhere around sixty was working at that level.

Face down on a table in a tiny medical examining room, Maureen nodded her head against the starched white pillow case. The ship's hospital sounded busy. Voices were everywhere, accompanied by steady zips of curtains opening and closing on metal rings.

Aide Lawton had taken Maureen's vital statistics, checked her blood pressure, ears, and temperature, listened to her heart and lungs.

"Yep, you're getting it, I'm afraid," she'd said. "Sometimes we can catch it before it grabs too tight a hold. You should have tried some Dramamine or a patch before coming aboard, I think. Do you always get motion sickness on cruises?"

"I've never been on a cruise until today," Maureen had told her. "And I never will again," she'd muttered while Stella Lawton made some notations on a sheet of paper.

"Take off your dress and lower underthings," Lawton had instructed. "The doctor will want to give you a shot."

"Wonderful," Maureen had groaned.

Lying flat now, letting her heavy eyelids

327

close and giving in to fatigue felt like heaven. Why was it she felt fine, just tired, when she was flat on her back or stomach? As soon as she stood up the world started spinning in slow motion.

The curtain to the examination room snapped quickly aside and two people came in. Lawton was in front, followed by a man Maureen assumed was the doctor. She opened her eyes briefly, but couldn't see anything but Lawton's jutting chest armored in starched white cotton. Her eyelids lowered again.

The doctor must have been reading over the notes Nurse Lawton had taken, for Maureen heard him saying "Mm-hm, mm-hm," in a low voice. "Well, it looks as if we'll have to give you a shot. I hope it helps. It will probably make you feel drowsy." His voice was deep, almost hypnotic.

Maureen nodded, not caring whether she would get a shot or not, and wondering how much drowsier she could possibly become. She heard them getting things, bottles or something, in preparation for the shot.

Lawton came over to the table. Maureen felt her rough cold hand as Lawton lifted the sheet off her naked backside and rubbed her left flank with cotton dipped in alcohol. "Isn't that cute?" she said, and Maureen vaguely knew she was referring to her clover-leaf birthmark.

Then she felt a different hand on her flank. This one was warm, a man's hand. Though it had been a long time since a man had touched her, in her haze she was surprised she was able to recognize it. He moved the sheet and poised the needle against her skin. The needle went in and came out in a flash, but the doctor's hand stayed a moment, then jerked away quickly.

"Lucky?"

Maureen's heavy eyelids flew open like a window shade that had snapped to the top.

The doctor quickly yanked the sheet over her backside. She saw the back of him, tall and broad-shouldered under a white coat, wavy salt-and-pepper hair. He picked up the sheet of paper with her vitals on it, and turned around slowly.

"Maureen Dixon," he read in a tight low voice. "Maureen *MacAfee* Dixon? From Miami?"

Maureen clamped her eyes shut. *Danny Lonergan?* Could it be? Her stomach flipped and a wave of dizziness gushed over her.

"Lucky? Is it you?" he asked with insistence.

Danny Lonergan! Oh God! Maureen's stomach did another flip. Danny Lonergan had just seen her bare behind for the second time. He'd even stuck a needle in it this time. Maureen reached over her shoulder and grabbed the top of the sheet, dragging it over her head.

"If you're Danny Lonergan," she mumbled into the pillow, her eyes still clamped shut, "this time I hope you're a doctor."

"Lucky! It *is* you!" Doctor Daniel Lonergan stepped closer to the table.

"Interesting," said Stella Lawton, standing near the opening, her hand on the examination room curtain, "you recognized this woman by just looking at her . . ."

"Thank you, Stella," Danny said with efficient detachment, ushering her out and closing the curtain. He turned back toward Maureen and placed a hand on the middle of her back. "Lucky? Can you sit up now?" he asked gently.

Maureen felt every finger of his hand through the sheet. Their warmth made an imprint onto the middle of her back.

Maureen stirred and rolled to her side,

clutching the sheet around her. "Okay," she said weakly. She pushed up with the elbow crooked beneath her. He took her other arm and assisted her to a sitting position with her legs dangling over the side. He searched her face, and then smiled.

"Lucky! God, I can't believe it! It *is* you! I haven't seen you since . . . the summer before I left for college. How long has it been?" He looked at his hands as if to tick off the years on each finger. "Let's see, that's . . ."

". . . a long time ago," Maureen finished for him.

Her head swam, but she tried to steady her gaze on his face. It was Danny Lonergan, all right. His baby-faced cuteness that had made all the girls in high school practically weak with adoration had become a chiseled handsomeness that would make them all swoon if they saw him now, Maureen decided.

"Danny," she breathed, noting his long white lab coat swinging open over a sea green polo shirt and light blue jeans. "Mother and I were talking about you recently."

He broke into a charming grin. "Really? Well, that's good news. How is your gorgeous mother?"

Maureen winced inwardly. Even Danny had

thought her mother gorgeous. The only thing he remembered about her was a clover-leaf-shaped birthmark.

"Mother's fine. She's here. I'm supposed to meet her for dinner at eight-thirty. That is, if I can stand. She'll be thrilled to find out you're a doctor. She . . . she always liked you." Maureen gripped her head as another headache assaulted her.

"And I always liked her," Danny said. His voice hung in the air as if he were about to add something more. "But she'd be disappointed that I'm not doing my job with her only child. Here, let me have a look to see that you're not sick with something more than just seasickness."

"*Just* seasickness," Maureen groaned.

"Ghastly, but curable."

He came nearer, and Maureen caught the scent of a light masculine cologne mixed with antiseptic and laundry bleach. He reached out and, with the fingers of both hands, felt the glands under either side of her jaws. Then he came even closer and peered into her eyes with a tiny light. He picked up a tongue depressor and lifted her chin with his other hand. Nervously she opened her mouth and said "Ah." Her head swam, and this time she couldn't be

332

certain if it was from the pounding headache, the motion of the ship, or the fact that Danny Lonergan's warm palm was cupping her chin.

"It's just seasickness," Doctor Daniel Lonergan said again.

"Just seasickness," Maureen echoed, but wasn't certain she believed either one of them.

In the dining room, a white-jacketed waiter with jet-black hair and a Spanish accent seated Rose near a window. She gazed out over the rolling, dark-green ocean as the setting sun sent a tiara of burnt orange and deep mauve spikes over the horizon against a darkening blue-gray sky. Around the large, high-ceilinged room, tables were set with deep pink and white linens, gold-rimmed white china, gold flatware, and two gold-rimmed crystal goblets at each setting. Each table was centered with a clear crystal pine tree lit from underneath to give off a rosy glow reflected from the linens.

String music served as accompaniment to the chatter of diners already seated as others entered. Waiters descended like a flock of butterflies to fill water glasses, bring buckets of chilling wine, and present trays of interesting crackers and breads, at the ends of which were perched swans of perfectly-sculpted butter.

Rose rested the point of her chin over the back of one hand, and leaned on her elbow toward the window. She'd made the reservations for this cruise on the spur of the moment, hoping moments later that she hadn't made a mistake. Her spontaneous show in the Jolly Roger Lounge had given her the thrill of fond memories, but she'd shocked her daughter, she knew that. At first she'd been glad she'd had that effect on Maureen. Now she wondered if she should have declined Buddy's offer to show off her stuff. Maureen was still so sensitive about Norman's death.

Rose made her wine selection; after a waiter poured it for her, she gazed out across the gathering darkness. She was sick to death of respecting Norman MacAfee's memory, if the truth were known. Might as well admit it once and for all. She'd acted spontaneously and adventurously before her marriage to him and, since his death, that old spirit seemed to rekindle of its own accord. She knew she'd pay for her antics at the Jolly Roger tomorrow with every bone and muscle in her seventy-two-year-old body. But if she died then, she'd be happy knowing she'd been to heaven with the thrill of performing in front of an audience again.

And seeing Buddy again.

"Is this a capacity party, or can you fit in one more?" a masculine voice said behind her.

Rose turned her head quickly. A tall, trim man with an engaging smile cocked his head and looked down at her. "I'd know the magnificent Rose MacAfee from Miami no matter how long it's been since I've seen her. You haven't changed a bit."

Rose cocked her head and smiled. He walked around and stood in front of her and she scrutinized his face, lingering on his dark blue eyes. "I wish I could say the same thing, but I'm extremely sorry I can't," she said warmly. "A gentleman would be of more assistance to a lady and not leave her struggling with a less-than-acute memory."

"It's the Irish kid who used to hang out by your back door."

A smile of recognition broke over Rose's face. She pushed out her chair and stood up quickly. "Danny? Danny Lonergan?"

He threw his arms around her and lifted her off the floor. "Mrs. MacAfee! Yes, but it's *Doctor* Daniel Lonergan now." He set Rose back on her feet.

"A doctor!" Rose beamed, remembering her husband's prophecy about the young Lonergan. "You look wonderful! I can't believe it's really you. Please join me. You'll make my party almost complete." She motioned to the chair opposite her and the two sat down.

Daniel reached across the table and took Rose's hands in his own and gazed into her eyes. "Mrs. MacAfee. It's great to see you, and to see you're still gorgeous as ever."

"And you still have that Irish blarney young man. Call me Rose, please." She looked anxiously toward the dining room door.

"Are you expecting a dashing date?" Daniel whispered, a tease in his voice. "Don't let me cramp your style." Then his expression sobered. "I heard Mr. MacAfee passed away. I'm sorry."

"Thank you, Danny. It's been almost a year. I'm starting to have some fun again, and don't I wish I had a dashing date!" She offered him wine, which he accepted. "I'm waiting for Maureen. You remember my daughter, don't you?"

Rose caught the look that crossed his features and knew she'd struck a sensitive chord. The notion pleased her.

"Yes, indeed, I remember Maureen. In fact, I saw her this afternoon. In ship's hospital."

"Doesn't she look wonderful?" Rose asked with a hopeful note. "Well, she would look wonderful, but I'm afraid she's seasick. She's never been on a cruise, and I think I should have pushed her to get something as a prevention beforehand." She took a sip of wine to give herself time to ask a most personal and devious question. "Are you the doctor on this love boat, or are you vacationing with your . . . wife?"

Daniel sipped his wine. "Yes, I'm the doctor on this love boat, as you call it. It's my work, for now."

He didn't mention a wife, or the lack of one, so Rose pressed further than she knew Maureen would approve of. "Did you also hear that Maureen is divorced?"

He set down his wine glass. "No, I hadn't heard that. I'm sorry."

"No need to be," Rose said quickly. "It should have been over long ago. In fact, it never should have happened in the first place. There have been a lot of changes."

Daniel gazed straight into Rose's eyes. "I see some things haven't changed a bit. The outspoken and direct Rose MacAfee is still as outspoken and direct as ever." He chuckled. "I always liked that about you."

"Thank you, Danny." Rose reached over and squeezed his hand. "So, tell me, what about you? What are the changes in your life? Do you have a family?"

"No, I haven't. I was never that fortunate." Rose plunged directly in once more. "Are you married?"

"I was once. It didn't last. A few years ago I lived with a very nice woman, but that didn't last either. I guess I'm just not cut out for settling down and staying in one place. I've moved around a lot, and I've been on cruise ships for about twenty years. I have friends all over the world. This life suits me fine." He took a swallow of wine. "And I suppose that makes me sound shallow, doesn't it? This isn't exactly brain surgery."

Rose smiled. "Not at all. I'm sure you have to be prepared for any emergency, given that cruises are either filled with people my age, or hardcore party-goers aging themselves by the glass. It makes you sound as if you know what you want and need in your life."

Daniel smiled. "I wouldn't go that far. Let's just say I don't mind what I've got."

"I used to feel that way, too," Rose said.

338

"When I was in vaudeville I thought I'd never want to leave. But I did it quickly, like ripping off a bandage. Fast, so the pain only lasted a few minutes. Then Maureen arrived, and that made it all worthwhile."

He smiled into her eyes. "Did you ever feel you were missing something? I mean, by making a snap decision to leave something you loved doing?"

Rose gazed out into the darkness that joined the sky and the sea. "There were extenuating circumstances."

Daniel followed her gaze. "There always are."

"Did you?" Rose drew her focus back to his face. "Feel you were missing something, I mean?"

"Still do."

"What do you think it is?"

"If I knew, I'd go looking for it!" he laughed. "It's been so long, I don't know if I'd recognize it if I saw it anyway, whatever it is. You?"

"I recognized it."

Daniel's gaze was fixed on Rose's face. She shifted uncomfortably in her chair, and checked her watch.

"Maureen's late for dinner. It's almost nine.

339

I hope she's all right. I'm starving."

Daniel tapped his forehead with two fingers. "I should have said something. I had a nurse's aide take Maureen back to your room. I gave her a shot, so she's probably conked out for the night."

"I'm sure that's for the better. I hope she'll feel stronger tomorrow so she can enjoy this vacation. She didn't want to come, and now I suppose this is what I get for forcing her."

"You couldn't know. Seasickness happens to some and not to others. But, if you don't mind a change in dinner companions, I'd be thrilled to stay if you'd like."

Rose opened the menu, then lifted her wine glass and clinked it against Daniel's. "I thought you'd never ask!"

Gingerly, Maureen walked along the corridor toward the dining room. She wasn't one bit hungry, but she didn't want to let her mother down by leaving her to dine alone on their first night out.

As she walked she kept one hand on the wall, balancing each step, trying to avoid fixing her gaze too closely on the dizzying pattern in the gold and green Oriental carpeting.

340

She was wearing her purple flowered dress, and even the swishing movement of the full skirt added to her wooziness.

At the entrance to the dining room she stopped and slowly let her eyes skim over the diners and spotted her mother at a table near the window. A waiter seemed engaged in animated conversation with Rose. That didn't surprise Maureen one bit. Slowly she advanced toward them. Her senses registered the movement of the ship through the water, and her temples pounded. Perhaps when she sat down, the internal churning would stop.

The waiter moved away and then Maureen saw him. Danny Lonergan was seated across from Rose, his face riveted to hers as she spoke. His hands reached across the table to clasp hers. He looked positively enraptured.

Maureen's stomach clutched and her temples pounded harder. She turned too quickly and lost her balance momentarily. A passing waiter caught her arm and she asked him to assist her to the doors.

Back in the corridor, Maureen leaned her forehead against the flocked wallpaper. She had wanted to be the one to surprise her mother with the news that Danny Lonergan was one of the ship's doctors. But Rose had already found him.

Maureen remembered what Rose had said as they'd embarked on this cruise—she wanted another man in her life for romance . . . and for physical love.

And Rose had said she'd always adored Danny Lonergan.

"Well, you're up before the chickens!" Buddy Beers called cheerfully, if hoarsely, to Maureen from a deck chair at the ship's swimming pool.

She stopped a moment, then advanced toward him. "Good morning, Mr. Beers." Maureen assessed his red and blue plaid shorts and green and white plaid open-necked shirt. "I suppose it *is* early. I . . . I thought a swim might be good for me, and I wanted to do it before the pool got too crowded."

"Siddown, take a load off, dearie. And no 'Mister Beers' stuff. Call me Buddy. Cuppa java?" A waiter arrived with a tray holding a coffeepot and one cup and saucer and set them on a low wooden table next to Buddy's chair. "Joey, would you bring another cup, please? Got me a lovely lady to share the morning."

"Oh, no, thank you, Mr. Beers . . . Buddy. I'll just sit over there on the other side, maybe go into the pool."

"How're you feeling?" Buddy said as if she hadn't spoken. "You're still looking anemic. Well, you'll get your sealegs soon. You know," he scratched his thinning wiry hair, "I know just the ticket that'll clear up your head fast. One of old Doctor Beers's toddies for the body. Joey? Where are . . . there you are. How about whipping up two Bloody Band-Aids and an order of garlic toast?"

"Another bad night, Buddy?" the youthful waiter asked.

"Not me, sonny boy, and you know too much! Now hop to, and respect your elders."

Joey made a mock scurry. Maureen noted in the back of her mind that his pants fit tight around his buttocks. Rose would have certainly critiqued them approvingly. And she would have been equally pleased that Maureen noticed the way Joey's pants fit. In fact, Maureen was pleased with herself for having checked him out.

She felt a little sheepish about sneaking out of the cabin so early while her mother slept soundly in the next bed. And she'd been fighting anger, or something, lying in bed until

343

after three in the morning waiting for Rose to come in. She'd pretended she was asleep so she wouldn't have to hear all the details about what a wonderful evening Rose had had with Danny Lonergan. Worse, she was arguing with herself about begrudging her mother an enjoyable time with a friend. Why should that bother her? Shouldn't she be glad her mother was having fun?

"Here, dearie." Buddy interrupted her thoughts and handed her a tall glass of tomato juice with a scallion sticking up like a mast, the ubiquitous *Romance* logo waving jerkily from a swizzle stick. "This'll put lead in your pencil and you'll sharpen up and have some fun. Here's lookin' at you, kid!" He clinked his glass against hers and took a long swig.

Maureen dropped down in the lounge chair next to him. "What is it?" She peered past the scallion into the red depths dotted with specks of black pepper as wafts of garlic mist floated up from the basket on the table.

"Love potion number thirty-two-and-a-half. Took me thirty-one-and-a-half tries to get it right. Go ahead. It won't bite. Wait, I take that back. It *will* bite and you won't mind a bit!" He opened the red napkin in the basket, broke off a chunk of garlic bread, tore that piece in two, and handed half to Maureen.

"Uh, no thanks." Maureen frowned. Garlic bread for breakfast? She sniffed the drink. She could smell Worcestershire and Tabasco sauce, more garlic, and some other spice that permeated the concoction. She sipped tentatively. The end of the scallion went up her nose and allowed the pepper easy access. She sneezed.

"Aha!" Buddy shouted, raising one finger overhead. "The first phase of the remedy at work!"

Maureen lowered the glass and rubbed her nose. "Sneezing is part of the remedy?"

"Best thing for what ails you. A sneeze is like an orgasm. You're blinded for the duration of it, it jolts your body right down to your big toes, and when it's all over you feel like you've just pulled your finger out of an electrical socket. Nothing's been invented yet can beat that." He chewed a chunk of bread and took a long slurp from his drink. "You're gonna start to have fun any minute now, in spite of how hard you're workin' to avoid it." He gave her a knowing glance.

Maureen felt her throat and face grow warm. "I'm not . . ."

345

"Are, too."

"You don't even know me. Oh, I suppose Mother has told you some long and boring stories. Right?"

"Wrong. I haven't seen Rose since last night in the Jolly Roger. Where is that gorgeous hunk of womanhood, anyway? I suppose she got snapped up by some rich tycoon and is locked up in a stateroom with him right now." His voice dropped to almost a whisper. "Just like in the old days."

Maureen caught a note of sadness, or wistfulness, or something in his scratchy morning voice. She took a larger sip of the drink. What was that spice? She chewed absently on the garlic bread. The taste added to the jolt that had already assaulted her taste buds. She took another bite and found her mind awakening with the warming sun.

"What do you mean 'like in the old days,' Buddy?"

Buddy drained his glass and started chewing on the scallion. "Nothing much."

The Bloody Band-Aid was tasting better by the minute. She dipped into the basket for a second chunk of bread. "Go ahead, tell me," she urged, nibbling and sipping. "I know Mother must have been a terrific dancer."

"Terrific doesn't begin to do her justice," Buddy replied with a swell of pride in his voice.

"Tell me about it, Buddy. What was she like? What were you like? What was the traveling like?" Suddenly Maureen was ravenously hungry and overwhelmingly thirsty and enormously curious. "Do you think Joey could whip us up more breakfast?"

"Quicker'n a minnow in a lake full of catfish! You better drink a glass of warm water between courses." He signaled Joey and placed another order of Band-Aids and garlic bread and a pitcher of warm water.

"So tell me," Maureen urged again. She shrugged out of her robe and settled back in the lounge chair.

"We met back east," Buddy began, "in a railroad station in Albany, New York. She never did tell me if she was coming or going, and I didn't ask. I said I was hopping a freight up to Utica to join a vaudeville troupe and she told me she was doing the same thing. No sense in wasting money on a Pullman when a freight would get you to the same place in the same amount of time, she said. I saw the logic in that, but I knew she was greener than an unripe apple and there'd be no-accounts everywhere just waiting to pick her off the tree. So I figured I'd just ride along . . . and let her ripen up a bit."

"You wanted to protect her, didn't you, Buddy?" Maureen asked, warming inside at his words. "Didn't you think about . . . well, picking her up, too?"

"Heck, no. I wouldn't have done anything to hurt her. She was so all-fired beautiful and innocent, I had to stay with her night and day to fend off the undesirables and rich guys."

"You were in love with her, weren't you?"

Buddy looked out over the calming sea. "Didn't know if I was afoot or horseback half the time when I was around her." He drew his gaze back to Maureen and she noticed with astonishment that his hazel eyes held gold flecks similar to her own. "Except when the stage door Johnnies would gather. Then I was sharp as a tack."

"Was she in love with you?"

"A second-rate bones player and magic act like me? Your mother was as far as the moon beyond me. I was pretty wild back then, anyway. Lots of ladies on both arms. I thought the party could go on forever. Rose said I was the best friend she ever had, said we'd be friends forever. That was enough for me.

348

Didn't know what I wanted . . . until it was too late."

Buddy turned away and continued. "She had millionaires courtin' her. I'll say most of 'em made fools of themselves steppin' over each other at the stage doors. But she was all peaches and cream to 'em, never favored one over the other. And I kept the others at arm's length. Don't know how MacAfee got by me."

Maureen reached out and touched his arm. "Did Mother know you loved her?"

"Well, I never said, if that's what you mean. But everybody else did. I mean, I might as well have been wearing flags with it written all over. I knew she was too good for me, and I didn't want to put her on the spot by declarin'. You know what I mean."

"I understand." She bit back a few tears for the wiry little man sitting next to her, a man she liked more and more by the minute.

Joey set down a tray of reinforcement Bloody Band-Aids and garlic bread and poured a tall glass of warm water for Maureen. Buddy motioned for her to drain the contents and laughed when she grimaced.

"Tell me about the rest of the performers," Maureen said, genuinely interested.

"We were a classy bunch of entertainers,"

349

Buddy said. "Maybe we didn't play the top theaters — the Palace, or the Hippodrome — but we gave every audience all we had every time, and they loved us. Especially 'Rosie Greggs and her Fabulous Legs.' Once we played in a honky-tonk out west. It was a tough place. Sometimes they paid attention and sometimes they didn't, 'specially when they were grabbin' the girls or spittin' on each other." Buddy's voice hushed. "Then your mother came out on stage."

Maureen took a long swig of the Band-Aid, took a bite out of another piece of garlic bread, and leaned closer.

"All those chewin', spittin' horse's patoots made a lot of off-color remarks. She walked right off the stage into the middle of 'em, hands on her hips, and looks 'em right in their bloodshot eyes. 'I know you all are about to settle right down and watch a lady do her stuff for your pleasure and enjoyment,' says she, sweet enough to pour on pancakes. She didn't move, but I could see the muscles twitchin' in her jaws. 'And it's customary,' she goes on, 'for gentlemen to remove their hats when in the presence of a lady. I'll thank you all to do that.' They laughed again, and Rosie ups and kicks the hat right offa the biggest loudmouth in the place. Then she spins around like some kinda whirling dervish and starts kicking off all the hats around her. The drummer caught up with her and slammed the cymbal every time she knocked one off. I was hopin' she'd miss and knock the blocks offa half those jokers, but she was too good for that, too precise. All of a sudden the bunch of hooters sits down like an earthquake had opened the floor under 'em. You could hear the thud all around the room. They sent up an applause that rocked the place. And your mother, the classiest dame I ever met in my whole life, does a curtsy and says nice as you please, 'Thank you . . . gentlemen. It does one's heart good to know when discerning people like yourselves appreciate fine art.' I tell you I never saw the like again until Marlene Dietrich did it in *Destry Rides Again*."

Maureen drained her glass. There was a last lingering taste of garlic, pepper, and . . . what was that spice? She leaned her head against the lounge and closed her eyes, growing languid in the warming sun.

"Thanks, Buddy, for telling me those wonderful stories."

"Aw, Rosie can tell 'em better than I can.

She remembers everything. At least she used to."

"She never told me very much about her life on the road. But then, Father disapproved of her talking about it."

"I knew MacAfee would snuff out her spirit." Buddy's head spun around toward her. "Oh, dearie, I'm sorry I said that. I forgot for a minute you were MacAfee's daughter. I always did have the biggest mouth."

Maureen sat up and swung her legs off the lounge toward him. "No need to apologize, Buddy."

He swung toward her then, and took her hands. "You're as nice as your mother. I wish you were my daughter." His face instantly ruddied with embarrassment. "I suppose that sounds funny to you, but I always hoped . . ." His eyes filled.

"That's the nicest compliment I've ever had. Thank you." She leaned over and kissed his cheek.

The sounds of laughter and chairs scraping over the wooden deck signaled the arrival of more people. Maureen checked her watch. The time had passed so quickly while Buddy was weaving his vaudeville yarns that she hadn't noticed how late it had gotten.

"I should be getting back. Mother's probably awake and wondering if I've checked myself into the ship's hospital." Her laughter stopped short as the vision of Danny Lonergan holding hands with Rose jumped into her mind.

She stood up, pulling her robe with her. No wave of dizziness engulfed her. "Hey! What's in that magic potion?"

Buddy inched himself off his lounge and stood up, adjusting his plaid shorts. "You really want to know?"

"Yes, I do. Tell me!"

"Okay, you asked for it. Vodka, tomato juice, Tabasco, Worcestershire, salt, lime juice, pepper, garlic, dill, a raw egg . . ."

Maureen swallowed hard at the mention of the egg. "But what's that other taste? A spice or something."

"Oh, that's cloves."

"Cloves?" Maureen cocked her head. "What do they do?"

"Nothing, but people wonder about them being in there so much it takes their minds off their ailment."

Maureen laughed. "Buddy, you're the best. I hope you'll be my friend, too."

"You got it, kiddo."

He opened his arms and Maureen stepped into them. They hugged warmly as he pulled her robe around her, and she couldn't have felt closer to him in that moment if she were indeed his daughter. She was stunned to realize she felt closer to Buddy Beers than she ever had to Norman MacAfee.

Rose awakened to the sound of a knock on the cabin door. Sleepily she pushed herself out of bed and went to answer it. Vaguely she noted Maureen wasn't in the bed next to her and thought it was she knocking, having forgotten her key.

"Breakfast, Mum," a white-suited waiter easily in his sixties said when she opened the door. He breezed in with a tray and set it on a small table below the porthole. "My name is Sidney. If you need anything, please ask for me personally, Mum."

Rose had forgotten she'd put in an order for tea and muffins to be brought to her room in the morning. Dancing with Danny Lonergan until the wee hours of the morning had distracted her from everything but having a good time.

"Thank you, Sidney. That's very nice of

you."

"My pleasure to serve such a lovely lady, may I say," Sidney gushed. "I hear you're a famous dancer. I hope you'll honor us with a performance one evening."

"You're a friend of Buddy Beers, aren't you, Sidney?"

"We're acquainted." Sidney smiled a wrinkled grin. "He said . . ."

"A word to the wise, Sidney. Don't believe everything you hear from the overly-active memory of Buddy Beers."

Sidney bowed and left the cabin, closing the door quietly behind him. Rose refreshed herself in the bathroom, then settled down at the table, drank the tea, and ate both buttered muffins.

Much as she liked crowds, Rose didn't like them first thing in the morning. She'd learned early in life to take breakfast alone. Before she'd run away from home, she'd found sneaking out for breakfast a way of avoiding an abusive father. During her days traveling the vaudeville circuit she was constantly surrounded by people. Breakfast alone gave her a little time to think about something other than rehearsals and traveling. Something like love. Or the lack of it.

The only one Rose had ever enjoyed having breakfast with was Buddy. She and Norman never had breakfast together. He was already up and gone by the time Rose got up, and that suited her just fine. Maureen, too, got used to having breakfast alone early, Rose remembered. She thought it would be good for her daughter to know what an important time of the day that was for examining your thoughts. That must be where Maureen was now, having breakfast alone.

Later, Rose strolled along the deck breathing in the refreshing salty air, listening to the gulls, and nodding greetings to joggers and other strollers.

She headed for the prow pool, looking forward to stretching out in the sun and getting into the latest romantic novel from the pen of her favorite author. At least this publisher knew that women her age were out participating in love and sex, some even actively looking for it, preferring romance and fun to a life of crocheting afghans.

After rounding the upper deck cocktail bar, she stopped short and drew in a sharp breath.

Several yards away from her, Buddy and Maureen were locked in an embrace, and he was pulling her robe up around her shoulders.

They pulled back, gazed into each other's eyes, and both were laughing.

Rose gasped. Maureen? And Buddy? Much as it distressed her, Rose had been certain Maureen found him to be a distasteful remnant of her mother's past. Clearly that wasn't so. Maureen appeared to have overcome the animosity she'd shown in the Jolly Roger Lounge the night before.

Rose's mind swam. She stepped around the other side of the cocktail bar as Maureen started to walk in her direction. What had Maureen said the night before? She wished she could find another man like Norman. That was it. Rose's mind worked. Maureen must have meant that if she could find another man like Norman she would begin to live again, begin to have fun.

But *Buddy?*

He's nothing like Norman MacAfee, Rose thought, nothing at all. Buddy was in show business. Norman was in big business. Buddy's a bartender. Norman was a bar frequenter. Buddy probably doesn't have a pot or a window to his name. Norman had owned a good many pots and a million windows to throw them through.

Well, she'd have a talk with him, and with

Maureen, too. If they got too close, a lot of hurt could result. Rose leaned against the door of the cocktail bar and closed her eyes. Think, she instructed herself, think before you shoot off your mouth where it might do the most damage.

Rose did think.

Buddy was probably making Maureen feel comfortable. Just the way she used to feel with Buddy. Buddy had cared about her no matter how many mistakes she made. He thought everything she did was wonderful, marvelous. He thought she was beautiful no matter how many late nights had made her look haggard and drawn in the morning. He watched out for her, protected her, provided an arena for her to be her best self in, gave her loyalty and support. All the things Maureen needed from Norman as a father, from Larry Dixon as a husband, and never had received.

Was she starting to receive them now? From Buddy?

Rose felt an ache low in her stomach. Maybe she should visit the ship's hospital and ask Doctor Lonergan to check it out. No. This was an ailment that was too old for any doctor to fix. But it couldn't hurt to seek a

358

second opinion.

Buddy was right about Maureen's sealegs. Following the healing ingredients in his Bloody Band-Aids, a refreshing shower, and change of clothes, she held onto her equilibrium quite well. She didn't need a follow-up visit to ship's hospital. She didn't *need* one, but she wanted one. After all, it would be another night and morning before the ship docked at Hamilton. What was that old saying? An ounce of prevention was worth a pound of cure? Or maybe a quart of Buddy's magic potion, and a ton of conversation with an old friend.

Maureen stepped into the hospital waiting area at the beginning of the corridor, and spotted Stella Lawton coming out of an exam room.

"Hello, Ms. — what was it? Lucky, right? You still seasick . . . or something?" Lawton's lopsided grin suggested a smugness Maureen decided to ignore.

"Maureen Dixon. I seem to be cured for now. But I wonder if I might speak to Doctor Lonergan. Is he available?"

"He's in with a patient right now, but I'll

check."

"Oh, don't disturb him. I can come back."

"I'd rather disturb him, thank you. He seems to be having entirely too much fun for a doctor on duty." Farther down the corridor she knocked on the wall outside of an examination room, slid the curtain back, and walked in.

Maureen heard a burst of laughter, male and . . . her mother's. She wasn't sure if she should leave right then, or go down the corridor and see if Rose was all right. Was she truly sick? Maureen stopped a moment. Most likely this was strictly a social visit for Rose. She never remembered her mother being sick a day in her life, at least not that she'd admitted to.

"Lucky?" Daniel's voice called, and he appeared seconds later in the corridor. "How are you? Are you feeling better?" He came quickly toward her.

He looked good—great, in fact. Tanned, trim, healthy. Maureen took a long look as he strode down the corridor. Seeing him now took her back to those carefree days when they'd walked along the beach.

"Yes," she managed at last, "I'm much better. I guess it was just the rushing to get ready to come on the cruise, and . . ."

"Come down here. Your mother's here."

"Is she sick?"

"Rose? Of course not. She could withstand being in a paper boat in a hurricane!" He took her arm and leaned close. "She worked her way past Lawton, so you know how good she is."

"Mo!" Rose said when Maureen entered the exam room. "There you are! I was worried when you weren't in the room this morning. Are you all right?" She was perched on the edge of an examination table, bare tanned legs dangling off the side.

"Better than all right," Maureen responded, showing none of her feelings of . . . jealousy. *She was feeling jealous.* God, how ridiculous. There was no reason for that. Rose was her mother, after all. And Danny, Daniel Lonergan was simply an old mutual friend. They had a right to have dinner together or go out together. Didn't they? "Buddy fixed me right up. We had breakfast together."

"Breakfast?" Daniel cocked his head. "Not one of Buddy's famous remedy breakfasts."

"Does he have more than one?"

"Don't ask!"

Rose watched the two. "Be careful of Buddy's remedies, honey. His cures have been known to be much worse than the ailments. And don't take everything he says as gospel. I think he has a selective memory, and he does exaggerate."

"Really? I didn't get that feeling at all. He seemed to know so many . . . details."

Rose frowned. What could Buddy have said? she wondered. How far did he go?

Daniel jumped in. "If you ladies don't have dates for the evening, I hope you'll both consider spending it with me. Dinner, dancing, whatever comes along. There's a great show in the Yellow Bird Room tonight. The disco's open, or Oldies Night in the Pink Cadillac Room. What do you say? Make me the most envied guy on the ship."

Maureen's pulse quickened. She was afraid to be in Daniel's company. No reason for it, she just was. Yet, she wanted to be. But she had nothing to wear, at least nothing like the bangles and beads she'd seen on the diners the night before. Besides, she'd better take it easy. She didn't want to feel seasick again. The best thing for her to do was stay in her room and read.

But that would mean Rose would probably go out with him again alone. That wasn't a good thing, was it?

"We'd love to!" Rose answered for both of them. "What'll we do first?"

"Mother, I think I'll just . . ."

"Great!" Daniel interrupted. "I'll meet you both in the Jolly Roger at seven, and we'll make our plans from there. Dress comfortably. We can't let loose if we're in restrictive clothing!"

Rose lowered herself off the table with Daniel's help.

"Are you feeling all right, Mother?" Maureen was truly concerned.

"I'm feeling terrific. Just a little creaky this morning. Must have slept in a bad position." She gave Daniel a conspiratorial look that said *Don't mention I'm a wreck because of my hijinks of last night*. "We'll be there with bells on, kid!" she called out as she took Maureen's arm and headed down the corridor.

Rose and Maureen spent an enjoyable day lunching, sunning, browsing the shops, talking. This was the closest the two had been in years, and the impact of their reactions was not lost on either of them. Maureen especially. She realized now how the dominating presence of Norman MacAfee in their lives had diluted the kind of exciting relationship she could have been sharing with Rose.

She wished that Rose had told her more about her biological father. She wondered how much she'd inherited from him in looks, or temperament. But she'd never found a way to ask Rose for more details, and she'd sensed her reluctance to offer them. Whether that had been in deference to Norman or not, she wasn't certain. But Norman was dead now.

She'd always wanted to let Rose know she admired her for taking care of her baby, not letting her go during a time when having a child out of wedlock wasn't looked upon favorably. It took guts, and Maureen knew her mother had those, in spades. Maybe now that they were taking their first vacation together she'd be able talk to her about everything.

In a British boutique Rose bought a stunning dusty coral linen sheath for Maureen, who tried strongly to refuse it. While she tried it on, and Rose saw what the color and cut of the dress did for her daughter, she purchased it on the spot. The above-the-knee length and wide vee neck was flattering to Maureen's skin and figure.

Maureen silently wondered what Daniel would say when he saw her.

Next, Rose ducked into a beauty salon,

Maureen in tow, on the pretext of having her already-perfect nails redone. An exotic-looking, dark-haired young man named Roberto, who sported a sapphire stud in one ear, overwhelmed Maureen and before she knew it he was shampooing her hair and talking about the simply fabulous ways she could wear it to frame her simply fabulous cheekbones and even more fabulous eyes. He couldn't wait to "get at" her, he said, and wanted to experiment with eyeshadows in the new coordinating colors. Might as well have her nails done as well, Rose urged, and said she'd be back later to pick her up.

Covered up to her neck in a black and gold vinyl cape, Maureen was trapped in Roberto's chair, powerless to resist his artistic enthusiasm.

Rose and Maureen arrived at the Jolly Roger several minutes before seven. They were beset almost immediately by men of varying ages who clustered around as if Rose were a queen bee and Maureen her princess. They flattered and charmed, insisting upon buying them drinks, which Maureen and Rose refused. Then the men regaled them with stories of their travels and namedropped incessantly.

Rose basked. Maureen blanched.

"What is this, the judging panel for Most Beautiful Mother and Daughter in the World?" Daniel exclaimed when he met them promptly at seven.

"Is it that obvious?" Rose laughed. She adjusted the portrait neckline of her teal green taffeta dress, and flipped out the tips of her hair. Her eyes shifted to the door at the end of the bar as if expecting someone to come through at any moment. She turned back to the men. "Sorry, boys, our Number One Gentleman is here. I'll catch up with you later."

Maureen smiled nervously, shifted on the stool, and crossed her legs. Rose was shining more than she ever remembered. As for herself, she couldn't believe Daniel had included her in his assessment of beauty.

Roberto had enhanced her complexion with translucent powder and a blended blush of his own concoction, adding a dusting of three shades of moss and gray eyeshadow. He'd lined her eyes with charcoal and put on three coats of black mascara. Before he was finished cutting and styling her hair into a soft cloud around her face he'd put a rinse in it that softened the gray and brought out burnished copper highlights. Before she left he handed her a tube of lipstick he called cedar, and a lipstick brush, giving explicit instructions on how to apply the color.

All that and the dusty coral sheath, buff silky hose and matching high-heeled sandals, a slim gold chain at her throat, and perfect gold hoops in her ears made her feel like someone other than the Mrs. Larry Dixon whose skin she'd been living in for so many years.

"Lucky MacAfee," Daniel whispered. "I thought I'd never see you again." His deep blue eyes locked with her green ones. "I always knew you'd grow up to be even more beautiful than you were when we were kids."

Maureen felt stunned, as much by her own transformation as by Daniel's reaction — as well as her own. It felt as if her clover-leaf birthmark were branding itself into the stool seat.

"Well, hel-lo, Honey." The man called Roy whom she'd met after they'd first arrived on the ship stepped up to the bar and draped one arm around the back of Maureen's stool and the other around Rose's. He leaned into Maureen's ear. "I'd say cruising agrees with you."

She felt the moistness of his breath through her hair and in her ear, and instinctively jerked away.

"What do you say we get out of this dead

place and find a little more excitement? All three of us." Roy tottered backward. Daniel grabbed his arm and started to move him away.

"Seems like you've had all the excitement you need for one day," came a voice from behind Daniel.

"Buddy!" Rose was genuinely relieved and pleased to see him. His awful brown plaid three-piece suit could have been a Superman outfit as far as she was concerned.

He touched Maureen's arm. "How ya' doin', Miss Maureen? You're lookin' shipshape."

Rose saw what she thought was an intimate look pass between the two. The palms of her hands grew moist.

Roy backed away, none too steadily.

"Rosie!" Buddy rushed over to her. "Hey doll, you look like a million bucks!"

"All green and wrinkly, I know that old thing," Rose came back, laughing.

"Did I say that?" Buddy chucked her under the chin.

"Where's your pirate get-up? Aren't you working tonight?"

"Nah. I was hoping, that is, if you haven't made any plans, that we might have dinner together."

Rose looked over at Maureen and Daniel. "Well, Doctor Lonergan has already . . ."

Maureen butted in. "Great! Come join us, Buddy. You'll make our party even livelier."

"Well, thanks. I'd really like to!" Buddy's wrinkled face pleated in a big grin. "That is, if the sawbones here doesn't mind."

"Not a bit," Daniel said. "We'll make it a foursome. Let's go before the hordes hit the dining rooms. "What do you think about the Crystal Cockatoo room, Buddy?"

"A bit upper crust, but I'll try to cope."

"Before you start coping," Rose said, sliding off the stool, "let's get a different tie for you. Those green flowers are screaming to get away from that brown plaid jacket, and I fear I'm the one who can't cope." She took Buddy's arm. "We'll see you in the Glass Parrot."

"Crystal Cockatoo," Daniel corrected.

"Exactly," Rose said, winked, and drew Buddy away.

Maureen watched them leave, seeing the adoration that lit Buddy's face like the beam from a lighthouse as he smiled at her mother. She turned back and looked up at Daniel; his gaze was fastened on the retreating couple.

Daniel laughed. "Your mother is fabulous, Maureen. She looks wonderful, she sounds wonderful, and she's so full of life. She makes everybody around her feel alive, almost electric."

And that was only the beginning of the flow of compliments he showered over Rose during dinner with Maureen. She had to swallow the pangs of jealousy that threatened to erupt. Yet, he seemed nervous somehow. What did he have to be nervous about? She was the one barely holding herself together!

She was startled then to discover that there was something going on between Daniel and herself, and she was becoming more and more aware of it. This wasn't the way they'd been more than thirty years ago—tentative, taking a long time to get to know each other and savoring the moments. Now it seemed, without voicing it, they were almost picking up where they'd been so rudely interrupted by Norman MacAfee's decision about who or what was appropriate for his daughter. Maureen felt she and Daniel were starting all over again from a more daunting yet somehow more comfortable place. It was a curiously delicious sensation, and she enjoyed everything about it.

Maureen allowed herself to experience what was happening inside her in the company of Daniel Lonergan for the first time since their last walk on the beach.

Rose and Buddy never did meet them in the Crystal Cockatoo.

"Your daughter is a real peach," Buddy said to Rose as she looped a plain beige tie around his neck. They were in his cramped and cluttered quarters, and she had been hard-pressed to find any clothing accessory that didn't have stripes, plaids, or flowers all over it.

"Isn't she, though?" Rose answered. "I'm glad she's finally relaxing a little. I was afraid she'd be sick or bored for the whole cruise."

"I think she'll be just fine. She's a beautiful girl. So interested in things, so inquisitive. Makes a body feel good just bein' in her presence."

And those were the first of many compliments Buddy showered on Maureen while at dinner in the Treasure Chest with Rose.

His choice of subject was of great concern to Rose. After two hours of listening to him talk mostly about Maureen, it was with uncustomary weariness that she excused herself to go back to her stateroom early. She felt like reading, or playing solitaire, or something. But she didn't feel like partying. Or worrying about whatever might be growing between her daughter and Buddy.

Early Sunday, Mother's Day, Rose and Maureen awoke at about the same time. After breakfast in a dining room that crackled with the passengers' excited anticipation of the day ahead, they went back to their stateroom to prepare to disembark at Hamilton and explore Bermuda.

On deck, Rose's ever-increasing corps of admirers gathered around her, each hoping for a few moments of her time during the day. Maureen spotted Buddy in the background watching the whole scenario. For once, he was wearing something understated—a pair of blue plaid shorts and a pale blue polo shirt. She noticed how knotty his legs looked, and she smiled with affection for the little man who worked at staving off aging with as much vigor as did Rose.

In a flash of clarity, Maureen wished her mother would end all the flirting and collecting of suitors and settle on Buddy. She surprised herself. Was she also ready to accept replacement for Norman in her mother's life? Or did she just want to be certain Rose was taken care of? That was silly. Her mother didn't need taking care of—did she? Maureen remembered Rose's words about needing to be cared for, needing to receive love, needing to give love. Buddy was someone who'd been giving her that, albeit from afar, for more than half a century.

Maureen made a pact with herself on the spot. Her mission was clear. She was going to get Rose together with Buddy before this vacation was over—no matter what it took.

She waved to Buddy and pushed her way through the crowd. "Do you have to work today?"

"Nope. Clubs on the ship are closed while we're in port."

"Great! Why don't you come keep us company on the island?"

"No, babe. You and your mother go along. Looks like you have plenty of company ready and waiting."

Maureen saw the longing in his eyes as he watched Rose, classy in her slim white capri trousers and coral silk camp shirt, a black nylon fanny pack strapped around her waist. She was surrounded by white-haired gentlemen and overweight tourists. "They're a boring bunch. You'd be a lot more fun. You probably know lots of neat places we wouldn't be aware of."

"I don't think your mother would like me tagging along."

"Then you be my date." She linked her arm through his. "Come on. What do you say?"

He looked into her eyes and a big grin swept over his face. "Okay. I've always been a sucker for a beautiful woman."

Maureen smiled back. "And I'm just learning I can be a sucker for a fabulous compliment."

Arm-in-arm they strolled past Rose and her entourage to watch the gangway being lowered and secured. Buddy's eyes caught Rose's for a moment, and the unanswered questions he'd been asking himself for the last fifty years hung heavily in his mind.

When Rose left him the note that said she was leaving show business and implored him not to try to find her, he'd gone around in a state of numbness for months. She'd given no reason, but he felt it was his fault somehow. She was sweet, and he was so sweet on her he didn't know if he was coming or going most of the time. He'd held himself in check for the few years they were on the road. Then he'd made that one mistake. He'd wanted to apologize, yet he didn't feel sorry they'd made love.

Later he felt like a heel, but by the time he'd finally screwed up the courage to talk with her about it and ask her to marry him, she'd already left. He never would have made her quit the business. The last thing he would have asked was that she give up the very thing that brought her the most happiness. She probably never would have married him anyway, but he'd never had a chance to find out. He was forced into a silence that drove him crazy for most of his life. When he'd learned later that she married that MacAfee peacock, the worst of the stage door Johnnies, he could hardly contain his frustration and disappointment.

He hadn't the courage to ask Rose what had happened a long time ago. He had an inkling, but he put it out of his mind. For now.

Rose smiled beguilingly around the crowd of couples and single men who gathered near her. She caught sight of Maureen and Buddy strolling by, laughing and talking. Maureen looked more alive than she had in years. Another wave of mixed emotions swept over Rose. She was glad Maureen seemed to be having fun in Buddy's company, but she wished she'd focus her attention on someone else. This kind of connection with Buddy was . . . inappropriate.

She spotted Danny Lonergan coming down the deck, tanned and healthy looking in thigh-length faded jean shorts and a white polo shirt. The wind rustled his hair. He swung his arms easily, like a man who was obviously enjoying the glorious sunny morning. On impulse, Rose pushed through the group to get to him.

"Good morning, handsome," she called brightly.

"Hello, gorgeous!" Daniel bent down and kissed her cheek. "I swear you grow more beautiful every day."

"Flirt!"

"I learned from watching the best," he retorted, hugging her.

"Are you on duty today?"

"No, but I'm on call."

"That means you can go sightseeing with me, then."

"I don't think so. Besides, what if I took you to some romantic spot and my beeper went off? I'd have to leave you stranded and speed away."

"Don't worry about me. I can take care of myself."

376

"True. A flock of passing male seagulls would probably swoop down and save you, just like that flock of birds over by the gangway," he teased, motioning to the group Rose had just left.

"You're the only seagull I want to be with today. I'll take the beeping if it comes. Come on. Give me a real tour of Bermuda, not the usual thing."

"I've never been able to refuse you. I'll call down to the hospital and see if Lawton will parole me for the day."

When Daniel finished his call, he returned to Rose's side and slipped an arm around her waist. Rose looked up at him with adoration in her eyes. They strolled toward a gangway, and he spotted Buddy and Lucky . . . he supposed by now he should be calling her Maureen. Buddy, as usual, was telling her some kind of story, for she was laughing at his words and gestures. For a moment, Daniel wished he and Buddy could change places. Not that he didn't love being with Rose, but since the moment he'd seen Lucky's clover-leaf birthmark, his longing to be with her had escalated to the point where he didn't know a moment that hadn't included a thought of her.

Lucky looked wonderful with her hair blow-ing free in the wind, whipping beguilingly around her face. Her smile lit up her features. Her royal blue nylon fanny pack perched provocatively over one hip, and the pale blue cotton pants and white sleeveless blouse with the collar turned up under her hair made her look nineteen years old again, the way she had when they'd last strolled the beach together.

That was it! Now he knew what was missing from his life, what had been missing all along—the way he and Lucky had treasured their moments together. He hadn't had that feeling since. Other things always crept in, stealing his concentration from any of the women in his life. It wasn't their fault. It was his. He was always thinking of something else. Or was it *someone* else?

Rose watched Danny watching Maureen. She caught the look in his eyes and thought she saw loneliness, longing. She knew what she had to do. It was blindingly clear. She would get Maureen and Danny together before this cruise was over. It would be a challenge, with less than four days until they'd be back in Miami. Well, she'd accomplished a great many other things in less time. This would just be a new challenge, that's all. And if there was anything Rose Greggs MacAfee loved, it was a challenge.

The four caught up with each other on Front Street where Maureen was enthralled with the Bermuda shorts-clad policeman in a white helmet directing traffic from a human-size birdcage in the middle of the street. She thought his arm movements and commands as graceful as a dancer's, and somehow he waved a kind of magic over the four of them.

Daniel steered them to Asher's Cycle Livery where he picked out four mopeds.

"I don't know how to ride one of those," Maureen protested. "Can't we double up?"

"Not anymore. The law says one body to a bike. But don't worry. Cecil, here, will give you lessons." Daniel dropped his hand on the shoulder of a wiry little man with beefy arms and a chest-length scraggly beard.

"Roight, guv'ner," Cecil said with a gravelly voice. "Up you go now," he instructed all four to mount the bikes held stationary on stands.

They donned helmets and got up onto the bikes. Cecil walked around all four as they got the feel of the machines. "Brakes on the handlebars, that's it. Automatic shift. Now, then, stay to the left, use regulation hand signals,

379

mind the give way signs, don't look back, mind your speed, keep your shoes on, look right at the two-ways, lock up at the pubs, back before sundown, all injuries your problem. That'll do 'er. Any questions? Good. Have a nice day."

Rose was enjoying every second, but Maureen saw the terrified look on Buddy's face and knew his feelings mirrored her own. And then they were off. Maureen and Buddy did surprisingly well following Daniel and Rose through winding streets wide enough for only one car, past rows of quaint shops and restaurants, until they stopped at a unique aquarium-museum. Inside, they viewed a variety of marine life displayed in a natural reef setting, inspected treasures pulled up from sunken galleons, and watched the preening of flamingoes and other tropical birds.

Afterwards Daniel led them to an old fisherman's tavern perched on a rocky shoreline overlooking the crashing surf.

"Four ginger beers here," Daniel ordered as they scraped wooden chairs over the plank floor and sat down at a round dark wood table.

"I feel like I've been riding a horse," Rose said, rubbing her right buttock. "A very bony, narrow horse."

The ginger beer arrived and Daniel lifted his mug. "Let's toast to something. How about . . . a very special vacation?"

"Here, here!" Rose said, and took a swig.

"And to seeing old friends," Buddy said, clinking his mug to Rose's, "and meeting new ones," he added clinking with Maureen's.

"I'll drink to that," Daniel chimed in.

Maureen lifted her mug higher, caught up in the spirit of the moment. "And one more," she said quietly. "Happy Mother's Day to the most special mother in the world."

Rose's eyes filled. Buddy linked arms with Rose, forcing the two of them to drink like a bride and groom at their reception.

Daniel stared directly into Maureen's eyes. "You truly are lucky, Lucky," he said, and clinked her mug. "And very special yourself."

Rose reached out and took Maureen's free hand. "The most special daughter in the world. Thanks for coming with me."

"Enough of this bawling, now," Buddy said. "Let's eat!"

Over the mugs of ginger beer the four perused the menu. Turtle soup and turtle steak seemed to be the specials of the day. Maureen lifted her eyes and watched the other three studying the handwritten menu. They were an odd quad, she thought, smiling inside. Yet, there was a thread of energy running through them, connecting them. There was almost a feeling of family in a way that she never remembered feeling before or after her marriage.

"So, what'll it be, folks?" a blonde asked.

"Four orders of angels on horseneck for starters," Buddy said quickly.

"I'm not eating anything that's been on a horse's neck," Rose came back.

"Better place than it could be," Buddy countered.

"Wait, what is it?" Maureen asked.

"Oysters wrapped in bacon. Nothing too scary," Daniel answered.

"Let's do it!" Maureen chirped.

"You've never eaten an oyster in your life," Rose said. "What's come over you?"

"I don't know," Maureen answered, a hint of incredulity in her voice. She stole a glance at Daniel, who was gazing at her openly

"And four of those Bermuda Triangle specials," Buddy added.

"Where's that?" Maureen studied her menu and read the ingredients: Bermuda guinea chick lobsters, grouper fritters, and scallops.

"Inappropriate," Daniel announced. When

all three looked up at him, he said, "Add a bowl of conch chowder to each and make it what we are." They frowned and waited for his pronouncement. "The Bermuda Quadrangle."

With a groan the others gave in. The waitress raised her eyes heavenward, gathered up the menus, and placed the orders. They topped off the sumptuous repast with Bermuda bananas cooked in black rum.

Heading out again after lunch, the four followed Daniel over the world's smallest drawbridge, only eighteen inches wide, just enough to let a sailboat mast pass through. At the top of Gibb's Hill Lighthouse, they gazed toward every part of the island and far out to sea from this highest point on Bermuda.

"I thought you were pretty mean to drag us up here," a breathless Rose said to Daniel, "but now I'm glad you did. How many steps did we climb, anyway?"

"Just a hundred and eighty-five. I figured we all needed to work off that decadent lunch. Soon as you're ready, I want to show you my favorite part of Bermuda."

"After that I'll be ready to turn in the old nag I've been straddling all day," Buddy said. "I won't be able to walk for a week."

"I can't believe you're complaining," Daniel chided. "You never get tired!"

"I'm almost seventy-five years old, you young whippersnapper. I had to start getting tired sometime!"

Daniel next led the moped convoy toward the end of a causeway to Blue Hole Hill. He escorted them into the Blue Grotto, and told them that erosion by the tidal flow through limestone walls over thousands of years had formed the natural theater. Delicate mangrove trees shaded it, and the delightful Blue Grotto dolphins came out to entertain the appreciative audience.

Rose and Maureen applauded the dolphins' hula dancing, basketball games, and hoop jumping, then stepped up to shake fins with one of them and pat the sleek nose on its smiling face.

"I see why you love it here," Maureen said to Daniel as they watched Rose and Buddy communing with the dolphins.

"You'd love it here, too," he responded in a hushed tone.

Back on the mopeds they circled and rode along an abandoned railroad right-of-way that passed through woods and subtropical forests and bordered the boat-dotted Great Sound.

Lush and fragrant flowering plants, palmetto, and other trees in variegated greens decorated their ride, the path studded with oleander, poinciana, and spreading bougainvillea. At last they stopped on a pink sand beach just minutes off a main road, yet possessing a remoteness that made Maureen feel no one was around for hundreds of miles.

They strolled in separate directions. Rose came up behind Maureen and dropped down into the sand next to her. She sighed.

"This place is magic, Mother," Maureen said. "I'm glad you chose this trip, and I'm glad you made me come with you."

"I'm glad you're here with me. I'm having the time of my life."

"Me, too. I'm in love."

Rose sucked in a sharp breath. Could wishes come true that fast? She measured her words carefully. "Daniel always was a nice young man."

Maureen continued to gaze out over the sea. "I don't mean with Daniel . . . exactly."

Rose felt a heaviness in her chest. If Buddy was the object of Maureen's affections, she was going to be forced to tell a secret she'd locked up inside her for half a century, and then she could be risking everything in her relationship with her daughter. But she had no choice. She couldn't take the chance of something happening that would be disastrous.

"Maureen . . ."

"I'm in love, Mother, maybe for the first time in my life. I'm in love with this wonderful, beautiful place. I want to come back again and again. Or maybe . . ." her voice hushed, "I never want to leave. I feel more alive than I ever remember feeling. I'm in love with life. I guess that sounds corny, doesn't it?"

Rose stared at her daughter dumbfounded. She had the oddest feeling her pins had been knocked out from under her. This was good, wasn't it? At least Maureen hadn't said she was in love with Buddy.

"Hey, you two," Daniel called as he jogged barefoot down the sand toward them, Buddy managing to keep up. "Time we headed back and returned these bikes. Sun's starting to go down."

Buddy helped Rose to her feet. "I'm about to announce something no one has ever heard me say," she sighed. "I'm bushed, and I'm ready for one of those infamous rum swizzles I've heard so much about. Lead on, Doctor, to the healing waters of a nice relaxing pub."

When they'd returned the mopeds, Buddy headed for the nearest pub. Gallantly, he ordered Rose's rum swizzle before the rest followed him in. Maureen caught the glow in her mother's eyes when he presented it to her. When she asked what she could try, Daniel suggested an icy glass of Bermuda Gold, a liqueur made from loquat fruit, whatever that was. It had a lovely sweet taste and warmed her insides to meet the languor brought on by the nearness of Daniel — there was no ignoring that.

Over the jukebox came the strains of an old song from the fifties, "Bermuda Buggy Ride."

"How about it?" Daniel said, slipping his arm around the back of Maureen's chair.

"How about what?" she drawled, the Bermuda Gold affecting her nerves in a most relaxing manner.

"A Bermuda buggy ride?"

Rose picked up on it. "Great idea, but include me out. Maybe the tightwad here will treat me to dinner and get me back to the ship in one piece. I plan to turn in fairly early, for me."

"What? The indomitable Rosie Greggs admitting her dogs are barkin'?" Buddy leaned back, palms up in mock amazement.

"My dogs need pampering so they can live to bark tomorrow, wise guy," Rose came back good-naturedly, giving him a poke in the ribs. "You kids go ahead. Wake me in the morning, sweetie."

"See you tomorrow." Daniel waved to Rose and Buddy and escorted Maureen out of the pub.

"Oh-h," Maureen breathed as their buggy drew them along the harbor at sundown. "It almost feels as if we could hold out our hands and keep the sun from sinking into the sea."

"It's part of the magic of that liqueur you drank in the pub. Makes you see things through Bermuda Gold-colored glasses."

"It's more than that."

"Yes, it is."

Maureen fell silent. The rhythmic clop of horseshoes on pavement and the silver wash cast by the slowly rising moon stealing over the lush Bermuda scenery lulled Daniel into a romantic mood. But it was more than that and he knew it, although the atmosphere was pretty powerful. The fact that Lucky MacAfee lay in the crook of his arm was the real reason for his mood. He stole a glance to try to read hers, but all he could see was preoccupation.

The driver urged the horse along a narrow street. Feeling apprehensively brave, Daniel turned his head very slowly, leaned forward and kissed Maureen softly on the lips. He felt her bottom lip quiver slightly when he released her. He leaned back against the buggy seat and closed his eyes. He'd be damned if he'd apologize for something he'd wanted to do almost from the moment he'd laid eyes on her again in ship's hospital.

Maureen was barely breathing. Her head whirled with a vortex of emotion. Excitement, regret, wonder . . . then desire . . . need . . . anticipation. . . . fear. And questions, questions.

"Why did you kiss me?" she whispered.

"Because I wanted to, and because it felt nice."

"Was it . . . honestly me you wanted to kiss?"

Daniel made a show of looking around the small carriage. "I don't see anyone else here . . ."

"So if someone else *was* here, like . . ."

"You didn't let me finish. I was going to say I don't see anyone else here named Lucky

MacAfee, and it's Lucky MacAfee I wanted to kiss. There."

She fixed her eyes on the driver's back. "I'm Maureen Dixon. It's been a long, long time since I was Lucky MacAfee."

"You're still Lucky to me. And I want to kiss you again."

Maureen turned her face toward him. "And with all my heart I want to kiss you," she whispered.

He lowered his head and claimed her lips softly, fully, then more completely. With one hand he caressed the side of her face and wound his fingers in her hair. She was tentative, testing at first, then responded completely, her hand slipping up his arm over his shoulder.

"I wanted that even more," he murmured when their lips parted.

"Me, too," Maureen whispered, grateful for the darkness surrounding them.

All too soon, the driver and horse drew their buggy along Front Street to the Customs House Shed and came to a stop.

Arms around each others' waists, Maureen and Daniel strolled to Rum Runners Pub and climbed the stairs past a variety of marine artifacts lining the walls. They ordered crocks of

Bermuda onion soup, glasses of mineral water, and shared a special open grilled sandwich of ham, tomato, cheese, mushrooms, and onion called Load of Mischief. Against the sounds of two couples involved in a serious darts game, Daniel talked glowingly about Bermuda.

"Every time I come back here I think more and more about disembarking from the ship for the last time and living here." When Maureen's eyes grew brighter over the candle pot, he continued. "The pace is slower, the people friendly, and the Bermudian children are wonderful."

"You'd live here? You mean you'd give up practicing medicine?"

"Not at all. I could put my experience and talent to good use in a hospital or clinic. Every time I stop here I have the feeling I don't want to leave. It gets harder every time."

"I felt like that when we stopped on the beach today. It was a strange feeling that came over me."

For a long moment the two held a meaningful gaze, until Daniel broke into the moment and looked at his watch. "I hate to do this," he said, "but I have to get back on board. I've drawn the first shift early in the morning, and I'd better get some rest. We had a fairly strenuous day for someone of my advanced age," he said with a grin.

"I understand," Maureen replied. "It was a strenuous day for anyone of any age."

They paid the check and headed out and down the street to the ship dock. Maureen was ready to go off to bed, still dreamily engaged in the romance of her own Bermuda buggy ride and Daniel's kisses.

"Except for Rose and Buddy," Daniel said. "I suppose if we had enough energy to check, we'd find them dancing their legs off in a nightclub somewhere. Your mother is an amazing woman."

"Buddy's pretty amazing, too."

"I know." Daniel cocked his head. "Is there a problem between you and your mother that I may have aggravated somehow?"

Maureen stopped walking. "Do you . . . are you . . . attracted to my mother?"

"Of course I am. She's wonderful, fun, warm, beautiful, amazing . . ."

Maureen started walking, hands in the pockets of her trousers. She hurried up the gangway and down the corridor toward her stateroom.

"Wait a minute." Daniel came up quickly behind, caught her arm, and turned her to face him. "You don't think . . . is that what you meant when you asked if it was you I really wanted to kiss? You think I'm attracted to Rose romantically? Physically?" Maureen's silence told him volumes. "Lucky . . . I'm attracted to your mother for all the things I said, but not romantically." He gathered her into his arms with renewed strength and kissed her until her loss of breath made her go limp in his arms. "I hope that explains who else I think is beautiful, warm, fun, and all those things, and to whom I *am* attracted by the other two elements." Then he turned and headed back down the corridor.

Maureen watched until he disappeared around the corner. She stepped into the dark stateroom. Rose must be sleeping. She thought about waking her, but decided against it. Tomorrow would be another lovely day on Bermuda and she'd share thoughts about her new feelings with her mother then. In the bathroom, she changed into her nightgown, brushed her teeth, washed her face, and decided she was too keyed up to sleep and wanted her mother to wake up and talk to her, help her sort out the flood of new feelings that had come over her with Danny—they were beyond his youthful name now—*Daniel* this evening. She came out of the bathroom and snapped on the light.

Rose was not there. And her bed had not been slept in.

Maureen threw on a robe and left the room barefoot. Could something have happened to her mother? Rose was awfully tired when they'd left her and Buddy in the pub earlier. Maybe she was sick. She decided to go to the hospital and see if Rose was there.

Daniel was going over some reports when she ran into the hospital.

"Daniel! I'm so glad you're here. Is my mother all right?"

"I have no idea. I haven't seen her. Why?"

"She wasn't in the cabin, and she hasn't been. I thought maybe she got sick and she was here. She was very tired when we left them. You heard her. Where could she be?" Maureen ran a frantic hand through her hair.

"Now calm down. Don't worry. Buddy would take care of her. I told you we should have checked a nightclub."

"You heard him! He's seventy-five years old. He was practically folding up!"

"Buddy? Hardly. He's made of iron. Did you call his room to see if he was there?"

"No, I didn't think of it, truthfully. I don't

even know where it is."

"Come on. I'll show you." He took her down a hallway to a set of back stairs, down those, and down another long hallway to a door at the end. "This is it."

Daniel knocked on Buddy's door. No answer, but she thought she heard something. He knocked again.

"Who is it?" came Buddy's muffled voice.

"Me," Daniel said. He pushed open the door and stepped into Buddy's room, Maureen close behind. "We've been wondering . . ."

A light snapped on. Daniel stopped and Maureen came around beside him. Buddy sat up in bed, the sheet pulled up to his chin. The sheet alongside him moved and lowered. Rose sat up and propped the pillows behind her.

"If we'd known you were coming we'd have baked a cake," she said lightly.

Maureen stood speechless, her mouth open.

"See?" Daniel said. "I told you Buddy would see that Rose was taken care of. You had nothing to worry about." With two fingers under her chin, he pushed her mouth closed. "Sorry we dropped in unannounced. Have a nice night."

He turned Maureen and pushed her through

the door, closing it carefully behind them. She walked as if in a trance.

"You all right?" Daniel asked.

Maureen found her voice. "My mother . . . and Buddy . . . they were . . . they were . . . what were they doing?"

Daniel scratched his head. "Well, if I can trust my memory, I think they were probably making love."

"What? How could they? They're . . . they're . . ."

"Old enough to know better? Well, three cheers for them. May they always be young enough to ignore that old saw."

Maureen's frustration mounted. "Leave it to my mother. No doubt she forced him into it."

Daniel chuckled. "Really? She did a great job of concealing the whips and chains. Your mother's pretty clever for a senile old broad."

She whirled on him. "You think it's amusing, don't you, finding my mother in bed with a . . . man?"

"Not in the least. I find it heartwarming, hopeful, and a damned good idea." He touched her arm.

Maureen pulled away. "Well, I think it's appalling behavior. What will people think?"

"Anyone who might have the right to take

396

issue with it is dead," Daniel said quietly, his expression serious.

Maureen could say nothing more. She turned and left Daniel in the corridor and went to her stateroom. It was a long hard night for her. Her mind churned and wouldn't shut down. She dozed but never slept.

And Rose never did come back that night.

Monday morning Maureen left the ship early and went into Hamilton. She wanted to be alone, to think. On Front Street she found a cedar-paneled coffee shop already busy with early-rising tourists and locals. She ordered scones with orange marmalade and capuccino, a breakfast she'd never find at home.

After breakfast she walked along Front Street peering into gift and antiques shops. She passed the policeman in the birdcage and again watched with fascination as he gracefully swung his arms and torso to the musical rhythm of the awakening island. She smiled. How lucky were the Bermudians who passed the birdcage and got to start every day with unique moments of entertainment.

At Trimingham's Department Store she admired a window dresser changing his display of spring wearing apparel to summer English and Continental clothing. Past the British Airways building she turned up Chancery Lane, a picturesque street paved with brick walks and lined with potted trees and plants and gift shops. She stopped in at The Little Mermaid and purchased a conch shell. Winding her way in and out of the shops and ending again on Front Street, Maureen filled a handled bag with treasures she'd found, among them two handpainted scarves, a long multi-strand necklace of colorful seaside materials, and three books on the Island's history, homes, and natural wonders.

Toward mid-afternoon, she stopped at a harborfront restaurant and sat on the open deck eating a spicy concoction called Bermuda Rockfish Chowder. The place appeared to be a gathering spot for Hamilton's working women, and she caught snatches of conversation among the tables of three or four around her. One group in particular appeared to be affiliated with a travel agency, and she caught snippets of information about the booming travel industry and the lack of qualified staff to meet the needs and demands.

Before heading back to the ship, Maureen walked along the harbor listening to the sounds of a ship arriving, the clang of buoy bells, the clatter of rigging on boats. She thought about everything, from her childhood with Rose and Norman, to the time when she knew Daniel, to when she married Larry, and to later when they divorced.

She dropped down on a bench and thought about Daniel some more. Had it only been a few days since he'd touched her bare backside and recognized her birthmark? Was it only a few days since she'd sat in her Miami office in a gray suit? Was it only a few hours since Daniel had kissed her and stirred something deep inside her? Was it her mother and Buddy in that bed, or was it a dream she'd had—a dream to mask the reality that . . . she wished it had been herself and Daniel.

The day had grown warm and sticky, and her emotions were running high. She reached into her purse for her mirror and a tissue, then blotted the moisture that had formed under her eyes. She stopped abruptly. Hazel eyes with gold flecks stared back with a sharpening glint of recognition. *The same gold-flecked hazel eyes as Buddy Beers!*

A couple of sailors spoke to her, and several locals waved as they passed. Rising, she greeted them vaguely, then started walking back toward the ship. *Buddy Beers's eyes*. Her step quickened and a smile played around her mouth. Then a light laugh broke through her lips. She knew it now. Rose had been just as much in love with Buddy as he'd been with her! They'd loved each other, and she was born of that love!

Suddenly she felt at home, truly at home for the first time in her own skin on a foreign island. And more.

She knew she'd fallen in love with Daniel, and she never wanted to lose these new feelings. That meant she had to make things happen instead of letting things happen to her.

And most important — she couldn't wait to talk to Rose.

Buddy's arms reluctantly loosened around Rose's back. He sighed the sigh of a satisfied man. They leaned against the ship's rail and watched the hubbub along the Front street dock.

"There's Maureen," Rose said, pointing to a figure walking briskly along the quay.

"How can you tell?"

"Mother's intuition."

Buddy turned toward her and took her face

between his two hands. "How about father's intuition? Do you believe in that?"

Rose closed her eyes. When she opened them she saw tears in Buddy's. "You believe in it . . . don't you?" she whispered.

He nodded. "It hit me like a ton of bricks. But I won't totally believe it until I hear you say it out loud."

Rose curled against his chest, and Buddy's arms clasped her tightly. "I've never told a soul."

"Tell me. I'm the right one to tell first."

Rose breathed deeply. She leaned back in the circle of Buddy's arms, her hands clasping his narrow shoulders through yet another plaid shirt. "Maureen is . . . your daughter."

Buddy's tears spilled down his cheeks. "I knew it the morning we met by the swimming pool."

"You did? How?"

"Don't ask me, I couldn't tell you. But I did."

"I felt something had connected between you two, but I was afraid it was something else . . . do you think Maureen has it figured out?"

"No. But don't worry. I won't give away your . . . *our* secret. I understand now why you disappeared back then. We made love once. A couple of months later you were gone. I thought I talked you into something you didn't want to do. I just wish you could have told me about the baby . . ."

"You have a right to hate me for what I've done to you," Rose whispered.

Buddy wiped his eyes and shook his head. "It was my fault. I was pretty wild in those days. You had no way of knowing that if you'd just crooked your beautiful little finger, I'd have been tame as a tired tiger. And . . . to have a child . . ." His voice trailed away, heavy with emotion.

"I hope you can forgive me for doing what I thought was right."

Buddy let out a long sigh. "No need. I've blamed myself for fifty years, and I haven't stopped thinking about you for as long."

"I drive you crazy, don't I?" Rose said, slipping her arms around his neck and holding him close.

"Yeah, but with me it's not a drive, it's a short putt when it comes to you." He hugged her hard.

"I'm so sorry," Rose whispered. "I should have told you. I just thought you wouldn't want to be tied down with me and a baby.

You loved vaudeville, loved performing. I couldn't ask you to leave that. And I didn't want to bring up a child on the road. I wanted a good solid homelife for her. Norman had been coming around. He was good to us both. He knew Maureen wasn't his. He couldn't produce children of his own. He was grateful. God, I've made a mess of things by trying to do right, haven't I?"

Buddy rubbed her back, then gazed lovingly into her eyes. "Let's not talk about any of that. Rosie, baby, I loved you from the moment I laid eyes on you in that railroad station. If you'd even given me a crumb, I'd have gone to work digging ditches just to be with you and . . . our baby." He said the last with hushed awe.

Rose's eyes sparkled bluer than the sky. "You loved me? I didn't know that. Why didn't you tell me?"

"I wasn't good enough for you. And I thought you just wanted to be friends."

"What a crock of baloney that is! I thought you were the most wonderful man in the world. I fell in love with you the night you sang "Let Me Call You Sweetheart" in Utica, our first show together. I was this gangly kid who thought she was gonna be a hot

403

showgirl. But you were a star, a real star. Why would you even look at me twice?"

Buddy kissed the tip of her nose. "Lord love a duck, are we a couple of dumb ringers! We shoulda stopped acting long enough to talk to each other." He cupped her face and kissed her sweetly. "But, Rosie, honey, I don't want you to disappear again. I don't want to live without you from now on. Whaddaya say? I'll get off the boat and we'll live in Miami or wherever you say. Please, Rosie. Think about it. Take all the time in the world."

"I have. I've thought about a lot of things. There isn't all the time in the world. The only time to count on is now. Let's go someplace quiet and figure it all out."

"What about Maureen?"

"I don't know how she'll take any of this. But she doesn't need sheltering anymore. She needs truth, and she needs to get hold of her own life. I'm going to have a lot of hard decisions to make and thinking to do . . . and a heart-to-heart with Doctor Daniel Lonergan."

Ship's stewards were rushing about making ready to leave Bermuda. The kitchens were gearing up for dinner, the nightclubs making ready to open the moment they were out of port. And Doctor Lonergan had just returned to his quarters after a long day on the island seeing old friends, exploring old haunts, asking new questions.

He opened the door to a light knock.

"Hello, Daniel, may I come in?" Maureen waited in the doorway wearing a newly acquired pair of palm green Bermuda shorts and a white shirt tied at the waist. Strings of tiny shells swung from her earlobes.

Daniel did not conceal his surprise and delight. "Lucky! Of course. Please."

She strode in, purposeful, he thought, strong, all remnants of reticence gone.

"We need to talk. Actually, I'll be selfish about this and say I need to talk, and I need you to listen."

"Go." He sat down on the bed, his face turned attentively toward her.

"This is a great place. Bermuda, I mean, not the ship. Well, the ship is great, too, once it quit making me sick. Seeing my mother in bed . . ." When Daniel tried to speak, she stopped him. "Wait. I'm over the shock. Really, I am. I felt like a little girl. You know how it is, we never think our parents would do *that*. But why not? Truth is, I envy her. I envy her free-spirit, the stamina it must have taken all those years with my . . . Norman . . . to keep that spirit under control. She felt like going to bed with Buddy, and so they . . . just did it . . . went to bed. I mean, there's nothing wrong with that, is there." It was a statement, not a question. "So what if they're over seventy, right? Doesn't mean a thing, does it? Just because one is of a certain age doesn't mean one doesn't still think about . . . desire . . . want to . . . well, you know." She ran a nervous hand through her hair.

"Right!" Daniel said, catching on to her mood. "Reaching a certain age gives one the right to say right out if they think . . . desire . . . well, want to . . ." He stood up and walked over to her.

Maureen didn't move. She couldn't have if she'd wanted to. If she didn't touch him in the next thirty seconds she knew she'd self-destruct. When he lightly placed his hands over her hips she shuddered.

". . . Make love with the one person they've been thinking about all their lives," he finished, his voice low and dusky, "the one person they couldn't have who would have made everything else in their lives worthwhile, and made everyone else in their lives pale in comparison."

Slowly, Maureen slid her hands up over his arms, his shoulders, and circled them around his neck, entwining her fingers in the back of his hair. "Exactly," she whispered. "And two people shouldn't wait any longer than thirty or so years to do that, make love I mean. Should they?"

"Exactly," he concurred. He lowered his arms under her buttocks and lifted her off the floor. "If that's about to happen," he whispered hoarsely, "then I'll be branded as 'lucky' as you are.

She dropped her head and, letting her hair fall over his face, kissed him fully and satisfyingly. He turned and lowered her onto his bed, and took his time removing first her clothes and then his. Maureen closed her eyes and basked in his loving appraisal of her body with his eyes and hands. He turned her on her hip and kissed the clover-leaf on her backside, ending with a little nip.

She jumped, then laughed, turned over and gathered him as closely as she could against the length of her naked body. With his lips, his voice, his fingers he elicited in her every sensation she could imagine and then some. And she experienced what Rose had told her she should, that day in the office. She couldn't stop touching him, exploring his trim body with her own hands and lips.

When at last they came together in the complete embrace and he was buried deep inside her, Maureen knew that this was where she truly belonged.

"We're agreed then?" Rose asked Buddy as they walked down the corridor. "We ask Danny to bring Maureen to the Yellow Bird Room tonight after dinner. We'll tell them then."

"Agreed. But we don't have to tell Maureen . . . everything, just yet. It's really okay with me, sweetheart." Buddy rubbed her back as they walked.

"I know it is. But by tomorrow, I swear she will know you're her father. I hope she'll understand. If she does, then we'll really be launched." Rose didn't want to think what would happen if Maureen didn't understand.

"Whatever you say, darlin'. Here's Daniel's room. If he's in we could tell him right now." He knocked on the door.

A muffled "Who is it?" came from the other side.

"Buddy. I need to talk to you." He opened the door and he and Rose stepped in.

Daniel and Maureen sat up in bed, he smiling like the Cheshire Cat and she fixing her hair nervously. They both looked like teenagers who'd been caught in the back seat of his father's '57 Chevy.

"Hello, Mother," Maureen said shyly. "There's a cake in the oven."

Maureen and Daniel sipped rum swizzles served in hurricane glasses with red heart-topped stirrers which sported tiny blue and white banners emblazoned *Majestic's Romance on the High Seas*. A note had been slipped under the door, following Rose and Buddy's hasty departure, giving them instructions to be in the Yellow Bird Room and seated at the reserved table at the front of the stage by eleven.

"Mother said I needed to make some changes," Maureen said. "She told me this vacation would do it. Why are mothers always right?" She smiled lovingly into Daniel's eyes, and ran her fingers along his forearm.

"It's in their genes." He leaned over the small round table and kissed her lightly on the lips. "What do you think she'll say about our plans?"

"They're pretty drastic, aren't they? Staying in Bermuda, me working in a travel agency, and you setting up a medical practice. I think she'll say it's wonderful, and she'll be happy for me. At least I hope she will. I do worry about her, though. Her age, and alone in Miami. She has her friends, but I'm still going to worry about her. What if she gets sick?"

"I'll make a house call."

"The drive will be murder," Maureen came back.

"I'm still stunned we had the same idea."

"Which one?" Maureen sucked the end of the stirrer and laid it on the table. She looked up into his eyes provocatively.

"That one, too. I mean the one about we both stay in Bermuda, live there."

"It's the scariest . . . and the nerviest thing I've ever done."

"Except for the time on the beach when I found you squatting in the bushes."

She dropped her head over her arms and wailed, "I'm mortified that you can even bring that up."

"You love it! And I love you, and I adore your clover leaf."

"I do love it, and you, and the fact that you still like my clover leaf. Danny Lonergan, I adore you. I've loved you all my life. Mother always knew that, too. She's pretty incredible."

"That she is." He looked around. "I wonder what's keeping those two."

"They're probably back in the room making love."

Daniel feigned shock, and covered his heart with his hand. "Shame on you for what you're thinking," he whispered.

Suddenly the lights went out and the room was lit only by the glass-shrouded candles on tables all over the club. A drum roll rumbled and a spotlight shone on the golden yellow curtain that swept across the stage.

"Ladies and gentlemen," a disembodied voice said over a sound system, "tonight we have a special treat for you. Direct from vaudeville and opera houses across the United States, and from behind the bar of the Jolly Roger Lounge of the great *Romance on the High Seas,* the two and only," the voice escalated, "that wild and crazy man, our own Buddy Beers, and his lovely former, present, and—at last, so I hear!—*future* partner, Rosie Greggs and her Fabulous Legs!"

Applause swelled around them as Maureen and Daniel stared at each other.

Then their eyes were glued to the circle of light on the curtain. It snapped open and Buddy stood center stage with Rose perched on his shoulder, one arm draped around his neck and the other flung up over her head. Her hair was piled high and studded with sparkling beads and a hot pink plume.

He set her down carefully and she spun out to the edge of the stage, tall and amazingly leggy in pale fishnet stockings, taupe character shoes, and a one-piece, hot pink costume with sheer sleeves and a sweetheart neckline. She looked almost as she had in the only picture of her show business days that she'd ever shown to Maureen.

Rose leaned over and threw a kiss toward her daughter. Starkly, Maureen was struck in that moment that even with years of performing the duties of a corporate mogul's society wife, the smell of greasepaint and the applause of the crowd still bubbled in Rose's blood. And she knew Rose was reliving a dream. Happily, she threw a kiss back to her, thrilled to be sharing the dream with her.

Rose did a side dance back to Buddy, and the orchestra struck up the chorus of an old show tune. Buddy and Rose had rewritten the words, and together they sang them directly to Maureen and Daniel.

"Oh, we ain't got our youth or our money . . .
But we're in love and we're funny . . .
So we'll travel the sea,
Seein' what we see . . .
Side by side . . ."

They finished their song to thunderous applause, and then another drum roll sounded.

"Oh, no," Maureen said, clutching Daniel's arm. "Wait till you see this."

Rose backed up, Buddy took a wide-legged stance. Rose gave a small leap, cartwheeled, and landed in a leg spit in Buddy's arms.

Daniel was on his feet whistling and applauding and shouting, "Bravo! Bravo!"

The audience followed all around the room. Maureen's eyes filled and the tears streamed down her face. Buddy set Rose back on her feet and motioned to Maureen and Daniel, beckoning them to join them on stage. Daniel sat down with a thud. But Maureen, caught up in the whirlwind of her mother's personality and love, and at last letting her own spirit free, grabbed his arm and dragged him to his feet. He stumbled behind her.

The four embraced each other in the truthful glare of the Yellow Bird spotlight.

"Mother," Maureen shouted over the ongoing applause, "I'm moving to Bermuda. Daniel and I are going to get married!"

"Oh, baby!" Rose hugged her. "I'm so happy for you! Buddy and I are getting married, too! We're going to cruise around the world on the ship! And I have other news I hope you'll be just as excited about!"

"I know, Mother . . . and I am!"

With shining eyes, mother and daughter embraced closely.

The orchestra struck up another chorus. The four looked at each other. Rose lined them all up and, arms linked, they sang the final chorus side by side, laughing, hugging, and kissing when the curtain closed.

On Father's Day, in June, a double wedding was performed among the mangrove trees in the ancient stone Blue Grotto on the romantic island of Bermuda. The daughter of the first bride wholeheartedly gave her mother's hand in marriage. And the father of the second

414

bride proudly kissed his daughter and presented her to her handsome groom.

At the moment of pronouncement, four
dolphins burst out of the crystal clear water
and clapped their fins in approval.

When Lilacs Bloom

by Clara Wimberly

Georgia Lee stood up and smoothed her hands down the heavy hand-knit sweater that she wore over tailored gray slacks. Then she walked slowly through the antique store. Business was slow today because of an unusually cold and bitter spring storm. There just didn't seem to be many people out on the wet, slippery streets of Charleston, and most of the garden tours were over for the season. The azaleas bloomed early here, much earlier than they did back home.

She stopped, frowning at her thoughts, her brown eyes growing dark and troubled. What on earth was wrong with her today? Charleston was her home now and she couldn't imagine why she'd felt such a sudden rush of longing.

She glanced around the shop, letting her eyes move lovingly over the gleaming wood patina of antique tables and cabinets . . . over the breathtaking array of glassware and lamps that she had bought with such joy. The entire shop gave her joy.

She stopped, frowning again and slowly shaking her head as she tried to stop the thoughts that came, unbidden, into her mind.

"This is what you wanted," she whispered. "Independence . . . a shop of your own . . . a man who loves you and wants to marry you . . ." She sighed and waved her hand helplessly over the array of beautiful old furniture, so carefully arranged and preserved.

She wished she were busy, wished that the weather outside weren't quite so gloomy. And she wished that Glen, her fiancé, was not away for the day on a buying trip.

She heard the jangle of the bell as the front door opened and the mailman stepped inside, wiping his booted feet on the welcome mat.

"Hi," she said, feeling foolish that she sounded excited by so simple a thing as a mail delivery. "Come on in,"

"No," the mailman said, smiling toward

her. "Don't want to track up your nice floors. Got a lot of mail to deliver today and I think I'm coming down with a cold."

"Oh, that's too bad," she said, taking the stack of mail from his outstretched hand. "Well . . . hope you get to feeling better."

Georgia walked to the back of the shop and placed the mail on her desk, then turned on the old lamp that threw a soft green glow through its antique globe.

She murmured softly when one of the letters slid across the desk and she saw the address . . . the very place she had been thinking of . . . Alabama . . . home.

"Amelia Lee's Lilac Inn," she whispered as she read the perfectly scrolled handwriting in the upper left-hand corner. Georgia smiled with pleasure, remembering the day her ex-mother-in-law had announced she was naming her new bed-and-breakfast inn for her favorite flower.

Georgia had been divorced for two years from Amelia's son, Thomas, but the divorce had not weakened the motherly bond between her and Amelia Lee. They had remained close, even though they had to rely on letters now. Georgia loved her dearly and had always regarded her as a second mother.

She picked up the envelope, turning it over curiously before impatiently ripping open the flap.

She leaned back in her chair, smiling and preparing for the pleasure of Amelia's quaint and sometimes salty words. For all her wealth, Amelia Lee was a throwback . . . a pioneer mountain woman stuck in modern-day society. A woman who still spoke bluntly, who hoed her own garden and took more pride in her flowers than she did in her wealth and position.

Georgia read aloud, enjoying the sound of Amelia's words.

"My dear Georgia, The weather here has been simply atrocious, what with rain and fog one day, then snow and sleet the next. But then, you remember how it is in North Alabama in the springtime. And I don't have to tell you that here on the mountain, conditions are usually even worse. But I'm bearing up all right, considering I'm even older than most of the antiques you have in your lovely shop."

Georgia laughed, hearing Amelia's scratchy little voice in her mind. She could almost see her twinkling blue eyes and the soft feathery hair as pale as the angel hair that always decorated her Christmas trees.

She turned back to the letter.

"Did I tell you that Tracy is going to work at the Inn this summer?"

Georgia frowned. Her daughter, Tracy, had *not* told her she would be working for her grandmother, and she was a bit surprised. Tracy was ever the sophisticate and she couldn't imagine the twenty-two-year-old beauty stuck on the mountain all summer. And she felt a twinge of disappointment. She had hoped Tracy would come to Charleston for the summer. She wanted her to get to know Glen. Maybe then her daughter would stop making those not-so-subtle remarks about getting her mother and dad back together.

Georgia read on.

"I suppose I should just come right out and tell you why I'm writing this letter." Georgia frowned again, her eyes scanning quickly ahead. "I'm not well, darling. And this time there seems to be more wrong than the usual nagging old migraines and the ever-present arthritis. That's one of the reasons, I'm sure, that your sweet Tracy so readily agreed to come this summer. So, I have a very big favor to ask of you, Georgia. If I could have all of you together here this spring . . . one last time, my last days would not seem so cold and lonely."

"Last days?" Georgia murmured, letting her eyes move upward to read the lines again. "Dear Lord," she whispered. "She's dying."

"Please don't be upset . . . I can't stand it when people worry about me, and Lord knows, Thomas is worrier enough for one tiny little woman like me. So, I don't need you fretting about me, too. But what I do need, my darling, is your company . . . to see your face and your laughing brown eyes when I wake up in the morning and when I go to sleep at night. Is that asking too much? I know you're busy . . . a career woman now, Tracy says. But perhaps your partner . . . what was his name . . . Glen? Perhaps he could mind the shop while you're here. And I'm sure he wouldn't mind postponing the wedding for a little while. It would mean so much to me. With all of us together, I would be able to see the lilacs bloom . . . just one more time."

Georgia sobbed and held the letter to her breast. Amelia . . . dying? It just didn't seem possible. Not the feisty little woman who moved so quickly through the big house, giving orders and making sure everything was perfect for her guests. Her mind was as alert and clear as ever and those sparkling blue eyes could still rivet one to the floor when she was angry.

"But of course, I'll have to go," Georgia muttered aloud.

Even if it meant seeing Thomas again for the first time since their divorce.

Georgia frowned and stood up. Thomas . . . just the sound of his name, even after all this time, still had the power to make her heart skip a beat. She had spent the last two years trying to forget him, trying to convince herself that divorcing him had been the best thing for both of them. After a near-fatal car accident that almost caused him to lose his legs, after he learned that he would never play professional football again, he had become bitter and sarcastic. He had started to drink too much, to stay away from home for long periods of time.

It hadn't seemed to matter to him that at the age of thirty-eight he was past the age of retirement, according to usual pro football standards. Before the accident he had continued playing, despite pain and injury, due to pure stubborn pride and the fact that he kept himself in superb physical condition. Perhaps it would have been different if he had been allowed to make the decision to quit. But as it happened, so suddenly, so finally — that decision was made for him. And Thomas had not been able to accept it. That and his bitterness had ruined their marriage, a marriage that Georgia had thought would last forever.

Georgia had even wondered if there were other women during those last torturous ten years, but the mere thought of her husband, the man she had adored since college, holding someone else ... kissing someone else ...

"Oh, God," she whispered, feeling the old bittersweet longing rush over her. She hadn't been able to banish those feelings, hadn't forgotten the love they shared for twenty-five years. But she was the only one who knew that. She had learned it with heartwrenching despair every night since leaving Alabama.

Georgia had tried to be patient and positive about Thomas's injuries, even though it killed her to see him in a wheelchair. And she thought it was even worse when he graduated to canes and braces. Seeing the man she loved so helpless and vulnerable ... the strong, powerful man whose strength was his pride — it had hurt so badly. Seeing him stumble and fall, then curse and pull himself up again, had simply broken her heart. He wouldn't let her help; he hadn't wanted anyone to help. And he had finally pushed her away. His stubbornness and pride had made it impossible to accept her help and, finally, even her love. It had hurt with an agony that, even now, pierced her heart.

Tears filled her eyes and she wiped them away with a sad impatience. She would save her tears for Amelia, she told herself. She was the one who deserved her sympathies now. Georgia simply couldn't imagine Amelia ill.

Georgia smiled despite herself as she remembered Amelia's penchant for gloomy predictions. It had even become an affectionate family joke. Every year after a wonderful, joyous Christmas and New Year's celebration, Amelia would become quiet, even a little depressed after the holidays. She would begin to long for spring, and for the flowers to sprout from the rich Alabama soil. And sooner or later, she would always utter the same phrase. It happened year after year.

"If I can just live to see the lilacs bloom,"

she would say. "When lilacs bloom, this old body just comes alive. But I don't know . . . spring seems an awfully long way away this year."

"When lilacs bloom," Georgia whispered now, her dark eyes sparkling with tears. Amelia had even mentioned it in her letter today and something in the sweetness of her words, something in the poignant urging, made Georgia feel protective and strong.

"I'll be there, Amelia," she said, pulling herself up and drying her eyes. "And if it's within my power, my darling, you will see your lilacs bloom again."

It took Georgia several days to get her business affairs in order and to pack what she would need for a long stay. Luckily, by then the weather had improved considerably. She thought it might even be a pleasant drive from the coast of South Carolina over to Alabama. And she might have looked forward to it if her guilt over postponing her wedding to Glen was not quite so great.

"But darling, why do *you* have to go?" he asked as he watched her pack.

Georgia turned to him, noting the impatience and concern in his pale blue eyes. Even now, though he was obviously upset about her decision, his eyes were still calm and steady. That was one of the things that had first attracted her to the tall, slender man. He was so cool . . . so sophisticated. And perhaps after those last stormy years with Thomas, he had seemed like a safe, comfortable haven.

"I told you, Glen . . . Amelia is like a mother to me. After my own mother died several years ago, I even began calling Amelia Mother . . . I even sent her Mother's Day cards after I moved here." She continued packing, hoping he would relent. She didn't want to argue about this and she especially didn't want to argue with Glen.

"I understand that," he said, his voice calm and reasonable. "But I'd feel better about it if she were in a hospital somewhere . . . or a nursing home . . ."

"Glen," she said, turning softly-accusing eyes toward him.

"Oh, honey . . . I don't mean it the way it sounds. I'm not being heartless, but honestly, wouldn't she be better off in a home until she . . ." Seeing the tears in her eyes, he looked a bit shamefaced and paused, coming to take her in his arms. "I'm sorry . . . it's just that I'd feel much better . . ." His fingers smoothed back the dusty blond hair that had fallen over her forehead. ". . . if your big, famous jock of an ex-husband weren't going to be around."

She frowned and moved out of his arms, turning back to her suitcase. "That's ridiculous," she said, her voice soft and muffled. "Thomas and I have been divorced two years now . . . I haven't seen him since then . . . the day I left Alabama. And if you knew Thomas and how stubborn he is, you wouldn't even think such a thing. He didn't want me then, and he doesn't want me now."

"Are you telling me he's not still attracted to you? He'd have to be crazy." Meaningfully, he let his eyes wander over her tall, slender figure, the curve of her hips, the mature yet still very desirable body.

His blue eyes were cool and unreadable. For one impatient moment, Georgia wished he would say what he meant . . . even get angry. If he was jealous, he should just come out and say he was jealous. At least Thomas . . .

She stopped her thoughts, turning to Glen and putting her hands on his arm. "I'm sure he has quite forgotten all about me by now," she said. "Thomas probably has a flock of women after him; he always did, and now that I'm out of the picture, I imagine he's enjoying it very much." She reached up to kiss him, noting the coolness of his lips and the way he sometimes didn't close his eyes when she kissed him.

"Well . . ." he murmured, pulling her close. "Perhaps I wouldn't feel quite so threatened if you'd ever said you love me."

Georgia sighed and frowned up at him. "Glen . . . please. We're getting married . . . I want to marry you. We have so much in common, we have such fun together and I care about you . . . I really do. Isn't that enough? Don't you think its unreasonable to expect a full-fledged, passionate romance, too . . . at our age? Isn't it much more sensible to marry for friendship and companionship?" She shook his arm a bit for emphasis, seeing his closed look and hearing his sigh of impatience.

He bent to kiss her, smiling when she pulled away. "I suppose you're right," he said. "I suppose I should just count my blessings that I found someone like you. And who knows . . . perhaps in time, you might grow to love me . . . passionately . . ." he said, his arms tightening, his hands moving down to her hips. ". . . the way I love you."

After Glen left, Georgia stood for a while frowning at the door. Was she being unfair, expecting him to understand, expecting him to marry for the same reasons she was? Despite his cool, calm exterior, she suspected what Glen really wanted was the hot, blazing love affair of youth. And as she stood thinking, she wasn't sure she would ever be able to give him that. She wasn't sure she could ever feel that excitement and passion for anyone except . . .

"God," she muttered, turning and pulling the top of the suitcase closed and zipping it impatiently. "Just stop this now." She had to get Thomas out of her thoughts long before she reached Alabama. She simply had to.

Georgia started early the next morning, but it was a long drive. Still, she turned off the interstate in Chattanooga at the Lookout Mountain exit, unable to resist taking the longer, more scenic route across the mountain. The road skimmed the top of the mountain chain, extending from Tennessee through Georgia and into northern Alabama.

"America's most scenic one hundred

miles," Georgia said to herself. She smiled as she maneuvered the car around hairpin curves, up and up past gracious old homes, past thick waxy branches of mountain laurel and feathery evergreens that hung over the road in dark clusters. And once on top of the mountain the road became straight and flat, extending along the plateau toward the south. The late-afternoon sun to the west was spectacular, just as she knew it would be. But she didn't stop at any of the overlooks; it was getting late and she wanted to reach the inn before dark.

She sighed as she passed the beautiful castle-like structure of Covenant College that rose like a sentinel before the green valley below. The setting sun turned its surface to a soft, muted gold.

As she grew nearer to home, her heart began to pound. She even felt her mouth growing dry, her breathing shallow and quick. And then she finally saw the moss-covered stone fence and the wide driveway beneath more arched stonework with the ornately scrolled sign that read, "Amelia Lee's Lilac Inn". Georgia took a deep breath, willing herself to be calm. She couldn't believe that the prospect of seeing Thomas again had her so nervous, not when she should be concentrating on Amelia and her well-being.

The house was as beautiful as ever, still well-kept, still bearing the clean, classic lines that she loved so well. It was a big, rambling old house with the evidence of several additions added over the years. The front was pristine white clapboard, with dark plantation-green shutters at the long gabled windows, but at the back, mellow, rose-colored bricks blended with the white wood. A long porch, screened against the summer's onslaught of insects, ran along the side of the house, ending at a bricked courtyard in back that was usually filled with pots of flowers. The house was surrounded by huge trees and nearer the house, clumps of lilac bushes stood, heavy with unopened blossoms.

As Georgia pulled her car slowly up the circular drive to the front door, she smiled, seeing the welcoming glow through the sparkling windows and feeling an unexpected tug of longing rush toward her heart.

She opened the door, glancing up at the towering canopy of fragile spring leaves. Clumps of azaleas against the house were just beginning to bloom in myriad rose-colored hues. A few white ones intermingled, made more brilliant by the comparison.

"Mom!"

She turned to see Tracy jogging toward her from the house, hurrying toward the car with a graceful, long-legged gait. She had her mother's tall, slender build, but the shining sandy hair was her father's—as were the gray eyes that revealed every emotion and sometimes turned dark and stormy when she was hurt or angry.

Georgia laughed and took her daughter in her arms and they rocked back and forth before standing back to look at one another.

"Mom, you look terrific," Tracy said with a mischievous lift of her eyebrows. "Wait 'til Dad sees you."

Georgia frowned and turned toward the car. "I've been here less than five minutes, little matchmaker, and you're already starting."

"Sorry," Tracy said with a breezy wave of her hand.

Georgia glanced at her, knowing full well she wasn't sorry. She was willful and stubborn, just like her father. And if she ever got an idea into her pretty head, she usually didn't let up until her mission was accomplished. Georgia didn't have the heart to tell her that this was one time she would be disappointed.

"How's your grandmother?" Georgia asked, glancing toward the house, and wondering where Amelia was.

"Oh," Tracy said, turning away to help with the luggage. "She's . . . she's resting."

"I just couldn't believe it when I got her letter," Georgia said. "Did this happen suddenly . . . or has she been ill for a while? I know how secretive she can be at times, where her health is concerned."

"Uh, Mom . . . before we go in . . . maybe I should tell you that Dad doesn't know anything yet."

"Doesn't know? But—"

Tracy frowned and walked on ahead, her shoulders slumping from the weight of the luggage. "For the time being, Grandma Amelia would like him to think you're only here for a visit."

"But Tracy . . . darling . . . she shouldn't keep this from him. You know how protective your Dad is of Amelia . . . how he adores her. And I don't think this is something we should—"

"Please Mom," Tracy said with a sheepish look. "It's what she wants . . . just for now

434

. . . please?"

Georgia sighed, knowing full well that it was useless to argue with Amelia once she'd made up her mind.

"Oh, all right. But it's a terrible secret and I hope it's only for a short time. You know I could never keep a secret from your father."

Tracy wiggled her eyebrows suggestively as she glanced at her mother. "I know. That's the way it is, I hear, when you love someone."

Georgia groaned and rolled her eyes, opening the front door and placing the luggage inside. Then she stopped, just letting her eyes take in the beauty of the old place that was already filled with the glorious fragrance of lilacs. The gleaming wood floors, the warm Oriental rugs, the elegant white wood molding. The house was always sparkling clean and bright, and Georgia found herself wondering again how Amelia managed it. It was the perfect blend of elegance and warm mountain coziness; for a moment Georgia simply let herself feel it welcome her back home.

Just then a young man stepped into the hallway. Georgia saw her daughter's quick frown and the way she stiffened noticeably. He was about Tracy's age and Georgia's eyes widened with speculation as she noted his rugged build and good looks . . . and his cocky masculine stance.

"Here," he said, motioning toward the suitcases at the doorway. "I'll take those up for you."

"No," Tracy said quickly. "We can manage on our own, thank you." She clamped her lips together in a thin, stubborn line.

Georgia turned to stare at her daughter and saw the defensive flash in Tracy's gray eyes.

The boy grinned, his blue eyes raking slowly over Tracy's figure and up to her face. Georgia was surprised to see the warm flush that crept over her daughter's lovely peach-colored skin. She couldn't remember ever seeing her extroverted daughter blush.

Georgia looked for a moment from one to the other . . . then at the boy's amused blue eyes. They looked knowing and full of confidence as they stared into Tracy's stormy ones. Georgia smiled and stepped toward the boy, extending her hand.

"Hello, my name is Georgia Lee. I'm Tracy's mother."

"Yeah, I know," he said, grinning and taking her hand in a firm clasp. "Mrs. Lee told me you were coming. Besides, you two look enough alike to be sisters. I'm Bo Cavanaugh . . . Mrs. Lee hired me to do odd jobs here at the Inn for the summer."

Georgia smiled, seeing the impatience on Tracy's face. There was something going on between these two, she decided. Definitely worth watching.

"Well, Bo . . . I don't know where my daughter's manners are today. But personally, I'd be delighted to have you carry this luggage up to my room."

Bo grinned and moved past Tracy, faintly brushing against her shoulder as he did. Then he and Georgia stood at the foot of the stairs smiling as the girl gave a low, muttered growl and stalked up the steps ahead of them.

The young man left the bags in the west bedroom, one of Georgia's favorites. It was at the back of the house and Georgia could see past the gardens and down into the valley. The trees below the house were kept trimmed just for the guests' pleasure. Georgia turned from the window, glancing at the pale-rose-and-dark-blue rug, at the mahogany

437

furniture, and the carefully selected antique lamps and accessories. Amelia Lee was the one who had instilled a love of antiques in Georgia in the first place.

She turned to Tracy, seeing the faint blush still on her cheeks. "What on earth has Bo Cavanaugh done to you? You were as prickly as a porcupine with him just now."

"He deserves it," she said stiffly. "He thinks he's God's gift to women. He's used to having any girl he wants simply fall at his feet and I, for one, don't intend to be one of his harem. He's arrogant and cocky and just a tad too masculine for me."

"Too masculine?" Georgia asked, smiling. "Gee, I didn't know a man could be too masculine."

"Oh, Mom . . . you know what I mean. He's a chauvinist . . . a Neanderthal. I just don't like him, that's all."

Georgia began to unpack, smiling as she remembered something from her past.

"You'd better be careful. I seem to recall using very similar words to describe your father once upon a time."

"Dad? Oh, I can't believe that. Why, Dad is the most . . . he's the sweetest, most sensitive man I know. I wish all men were like

438

Daddy."

Georgia smiled, recalling how Tracy had always been a daddy's girl. "A man is different with his daughter than he is with his wife."

"Well, I guess that's true." She smiled at Georgia, that look of mischief returning to her gray eyes. "So . . . Dad was a tough guy, huh? A macho kind of man who swept you off your feet. Tell me, Mom . . . did he have a reputation back then . . . was he a handsome stud? A lot of my friends think he still is."

Georgia frowned at her daughter. She could feel her face growing warm and she wished she hadn't started this conversation.

"For heaven's sake," she muttered. "A stud? What kind of question is that to ask your own mother?"

"Ha," Tracy said, smiling and rocking back on her heels. "Now who's blushing? Well, well, well . . . I think that answers my question pretty well."

"Tracy Lee," Georgia said, smiling despite herself. "You just stop this right now. You're embarrassing me. And don't think you're going to start this matchmaking between your father and me again. Thank goodness he doesn't live in this house or you and Amelia would probably—" She stopped, seeing the grin on Tracy's face and the way her gray eyes sparkled with fun.

"Tracy . . ."

The girl shrugged and threw up her hands. "I guess we forgot to tell you that Dad's moved into the inn, didn't we?"

"Oh, no," Georgia muttered, sitting on the bed and staring at her daughter. "Forgot, huh?"

"He's having some remodeling done at home, so . . ." Again Tracy shrugged. "As a matter of fact, I believe his room is . . ." She leaned toward the door and pointed down the hall. "Right . . . next door."

Georgia's gaze moved to the hallway and down toward the end of the stairs. He was standing there . . . her tall, familiar, and very masculine ex-husband, his broad shoulders seeming to block out some of the light as he moved toward her room. She took a deep breath and her eyes grew dark and dusky as she watched him. She couldn't see his face because of the evening shadows that had moved into the hallway. But she could see the limp as he walked, the way he leaned heavily against the cane in his right hand as he came closer.

Tracy saw her mother's perplexed look and moved quietly toward the door. "Speak of the devil, huh?" she said sheepishly. Then hurriedly, she sped down the hallway and past her dad with a breezy wave of her hand.

Georgia rose to her feet, unable to take her eyes off him. She felt a bit like she had that first time she'd seen him in college . . . overwhelmed, her insides tingling with excitement. Breathless.

Her eyes skimmed over him, from the dark skin at the neck of his shirt to the flat, trim stomach. He wore soft faded jeans that fit his muscular legs well and made them look long and lean.

"Hello," she said quietly when he stepped into the room. He seemed to tower over her and his eyes were as gray and tempestuous as the day she last saw him. He hadn't changed except that the leg braces were gone. The cane and his slight limp gave him a vulnerability that was mysterious and completely appealing. If anything, he had grown even more handsome.

"Hello, Georgia," he replied in a deep, quiet voice. "Welcome home."

* * *

"Well," she said, wishing her voice didn't sound quite so shaky. "I see you're better." She glanced down at the cane. "Only one cane now."

"Much better," he murmured. "Well enough to go back to work."

Her eyes widened. "Not . . . not football?"

His smile was slow and warm. "What else but football? I'm the new high school coach. Not quite so glamorous, but every bit as rewarding."

"Why, that's . . . that's wonderful," she said, staring at him and wondering at his new air of calm and contentment. Had her leaving made such a big difference in his life? For the better, it seemed.

Something about him was changed. He had an easy demeanor that was even more appealing, more masculine than ever.

Georgia turned away and pretended to be busy unpacking. He stood leaning on his cane, watching her as she walked back and forth from the bed to the closet.

"I . . . I didn't know you would be here," she said, glancing his way and noting his amused smile.

"Does it bother you?"

"No . . . no, of course not. It's just that I . . . I . . ." Damn him, why did he always do this to her? Even now, at their age, and after all their years together, he still had the power to make her stammer and blush like a young girl.

"What?" he asked, his voice soft. When she didn't answer he took a step closer. "Georgia, I want to . . ."

As he came nearer, Georgia whirled around to stare into his shadowed gray eyes, afraid he might actually touch her.

"Don't," she said, backing away. "Just don't come any nearer . . . and don't tell me what you want. It doesn't matter to me anymore what you want."

"Oh?" he said with a mocking lift of his brows. "Doesn't it? You seem awfully nervous . . . for a woman who knows exactly what she wants . . . and what she doesn't. But perhaps you've jumped to conclusions here about what I want, Jo."

Georgia gritted her teeth and stared into his eyes. She hated it when he called her Jo . . . if only because it had been his pet name for her years ago and she felt he was only using it now to make her uncomfortable . . .

to try and establish some sort of intimacy that she didn't want.

"Don't call me that."

"Damn," he muttered. "You *are* a bit touchy, aren't you? And as stubborn as ever. I thought two years away might have made you more . . . mellow." He grinned at her, obviously unfazed by her anger and bitterness.

That surprised her. Two years ago he would have been in a full-blown fit of anger by now.

"Thomas," she said, sighing. "Just say whatever it is you wanted to say and then go. I've been driving since dawn and I'm tired. I—"

"I wanted to congratulate you," he said, choosing his words slowly and carefully. "I hear you're getting married again."

"Yes," she replied. Somehow that wasn't what she expected him to say. "I am." She turned away busying herself with something totally unimportant.

"You're making a mistake, you know." His voice, soft and husky made her frown, then whirl around to face him.

"What?"

He took a step closer, pushing the cane

away with some of his old ferocity. As she stared into his eyes, into those ever-changing stormy eyes, she saw him reach for her, felt his strong hands clasp around her arms and draw her slowly, deliberately toward him.

His mouth closed over hers, smothering her protests and making her feel weak and unsteady. The touch of him, after all this time, the taste of his mouth, so familiar and yet so new . . . it was almost more than she could bear. It was as if they were young lovers united after a long separation that had left them yearning for each other.

For the first time in a long while, Georgia reacted without conscious thought. She responded only with emotion, with her need for what no one else had ever been able to give her. Her arms moved around his neck as she returned his kiss, as she savored the taste of him, the scent of him, and the solid feel of his muscular chest and shoulders.

She felt the back of her knees touch the side of the bed, felt the hardness of Thomas's body against hers and suddenly a quick flash of dismay washed over her. What was she doing? What was she thinking?

She wrenched away with a gasp, staring into his eyes, those eyes that once had been able to see straight into her heart.

His laugh was soft . . . triumphant as he returned her gaze, and she knew she hadn't been able to hide the flame of desire still burning there for him.

"Does he make you feel this way?" he whispered, his eyes taunting, his look challenging. "Tell me," he urged, reaching out to trace his fingers over her lips.

She closed her eyes, feeling faint, feeling all the glorious, delicious feelings of passion they had always shared. And feeling guilty because of Glen.

"Don't," she whispered, moving aside and away from the warmth of his body. "Don't do this Thomas."

"Why?" he asked, turning toward her with a slight limp. "Why shouldn't I? You might have fooled yourself into believing it's over between us, Jo," he said, his voice husky and emotion-filled. "But I haven't. Not for one single, lonely, miserable night have I ever convinced myself of that."

She laughed—a harsh, humorless sound in the quiet of the room. "Maybe you should have a drink," she said, intending to punish him for making her feel this way, responding with an instinct to hurt him and push him away. "Maybe you should just call up one of your many women friends . . . or maybe—"

He took her arm, turning her around to face him. "Or maybe I should just lock the door and show you exactly how wrong you are."

Georgia couldn't seem to breathe as their eyes met again.

"Rape is, hardly your style," she finally managed, lifting her chin defiantly.

He smiled then, causing a deep groove to appear beside his mouth and making his gray eyes sparkle. "No," he said, still smiling. "I'm glad you haven't forgotten."

She clamped her lips together and looked away from his knowing gaze. It had always been a delicious secret between them—that wild, overwhelming passion, her willingness to make love with him, anywhere . . . anytime. She saw that he remembered . . . and knew she had walked right into that one.

"Do I have to remind you that *you* were the one who pushed *me* away, Thomas?" Tears welled against her will and she wiped them away impatiently. "After the accident you didn't want my help; you made it clear on many occasions that you didn't need me or anyone. And you locked me out of your heart and out of your thoughts. Then you substituted liquor and clubs . . . women . . . anything you could find to keep you away from me." She sobbed then, not meaning to. And she turned away to walk to the window, staring sightlessly at the night sky above the mountain.

"I haven't had a drink since you left," he said with a note of quiet humility that surprised Georgia. "And you're right . . . I did push you away. Only because I felt so inadequate, because I felt like such a failure and I couldn't bear for you to see me that way." She heard him moving across the floor, but she held herself stiffly, not turning away from the window. "But there was never another woman. Jo . . . never . . . not ever." His voice was a soft growl of protest and she could feel his breath against the back of her neck. "There's never been anyone but you . . . and there never will be."

She turned then, searching his face as tears streamed from her eyes. "Why are you doing this?" she asked, feeling confused and wishing he didn't make her feel so vulnerable, so needy. "I have a new life now; I'm going to be married. Why, after all this time, are you doing this . . . making me feel so . . .

so . . ."

He took her arms, staring down into her eyes and shaking her slightly. "Because I love you, dammit. And because, despite all my stupid mistakes, I think you still love me."

He made no effort to pull her into his arms or kiss her, but merely stood waiting, staring into her eyes expectantly as if she could end his agony with one word.

She felt her heart pounding, felt her knees growing shaky as she watched the shadows in his eyes and saw the hope. It shook her . . . humility was a foreign thing in the man she once knew, and for a moment she was speechless.

"No," she whispered, willing herself to think of Glen and her loyalty to him. "No, Thomas . . . you're wrong. I don't."

"Don't what?" he persisted, his voice soft and deceptively quiet. "Can't even say the word, can you?"

Tears came again and she put her fingers against her lips to still their trembling. She blinked and faced him straight on. "I want you to leave my room, Thomas . . . please. I'm tired and this conversation is too . . ." her voice cracked and she dropped her gaze, confused by her own weakness.

"Baby," he muttered, stepping forward as if to comfort her, as if to take her in his arms. But he saw her chin go up, saw the confusion and pain, and slowly stepped away. "All right," he sighed. "I'll go. Get some rest . . . because this isn't over, sweetheart. It will never be over until you can look me in the eye and tell me straight out that you don't love me anymore."

She watched him limp slowly across the room and the difficulty of his movements caused an odd, sharp pain in her heart. And for a moment . . . only for a moment, she considered going to him, putting her arms around him, and telling him that he was right . . . she did love him. She would always love him. But she couldn't seem to make her legs move.

He bent to pick up his cane, then turned to her once again.

"Good night."

As he turned and walked away, she couldn't seem to take her eyes away, couldn't seem to dismiss the way the soft jeans fit his long legs or the way his height and broad shoulders made the doorway look narrow and small. He was still incredibly handsome, incredibly sexy . . . and, God help her, she wanted him just as wildly as she had in her youth.

Georgia took a long, cool shower and dressed in a soft ivory silk gown and negligee. She smiled at the scent of lilac soap and bubble bath, thinking that it wouldn't be long until the house would be filled with real lilac blossoms and not just scented oil from a gift shop. For a moment, she frowned, thinking of Amelia and anxious to see her and find out for herself what was wrong.

She turned down the bed and slid with a sigh between the soft sheets, and reached to call Glen and tell him she had arrived safely.

"I'm glad you called," he said when he heard her voice.

"I'm here," she went on, letting her eyes wander with pleasure over the beautifully appointed room. "And it's as beautiful as ever. I wish you could see this place; you'd love it."

"Maybe I will someday," he replied. "How's Mrs. Lee?"

"I really don't know yet. She was in bed when I arrived. I had stopped to eat on the way and since it was such a long, tiring trip I'm going right to bed."

"So . . . you didn't . . . you didn't see anyone?"

"Well, yes, I saw Tracy. I told you Tracy was here. And . . ."

"And?" he repeated. "I don't like the sound of that."

"Glen," she protested softly.

"Is *he* there? The famous All American tackle from Alabama?" His voice was uncharacteristically sarcastic.

"If you're speaking of Thomas, the answer is yes, he is. And . . ." For the life of her she couldn't make herself utter the words he wanted to hear.

"And . . . I have nothing to worry about?" He said the words for her in a light, cajoling voice.

"No," she said, aware of her confusion. "Of course you don't." She felt like such a fraud. She didn't want to hurt him by telling him about her bewilderment over the way Thomas made her feel. And yet she hadn't been able to tell Thomas what he wanted to hear, either. She sighed, suddenly feeling very tired and very irritable.

"You're exhausted," he said. "I'll let you get some sleep. Call me tomorrow?"

"Yes," she answered. "I will."

She was surprised at how well she slept. And in the morning, when she first opened her eyes, she smiled, delighted with the sound of a mockingbird just outside her window. She'd always loved mockingbirds. She could remember how she and Tracy used to laugh when one of the feathery creatures would switch from a beautiful birdsong to a shrill, raucous imitation of a crow. She was still smiling when she got out of bed and dressed.

Georgia walked down the stairs and through a sitting parlor, then toward the back of the house where the guest dining room overlooked the flower-filled courtyard. She listened for voices and looked about for signs of guests, but the house was quiet and peaceful. Just the fact that Amelia had no guests was disturbing, knowing that she loved nothing better than a house full of people.

She stepped into the dining room and saw Amelia and Tracy talking. She went immediately to her ex-mother-in-law, taking the tiny woman in her arms and bending to hug her. She stepped away and looked into her sparkling blue eyes.

"Why you look . . . you look wonderful, Amelia," Georgia remarked, feeling a mixture of surprise and relief.

But there was no time to question her before Thomas stepped into the room.

Amelia's smile was immediately gone and as she turned to sit down, Georgia thought she saw her glance uneasily toward Tracy. Amelia cleared her throat loudly and frowned toward Georgia as if to remind her of their secret.

Georgia felt her face growing warm as she looked toward her tall ex-husband and met his steady gaze. She quickly looked away, smiling at Amelia and pretending that Thomas didn't cause her pulse to race, or that the small tingle in the pit of her stomach had anything to do with his presence.

He was quiet as they ate breakfast, chatting and laughing with Tracy and Amelia. Georgia felt for a moment as if she were a stranger, as if she didn't quite fit into this small, close-knit family. And that disturbed her more than she would have thought.

"You know what I'd like to do today?" Amelia asked, her voice bright and strong. "I'd like to ride to Cloudland Canyon . . .

take a picnic and walk through the woods. See what wildflowers are blooming and just listen to the birds." She stopped, looking about the table as if waiting for everyone's response.

"That sounds wonderful," Tracy said. "Count me in."

Georgia glanced toward Thomas and caught his eyes on her. She felt a small catch in her throat at the look on his face, at the tender warmth and the quiet little smile.

Cloudland Canyon had been their place . . . their favorite getaway . . . the place where Thomas had first told her he loved her.

"But . . . but are you sure you feel up to it?" Georgia asked, trying to think of any excuse not to go.

Thomas frowned and turned to look at his mother, then back to Georgia. "Why wouldn't she?"

Tracy and Amelia both glanced at her and she stammered something quickly about the weather and the rough terrain before picking up her glass of water to hide her awkwardness.

Later, when all of them had left the dining room to get ready, Georgia walked to the windows, staring thoughtfully out at the trees and the beautiful landscaping. Something about this was not quite right . . . something about the way Amelia and Tracy looked at one another. But it wasn't anything she could really put her finger on. Finally she sighed and turned to go upstairs to change into jeans and sneakers.

Later they all met outside and Georgia smiled, seeing that Bo Cavanaugh would be joining them. He was already seated in a jeep with Tracy glowering in the seat beside him. Amelia was in the back with a large wicker basket. Thomas slid a drink cooler onto the floor beside his mother and turned toward Georgia, who was standing near his pickup.

Georgia stared at Amelia and Tracy but they wouldn't even turn and look at her. She knew very well what they were doing by forcing her to ride with Thomas. And even though it irritated her somewhat, she also felt slightly amused. When Thomas came to the truck and opened her door, Georgia merely smiled and, without a word of protest, climbed up.

As they pulled out onto the main road behind the jeep, Georgia turned to Thomas.

"Was this your idea?"

"Nope," he said, glancing her way with a smile. "Believe me, when Amelia and our daughter get together they don't need any help. Their schemes leave me in the dust."

Georgia laughed, hearing the teasing note of pride in his voice. She knew how much it pleased him that Tracy and Amelia were close. It pleased her, too.

They drove for a while, not talking, but simply enjoying the beautiful scenery.

"Oh," Georgia sighed. "I'd forgotten how much I miss this place."

Thomas turned toward her, his gaze lingering for a moment before he turned his attention back to the road. But he didn't say anything.

Georgia motioned toward the vehicle in front of them.

"Tracy seems a bit hostile toward Amelia's new employee."

Thomas grunted, turning toward her again with that brief, mysterious smile. "She's not used to having anyone tell her what to do and that rubs her the wrong way. Bo is a pretty confident young man, just as used to having his way as Tracy is."

"Yeah, well . . . despite all that, I think

she likes him." Georgia said thoughtfully. "Sometimes things are not always what they seem."

"Yeah, tell me," he said wryly. "I know all about that."

Seeing the serious look cross his face, Georgia quickly changed the subject, not ready to get into another difficult conversation. Finally they both grew silent.

Then, unexpectedly, Thomas reached for her hand, glancing toward the road, then back down at the ring on her finger. He looked into Georgia's brown eyes and saw the warning there, but merely smiled.

"What's this guy like anyway?" he asked.

She lifted a brow, giving him a haughty look as she pulled her hand away. "Glen is very nice. He's sophisticated and quiet . . . unassuming. He has a very calm disposition," she added, throwing him a pointed look. "He doesn't push and he doesn't have the tiniest drop of male chauvinism in him."

"Oh," he said, still watching the winding road. "A cold fish, huh?"

Georgia's eyes flashed as she turned toward him. "Just because a man behaves like a gentleman and knows how to treat a lady does *not* mean he's a cold fish."

They were inside the park now and Thomas didn't say anything until he had pulled the truck into a parking space, motioning to the others to go on ahead. Then he turned to her, letting his hand rest on the seat near her shoulder. He looked into her eyes and his voice was quiet.

"Do you feel any of the things with him that you once did with me?" he asked. "Do you wake up in the night, wanting him . . . does he make you want to make love on the beach . . . in the back seat of a car?"

His voice was gruff and low and as he leaned toward her, she caught the scent of his shaving lotion. She reached for the door handle, feeling suddenly breathless . . . even dizzy.

"Stop it," she said, her voice breathy with anger. "I told you last night . . ." How could she tell him that she and Glen had never made love? Or give him the satisfaction of knowing that she had never been able to let anyone else touch her that way.

Thomas reached for her, pulling her back into the truck against him until her mouth was just beneath his.

"Just answer that one question . . . and I'll let you go."

"I don't have to answer your question," she gasped. "I don't have to tell you anything." Finally she sighed, seeing the determination in his eyes and knowing he was not going to relent. "Yes," she whispered, her voice trembling with anger. "Yes, he makes me feel wonderful. He makes me feel like a complete woman. I feel wild when I'm with him . . . wild and—"

His mouth stopped her words, moving seductively against hers, as his hands touched and teased, and made her move toward him against her will. She groaned softly and pushed him away, looking up into his eyes.

"Liar," he whispered. "You never were very good at lying."

She pulled away from him then, seeing the glimmer of triumph in his eyes, seeing his knowing smile. She shoved against the door and stepped down to the ground with a soft grunt, then turned away from the parking lot to find the others. She glanced back at him over her shoulder and saw him still sitting in the truck, watching her.

Did he have any idea how he affected her still? Or did he feel as confused and vulnerable as she? She had not expected him to be this way, so quietly coaxing . . . even his impatience seemed to have a new restraint. And she found herself looking into eyes that, while still stormy, were also warm and tender, and filled with a dark sadness that she did not quite understand.

She was helping with the picnic when Thomas emerged from the woods. She'd barely had time to ask Amelia how she was feeling, getting only a vague reply before the tiny woman changed the subject. Georgia could understand that she didn't want to talk about it . . . how terrible it must be to face one's own death. But somehow, she was beginning to get the feeling that wasn't it at all. She was even wondering if Amelia was as sick as she claimed to be.

They ate, talking and laughing and enjoying the cool mountain breeze and the sounds of the birds. Off in the distance, they could hear the muted roar of the falls far below in the canyon. It called to Georgia more than once, and she couldn't help remembering the time she and Thomas had hiked down to the falls in the very early spring . . . the time they had found a quiet, secluded place and let their passions carry them away.

She glanced at Thomas and found him watching her. He smiled and looked away,

461

but not before she saw the hurt in his eyes. What could she say to him? What did he expect her to say? Did he think that she could just forget everything that happened . . . that she could just dump her newfound life in Charleston and come running back?

She turned to Tracy and saw an odd little look on her face. She and Bo were talking quietly and he reached for her hand, urging her softly to walk with him. Georgia's eyes widened when she saw the look on Tracy's face, and saw her faltering, almost shy smile as she glanced toward her mother.

She frowned at Tracy, nodding her approval and grinning broadly at the blush on her daughter's face. When Tracy finally relented, Georgia turned toward Thomas. He was watching them, too, and his look was sad and strained.

"Thomas?" she said, placing her hand on his forearm. "What's wrong?"

He sighed and gave a quiet little laugh that sounded hollow. "Life passes so quickly," he said, turning to look at her. "Watching them, for a moment I felt as if I were seeing us. It doesn't seem possible that it's been almost twenty-five years."

Georgia glanced at Amelia, who had

grown very quiet. Her eyes were bright, and after a moment, she stood up from the bench. "Why don't you two walk over to the path that looks down into the canyon? I'll pack everything up."

Georgia didn't argue; she found herself wanting to talk to Thomas alone, wanting to see the sad look leave his eyes and wanting to reassure him that he hadn't lost Tracy if that was what he was worried about.

They stood for long, silent moments with their arms resting against the wooden rail at the edge of the mountain. The sound of the falls was clearer now and here, the breeze seemed to carry with it the cool mist from the water, even though it was in the gorge, hundreds of feet below.

"You don't have to worry about Tracy, you know," she said, looking up into his face and trying to see his expression. "She was always a daddy's girl and no matter what happens, you're never going to lose her."

"It's not Tracy," he said, turning to her. "It's you . . . us."

Georgia didn't answer. She sensed some long-hidden pain within him that he had never let her see before.

"I look at Tracy and I see how quickly

things change. First she'll be walking down the aisle in a beautiful white gown, and next thing we know, we'll be grandparents."

The sadness in his eyes made her forget her resentments. She reached out to touch his face and he turned, kissing the palm of her hand, then taking it in his to press it tightly against his chest.

"When I woke up after the car accident, I thought my life was over. I thought if I couldn't play football again that my life would be meaningless. And I'll admit, I pushed you away then . . . I was hurt and confused . . . I felt as if I had somehow let you down, let everybody down." He tapped his finger against his head. "I must have been crazy . . ."

"No," she whispered. "You were never crazy. I know what the accident did to you, Thomas. I know what football meant, but—"

"But I shut you out," he whispered, his eyes almost black now. "And I made the biggest mistake of my life by letting you go without a word." He lifted her hand, kissing her fingers and looking into her eyes. "I'm sorry, Jo . . . I'm so very sorry for everything. You were my love . . . my best friend . . . and I pushed you away . . . and I know

I hurt you. But whether you believe it or not, if I could go back and change one thing, it would be what I did to you. Not the accident, or my legs . . . not the loss of football . . . just hurting you. Because you were everything to me . . . you always have been and you always will be . . . everything."

"Thomas," she whispered, unable to believe the change in him and unable to bear the sight of tears shimmering in his eyes. "Oh, Thomas." She clutched his shirt, pulling herself nearer until she was in his strong arms, until they held each other tightly, almost desperately there above the canyon . . . there where it all began so many years ago.

He let her go only when a couple passed by with two young boys. They heard the children giggle and Thomas turned to see them staring and grinning. He put his arm around Georgia and pulled her with him back toward the picnic tables.

"What must they think of us?" Georgia whispered. She slid her hand around his waist, giving in finally to the urge to hold him close.

He chuckled softly and his hand tightened

465

against her waist. "You never worried about that before. Remember that weekend in Florida . . . on that little island where we walked down the beach early one morning . . . and we thought it was deserted?" He looked down into her face, his grin teasing and full of mischief.

"Oh," she said, shaking her head. "I'd forgotten that. I was embarrassed to tears . . . it's a wonder we didn't cause that old man to have a heart attack."

"He probably enjoyed it."

"Thomas," she scolded. But she couldn't stop smiling. "Well, I couldn't help it if you were always so . . . so . . ."

"In love?"

He stopped then, pulling her around into his arms and kissing her again. When Georgia stepped away, she looked up into his face with a perplexed look.

He took her face in his hands. "I asked you last night to look me in the eye, Jo . . . and tell me straight out that you don't love me anymore."

"Thomas," she said softly, pulling away.

He stood watching her, one hand on the walking cane, the other on his hip. "I love you, Georgia. But I'm not going to push you, because baby, this is one thing I want you to be real sure about. I know you still love me . . . I can see it in your eyes . . . feel it in the way you kiss me. And whether you want to admit it or not, I see it in the way you look at me and I know you want me just as much as you did that morning on that island in Florida."

She didn't reply, didn't bother denying his words, because she knew they were true. Because he'd hurt her, she had fooled herself into believing for two years that it was over between them. But she knew that if she'd been here all along, where she could see him, where he could touch her and kiss her, she might have been back in his arms and his bed long before now.

She turned and walked away. She just wasn't ready yet. She wasn't ready to break Glen's heart, and she wasn't ready to believe that Thomas had really changed.

The rest of the day, just as he promised, Thomas didn't push, didn't say another word about her coming back to him. But his eyes spoke volumes and Georgia found herself transported to another time, another place, where all he had to do was look at her that way. She had always been a fool for Thomas.

Lee, and, heaven help her . . . she still was.

Riding back to the inn, she watched the jeep ahead of them as it moved through the late afternoon shadows. She could see Amelia's gray head bobbing as she talked, see her reach forward to pat Tracy on the arm for emphasis. And several times, she saw her lean her head back with laughter. Even in separate cars, Georgia could almost hear that laughter and see the twinkle in her eyes. And she wondered at the small woman's spirited good nature and her energy. She didn't look at all like a woman who was dying.

"Thomas," she asked, still watching Amelia in the car ahead. "How is Amelia? Has she been feeling well?"

"Yeah, as far as I know. She still has enough energy for two women. Why?"

"Oh, nothing," she said. As much as she wanted to tell Thomas about his mother, she had promised she wouldn't. She turned to look at him, at the lean jaw, the way his sandy hair had turned lighter at the temples, and the way his eyes concentrated on the road.

Suddenly, those eyes turned toward her, fixing her with a steady gaze. "What is it?"

He had been right earlier . . . she was

never a very good liar, especially not with him.

"Has your mother been to a doctor lately?"

"No," he said, growing concerned. "Georgia . . . what's this all about? I noticed earlier when you asked her how she was feeling . . . she acted a little strange."

Georgia frowned, getting that feeling again that something was just not quite right.

"Thomas . . . what did Amelia say about my coming home for a visit?"

He shrugged. "She said you wanted to see Tracy . . . that you were homesick . . . and I remember she was very perturbed with me because I hadn't already asked you. Said she'd have to take matters into her own hands." He grinned. "She's been nagging me since you left about that. And I specifically remember her saying something about your wanting to see the lilacs bloom at the inn."

"Ha," Georgia said. She couldn't believe the nerve of that little woman, or how she could twist things around to suit herself. She simply couldn't believe it.

"What?"

They were turning into the driveway. "Nothing." Georgia smiled at him. "I'll tell

469

you all about it . . . later."

The next few days were wonderful for Georgia. The weather was beautiful . . . cool in the mornings and evenings, and warm during the day. The only glitch was she couldn't seem to get Amelia to tell her anything. In fact, she managed to avoid being alone with Georgia and used the excuse of being tired or not wanting to talk about anything 'morbid'. Finally Georgia stopped asking.

She began spending almost all her time with Thomas, and although there were occasions when he would pull her against him and kiss her, he didn't ask her to come back to him and he didn't press her to say she still loved him.

But they were growing closer; she couldn't deny that.

He took her to the high school stadium one afternoon. They walked around the field, and when he sighed and stopped, letting his eyes roam, she saw something on his face she hadn't seen in a long, long time . . . not since his accident. There was pride in his eyes . . . and contentment . . . and that look made her heart grow warm and tender.

She walked to him, slipping her hand in his and looking up at him. "It's good to see you happy."

He smiled. "I am, you know, except for one thing." His smile was wistful and sweet as he returned her gaze. He lifted his hand, letting his fingers caress her face, but he made no effort to pull her into his arms. He sighed and looked around the field. "This is where I belong," he murmured. "You know how I get in the fall of the year . . . the smell of damp earth and grass . . . the scent of woodsmoke in the air." He shook his head and his eyes held a sense of wonder.

"Kickoff time," she said with a knowing smile. "The beginning of football season."

"Yeah. But here . . . at a small high school, it's different. The excitement is still there . . . the youthful expectancy . . . do you know what I mean?"

"Yes," she whispered. "I think I do. We used to go to all the home games when Tracy was in the band. And you're right . . . year after year, the excitement was just as great. New players . . . a new team." She sighed with pleasure, remembering those days.

"It's the kids," he said. "The boys. God,"

he added, smiling and raking his hand through his hair, "these kids think they can do anything . . . they don't think anything can keep them from fulfilling all their dreams. And I think that atmosphere was just what I needed." He looked at her again. "I love it here, and if I'm lucky, they'll let me stay for a long, long time."

"Luck," she said, smiling up at him. "And a winning season."

"You got that right." He laughed and took her hand and they moved back toward the truck.

"You can do it," she said. "You were always a good coach, even with your pro teammates."

He chuckled softly. "Yeah . . . I guess I was the old granddad of the team."

"You don't look like a granddad to me," she teased, her eyes openly admiring.

"The house will be finished soon, Jo," he said, his eyes turning serious. "I want you to see it."

"All right."

"I want you back in that house with me, baby. And I want you here with me every Friday night." He waved his hand back toward the small stadium. "Sitting in the stands, rooting for our team. I want us to go to the pizza parlor after the game and celebrate with the kids . . . I want us to go to Mother's for Sunday dinner . . . to the beach in summer and to Gatlinburg in winter. Just the way we always planned. Does that sound boring to you now?"

She looked up at him, tears in her eyes. They were all the things they had planned, once he retired from football . . . once they were back home in Alabama for good.

"No," she whispered. "It doesn't sound boring at all . . . it sounds like heaven."

His eyes grew bright as he stepped closer, imprisoning her against the truck as the lengthening shadows of evening stretched across them and the football field below.

"Tell me then," he whispered. "Tell me if you can that you don't love me anymore, Jo. Tell me that you really love this guy in Charleston, and want to marry him. And I'll never mention it to you again."

"I can't," she whispered, standing on tiptoe to reach his lips. "I can't tell you those things . . . because they aren't true. I do love you, Thomas . . . as much as ever . . . more even. And I don't want to leave . . . I don't ever want to be apart from you again."

473

"Oh, baby," he sighed, whispering against her searching lips. "That's all I wanted to hear."

They rode back up the mountain and out toward the inn in a happy daze. They laughed and reminisced, touched and caressed. And once, Thomas even pulled the truck off the road to turn and gather her in his arms. His kiss was long and hard until she felt herself growing breathless and giddy.

She couldn't wait to tell Amelia and Tracy the good news.

They came into the house quietly, stopping in the hallway to embrace again. They heard the low murmur of voices coming from the parlor and they both turned to go in. But just outside the door, Georgia reached for his arm, holding him back and putting her fingers to her lips when she heard the topic of conversation from within.

"Do you think it's working?" Tracy asked.

"Well, of course it's working. Those two have always loved each other. All I had to do was simply get them back together so they could remember that."

"But Grandma, what if Mom tells Daddy that you're sick? He knows it's not true. What if he thinks—"

"Oh, pish, child. They'll be marching down the aisle for the second time before that ever happens. And by then, it won't matter anyway."

Thomas glanced down at Georgia, seeing the look on her face and the gleam of realization in her brown eyes. And he watched curiously when she stepped softly into the room.

"How could you do this?" she asked, her voice fairly trembling with anger. "How could either of you let me think that Amelia was dying? Didn't you care how much that would hurt me?"

"Mom," Tracy gasped.

Thomas stepped to Georgia, putting his arm around her and frowning with concern down into her troubled eyes. "What's this all about?"

"Oh, my dear," Amelia said, looking at both of them sheepishly. "Let me explain."

Georgia sighed and shifted her feet restlessly, crossing her arms over her breasts. "Your mother wrote me a letter, Thomas . . . a letter telling me that she was dying and—"

"I never said I was dying," Amelia said, lifting her finger in the air as she corrected Georgia. "I said I wasn't well . . . and who is at my age? I said I wanted us all here together this year when the lilacs bloom."

"I specifically remember the words . . . *last days,* Amelia." Georgia said dryly, her brown eyes sober and stern.

"Oh," Amelia said, waving her hand in the air. "Did I say that? Well, you know how I am after Christmas. I have always had a hard time believing the good Lord would let me live to see another glorious spring and smell the lilacs. Why, Thomas's own father used to say he hoped they had lilacs in heaven, or I wouldn't stay." She laughed weakly, and glanced apologetically toward her son.

"Don't change the subject, Mother," he said. "Why did you do such a thing? Why did you lead Georgia to believe that you were seriously ill . . . and even dying?"

Amelia bit her lip and for once her blue eyes were cloudy and troubled. "I'm sorry, darling," she said to Georgia. "I meant to explain as soon as you came, but then I wanted to wait until you and Thomas had time to . . ." Her voice trailed away as she looked at both of them beseechingly. "Well, I thought you could see I was healthy as a horse."

Georgia sighed and shook her head. She glanced at Tracy, who was trying hard not to laugh. Georgia grinned and her shoulders began to shake until soon she was laughing out loud and opening her arms to Amelia.

"Amelia . . . you are a scamp. An evil, scheming little scamp. But I'm so relieved that you aren't sick that I can't even be mad at you."

Amelia came into her arms, hugging her, then turning to look accusingly at her tall, handsome son.

"I wouldn't have had to resort to such a thing if my son had gone after you the way I begged him to do. All I wanted was to see the two of you together again, here where you belong."

Georgia turned and put her arm around Thomas's waist, looking up at him. She saw Tracy's hopeful look, heard Amelia's soft gasp.

"Ohh," Amelia said. "Has it happened? Are you two—"

"Yes," Georgia said softly. "It has happened. Your scheming plan worked very well, my darling interfering little mother-in-law. The first time I saw your handsome son again, I just fell in love all over."

"Oh, Mom . . . Daddy," Tracy said, rushing forward to put her arms around both of them. "This is great. Oh, I'm so happy."

"And look," Amelia said. "Look what else has happened."

All three of them turned to see Amelia as she stepped to the table and picked up a large crystal vase. It was overflowing with lilacs that hung in rich, heavy clusters over the glass rim. There were white ones mingled among the traditional lilac colors and the glorious fragrance wafted across the room to enclose all of them in the familiar scent that Georgia remembered so well.

The sweet scent of home.

And she realized that over the years she, too, like Amelia, had come to equate peace and well-being with the scent of the lilacs.

She looked up at Thomas and reached to kiss him.

"It looks as if I made it home just in time."

CATCH A RISING STAR!

ROBIN ST. THOMAS

FORTUNE'S SISTERS (2616, $3.95)
It was Pia's destiny to be a Hollywood star. She had complete self-confidence, breathtaking beauty, and the help of her domineering mother. But her younger sister Jeanne began to steal the spotlight meant for Pia, diverting attention away from the ruthlessly ambitious star. When her mother Mathilde started to return the advances of dashing director Wes Guest, Pia's jealousy surfaced. Her passion for Guest and desire to be the brightest star in Hollywood pitted Pia against her own family—sister against sister, mother against daughter. Pia was determined to be the only survivor in the arenas of love and fame. But neither Mathilde nor Jeanne would surrender without a fight. . . .

LOVER'S MASQUERADE (2886, $4.50)
New Orleans. A city of secrets, shrouded in mystery and magic. A city where dreams become obsessions and memories once again become reality. A city where even one trip, like a stop on Claudia Gage's book promotion tour, can lead to a perilous fall. For New Orleans is also the home of Armand Dantine, who knows the secrets that Claudia would conceal and the past she cannot remember. And he will stop at nothing to make her love him, and will not let her go again . . .

SENSATION (3228, $4.95)
They'd dreamed of stardom, and their dreams came true. Now they had fame and the power that comes with it. In Hollywood, in New York, and around the world, the names of Aurora Styles, Rachel Allenby, and Pia Decameron commanded immediate attention—and lust and envy as well. They were stars, idols on pedestals. And there was always someone waiting in the wings to bring them crashing down . . .